SKELMERSDALE

FICTION RESERVE STOCK L60

D0318580

Dedicated to my mother, Evelyn, and her three sisters,
Doris, Elaine and Catherine, who taught us all
the joys of sisterhood and faith

Delia Parr

Abide with Me

Steeple
Hill®

Published by Steeple Hill Books™

STEEPLE HILL BOOKS

Steeple
Hill®

ISBN-13: 978-0-373-78569-8
ISBN-10:   0-373-78569-0

ABIDE WITH ME

www.SteepleHill.com

Printed in U.S.A.

ACKNOWLEDGMENTS

Writing a book about the relationships between sisters would not have been possible without the support of my own sisters. Pat and Joanne are my biggest cheerleaders. Carol Beth is my first "editor," who saves me from making dumb mistakes that wind up on my editor's desk. Like Joanne, she is also a registered nurse, so I have a medical expert at my fingertips while I'm writing. Pat's work with senior citizens also gave me insight that I used in creating some of my characters. Kathy and Susan have already gone Home, so they watch over me, too. My friend, Jeanne, is my sister-by-affection. A retired chemistry teacher and licensed real estate agent, she provided insight into the world of real estate that proved very helpful while writing the book. Unlike the Long sisters in the book, however, we have a brother, John, who has somehow survived growing up with six sisters!

I would be remiss if I did not acknowledge the great support and love I receive from my children, Matt and his wife, Ileana, Brett and Elizabeth. I am so proud of you all!

Chapter One

❧

Surrounded by animated conversations and mouthwatering aromas, Andrea Long Hooper waited for her sisters in one of The Diner's corner booths, gazing out the plateglass window to distract herself from being overwhelmed by memories of Sandra.

Bright July sunshine reflected on the windshields of the cars that eased by on Welles Avenue and circled around the old bronze monument that anchored the community. While some residents drove off to start another workday, still others filled the commuter rail that bisected the town of Welleswood, carrying them across the Delaware River to work in nearby Philadelphia.

Inside The Diner, the regulars, mostly retired folks from the nearby senior-citizens complex, sipped at coffee and enjoyed the daily special: one scrambled egg, one strip of bacon, a small glass of orange juice and coffee or tea with unlimited refills. No substitutions. All for $1.95. Served daily, from six to eight.

Only a few years ago, Welleswood's business district along the main street had been an odd mix of thrift shops, convenience stores and empty storefronts that kept The Diner sorry company. Concrete sidewalks, dark with age and automobile soot, had invited little foot traffic, other than neighborhood children making their way to school or the community swimming pool, which was a relic from a community-building program during the Great Depression. A lone gas station at the far end of town had closed, along with the lumberyard and movie theater, all victims of suburban flight in the sixties and seventies that had left Welleswood gasping for breath.

Not anymore.

With no small measure of pride, Andrea glanced up and down "the avenue"—only newcomers ever called Welles Avenue by its official name. The Town Restoration Committee, formed twelve years ago by a coalition of local businesspeople, town politicians and concerned citizens, had helped to breathe new life into the town that she and her family had called home for four generations. Armed with federal and state grant money, along with a daring business plan that had incited equal numbers of avowed enthusiasts and raucous critics in the early going, the committee had achieved phenomenal success.

Welleswood's renaissance was nearly complete. Restored sidewalks, replete with brick walkways, new light posts, benches and gardens filled with potted plants from early spring through late fall, invited strollers and window shoppers, along with buyers. With restored storefronts, trendy shops offering everything from apparel to handcrafted specialties, several jewelers and banks and a handful of small, upscale restaurants drew shoppers weary of chain stores and malls. The movie theater had been lovingly restored as a community theater, and the lumberyard had been converted into Antiques Row. The town itself had purchased the gas-station property and replaced the eyesore with a Community Center, shared by the town's teens and seniors.

The renewal of the business district had other, well-anticipated effects. Property values soared. Church attendance also increased. Folks started moving back to Welleswood. Others planted deeper roots.

And through it all, The Diner remained a quaint little restaurant that offered generous servings of homemade food along with a comfortable place to rest, either before or after shopping. No one ever suggested it was time to leave to make room for someone else, either. A place just like…home.

For Andrea and her sisters, there was simply no place more fitting than The Diner for holding their Sisters' Breakfasts, a tradition they had followed for years, commemorating the birthdays of their beloved sibling and parents, instead of the dates on which they had left this world to go Home.

As the town's only real estate agent, Andrea had done well. Remarkably well, considering she started her agency with little more than courage and a belief that her hometown deserved better. The lean years she had spent as a widow, raising two children on her own, had given way to a comfortable living, especially now that Rachel and David were grown.

But Andrea was in no mood to think about her success. Not today.

Especially not now.

She patted the worn red vinyl cushion at her side and traced several cracks with her fingertips. She bowed her head and swallowed a lump in her throat as memories from nearly every one of her fifty-seven years tugged at her heartstrings. This was the first time she and her sisters would gather here for a Sisters' Breakfast without Sandra, and Andrea could not help but wonder if the next breakfast would be for her own birthday. Facing the death of a loved one was hard. Facing her own mortality cut a deeper swath of fear in her heart than she imagined possible.

Before she could take another step down the path of self-pity, she heard the bell over the door tinkle, looked up and saw Jenny coming inside. Andrea smiled and waved her baby sister over to the booth and tried not to let her brows furrow too deeply.

Jenny Long Spencer was forty-two, but looked more like sixty-two today. Every one of the twelve hours Jenny had worked overnight in the emergency room at Mercy General across the river in Philadelphia had etched exhaustion on her face. She walked as if she had the weight of the world on her slumped shoulders, and her scrubs were wrinkled and splotched with a variety of stains. Her makeup had all but disappeared, her lopsided ponytail bounced as she walked, and her eyes were red from weariness as she dropped into the seat opposite Andrea.

Jenny had always claimed that she enjoyed her role as breadwinner while her husband, Michael, stayed home to raise their two young daughters and wait for his muse to inspire him yet again. Today, however, she looked so tired that Andrea could see firsthand how hard Jenny had to work while Michael was at home....

"Gosh, it feels good to sit down!" Jenny admitted.

"Unusually busy last night?"

Jenny scratched the tip of her nose, tipped her head back and slowly rotated her head, stretching taut neck muscles. "Not really. Just your typical summer night in an urban hospital. An emergency appendectomy. Two car crashes. One motorcycle accident. A couple of stabbings and gunshot wounds. No fatalities, though," she managed.

Andrea shook her head. "I honestly don't know how you do it, or why you'd want to do it. Not when you could be at home—"

"I work there because I'm a good ER nurse and because it's what Michael and I decided is best for us," Jenny said defensively. "Where's Madge?" she asked, clearly anxious to change the subject.

Before Andrea could answer, the restaurant's owner, Caroline, arrived with a tray. "Running later than you. As usual. Here's your decaf and a fresh iced tea for you, Andrea. I'll keep an eye out for your sister, too," she teased, then promptly moved to the next table.

Jenny's frown turned into a grin. "You can't get away with a thing here, can you? Poor Madge. We'll have to make sure we put something special on her tombstone…something like, 'She finally made it on time.'"

Andrea rolled her eyes, relieved that Jenny's natural good humor had returned. "I don't even want to think about what you'd put on mine. Or anyone else's tombstone, for that matter," she added, if only to divert her thoughts away from the very real possibility that a tombstone was in her own near future. "You know Madge. She had a last minute stop for something. Or a last minute phone call. Or a meandering drive in her new convertible. Or she lost track of time working in her garden."

Jenny added some cream to her coffee. "Sandra used to get so mad at her. She nearly missed one of her doctor appointments once because Madge was late."

"Speaking of Madge…" Andrea pointed to the window. "Here she comes."

By the time Jenny looked out of the window, Madge had pulled into a parallel spot across the street.

Andrea shook her head. "That's about the…the…"

"The purplest car you ever saw?" Jenny giggled. "Is that even a word? Purplest?"

Andrea nodded and turned her attention back to Jenny. "I suppose it is. She even made Roy, down at the car dealership, write it on the order. The convertible had to be the purplest it could be, despite the fact there was only one possible purple color the factory could use. I guess it just made her feel better to tell them what she wanted."

"Like the lavender top?"

Andrea chuckled. "No. They wouldn't even attempt that. The car came with a white top, but Russell made a few calls and found a place to custom order the lavender one before Madge even saw the white one."

"Well, I like it."

Andrea shook her head and stirred some artificial sweetener into her fresh tea. Madge had a storybook life: a devoted husband, Russell Stevens, who spoiled her; two successful, grown sons, Drew and Brett, who loved their mother to pieces; a valued place in the community. Madge also had both the time and the money to be as eccentric as she wanted to be, and because she was such a giving soul, most people forgave her most anything.

Andrea wondered what it might be like to have someone in her life to carry the financial burdens, then immediately snipped a tiny ribbon of jealousy that almost wrapped around her thoughts. "The car suits Madge, but honestly, I'm getting a little worried," Andrea admitted. "She's a little too obsessed with the color, if you ask me. Did you know when she ordered her annuals for her garden this year, she insisted that every flower had to be purple? She went online, got a list of every flowering plant with purple flowers that would grow in this area and took the list straight to the nursery! And that was after she bought new cushions for her patio furniture, all in purple."

Jenny took a sip of coffee and let out a sigh. "That's just her way."

"Well, it's harmless enough, I suppose. It's just odd."

"Sandra's favorite color was purple. Remember?"

Startled, Andrea nearly choked on her tea. When she cleared her throat, she looked straight into Jenny's eyes. "You're right. I'd...I'd forgotten."

Jenny offered a warm smile. "I think it makes Madge feel closer to Sandra. They spent an awful lot of time together. It's been nine months now since Sandra died, and I think it's Madge's way of saying, 'I remember you, Sandra, and I miss you.' Even if Madge doesn't realize it herself."

"What don't I realize?" Madge asked as she nudged Jenny to move over to make room for her to sit down. She laid a bakery box in the center of the table and slid in beside her younger sister.

"Time. Being on time is important," Andrea prompted gently, still mothering the sister who was younger by only two years. Old habits die hard.

Jenny stared at the bakery box and squealed. "Spinners! You stopped for Spinners!"

"They were Sandra's favorite so I thought we should have them today. In her memory," Madge suggested. Her eyes filled with tears, and she toyed with one of her amethyst earrings, the most recent of the gifts Russell invariably brought home with him from one of his sales trips.

Her words were barely spoken before Caroline appeared with a mug of decaf for Madge and a plate for the Spinners. "Here you go." She set the mug in front of Madge, opened the bakery box and lined the plate with the Spinners, which were bite-size pieces of sweet dough spun with cinnamon and smothered with either vanilla or chocolate icing or glazed with sugar. "Enjoy. I'll be back in a minute for your order," Caroline said, and carried the empty box away with her.

Jenny shook her head. "Caroline's such a dear. If I take outside food into the hospital cafeteria, they're ready to call a guard!"

"This is The Diner. She wants her customers to feel at home," Madge countered.

"Sandra once walked all the way to McAllister's to get Spinners during a blizzard. Remember?" Andrea took a chocolate Spinner and offered the first "Sandra story," officially beginning the Sisters' Breakfast. Tradition called for sharing memories, happy memories—from childhood to adulthood and anything in between.

"But that's not the whole story," Madge insisted.

"Walking two miles to anywhere in a blizzard is a story in and of itself," Andrea insisted.

Madge finished a sugar Spinner and tilted up her chin. "Anyone can walk two miles in a blizzard, but only Sandra would have enough nerve to go around the back of the balcony, climb the stairs to the residence on the second floor, and insist that Mr. McAllister go downstairs and open up the store so she could buy some Spinners."

Andrea's eyes widened. With her mouth full, she could not voice a question, but Madge simply patted her arm.

"Sandra was…Sandra. She always knew what she wanted, and she always knew how to get it. Besides, she just didn't go to the bakery to get some Spinners for herself. The blizzard hit midday, remember?"

Andrea nodded as she tried to swallow the last bite.

"Well, she knew the bakery had been forced to close down without selling out, and she also knew the road crews would be out working all night clearing the streets. So she convinced Mr. McAllister to sell her a few dozen Spinners, along with everything else he had. Then she loaded up her sled, walked down the avenue to the public works garage, dropped off the sweets from the bakery and got herself back home."

"Just in time for *Jeopardy*," Jenny added. Her eyes grew misty.

Andrea took a long sip of iced tea and wrapped her hand around the glass. "You both knew that story. Why didn't I?"

Jenny shrugged her shoulders.

Madge's eyes twinkled. "You're always working. Besides, you don't know everything, even if you are the *old-*

est," she teased. "That's why we're here together, isn't it? To share our stories?"

Caroline interrupted to take their breakfast orders. Andrea was grateful for the extra time to think of her own Sandra story, and she was ready by the time Caroline left. She glanced at Jenny. "When Sandra left to get married for the first time, how old were you? Three?"

Jenny tilted up her chin. "I was four, thank you. And very mature for my age."

Andrea grinned. "Then you missed the infamous black slip story."

Madge's eyes widened. "You're telling *that* story?"

"Of course. I don't think I can *not* tell that story."

"I know all about the black slip," Jenny insisted. "When she was a teenager, Sandra had a part-time job cleaning for some elderly lady who lived nearby, and she spent every dime on lingerie. Beautiful, expensive lingerie."

"Mrs. Calloway," Madge offered, and her eyes lit with a flash of sudden intuition that Andrea did not miss.

"Anyway," Andrea continued, "Sandra's black slip just disappeared. She blamed Madge. Madge denied taking it, and from there, a monumental shouting match. Of course, shouting and screaming never resolved anything. Sandra and Madge each held their ground. For weeks after, Sandra would make snide remarks, blaming Madge for the missing black slip, and Madge would play the wounded victim of 'rash judgment.'" She shook her head. "Then Mother found the black slip when she was housecleaning. The slip was stuck behind Sandra's bureau, caught between the bureau and the wall. Mother said it looked like the slip had somehow gotten wedged behind the bureau after sliding off the laundry she piled on each of our bureaus on wash day. Sandra was grounded for a month."

Madge's cheeks blushed pink. "And she spent even longer apologizing."

"And well she should have," Andrea cautioned.

Caroline arrived with plates piled high with steaming hotcakes and browned sausages. After quickly refilling their beverages and removing the now-empty Spinner plate, she left the three sisters to enjoy their breakfasts.

Andrea slathered her stack of hotcakes with butter, cut off a generous piece and savored the bite.

Madge poured low-calorie syrup on top of her stack and watched the syrup ooze over the sides. She cleared her throat. "Actually, I have a confession to make. To both of you. I—I had taken Sandra's black slip and hid it behind her bureau. I was just playing a joke on her. I didn't think she'd get so angry…but things just got out of hand, and I didn't know how to stop it or what to do…."

Andrea sputtered and choked on her tea.

Jenny's eyes twinkled. "You really *had* taken the black slip?"

Madge nodded. Her eyes glistened with tears. "I promised Sandra I'd tell you that today. On her birthday. That she had been right about the black slip," she whispered. "I took it, and the argument was my fault. After all these years, I never really thought it was important to confess to that. Not to Sandra or either of you. I'd already prayed for forgiveness from God, but I never asked Sandra to forgive me. Not until she got sick. I told her right before…right before she left us to go Home."

Andrea raised her glass of tea. "To forgiveness."

Madge and Jenny raised their coffee cups, and they gently clicked their cups and glass together.

"Sandra had the biggest heart and most generous spirit of anyone I've ever known," Jenny murmured.

Andrea swallowed hard before she took a sip of her iced tea. "She was a good friend, not just to me, but to a lot of people."

Madge bowed her head for a moment. "She was more than just my sister. She was my shopping buddy and my gardening buddy, as terrible as she was, and she was my…my best friend." She let out a deep sigh, paused, and then said, "I don't know about either of you, but I hope it's a long, long time before we have to do this again."

"Do what?" Jenny asked. "Have a Sisters' Breakfast? Kathleen's birthday is in October, you know. Mother and Daddy's aren't until March."

"No. I like the breakfasts. I like the tradition. I like sharing memories with each of you." She reached out and took hold of Andrea's and Jenny's hands. "I hope we have years to be together. I hope…I just hope I don't lose one of my sisters again. Not for a long, long time. That's all."

Andrea gulped hard and squeezed her sisters' hands. "I pray we do, too. According to His will," she added, certain that now was definitely not the time to share her news. She did not have to start chemotherapy for two weeks yet. Actually, she had a consultation tomorrow with the doctor to discuss the particulars of the process that would take a full year to complete. With all the experience she and her family had had with cancer and the treatments used to cure that hideous disease, she did not expect any surprises tomorrow. She did have questions, though, and decided it might be best to wait until she knew more before telling her sisters and asking for their help and their prayers.

Unless tomorrow held news she would not be anxious to share with anyone, most especially the sisters who were still grieving for Sandra, who had so recently been called Home.

Chapter Two

Andrea sat in her parked car outside of the urologist's office under the shade of a swamp maple tree large enough to cast a shadow that covered her entire station wagon. Her purse was at her side on the passenger seat. Her bottle of iced tea was in the cup holder. Her mind was focused on prayer.

Head bowed, she took small, measured breaths and kept her hands loosely steepled as they lay on her lap. Just the word *cancer* had the power to send shivers down her spine and arouse all the memories of her loved ones and their suffering she had stored in her mind, casting images of pain and suffering that made her heart beat so fast she grew dizzy.

Keeping this ten o'clock appointment to hear the particulars about *her* cancer recurrence would have kept her paralyzed in her seat if not for the power of prayer and the presence of the angels who had been sent to protect her from her own fears.

"According to Thy will, with the blessing of Your grace," she murmured. She believed in God, and in His protection. She believed in the power of prayer. She *believed*. And with that belief came a gentle peace that washed over her, calmed her racing heartbeat and gave her the strength to make it from her car and into the doctor's office with more dignity that she thought she might be able to muster today.

She entered the office and immediately cast aside the memory of her last visit when she had had a checkup at the other office Dr. Newton shared with several partners closer to the hospital. During the cystoscopic examination that day, more commonly referred to as a cysto, the doctor had discovered and removed several small growths in Andrea's bladder and sent them for biopsy. The visit itself had become a blur, but the clinical setting Andrea remembered in the examining room did little to assuage her unease today, despite the fact that she would be keeping all of her appointments here, in the doctor's office, which was closer to Welleswood.

The second blessing of the day came when the receptionist quickly ushered Andrea directly into the doctor's office. No forms to sign. No referrals to submit. No waiting. Just a gracious welcome and immediate escort to a private office with a comfortable upholstered visitor's chair facing a window that provided a spectacular view of an outdoor garden.

The doctor's desk itself looked like no desk that Andrea had ever seen in a medical office. It didn't hold files or a telephone or a computer screen. Instead, this small antique lady's desk cradled treasured family pictures and trinkets and a vase of wildflowers. A door next to the desk led outside to the garden, which, Andrea guessed, was the source of the flowers in the doctor's office.

With assurances that the doctor would be in momentarily, the receptionist left, closing the door. Through the window, Andrea could see the private garden was protected on all sides by a tall fence, bordered by lush hedges and flowerbeds bursting with riotous color. Elegant wrought-iron benches faced the open center of the garden, where Andrea glimpsed some sort of tiled patio. She noticed a number of low garden lamps and imagined how beautiful the garden must look at night. No matter the hour, the doctor would always have a private haven at her fingertips.

Andrea was half tempted to step outside, to enjoy the sweet fragrances of the flowers, when Dr. Newton suddenly appeared in the garden door, cradling an oversize calico cat in her arms. "Why don't we talk outside? I'm afraid to bring Muffin inside the office. Too many patients are allergic, though I didn't note that on your records."

Startled, Andrea followed Dr. Newton outside. They sat together on one of the benches. Dr. Newton settled the cat on her lap and stroked the calico's head, and another cat, a small, dark tiger cat, wove in and out of Andrea's legs. The doctor chuckled. "I hope you like cats."

Andrea leaned down and picked up the tiger cat. Already purring, the cat curled up on Andrea's lap. "As a matter of fact, I have a few of my own. Three actually," she murmured, grateful for this added blessing to the day.

"I thought you might be a cat person."

"Only recently," Andrea admitted. "I wanted a little companionship. With my schedule, having a dog was out of the question. But cats are easier to manage, especially when you get several from the same litter. My brother-in-law is a sales rep for a pet-food company so I get most of what I need for the cats from him. Cats are more independent, too."

"Independent? Like you?" the doctor remarked with an raised brow. "Most of my patients prefer to spend the night in the hospital after surgery."

Thinking of last year's surgery, Andrea's blushed. "You said it could be same-day surgery."

"I also said you might want to consider spending the night," the doctor reminded her. "The tumor was a little more expansive than I originally thought."

"My sister Jenny is a nurse. She was able to help," Andrea countered, hoping the doctor would also remember how well Andrea's post-op checkup had gone and how well she had continued to be in the months afterward. "She will again. Provided I need help." She took a deep breath, but she did not stop petting the cat on her lap. "How much help…that is, I'm not quite sure what to expect from the treatments," she murmured.

Then she corrected herself. "No, that's not true. I've lost four family members to cancer, and I know what to expect from the chemotherapy. The nausea. The fatigue. The loss of appetite, as well as my hair…" She stopped before her voice broke.

"What type of cancer?" the doctor asked gently.

"Breast. Bone. Stomach. Liver. Brain. Take your pick," Andrea said quietly. "We're an equal-opportunity host family. Unfortunately, we're not an equal-opportunity *surviving* kind of family."

Dr. Newton shook her head. "Not all cancers are alike. And not all chemotherapy treatment is the same, either, Andrea. In fact, your chemotherapy will be very different from what you've experienced with your family before. Based on the biopsy results and the early stage of your cancer, despite the fact that this is a recurrence, the standard chemotherapy treatment involves coming to my office here to have the drugs injected directly into your bladder via a catheter—with minimal preparation on your part, I should add. After two or three hours at home, you simply void the drugs out of your bladder. You won't get nauseous and you won't lose much of your appetite, if any. You probably will experience some fatigue as the treatments progress, but you will definitely not lose your hair, although you might be tempted to continue to keep it very short. Many of the patients complain that their hair gets very coarse and somewhat unmanageable. Now probably wouldn't be a good time to start to color your hair, though."

Andrea knew that her skepticism was etched in every feature of her face, but she couldn't help it, any more than she could stop herself from reaching up and touching her salt and pepper hair. "That's it?"

Dr. Newton chuckled. "Well, let's not pretend this isn't serious or life threatening. It can be, Andrea. But in your case, yes, that's it. Chemotherapy will be once a week for six weeks, then once a month for nine additional months. We'll monitor your progress very carefully to make sure the chemotherapy is effective and doing its job."

Andrea blinked several times, anxious to hold on to this

good news just a little longer before this blessing disappeared almost as quickly as it had been given. "There's bad news, too, isn't there?"

"Yes," Dr. Newton said. "You'll have to be monitored for the rest of your life. Eventually, that means I'll only see you once a year. Eventually. But the bad news is that you're going to be my patient, or someone's patient, for life. As long as you come for your checkups, the odds are that there's no reason to believe you'll have a recurrence or at least one we can't handle, just like this one."

Effective chemotherapy. Recurrence. Odds.

Andrea had heard those words before—from Daddy, Kathleen, Mother and then Sandra. All of them had lost their battles. Eventually, each had failed to beat the odds. Each had had chemotherapy that ultimately proved ineffective.

Would Andrea follow this dreadful family tradition, or would she begin a new one called *survivor?*

If she should survive and beat cancer, why? Why her? Why not Daddy or Kathleen or Mother or Sandra? Why?

She shivered and blinked back tears as she whispered silent prayers for courage. She *could* beat cancer. She could be a survivor. With His grace. According to His will.

"When…when will we start the chemotherapy?"

"That depends," the doctor murmured. "Have you had anything to eat or drink today?"

Andrea stiffened. "Today? Just some iced tea earlier. About seven."

"Then let's start today. While Nancy gets the chemotherapy ready, I can explain precisely how it's done. I can also give you a key to the garden. There's an outer door you can use when you want to come to visit. That's why the garden is here. For my patients. Feel free to use it anytime." She checked her watch. "It's ten-thirty now. By eleven, you can be home. By one-thirty or two o'clock, you can be back at work. Unless you have an appointment between now and then?"

"No. I cleared my schedule until four. I—I wasn't sure how long I would be here. Today? Are you sure we have to start today?" she gushed as panic sent her heartbeat into double time. The prospect of being able to start chemotherapy today did appeal to her, but she hadn't talked to her children or her sisters yet, to tell them about her treatments, nor had she prepared herself for beginning her journey toward recovery today. "What about…the referral for the insurance company? I didn't bring one today. Maybe—"

"We'll take care of that."

"Oh. Then…you're sure? You're sure we should start today?"

"Why not? Let's make today your first day toward full and complete recovery." The doctor stood up and set the calico cat down on the ground. Within a heartbeat, the tiger cat leaped off of Andrea's lap and scooted away.

The doctor held out her hand. "Shall we?"

By noon, Andrea had been home for half an hour. Her cell phone had been turned off, the machine was answering her home telephone was on, and she'd set the alarm clock, in case she fell asleep. She was lying on her tummy in her bed, watching the clock on her nightstand. "Time to roll, girls," she murmured to her three cats, who were all in bed with her. Each treatment required that she spend half an hour in four different positions, to ensure the inside of her bladder was coated and treated with the chemo drugs.

It wasn't a terrible way to spend a few hours, although resting was not something Andrea often made time to do for herself.

Unfortunately, none of the three sister cats made any attempt to move, and Andrea rolled onto her left side as gently as she could. Two of the cats rearranged themselves along the back of her legs, while Redd, the smallest, curled up next to Andrea's cheek. Normally loving cats, yet independent, the "girls," as Andrea called them, seemed to have an intuitive sense that something was different. From the moment she'd returned home from her first treatment, the cats had stayed close, as if they knew that she needed them next to her. It was yet another blessing in a very odd day.

Andrea looked around the bedroom, glancing up at the white border covered with ivy that she'd stenciled near the ceiling, after she'd painted the walls a very dark green. Every time she was in the room, she felt as though she had stepped deep into a forest where she felt safe and protected from the outside world. She smiled when her gaze rested on the pictures of her two children. Rachel, her first-born after several miscarriages, was now thirty, and looked so much like her father, she kept his image alive. Unfortunately, she had her mother's stubborn streak and drive. A successful engineer, Rachel lived in Boston with her husband and their two daughters. Andrea's son, David, was going to be twenty-eight in a few weeks, but although he was close in age to his older sister, he was completely opposite in temperament. Easygoing and spontaneous, David lived in the woods, in a small cabin in the New Hampshire, eking out a living as a cooper, making wooden barrels with seventeenth-century techniques and loving every minute of his austere lifestyle.

Andrea loved them both with a depth of feeling that never ceased to amaze her.

She was frightened that Dr. Newton might be wrong about effectiveness of the chemotherapy, but she was more afraid of letting her children sense her fear or think that she might not be there for them much longer. Blinking back tears, she snuggled against Redd.

Right now, Andrea needed time to get used to the idea that she was facing a year of chemotherapy. She needed time to get used to the idea she might, indeed, be her family's first cancer survivor. She needed time to think of all the things she should do, just in case she wasn't. If she had put one of her notebooks on her nightstand, she might have actually started one of her infamous "to do" lists. She needed time to…

"To pray," she murmured aloud. Prayer was going to be the only way she would survive the next year. She checked the clock, rolled onto her stomach, waited for the cats to get settled again and spent the next half hour praying for strength and wisdom and gratitude for the blessings of this day. She also prayed that the chemo drugs inside her body would work well and keep in remission the cancer that threatened her life. And she prayed for the courage to face the plan He had designed for her life, even if that meant being called Home sooner than she had thought.

As she prayed, a seed of hope began to grow inside her. If Dr. Newton was right—if the chemotherapy went well, with no noticeable side effects—then Andrea might be able to get the weekly treatments finished before she had to tell her children or her sisters anything at all. She could side-step their questions about the biopsy. Yesterday, with Sandra's birthday occupying their thoughts, Jenny and Madge hadn't even asked about the biopsy results. To be fair, Andrea *had* already told them that the results weren't expected for a few more weeks.

If she could finish the six weeks of treatments before she told her family, she would stand a better chance of convincing them that her chemotherapy treatment was different from the treatments Sandra had endured—or Daddy or Kathleen or Mother, for that matter. Andrea would be able to convince them that she was going to be a survivor, because they'd be able to see it for themselves.

And by then, she would have a better sense of just how taxing the next year was going to be.

Now *that* was a plan!

Whether inspired through prayer or her own sense of independence, Andrea liked it—a lot. Her mind raced ahead to the schedule of doctor's appointments she had set up for the next five weeks. All were early-morning appointments, so she could continue to work, showing homes or attending settlements in the afternoons. Nothing unusual there. She always talked to her children at night, when they were finished with their work for the day. No problem there, either. Since Jenny worked nights and normally slept most of the day, and Madge was usually busy with her volunteer activities, Andrea was convinced she had hit on the perfect plan.

There were some adjustments she would have to make. Getting extra rest, instead of the usual five or six hours of sleep each night, was a given. She also wanted to make an appointment with a nutritionist. Dr. Newton had been quick to respond to Andrea's question about diet with honesty. Other than suggesting a low-fat diet, she could only second Andrea's suggestion to consult a nutritionist. Andrea could search the Web, too. Other cancer survivors often offered tips that doctors may have overlooked or dismissed. Tips of that kind had helped to make Sandra more comfortable, and Andrea made a mental note to spend some time searching the Web tonight. She also decided to hire an additional real-estate agent for the office and scale back on her hours. Her children and her sisters had been asking her to do that for a number of years now, so they wouldn't be unduly suspicious if she hired someone to help her at the agency, with "help" being the operative word.

Andrea had no intention of letting the reins go slack when it came to her business, or any other part of her life, for that matter. She was in control now and she would be in control of her life for the next year—she was determined to keep her life so normal no one in town would suspect a thing.

Twenty minutes after she had made her final roll to her back, a knock at her front door made her freeze in place. The sound was followed almost immediately by the door opening, which set off the security alarm.

"Yoo-hoo! Andrea? It's just me. I can't believe I caught you at home. Wait till I show you what I found for your kitchen! Wait a second until I turn off your alarm. I can't believe you set that alarm during the day!"

Andrea groaned and closed her eyes, but try as she might,

she could not come up with a single plausible reason she could give Madge for not getting out of bed…except the truth.

So much for her plan.

Trouble was, she had less than sixty seconds to come up with another one.

Chapter Three

Madge tapped the code, 1919, into the pad to deactivate the house alarm. She turned and glanced around the living room that crossed the front of Andrea's five-room bungalow and headed straight for the kitchen, clutching her "find." Her heels tapped on the gleaming red oak floors. "I didn't bother to wrap it. I was going to—"

She took two steps into the antiques-filled kitchen, paused and pursed her lips. No Andrea. If she was in her home office, she could have met Madge in the living room. Must be in the bathroom? Madge set her pocketbook down, unwrapped the newspaper from the pitcher she had found at the thrift store, and set it in the center of the black-and-white enamel table. "A perfect match," she whispered, quickly tucking the newspaper into the old enamel slop pail Andrea used as a trash can. "Filled that right up, didn't I?"

Frowning, she made a mental note to find a decent-sized trash can for Andrea, one that would match the rest of the black-and-white enamelware that served a dual purpose in Andrea's kitchen.

All of the pieces her sister had collected over the years, from the small antique stove to the washstand and the enamelware hanging on the walls, were both decorative and functional, unlike the appliances in the ultramodern kitchen that Madge claimed was her favorite room in her house. How Andrea could manage without a dishwasher or a refrigerator with an ice dispenser in the door was no mystery. She barely cooked for herself and rarely entertained. She was not home long enough, not with running that real-estate agency of hers.

Madge shrugged. To each her own. Tapping her foot, she checked her watch. She had half an hour before her meeting with the Welleswood Beautification Committee, to plan the fall plantings for the avenue. She had hoped to spend that time with her sister. She grabbed her pocketbook, turned, walked back into the living room and gazed toward the small hallway that led to the bathroom, two small bedrooms and the office. The bathroom door was open.

Maybe Andrea was on the phone. Madge had taken only a few steps toward the hallway on her way to the office when she finally got a response from her sister.

"I'm in here. In my bedroom. Come on in."

Madge smiled with relief and hurried her steps. "Finally redecorating? I warned you that you'd get tired of that dark green paint." She stopped just inside the doorway of Andrea's bedroom. The light in the room itself was far too dim, with the shades pulled tight behind the white lace curtains.

Andrea was not checking new paint colors or hanging new curtains or even changing the sheets on the bed. She was lying flat on her back in bed with her cats settled beside her.

All three cats looked up at Madge, stretched or yawned and settled back down with Andrea, who offered a weak smile and patted the bed next to her. "It's just a headache. I was trying to nap. Here. Come sit and talk to me while I wait for the aspirin to kick in."

Madge narrowed her eyes. Her heart began to race the moment she remembered that Andrea had been waiting for the results of her biopsy. "You don't get headaches. You never sleep on your back. And you…you haven't taken a nap since you were six months old."

Andrea closed her eyes. "How would you know I stopped napping when I was six months old? You weren't even born yet," she teased.

"Mother told me. And don't try to change the subject. What's really wrong?"

Andrea let out a sigh. "I told you. I have a headache. Maybe it's…it's my first."

Madge tiptoed to the bed, set her pocketbook down on the mattress and eased herself to sit beside her sister. Gently, she stroked the top of Andrea's head, and she knew—she just knew—that the results of the biopsy were not good. Tears welled and spilled down her cheeks. Emotion choked her throat. "You're sick. You're sick again, aren't you?"

Andrea moistened her lips, opened her eyes and took hold of Madge's hand. "I feel fine. I'll be fine. The nodules they removed…well, I have to have a few treatments and then I'll be good as new again. I had my first one this morning. That's why I'm in bed. I have to lie in four different positions for half an hour each to coat the inside of my bladder. I set the alarm—"

The alarm in the bedside clock went off, interrupting Andrea but startling Madge. As Andrea sat up, all three cats scattered. One knocked Madge's pocketbook to the floor and the contents spilled out. Her keys hit the floor with a clang and something, presumably her lipstick, rolled away, but all Madge could think about was the fear that wrapped around her heart.

Andrea had cancer.

Again.

"Why? Why does this have to happen again?" Madge cried, and dissolved into tears as Andrea's arms wrapped around her shoulders.

"Hush now. It's not so bad. Really," Andrea crooned.

When Madge's tears were spent, she sat back, hiccuped and wiped her eyes. "I'm sorry. I'm such a baby."

"Yes, you are," Andrea teased. "But you're a lovable baby."

Madge hiccuped again and swiped at her cheeks. "Jenny's supposed to be the baby. She's the youngest. I'm older. I should be…more in control."

"You're younger than I am."

Madge chuckled. When it came to age, she had no desire to be a single day older than she really was.

"And you certainly look a lot younger than me," Andrea said.

Madge ruffled her sister's hair. "You could look younger, too," she whispered, then realized Andrea had done it again. "You're changing the subject. Just like you always do."

"You're not crying anymore, are you?" Andrea countered.

For some unknown reason, fresh tears welled and Madge tugged on her sister's hand. "It isn't fair. It just isn't fair. We just lost Sandra. We can't lose you, too. We just can't!"

"God has His plan for each of us, and with His grace, I'll make a full recovery," Andrea responded.

Madge listened attentively while Andrea explained what the course of the next year would be like. Doubt tugged at her spirit even as her heart grew hopeful. "Your doctor does sound more positive than Sandra's did," she ventured.

"She is. All cancers are not the same. I'm blessed to have a good one."

Madge leaned back, pulled her hand away and stared at Andrea as a chill raced up and down her spine. "A good one? There's no good cancer, Andrea. There's awful cancer. Horrid cancer. Debilitating cancer. Disfiguring cancer…"

"And curable cancer. Mine's curable. Or it should be. And it will be," Andrea added. She took a deep breath and her expression grew serious. "I'll…I'll need a little help."

Madge brightened, hiccuped again and shook her head. "I'm sorry. Did I hear you right? Did you say 'help'? You'll need a little *help?*"

Andrea sighed. "Yes, I did. A little. Only a little help."

"Caretaker duty is all mine," Madge insisted.

Andrea rolled her eyes. "I don't need you to drive me back and forth to the doctor's office for treatments. I'm perfectly capable of driving myself. I told you. These treatments are different. I was thinking maybe—"

"Sandra let me take her for her treatments."

Memories. Bittersweet, but precious memories of the

months she had spent with Sandra washed over Madge. "I can't take the cancer away. If I could, I would give anything to make that happen. But I can be there with you. Keep you company when you have to wait at the doctor's office. Take care of your referrals and insurance forms. I can take you home, tell you stories to help pass the 'rolling time.' Let me do something. Anything," Madge pleaded.

She watched Andrea carefully. First, she saw her sister's backbone stiffen as if her spine had been laced to a broomstick. Andrea's dark brown eyes hardened. Her lips pursed. Her eyes closed for a brief moment, and when they opened, she looked at Madge with soft and misty eyes.

"You win. I hereby appoint you Chief Caretaker, in charge of transportation, but you can never, ever be late. Ever."

Madge frowned, even as her heart began to fill with hope.

"All right." Andrea gave in further. "You can handle the doctor's referrals and the insurance forms, too."

Half a smile.

Andrea narrowed her gaze, but Madge knew her sister was very close to a line she would not cross. "And my gardens. You can tend to them. Such as they are. But that's all. That's my final offer."

Madge grinned from ear to ear. "I'm a much better gardener than I am a storyteller anyway." She got off the bed, scoured around the floor to retrieve her keys and the rest of the junk she kept in her pocketbook and straightened her outfit, a lovely purple dress and matching bolero sweater she had bought only last week. "Speaking of gardening, I'm late for a meeting. We're planning the fall flowers for the avenue."

When Andrea moved as if to get out of bed, Madge waved her back. "No. Don't get up. I can see myself out. I'll meet you for lunch tomorrow at The Diner. Twelve o'clock. No. Better make that at one o'clock. I have a meeting at church at eleven. Eleanor Hadley has an idea for a new women's ministry she heard about from her cousin in Connecticut. I'll bring my calendar and we'll set up our schedule," she insisted, and got out of the room before Andrea could argue with her.

When Madge got to the front door, she turned and went back to the bedroom. Andrea was restoring the bedclothes back to order. "What about Jenny?"

Andrea glanced down at the bed. "I suppose I'll have to stop by to see her tonight before she goes to work."

"And Rachel and David?"

Andrea turned and faced Madge, wearing an expression that invited no discussion. "I'm going to wait a few weeks. That way I'll have a better sense of just how good I'm going to feel…and I can reassure them…."

Madge nodded. "Okay. Then it's just us. Just the sisters for now. You and me and Jenny."

Andrea nodded. "Just us. And all the angels He can spare," she whispered.

Madge swallowed hard. She managed to get outside to her convertible and drive halfway up the block before she pulled over and parked under the shade of one of the ancient oak trees that lined both sides of the street. She hit the switch and got the top up, turned the air-conditioning to full blast and pressed her forehead against the steering wheel. Her sobs came in heavy waves, and she gripped the wheel so hard the bones in each of her hands ached.

Not again.

She could not do this again.

Not now.

Maybe not ever.

For eighteen long months, she had stayed by Sandra's side and watched helplessly as cancer gnawed away and destroyed all the beauty with which Sandra had been blessed since birth. Short gray, unruly spikes of hair had replaced the golden waves that had been Sandra's glory for all of her life, although she had helped Mother Nature along by lightening her hair, which had darkened with age. Pain had doused the sparkle in her dark blue eyes, and her full figure had grown gaunt, even skeletal, by the time death had offered sweet release and the Lord had come to take Sandra Home, silencing her infectious laughter forever, at least in this world.

Cancer.

Cancer had turned everything Sandra was into something...ugly and grotesque, even inhuman. A scrapbook of memories opened and images flashed through Madge's mind. She caught her breath and held it for a moment to try to silence the sobs that tore through her throat.

When she finally regained control, when her body was limp with exhaustion, when the well of her tears had gone dry, only then was she able to hear the whisper that cried out only loud enough for her heart to hear. As insidious and evil and destructive as cancer had been for Sandra or Kathleen or Mother or Dad, nothing had been able to destroy the beauty of their spirits. Nothing.

And it was that thought that gave Madge the courage to help her sister Andrea now.

Chapter Four

What on earth had possessed Andrea to give in to Madge? What had she been thinking?

In all honesty, she had been unable to think beyond the increasing pressure in her bladder or the relief that Dr. Newton had been right. Andrea had felt no pain from the chemo, although she had been a little frustrated at being forced to lie down for two hours in the middle of the day. But most of all, she had been thinking how she simply could not hurt Madge's feelings.

Still, by the time she got back to her office, she had kicked herself twice over for agreeing to let her sister take her for treatments, figuratively speaking, of course. Unless Andrea wanted to be late for her appointments or carry the stress that she might be late, she had to think of a way to either change Madge's habit of losing track of time or tell her sister that she had changed her mind.

Andrea opened the rear door to the agency, slipped inside and bolted the door behind her, even though she routinely left her car unlocked only a few feet from the back door. Located in the heart of the business district, her one-woman office occupied one of the old storefronts that had been carefully restored after she had purchased it over ten years ago. Not remodeled—restored, at least at the street level. She rarely went to the second floor. The upstairs, once the living quarters for the original owners, was a disaster, having been being used as a storage area for a short-lived pharmacy, wallpaper outlet and a news agency over the years. With rents at an all-time high, Andrea wondered if she really should do something about the wasted space overhead.

"Someday," she mumbled, and made her way along the narrow hallway that ran down the center of the main office. Wide-planked floorboards beneath her feet carried the scars inflicted by years of use, but shone beneath several coats of polyurethane. Bead-board paneling, stripped of half a dozen coats of paint, lined the lower half of the office walls, below pale blue, freshly-plastered walls.

She passed by the restroom and two conference rooms on either side of the hallway and went straight to the front office. Her office—her home away from home—held memories that swelled and washed over her. She swallowed the lump in her throat. Cancer threatened her life, true. But it also threatened the quality of her life, both present and future, and she was not going to see all that she had worked so hard to achieve fall by the wayside because of an…an illness.

She paused and glanced around. The picture window showcased photographs of properties she had listed for sale, both residential and commercial, for pedestrians. Nearly half had a "Sold" banner tacked on top of the photograph, and she needed to update the display as soon as the new photographs were ready.

To her left, five wing chairs, upholstered in a blue-striped fabric, were grouped around an old mahogany coffee table. A stickler for neatness and order, Andrea refused to allow the table to become littered with piles of brochures or pamphlets; instead, she kept a bowl of fresh fruit in the center, along with several milk-glass dishes filled with hard candy. The brochures and pamphlets were neatly stacked on shelves on the wall, below framed photos of the local girls' T-ball and softball teams, which Andrea's business had sponsored over the years. The photos reminded her that she still had to inform Carol Watson about whether or not the realty would sponsor the newest sports endeavor in town, a girls' crew team.

"I'll save that decision for another day," she whispered and headed across an Oriental rug to get to her massive L-shaped desk—the command center where she spent most of her time. She slid her briefcase under the desk and sank into her high-backed upholstered chair. There was nothing antique or low-tech about her desk or the tools it held. The computer, fax machine, laser printer, telephone and answering system were all state-of-the-art, although with technology changing so fast, she would probably be updating her equipment within the next year.

She checked her messages first and took notes. Of the six calls she'd received, three were from prospective clients, including the Davises, who canceled their four-o'clock appointment. One was from Carol Watson. Decision made. She would call Carol tonight and agree to sponsor the team. Another message was from Doris Blake, a retiree who had recently relocated to Welleswood after a career in real estate. She was looking for part-time work. Andrea wrote down her number, just in case.

The last message was from Jane Huxbaugh demanding to know the status of the proposed sale of the house she had inherited from her uncle, the late Anthony Clark.

Andrea tapped the eraser of her pencil on her notepad. Jane was not the most disagreeable client Andrea had ever had, but she surely ranked in the top ten. In all fairness, however, Jane had a right to be anxious. She had accepted a proposal to purchase from a prospective buyer, Bill Sanderson, early last week. To Andrea's complete consternation, Sanderson had not returned a single one of her telephone calls or responded to any of her e-mails asking him to come in and sign the formal contract. She assumed he simply had been delayed in returning from one of the long-distance hauls he made as a truck driver. Not that Jane would care. She wanted the house sold. Yesterday.

Determined to see this resolved, Andrea pulled out the Sanderson folder and sorted through the paperwork. She set the CIS, Consumer Information Statement, aside. Operating a dual-disclosure agency, representing both sellers and buyers, required a strong set of ethics, and the law was very clear about her responsibilities to both parties. Beneath the proposal to purchase, she found the contract, lifted her phone and tapped in Bill Sanderson's home telephone number.

"We're sorry. The number you have dialed, 555-2608, has been disconnected."

"Great," she muttered, checked the number he had listed for his employer in upstate Pennsylvania, and dialed that number as she tried to keep her heart from racing.

"AAA Hauling. Henry here."

She cleared her throat. "This is Andrea Hooper, with Hooper Realty. I'm trying to locate Bill Sanderson, one of your drivers."

A snort. "You and the state police from here to Colorado. Feds got involved, too. Landlord called yesterday. Get in line, lady."

"S-state police?"

"Sanderson left four days ago with a van loaded with computers and headed for Denver. Ain't been heard from since."

Andrea closed her eyes to organize her thoughts. "That's terrible! He must have had some sort of…accident?"

Another snort. "Ain't that wishful thinkin'! We got the van. Found that in Ohio. Empty, of course. I wouldn't go wastin' any hopes you got on that thievin', sneaky—"

"Thank you," she managed, and quickly hung up. Heart pounding, she leaned back and steepled her hands. So much for that deal. Exactly why Sanderson had gone to all the trouble of pretending to be serious enough to purchase a home here did not really matter. She had been in this business long enough to know better than to guess at the motivations of any of her clients, buyers and sellers alike, but she thought she was a fairly decent judge of character.

Apparently, she was not.

As for the check that he had given to her as earnest

money, she assumed she would hear from the bank that it was not going to be honored.

She also knew for certain that Miss Huxbaugh was going to be rip-roaring mad.

At seventy-seven, Jane Huxbaugh was a fixture in Wel-leswood, well-known for her thriftiness and her gift for making snide remarks, which was almost as legendary as her temper. Andrea had no desire to light a match to that woman's temper. It had burned her once too often. But un-less Andrea came up with a buyer fast, she would be well-advised to tell Jane the bad news in person, rather than by telephone.

Andrea swiveled around in her chair, stared out the front window and twirled her pencil while she mulled over her options. She could wait until tonight and visit Jane at home. Or she could leave now and walk the two short blocks to see Jane at the hospital auxiliary's thrift store, one of the last holdouts from yesteryear, where she volunteered week-day afternoons. Or she could…

She laid down the pencil, sorted through the folders for prospective buyers until she found the one she wanted. Cindy and Paul DiMayo were highly motivated buyers. They had a number of deadlines looming that had intensi-fied their search for a new home. Paul was scheduled to start a new job at the end of September, their apartment lease ran out around the same time and they were expecting a baby, due August twenty-seventh, less than a month from now. Under all these circumstances, they were more than a lit-tle anxious to settle into a home before the baby arrived.

The young couple also had been prequalified, a decided benefit, particularly in this case.

Andrea wrinkled her nose. Sanderson had been prequalified, too.

She dialed the DiMayo's number. When Cindy answered, Andrea let out a sigh of relief and checked her watch. It was only three o'clock. Maybe she had time to turn this day around after all.

On their second walk-through of the house, Paul paced the perimeter of the empty living room and nudged the sheer curtains that had fallen to the floor, along with the rods and brackets that had once held the curtains in place. "How long did you say it's been vacant?"

"Nine months. The property is part of an estate," Andrea replied, wiping a bead of sweat from her forehead.

Cindy poked her head into the kitchen and wrinkled her nose. "That red indoor-outdoor carpet has to go!"

"Careful! Don't go in there unless Paul's got a good hold on you," Andrea warned as she approached her very pregnant client. "See the ripples in the carpet? It's not safe."

Paul escorted his wife into the kitchen and lifted a brow.

"It's a throwback to the forties or early fifties," Andrea admitted as she followed behind them.

Paul chuckled. "Early neglect is my guess. Just like the rest of the house. They pulled up the carpet in the bathroom and took half the tiles with it. Guess they decided not to try again in this room."

"This way you can pick out your own flooring," Andrea offered. No matter how she had tried, she had not been able to convince Jane to make a few minor repairs, like rehanging the curtain rods and curtains or tacking down the kitchen carpet. Turning on the central air-conditioning would have helped, too, but Jane was too busy watching her pennies to realize her thriftiness was going to cost her lots of dollars in the end.

"Poor little house," Cindy whispered. "It just needs a little TLC."

Paul groaned. "And lots of elbow grease."

Cindy looked up at him and smiled. "You have great elbows."

"And the price is right," Andrea added. "In fact, there are a number of options we can explore together to help you get the extra money you'd need to do some cosmetic repairs. The house is sound structurally, and it's a good starter house. You could settle quickly, too."

Cindy beamed and rested her hand on her tummy.

Paul cocked his head. "How quickly?"

"Quickly enough to get you into the house before the baby is born. Why don't we go back to my office where the air-conditioning is running, and go over the details?"

The day certainly had taken an upswing. By four-thirty, Andrea had a deposit and a signed contract in hand, and she had called in almost every favor she was owed, just to make this sale happen, but now she had to see Jane at home. The thrift shop closed promptly at four. She returned calls, sorted through the mail, decided there was nothing that could not wait until tomorrow, grabbed her briefcase and locked up the office.

Determined to finish the day's rescue, she acted on sudden inspiration and walked a block down the avenue to Blackburn's. Once inside the jewelry store, she saw the owners, Ray and Georgina, were busy waiting on customers, so she went straight to the display case along the right wall. She studied the watches inside the case and decided the prices were a little too steep for her needs. When she turned to leave, Georgina was approaching.

"Don't tell me we don't have something you like," she teased.

Andrea chuckled. "Actually, I'm just looking for a work-day watch. Something with an alarm on it?"

"But not something that'll cost a week's salary. Hmm…" Georgina walked around Andrea, leaned over the display case and studied the contents. She shook her head. "I thought I had something… Ray, what happened to those Flick watches? The ones all the kids were buying?"

Ray looked up from the register and nodded. "They're in the back. What's left of them, anyway. Haven't sold one in weeks. We needed the space." He let out a sigh, pushed his glasses lower on the bridge of his nose and peered over the rims. "We talked about it last night, remember?"

Georgina grinned and shrugged her shoulders. "You talked. While I was trying to sew, remember?" She winked at Andrea. "Wait here. I'll bring them out. Since they're in the back, I can knock the price down for you, too." When she came back, she had a single watch in her hand. "It's got an alarm in it, just like you wanted, along with all kinds of other nonsense the kids like."

She held it out to Andrea. "See? You can even program the tune you want to play on the hour." She pressed one of the tiny buttons on the side, and the instant Andrea heard the tinny melody, she laughed out loud. She had to have this watch.

"Sorry about the color. Pretty garish shade, isn't it? I was hoping we had one of the white ones left—"

"No. It's perfect," Andrea insisted, and this time she did laugh out loud and promptly bought the watch.

Swinging her briefcase, she hummed the catchy melody as she walked around the block to get back to her car. On first glance, she thought someone was inside the car, but immediately dismissed that possibility. The closer she got, however, the clearer the image became. She stopped several feet from the rear of the car and waited, heart pounding, as the familiar figure emerged from the car and approached Andrea with outstretched arms.

She dropped her briefcase and stepped into the waiting embrace, uncertain whether or not she should strangle Madge or return the watch and buy a gag to keep her quiet, instead.

Chapter Five

Jenny wrapped her arms around her big sister, briefcase and all. "You should know you can't use the word 'good' and the word 'cancer' in the same breath with Madge, so don't get in a huff or holler at her for telling me. Russell isn't coming home for another two weeks. She had to sit down and talk to somebody. She just came to me to try to understand what you had told her."

She gave Andrea a squeeze. "Your office was closed. I figured even if you had an appointment nearby or went shopping, you'd have to come back for your car eventually, and I waited for you."

Andrea's body went slack for a moment. She gave Jenny a one-armed squeeze and stepped back. "I only told Madge because she caught me at home in bed. Another ten minutes, and I'd have been heading back to the office."

"She's scared."

"Me, too." Andrea sighed.

"Me, three," Jenny whispered. "You know that you're going to beat this, right?"

Andrea squared her shoulders. "That's what Dr. Newton tells me."

"She's right. I made a few calls earlier this afternoon and talked to two of the oncologists at the hospital. They both said—"

"You look exhausted," Andrea interrupted, changing the subject. "You're supposed to sleep during the day, remember? It's Thursday. You have to go to work tonight. Madge had no right to wake you up. Why didn't Michael stop her?"

Jenny grinned. "I switched with another nurse and worked a double on Tuesday, so I was off today. I don't have to go to work again until Sunday night, although I've got a zillion errands and appointments between now and then. Michael's got a great barbecue planned for six o'clock tonight—ribs, Silver Queen corn and a tomato-basil salad. Come for supper? The girls would love to see you."

Andrea toyed with her briefcase. "I have a stop to make. I can try, but I'm not sure if I can be there by six."

"We'll wait for you."

"I don't want to be a bother. Maybe another time would be better. I'll grab something at home."

Jenny tilted up her chin. "Maybe you should think about being a little less independent. Or maybe, big sister," she added with a grin, "you should think about the Blueberry Boy Bait that Michael made this afternoon for dessert."

Andrea groaned and switched her briefcase to her other

hand. "Mother's cobbler recipe, I gather. The one Sandra loved so much?"

Jenny chuckled. "Is there another?" She turned around, closed the passenger door, walked around and opened up the driver-side door. "I'll tell Michael six-thirty would be better," she offered. She watched the indecision on Andrea's face give way to acquiescence.

Andrea leaned into the car, tossed her briefcase to the passenger seat and slid behind the wheel. As soon as Jenny closed the door, Andrea lowered the window halfway, cranked the engine and turned the air-conditioning on full blast. A deep frown creased her cheeks. "Does Michael know?"

Jenny shook her head. "I wanted to ask you if I could tell him, first."

Andrea chewed on her bottom lip and nodded. "It's okay. He's your husband. You shouldn't keep secrets from one another. Just…just tell him not to say anything to anyone else. At least not for now, okay?"

Jenny swallowed the lump in her throat, but her smile went straight from her heart to her lips. "Okay. Thanks."

Andrea reached through the open window and tugged on Jenny's ponytail. "You're not always going to get your way, you know. I…I have to do this my way, and sometimes that's going to mean I'll need to be alone."

Jenny lifted a brow. "Like when you're cranky?"

Andrea pulled back and put both hands on the wheel. "I don't get cranky." She turned to face Jenny, and her lips curled into a smile. "But I do get even. Wait till you see what I bought for Madge. I'll show you after supper."

"Actually, I think Madge is coming for supper, too. With Russell away…"

"Even better." Andrea's eyes twinkled. "You'll get to see the look on Madge's face when she opens the package." She eased the car back out of the driveway before Jenny could ask for an explanation.

As soon as Andrea's car disappeared from view, Jenny crossed the street and headed home, taking a shortcut through Welles Park. Like other longtime residents, she could find her way through the maze of walking paths that sliced through the grounds of the former homestead, creating a cross patch of playgrounds, playing fields and woods that drew all the local children. The mansion near the entrance of the park had been built by Mary Welles Johnson, the founder of Welleswood, and now housed the Welleswood Historical Society, which frequently rented the beautifully restored old home out for wedding receptions, banquet events and the annual high school prom.

Jenny took the left fork in the path, passed the old carriage house, now home for Randy Baker, the park's caretaker. When she reached the gazebo on the shore of the small lake in the center of the park, she sat down on one of the wooden benches.

The air was scented with wild mint. A multitude of pale pink mountain laurel blossoms peaked over the sides of the gazebo. Several Canada geese slept along the banks of the lake. Scarcely a ripple touched the water.

A peaceful scene—one that soothed her heavy heart.

Cancer had come back to haunt her family.

One more time.

She moistened her lips, bowed her head and laced her hands together. She was too heartsick to even ask God why this was happening or to be angry that her family had to confront this dreadful disease again. Sandra's passing was too recent, and the loss of her parents and her sister Kathleen was still too profound.

Every night when Jenny worked in the emergency room, she saw such a great range of human suffering, some of it organic, but much of it caused by human hands. She should be immune by now. She was not.

Despite the brave front she presented to her sisters, she had been a nurse for too long to be able to accept the doctors' optimistic diagnosis for Andrea at face value. Sometimes doctors were wrong. Cancer was a disease far too unpredictable to label as curable.

She tightened her fingers as doubts shook her soul. What if Andrea's cancer proved resistant to treatment or had already spread? What if she, Jenny, was next? What would happen to her daughters, Katy and Hannah, if cancer claimed their mother, too? What would Michael do? How could he keep his dream of becoming a writer alive if he had to raise their children alone?

When tears welled, she brushed them away and battled her doubts with her strongest weapon: her faith. She did not know where her family's battle with cancer fit into the grand scheme of His plans for them, but she would not let doubt or fear destroy a lifetime of faith, even now. "But for Thy glory," she whispered as her heart poured out a litany of prayers. For strength. For courage. For hope. And in gratitude for all the blessings He had showered upon them all.

She touched her tummy and smiled. Before Andrea was halfway through her treatments, Jenny and Michael would welcome their third child into this world and into this family. Sharing their news now did not seem fair, not when Andrea was facing such a challenge. Andrea's health should come first and foremost, not Jenny's pregnancy.

She looked out at the lake and prayed for guidance. He would know the right time to share the joy that a new baby could bring to the family. And He would help her contain her joy...for just a little longer.

Jane Huxbaugh lived alone in the last house on the dead end of East Mulberry Street, next to the elevated transit line, affectionately dubbed E.T. by local residents. After nearly thirty years, a thick stand of mulberry trees, wild vines and evergreens created a private border between Jane's property and the right-of-way claimed by the D.V.R.T.A., the Delaware Valley Regional Transit Authority. At rush hour, trains sped by in both directions at seven-minute intervals, carrying residents back and forth from southern New Jersey to Philadelphia. The noise was so deafening, any attempts to have a conversation outside were useless, which certainly limited the use of Jane's summer porch at suppertime, even if the drooping screens had been tacked back into place.

It was now five o'clock. Andrea had no other choice but to park her car on the street under several messy, fruit-laden mulberry trees. She sidestepped her way to the front door and wiped her feet on the mat to remove any remnants of the blackish fruit. Staining Jane's carpet, even though it was threadbare, was definitely not a good way to open this meeting. Reaching for the tarnished brass knocker, she noticed it was hanging by a single screw and opted to knock with her knuckles instead.

A train whizzed by. Andrea waited several moments for the train to pass in the other direction and knocked again. She was wiping paint chips from her knuckles when Jane opened the door.

Scarcely five feet tall, Jane had to tilt her head back a little to meet Andrea's gaze, but then, she had to do the same with most folks, which did little to refute the impression that Jane's snooty attitude was deliberate. "You don't call first?"

Andrea winced. "Usually I do. I apologize. If this is a bad time, we could meet tomorrow. Either here or at my office, whichever suits you."

"What would suit me is a little courtesy and respect," Jane snapped. "I left a message for you first thing this morning, before you even opened. I expected to hear from you the moment you got to the office."

"I'm sorry. I had an appointment early this morning, and I had to tie up a few loose ends first."

Jane sniffed. "If you've got the contract, then I suppose you can come in now, inconvenient as it is."

Andrea drew in a long breath. "I have a contract in my briefcase for you to sign." Not a lie. Not the whole truth, either, but Andrea was not going to give Jane a chance to slam the door in her face before explaining why the contract she had in hand was not the one Jane anticipated.

The older woman stepped back and motioned for Andrea to come inside, where the light was dim and the air was stifling, as well as heavy with the odor of cooked cabbage.

"Kitchen table's set for supper. We'll have to sit in here," Jane grumbled. She removed several piles of clothing from the sofa and stacked them on the floor next to the coffee table, which was also piled high with newsprint, magazines and junk mail circulars. Jane plopped into her rocker, surrounded on both sides by bags and bags of yarn, and pointed to the sofa. "Sit."

Andrea offered a quick prayer for patience and courage, sat down and quickly explained what had happened to the original buyer. Before Jane could pontificate on her displeasure, Andrea handed her the contract that the DiMayos had signed a few hours earlier. "Their check is certified. They've already prequalified for a mortgage, and we can go to settlement in ten days," she said quickly. "That would be August third at ten o'clock in my office."

With skepticism on her face, Jane studied the contract and snorted. "Selling price is lower. Knew there had to be a fly in that sweet-smelling ointment of yours."

"But only by a few thousand," Andrea countered. "With the earlier settlement date, you won't be responsible for six weeks of taxes, and you won't have to pay for the repairs to the sidewalk and driveway, either." She held her breath and waited for Jane's response. Andrea had called in every favor she was owed to guarantee such a fast settlement. Absorbing the cost of the concrete repair work was unusual, but she had done it once or twice before. It seemed a small price to pay for the peace and goodwill she might get in return.

"Stupid law. Thanks to our illustrious mayor and his band of kowtowing commissioners. If the borough wants new sidewalks, let them pay for it. Nobody thinks about seniors trying to live on a fixed income," she replied, apparently none too happy about the new requirement that all concrete sidewalks and driveways in need of repair had to be fixed, normally by the seller, prior to any sale. She paused. "August third, you said?"

"At ten. Unless you'd like to make it later?"

Jane reached into her apron pocket, pulled out a handkerchief and dabbed at the perspiration beading on her forehead and above her lip. "If you intend to stay in business, you'd be well-advised to check out the folks you're bringing to Welleswood. This is a family place. We've got no room for somebody like that Sanderson fellow. As a matter of fact…"

Andrea only half listened while Jane offered her usual blend of snide comments and unsolicited advice. She was Jane's real estate agent. They had a business relationship, not a personal one, thank heavens. Andrea yearned for escape from the uncomfortable heat in the house and from Jane's company, but she refused to let this woman's diatribe drain her spirit. As the elderly woman whined on and on, Andrea pictured herself at Jenny's with her two nieces. Katy and Hannah were still so innocent. So precious. So untouched by the world.

"A pen! Have you got a pen?"

Startled, Andrea blinked. "I'm sorry. Did you say—"

"I said I need a pen." Jane lifted a craggy brow. "Not one of those common plastic throwaways, either. A fountain pen, if you please."

Chapter Six

Andrea could smell the ribs cooking the moment she turned the corner, a block away from the old Victorian house that Jenny and Michael called home. After pulling into the driveway and getting out of her car, she patted her skirt pocket. Madge's gift was still there.

Still overheated after an hour in Jane's sweltering house, she ran her fingers through her damp, short-cropped hair and followed the sound of shrieks and giggles along the winding flagstone walkway that ran along one side of the house. She stood under the arbor beneath a crown of glorious honeysuckle and surveyed the scene in the backyard. While Katy and Hannah frolicked under an umbrella sprinkler, Michael stood on the upper deck, tending the ribs sizzling on a gas grill. The picnic table on the lower deck had been set for dinner. Jenny and Madge were sitting on lawn chairs in the yard, shucking corn, with a brown shopping bag between them for the husks.

Andrea watched Michael baste the ribs. He was forty-five, but he looked ten years younger than other men his age. The scrawny adolescent he had once been had matured into a middle-aged adult with scarcely an ounce of fat on his frame. Laugh lines creased his eyes and forehead. His neatly trimmed beard held flecks of gray, finally, but just enough to make him look distinguished. But it was the gentleness in his eyes that marked him as a treasured addition to their family.

Andrea closed her eyes for a moment, slipped back in time and remembered herself standing in her backyard on West Beechwood Avenue. Her husband, Peter, bless his soul, was putting together a water slide. Rachel and David, about the same ages as Katy and Hannah were now, were running under the lawn sprinkler waiting for Daddy to finish. Andrea strained to keep the scene clear, but it vanished as fast as it had appeared.

Swallowing hard, she wiped her forehead. She could scarcely remember Peter's face anymore or the feel of his arms around her when they'd stood at the foot of their children's beds to check on them late at night. His goodness and his patience and his love for her and the children: those qualities she remembered clearly; those she treasured…then and now.

"Aunt Andrea! Come and play!" Katy had spotted her and came running, squealing, toward the arbor with little Hannah toddling in pursuit. "Wanna see? I can run around the sprinkler with my eyes closed! Wanna see me? Wanna try?"

"Katy! Leave Aunt Andrea alone. She's still dressed from work," Michael called as he waved a welcome.

Andrea laughed out loud. At six-thirty, the temperature was probably still in the low nineties. Definitely a day to sit by the shores of the river with your feet in the water! Or to run under a sprinkler? She was half tempted to accept Katy's offer, and the moment Hannah tripped forward and wrapped her pudgy little arms around Andrea's bare legs to break her fall, Andrea made her decision. She grabbed her youngest niece, swung her up to her hip, stepped out of her sandals and grinned at Katy. "We'll race you to the sprinkler. Ready? Set? Go!"

Andrea took small steps to keep pace with Katy, and the three of them reached the spraying water together. Oh, but the water was cold!

"Tie! Tie!" Katy cried, and started running. "Catch me if you can!"

"Andrea! Have you lost your mind?" Jenny called.

"Oh, no! Andrea! What on earth are you doing?" Madge asked loudly.

Laughing, Andrea ignored both of her sisters, set Hannah down and lifted her face to the spraying water. It felt delicious. Then she quickly stepped out from beneath the water and shook the droplets from her face.

Katy grinned. "I guess Aunt Andrea is too old to play like me."

"She's certainly old enough to know better than to run under the sprinkler in her work clothes," Jenny teased. She handed Katy a towel and wrapped one around Hannah. "I have more towels inside. I'll send Michael—"

"No. I think I'd rather drip-dry," Andrea said. "It shouldn't take long in this heat. Besides, we're eating outside. It shouldn't hurt if I drip a little water on the deck."

While she used her hands to ruffle her hair back in place, she spied Madge sitting in her chair, apparently too shocked to do more than stare at her.

Jenny nodded toward the house. "I'm going to take these young ladies inside to change into dry clothes before dinner while Michael finishes up the salad. Why don't you talk to Madge and see if you can convince her you haven't taken the final leap into senility?"

Andrea shook the water from her skirt, remembered the present she had tucked into her pocket and grinned. Hopefully, the watch was waterproof. "Hurry back."

"Start without me. I won't be long, just in case you need me to perform CPR. Madge is as white as Mother's azaleas used to be."

While Jenny and Michael ushered the girls inside, Andrea took a deep breath and sat down next to Madge, who was shucking the last ear of corn without looking at Andrea. "You're going to get sick, running around under the sprinkler like that," Madge said.

"I am sick. I had chemo this morning, remember?"

Madge's hands stilled, and she looked up at Andrea with tear-filled eyes. "Of course, I remember. The question is whether or not you remember that you have to take care of yourself. Did it ever occur to you that you might catch a chill?"

Andrea laughed, stretched out her legs and wriggled her toes. "It's at least ninety degrees. The humidity is close to one-hundred percent. I seriously doubt I have to worry about getting a chill."

"Your resistance is down."

"Not after a single treatment. Later, yes. But not now. As

a matter of fact, I feel utterly refreshed. You might want to try it sometime."

Madge sighed and carefully removed every strand of corn silk from her manicured fingernails. "I prefer air-conditioning, which you have in your home, in your office and in your car, I might add."

"True. But Jane Huxbaugh doesn't. Try sitting in her living room for an hour like I just did, and you'd run under a sprinkler, too." She paused. "Although, maybe, you'd change into your bathing suit, and you'd have your matching cover-up and beach sandals with you, too."

Madge lowered her eyes. "Go ahead, make fun of me. But even if you're not going to worry about yourself, that doesn't mean other people will stop worrying. Or caring," she whispered.

Andrea's heart skipped a beat. "I'm sorry. I'm just teasing. I didn't mean to hurt your feelings." She let out a long sigh. "I sounded a little like Jane Huxbaugh, didn't I? I guess I was with her a little too long today."

Madge chuckled and leaned back in her chair. "That's okay. Anyone who spends an hour alone with Jane Huxbaugh deserves a medal. I sure wish I knew what made that woman so miserable. Brenna told me just the other day that none of the other volunteers at the thrift store want to work with Jane in the afternoons. Some of the customers have complained about her, too."

Andrea steepled her hands on her lap. "Disappointment can eat away at a person until there's nothing left but bitterness that taints everything beautiful in this world. Without faith, there's nothing. No friends. No hope. Not even any joy."

"That sums up the Spinster Huxbaugh pretty well,"

Madge admitted. "But her fiancé left her at the altar…what? Fifty years ago? I can't imagine the shame and embarrassment she must have felt at the time. Still, fifty years is a long time to be bitter."

"Unfortunately, it hasn't been long enough. Some people still want to know what happened that day, but she's never told anyone. I can't recall her fiancé's name at the moment, but he left town and no one ever heard from him again." Andrea did a little mental arithmetic. "I do remember Mother saying Jane was supposed to get married right after her fiancé returned from the war in forty-five. Miss Huxbaugh was nineteen. She's seventy-seven now. That would be almost sixty years ago."

"That's a lifetime."

"Not in our family," Andrea murmured. She opened her eyes again. She was only a year away from turning fifty-eight herself. "Neither Mother nor Daddy celebrated their fifty-eighth birthdays, not to mention Kathleen or Sandra." Kathleen had died a week shy of her thirty-fifth birthday. Sandra had been fifty-one.

Andrea cleared her throat. "As short as each of their lives were, I think they all understood something that has eluded Miss Huxbaugh all these years."

Madge cocked her head. "Such as?"

"They knew how to forgive others, as well as themselves." Andrea recalled the sermon their pastor had given a few weeks back. "Reverend Staggart said forgiveness stems from faith and the blessings we get from forgiving others is like a warm shawl. It wraps around our hearts to heal the hurts, ease the pain of disappointment and douse the flames of anger."

A silence rested between them. Then Madge finally spoke. "Speaking of shawls, that reminds me of something I need to talk to you about, but…that can wait." Her bottom lip trembled. "Can you forgive me for telling Jenny about your cancer? I didn't mean to interfere or break your confidence, but I just…I just needed to see someone and talk. Russell is still away.…"

Andrea reached over and gave one of Madge's earrings a gentle tug. "You're already forgiven. And I have a present for you to prove it."

Sniffling, Madge looked up, her eyes shining with anticipation. "You do? You have a present for me?"

Andrea leaned to one side and retrieved the soggy package from her skirt pocket. She handed Madge the gift, but did not let go. "Before you open it, you have to make me two promises."

Madge hesitated. "What kind of promises?"

"First, don't get offended. Second, you have to promise you'll wear it every time you're supposed to take me for my treatments."

Madge rolled her eyes. "I have a watch, Andrea. I have several, as a matter of fact. Just because I was late one time, *one time,* taking Sandra for her chemo doesn't mean I'll be late again." She rotated her wrist, and the sunlight danced on the amethysts and diamonds surrounding her gold watch. "This has a brand-new battery and it works perfectly fine."

Andrea let go of the present. "Not like this one. Go ahead. Open it."

Madge peeled back the water-soaked wrapping and opened the box. Her eyes widened. "It's wild! Wherever did you find one the exact color of my convertible?"

"It was easier than you might think." Chuckling, Andrea pointed to one of the silver buttons on the side of the watch. "Push that one. It's an alarm. On the days I have to go for chemo, you have to promise me you'll set it. When it goes off, you're not allowed to turn it off until you get to my house to pick me up. That way you'll be on time."

"I promise." Madge pushed the button, and the tune began to play.

Andrea held her breath, hoping Madge would appreciate the melody. If not, well, forgiveness was not a one-way street.

Madge's eyes widened. Her lips curled into a smile that stretched to a grin. When Jenny and the girls returned, Madge gave them a demonstration and they all joined in to sing along as they marched to the picnic table for dinner. "I'm late. I'm late. For a very important date. No time to say hello. Goodbye! I'm late, I'm late, I'm late."

Forgiveness reigned. Joy abounded.

Alleluia!

Chapter Seven

The following day, running late after a settlement that nearly did not happen, Andrea waited for the light, crossed the avenue and hurried to meet Madge for lunch. If someday she were to write a book about the ups and downs of real estate, today's settlement would have to be in the first chapter.

Both buyer and seller had arrived on time at the title company where Andrea and the other principals were waiting in the conference room, ready to proceed, but only the buyer's wife had come inside. In near panic, she told them her husband was still in their car, suffering from a full-blown panic attack. It had taken Andrea and the couple's attorney over an hour to calm the man and convince him that buying a home, even for the first time, was eventful, but not threatening. Though the settlement had proceeded smoothly from that point on, Andrea was way behind sched-ule. If her luck held, Madge would be running late, too.

The moment she entered The Diner and saw Madge in the corner booth, Andrea knew that luck had abandoned her. Madge had already ordered; lunch was on the table. Andrea braced herself for a well-deserved reprimand and slid into the seat across from her sister. "I'm sorry. You wouldn't believe why I got delayed. I tried to call you. How come your cell phone wasn't on?"

Grinning, Madge held up her arm, rotated her wrist and flashed her new purple wristwatch. "I had my alarm set so I wouldn't be late for our lunch date, and I turned off my cell phone so I wouldn't get distracted. Maybe I should get a watch for you."

Andrea grimaced.

"I ordered the grilled chicken and walnut salad with low-fat raspberry vinaigrette dressing on the side for you, too," Madge went on.

Andrea glanced down at her lunch. So much for the BLT, fries and coleslaw she had intended to order, despite the doc-tor's advice about the advantages of a low-fat diet. She man-aged a smile before she squeezed three slices of lemon into her tea and added half an envelope of sweetener. She took one sip, paused and glared over the rim of her glass at her sister.

"It's caffeine-free. You'll get a taste for it. It's better for you, so don't argue," Madge said righteously.

Andrea sighed, set down the tea and flagged the closest waitress, who happened to be Caroline, and handed over the glass of tea. "Would you mind terribly…?"

"One regular iced tea it is," Caroline said, and winked

at Madge. "I warned you she'd taste the difference." She glanced at Andrea. "I'll bring you a double. Since you're such a great fan of salads, I'll bring you a take-home container, too. You should box up half the salad before you add any dressing. Stays fresher, and it won't get soggy," she instructed before she left.

"You should eat the whole thing now," Madge suggested as she cut the chicken strips in her salad into bite-size pieces. "You probably didn't bother to fix anything for breakfast, and I doubt you'll take the time to make anything substantial for dinner. The least you can do is eat healthy and well at lunch. Honestly—"

"Since when did you get appointed my personal dietician?" Andrea interrupted, shaking her head and drizzling dressing on a corner of her salad. "You can drive me to the doctor's office. You can handle my insurance and tend my gardens. But my diet is off-limits."

Madge laid down her fork. "Somebody has to watch out for you. Eating right is…well, it's part of recovery. Sandra let me—"

Andrea cut off her words by laying her hand on top of Madge's. "I know she did. I know you did everything to help Sandra. In fact, you probably helped her more than the rest of us combined."

Nodding, Madge lowered her gaze. "She said I was the best friend she ever had in the whole wide world, but it didn't make any difference. No matter what I did or how hard I tried, I…I couldn't save her. I was her best friend! I should have done more. If I'd done more, maybe…"

Andrea sighed. "You couldn't save Sandra. You can't save me, either. That's not your job. That's God's job. It's His plan, not yours, and certainly not mine. You can't blame yourself for Sandra's death."

Madge laced her fingers together and rested them on the tabletop. She looked into Andrea's eyes. "About a week before Sandra slipped into a final coma, she…she told me something. I haven't been able to tell anyone what she said before now. Not even Russell."

Andrea drew a deep breath. "Do you want to tell me now?"

Madge nodded. "We were alone in her living room. Sandra was stretched out on her couch, and I was sitting on the floor rubbing her feet. She liked that a lot."

"I remember," Andrea whispered.

"She was in a lot of pain," Madge went on. "She spoke so softly, I had to strain just to hear her. She talked about Dan and Frank a lot and told me stories." Madge shook her head. "I'll never understand why she married either one of those men, not if I live to be a hundred."

"She had a one-track mind," Andrea murmured. "Unfortunately, when it came to men, she always got on the wrong track."

"She knew that, even before she came back to church," Madge countered. "Just like she knew she was going to die. She told me she was ready to go Home, but she felt guilty for wanting to leave her children behind and all of us, too. You know why?" She leaned toward Andrea. "She said she wanted to go Home because no one here on earth ever really loved her…and she knew He would."

Chills coursed through Andrea's body. Sassy, spirited Sandra. She hadn't lived life; she'd torn through life on her own terms, practically from the day she had learned how to walk. She had dated young, abandoned the faith her family embraced, married twice and divorced both husbands. A gifted artist, Sandra had been Teacher of the Year at South Jersey Regional High School, and a few years later, she was named Adjunct Faculty of the Year at the nearby community college. She had raised and educated two children, one from each of her marriages. Sandra's elder daughter, Lindsay, had also become a teacher. She was now serving with the Peace Corps in Africa, and her sister, Samantha, was an Army nurse stationed in Germany.

Surrounded by love and success, but with no faith to guide or sustain her, Sandra had felt alone and unloved. Only months before her illness had been diagnosed, she had rediscovered and reclaimed her faith—an answer to prayer for all of her family. Andrea and Madge and Jenny had stood by Sandra's side when she was welcomed back into their community of Believers. Little did they all know how soon He would call his prodigal daughter all the way Home.

Madge's words echoed in Andrea's mind. She was not sure, but she felt that the experience of facing her own mortality, ever since her first dance with cancer over a year ago, gave her the insight to understand Sandra's meaning and to help Madge to understand, too. "I think all Sandra wanted to know was love," she whispered.

Madge leaned back and looked down at her lap. The burden she had carried for nearly a year was etched in her expression. "I thought our love would be enough to make her want to stay—and to fight harder. It wasn't. It should have been."

Andrea shook her head. "Our love sustained her to the

end of her life. In your heart, you know that. But it was her soul that craved to be reunited with Him for eternity. If you believe He plants the seeds of desire in our hearts, then you also have to believe He called her Home. His voice whispered to her heart so she could go to Him willingly, even eagerly. That doesn't mean she didn't love us or want to stay with us. She just loved Him more."

Madge toyed with one of her earrings. "I never thought of it that way."

Andrea held silent and watched faith and relief ease the troubles from her sister's expression. When Madge finally looked up at Andrea, her eyes were clear. "How come you're so smart and I'm so...not smart?"

Andrea grinned and picked up her fork. If it made Madge happy to see her sister eating a salad, then she might as well do so with a smile on her face. "'Cause I'm the oldest."

Madge grinned back. "Yes, you are. By twenty-one months. And don't think for a moment I'll ever let you forget it." She glanced down at their salads and back up at Andrea. Her expression was solemn. "You're not ready to leave us yet, are you?"

Andrea dropped her fork, which bounced on the table and fell to the floor. "No, I'm not ready. Of course not."

Caroline arrived, set two glasses of iced tea on the table and retrieved the fork. "I'll be right back with a new one. Oh, I forgot your box. I'll bring that, too."

"Hmm. Make it two boxes," Madge suggested with a sudden twinkle in her eye. "We're going to take the salads home. Bring us a couple of double bacon cheeseburgers, well-done, fries and a side order of onion rings. That okay with you, Andrea?"

Laughing, Andrea nodded her approval.

"Good. Now, while we're waiting, I have to tell you about the meeting I had with the pastor and Eleanor Hadley about the Shawl Ministry. We organized the ministry several months ago, but it just hasn't caught on as quickly as we thought it would."

Andrea fixed her caffeinated iced tea and drank a full glass while Madge recounted her meeting, in more detail, no doubt, than what was in the official minutes. By the time she stopped talking, the meal was nearly finished.

"I have to admit that I'd never heard of anything like the Shawl Ministry before," Andrea said, genuinely intrigued by the idea of women gathering together to pray and knit a shawl for someone suffering from anything, whether a devastating illness or simply old age, sudden tragedy or merely loneliness.

"It is taking a little longer to get it started then we imagined," Madge reported, "but we all think it's something we have to do. We have the community center. We have the need, and Eleanor has been doing her best as the coordinator. Unfortunately, we just haven't been able to get enough women to join, so we came up with some good ideas about publicizing the ministry more."

Andrea nodded and checked her watch. She did not bother to remind Madge, yet again, that some women, Andrea, in particular, did not have the luxury of spending their days doing volunteer work. Not when they had to earn a living. "It's after two. I'm showing the Campbell house at three. Call me later, and we'll work out the calendar for my appointments," she suggested.

Madge's eyes widened. "I forgot! We were supposed to go over your chemo schedule so I could put it on my calendar."

"I've got to run," Andrea said, taking some bills from her wallet to pick up the lunch tab.

Madge snatched the check away. "This is my treat. Go ahead."

"Love you. Thanks!" Andrea was in a rush to get back to her office for a file she needed. If she was lucky, Madge would be so involved with her latest volunteer activity, she'd forget to call, and Andrea could drive herself to her chemotherapy appointments but that was probably too much to hope for. Standing at the curb, waiting for the light to change, Andrea mulled over the idea of the Shawl Ministry, and an image flashed through her mind of the bags and bags of yarn and knitting needles she'd seen yesterday piled next to Jane Huxbaugh's rocker. Andrea was far too busy and too preoccupied with her health to even think about getting involved with the Shawl Ministry, but getting Jane involved was another matter…although perhaps a little like thinking you could lead a horse to water and make it drink. Getting other people to welcome Jane Huxbaugh into a ministry presented another problem, and inspired such a clear image of horses stampeding in the other direction that Andrea dismissed the idea completely.

Green light. She stepped off the curb. For one moment, she was fully upright. In the next, she felt a thud and was airborne. Then she hit the street. Hard.

Chapter Eight

❧

The ambulance ride was a blur. The stay in the emergency room at Tipton Medical Center lasted until nearly eleven o'clock that night. The final diagnosis of Andrea's injuries was a relief: no broken bones. Still, a bruised left shoulder and a badly sprained left ankle were proof enough that the left side of her body had borne the brunt of her fall.

Exhausted but comfortable, thanks to pain medication, Andrea was propped in bed with a pillow behind her as yet another emergency-room physician arrived to review her chart and her test results one last time before releasing her. He was young enough to be her son, too, just like all the other professionals she had encountered at the hospital during her visit. Didn't anyone over the age of fifty work in hospitals anymore?

The young doctor stopped reading her chart for a moment, lifted a brow and shook his head. "A skateboard accident? Next time you'd be better off wearing protective gear," he admonished.

She sighed. "I was *hit* by a skateboarder. I was simply trying to cross the avenue on foot. I wasn't skateboarding."

He had the decency to blush. "Sorry. That makes more sense."

She tightened her jaw. She was annoyed that the skater had actually struck her, but she was more annoyed she had not seen or heard him approaching. "I'm just grateful I didn't break any bones," she admitted.

"You might not be," he warned. "Your ankle is severely strained. You're lucky you didn't tear a ligament. It's going to be a good six to eight weeks before you'll be able to put any pressure on that ankle and try walking again. If you'd broken it, you'd have been able to get a walking cast and had an easier time of it."

He wrote out a prescription, handed it to her with a set of preprinted instructions and signed her release. "Make sure you take the pain medication with food and follow those directions. Have you got any questions before I turn you over to your family?"

She swallowed hard. "How long before I can drive? I have to work, and I'm a real estate agent. I need to be able to drive. My car is an automatic," she offered as an afterthought.

He paused. "Rest up for a week. By then your shoulder won't give you any trouble, and you'll be able to maneuver about on crutches. You can try driving then, but I wouldn't recommend it."

She clenched her jaw. "Crutches. For six or eight weeks?"

He shrugged. "That's the best I can do. Don't forget to keep that ankle elevated. It's important. I'll send your sisters back again now. They've got a pair of crutches for you to take home, but it won't be easy going for a few days." He shook her hand. "Good luck. And watch out for skateboarders," he cautioned before he left.

Andrea tapped her fingers on the mattress. A week at home. Six to eight weeks on crutches. Five weekly chemo treatments. And no driving. How in glory could she manage all that and still run a business?

She closed her eyes and tilted back her head. "I don't mean to be ungrateful, Lord, and I truly am thankful that my injuries aren't very serious, but wasn't having my cancer come back again enough of a cross? Aren't I worried enough, wondering if I'll be able to keep working as usual throughout my treatments? Did I really need this, too?" she whispered.

All the fears and frustrations of the past few weeks rose up within her. And today's harrowing accident added enough pressure to overwhelm her. Suddenly, tears streamed down Andrea's cheeks. She brushed them away quickly, only moments before Madge and Jenny entered the cubicle.

Madge was carrying a pair of old wooden crutches, with some sort of stuffed gray critter on top of each armrest. Fortunately, the critters were not purple. "I had my neighbor bring these down for you. She broke her foot a few years back. Look!" Madge tugged on one of the critters. "They're squirrels. Aren't they cute? They'll help pad the crutches so your underarms don't get sore."

Andrea managed a smile while Jenny steered a wheelchair next to Andrea's bed and helped her from the bed to the chair. "Michael's waiting outside with your car to take you home. Madge and I will follow behind in her car. Ready to get out of here?"

Andrea gripped the arms of the chair. Despite being well bandaged, her ankle throbbed unmercifully, until Jenny raised the footrest and elevated Andrea's leg. She let out a sigh. "More than ready."

It did not take very long to reach the car, get strapped in and situated, but Andrea did not relish the prospect of reversing the process when she got home.

Michael eased her car forward. "I'll take it slow," he promised. "How are you doing so far?"

She grimaced. "Great. I'm sorry to be such a bother. Who's minding the girls?"

He hesitated. "Cindy Martin."

"But she's only eleven or twelve."

"She's twelve. Katy and Hannah have been asleep for hours, and Cindy's mom is right next door, in case there's a problem. They both wanted to do something to help. They're pretty shook up."

As they rounded a corner, Andrea braced herself by holding on to the dashboard with her right hand. "I suppose I made for quite a lot of gossip today, but I don't really know the Martins all that well. At least not well enough to think they would be that upset," she said.

Michael glanced at her quickly, then turned his attention back to the road. "You don't remember?"

"Remember what?"

"The skateboarder who hit you."

"I can't remember him because I never even saw him. If I had—"

"It was Jamie Martin."

"Oh." Suddenly it all made sense, and Andrea sighed. At fifteen, Jamie Martin was the daredevil of all daredevils, the reigning king of the skateboard world in Welleswood. The fact that he ranked first in his class, served as a junior advisor in his church youth group and was on a fast track toward becoming an Eagle scout rankled most adults more than a little. "Is he…was he hurt?"

"A few minor scrapes," Michael reported. "Jamie's always careful to make sure he's wearing protective gear."

Andrea snorted. "I wish he was as careful to avoid pedestrians."

"He's pretty upset about what happened," Michael said softly.

"So am I," she snapped. Her churlish words echoed in the car, and she shook her head. "The kids need a place to skate, a safe place," she murmured. "I thought the commissioners had been looking into that. What happened?" She shifted her aching ankle and saw her house down the block. She was almost home.

Michael chuckled. "They've been looking even harder since this afternoon. The mayor called an emergency meeting for seven o'clock tonight. Your accident apparently inspired renewed interest in that matter."

"Great," she muttered. As visible as she was in the community, she deliberately avoided politics and local controversies of any kind, although her role in Welleswood's renaissance had required that she participate in both for a while. Her name, no doubt, had been invoked more than once tonight, and her accident put her square in the center of the never-ending battle between the critics of skateboarding and the advocates.

As Michael turned into her driveway, she checked the clock on the dashboard. Eleven forty-five. Good. This horrendous day was almost over. She leaned back in her seat and relaxed. Nothing could happen in the next fifteen minutes to make the day any worse.

Ten minutes later, with her three "girls" nestled alongside her on the couch and Madge in the kitchen, Andrea learned how very wrong she could be. No wonder Jenny left with Michael without even coming inside. Anyone who had known Andrea for more than twenty-four hours would have known better than to do what Madge had done.

Andrea clenched both hands into fists and counted backward from ten to zero before she allowed herself to call out to Madge, who was in the kitchen tagging the casseroles that friends had dropped off for Andrea's freezer. "Let me get this straight. This afternoon, while I was being treated at the emergency room, you left and showed the Campbell house for me at three o'clock, even though you don't have a real estate license, which means, of course, that if anyone finds out, I could lose *my* license!"

Madge poked her head into the living room. "I know that, silly. I didn't go alone. Doris Blake went with me, but it was more like four o'clock by then. Doris has kept her license current, and she was happy to help. She promised to stop by to see you tomorrow and tell you all about it." Madge grinned maddeningly and popped back into the kitchen.

Andrea's heart took a quick leap and began to pound. Doris Blake was the woman who had called and left a message on Andrea's answering machine about wanting part-time work. "I don't believe this. You took Doris with you?"

Madge returned to the living room with a tray and set it on top of the coffee table. "You missed supper, so I fixed you some iced tea and a light snack. I bet they didn't feed you at the hospital, did they?"

Andrea's stomach growled. "As a matter of fact, they didn't." She nibbled on a cracker topped with cheese spread. "Don't change the subject."

"Why not? It always works for you."

Andrea tightened her jaw and stared at her sister. "This is important. This isn't a game. This is about my business. My livelihood."

"Exactly," Madge countered. "Which is why I asked Doris to be there today. I also know you can't shut down your office for six to eight weeks, but unless you have someone undeniably reliable and qualified, you won't give yourself the time you need to rest and recuperate from your spill today, either. Need I mention the fact that you have weekly chemo scheduled, too? That's why I spoke to Doris, and she's agreed to come work for you starting tomorrow. Well, actually, I guess, she really started today since she showed the house."

Andrea gasped. "You've hired her to come work for me?"

Madge beamed. "I knew you'd be surprised. Pleased, too, aren't you? And just a little amazed at how fast I can work? I might not have been in the business world like you've been all these years, but I've learned a lot, volunteering as much as I have. Besides," she added as her eyes filled with pride. "I remembered what you said when I told you I wanted to help you, even before you had your little mishap today. I've got caretaker duty chauffeuring you to your doctor's appointments. I'm handling your insurance paperwork and I'm going to weed your gardens. That's all."

She really could mimic Andrea's tone of voice well. She knew it, too, judging by the glint in her eyes.

"So, since you won't let me help you do anything else," Madge continued pertly, "I know Doris can. And she's qualified, too. Amazing how things all work out, isn't it?"

Andrea shut her eyes. Amazing indeed. In a matter of weeks, her entire life, both personally and professionally, had come unraveled. Try as she might, she was utterly and completely helpless to stop it or to make any successful attempts to knit her life back together. Instinctively, she grabbed the only lifeline that had any chance of saving her from total destruction.

Prayer.

Lots and lots of prayer.

She even said one for Madge, hoping her sister might be sent a blessing that would turn her attention to something or someone other Andrea.

Chapter Nine

The answer to one of Andrea's prayers arrived at her home promptly at ten o'clock the following morning.

Doris Blake was a unique women who defied easy classification. Nothing about her was average, yet not a single feature was extraordinary. But she made quite a memorable impression. At sixty-something, she wore her years with quiet dignity, helped by subtle, artfully applied makeup only another woman would appreciate. Her green shirtwaist dress and matching crocheted sweater were simple, yet professional. She wore her pale gray hair pulled back into a chignon at the nape of her neck. On her, the style was elegant rather than old-fashioned. Her presence was both friendly and businesslike, just like her voice had sounded yesterday on Andrea's answering machine.

Andrea liked and trusted her immediately. She knew her clients would, too.

With her foot elevated and resting on an ottoman in her living room, Andrea skimmed the portfolio that contained Doris's résumé, a copy of her real-estate license and references from former employers and clients, both sellers and buyers. Andrea closed the portfolio and handed it back to Doris, who was sitting in an upholstered chair next to her. "You've had quite an impressive career."

Doris smiled. "Thank you. I've been blessed. Not everyone gets to make a living helping other people find a special place to call home. But you must know what I mean. My sister, Betty, has told me what a wonderful difference you've made here in Welleswood."

Andrea swallowed hard, remembering how close she came to introducing that scoundrel Bill Sanderson to the community. "Your sister still works at the county library, doesn't she? Or has she retired?"

"She's still there, and she's as involved with the Welleswood Historical Society as ever." Doris paused. "After my husband, Francis, died, I wanted a change. We'd lived in Barnegat for over forty years, and everywhere I went, I ran into memories. When I finally decided to sell our home last spring, I accepted Betty's offer to live with her. I was looking forward to having her company and living somewhere new. Frankly, she's gone from home so much, I've gotten a little lonely and a whole lot bored."

She smiled. "Helping you at the agency is a real answer to my prayers, but I don't want you to feel obligated in any way. Madge can be rather persuasive, but she's also a bit impulsive. If you'd rather advertise for an agent to help you run your office while you recuperate, I understand, though I'm going to be completely honest and tell you I want the position very much."

Andrea smiled. "You're hired, but I have to be completely honest with you, too. The position is very short-term." She paused, debated with herself whether or not to tell Doris about her upcoming chemo treatments, then decided to keep that news in the family for now. "Once I'm on my feet again—"

"I understand completely. I'm not even sure I want something long-term. Not at this stage of my life."

"I don't blame you. As a matter of fact, I've always worked alone. I've never had an employee before," Andrea admitted.

"I'll stay and work for as long or as short as you need me."

Chuckling, Andrea shook her head. "It can't be this easy."

Doris smiled and shook her head. "I was thinking the same thing. I only left my message yesterday. I was hoping you'd call back, but to actually be hired within a day…"

Andrea cocked her head. "Have you got any other plans for today?"

"No, I kept the day open."

"Good. Let's go into the office together. I'm sure there are messages waiting. You can get familiar with the setup, though we'll have to rearrange things a bit now that the two of us will be sharing the workspace. We'll need to stop by Jenny's on the way. Somehow she wound up with my brief-case, and I need to check my calendar to see about the appointments I had for today. We should be able to catch the clients before they leave. They have a wedding today."

She pointed at the portfolio in Doris's hands. "Bring that along, too."

Doris stored the portfolio in her briefcase before she stood up. "Unless you have something here we can take so you can keep that foot elevated, we'll need to stop at Betty's, too. She's got an old needlepoint footrest you can use."

No argument from Doris about Andrea going to the office instead of resting at home.

No debate from Doris over the terms or length of her employment.

Only support and concern.

When He answered prayer, He could be…amazing.

Andrea could not wait to see what He had planned for the rest of the day.

By half-past noon, Andrea had a signed employment contract stored in the new folder with Doris's name on it, along with a full copy of the portfolio and notes of conversations she had had with two of the references Doris had provided. Andrea had her foot elevated on an antique needlepoint footrest that was very old and exquisite, and she was actually quite comfortable sitting in one of the wing chairs in her office. Doris had just finished a virtual online tour of the agency's listings after familiarizing herself with the office equipment.

"You can use my password online until you join the Tilton County Board of Realtors," Andrea told her, "and you should see Tim Fallon on Monday to order business cards. He can take your photo, too, and use the template he made for my business cards. I'll call him first thing to let him know you're coming and tell him to charge it to my account as well."

"You're not obligated to do that," Doris protested.

Andrea hesitated. "That may be, but it's how we're going to do it. Normally agents aren't hired for a few weeks, either. Have you got a cell phone?"

Doris rolled her eyes. "A necessary evil in this business. I hate cell phones, and I love them. Yes, I've got one."

"Good. You can pay for that." Andrea glanced around the front office and sighed. "What we really need is a pair of strong arms to help rearrange the furniture. If we add one of the tables from one of the conference rooms, we can set up the work area to accommodate both of us."

Literally, before her words could fade to an echo, her front door opened and Jamie Martin stepped inside. Through the picture window, she could see his father, Shawn, watching from across the street, but she directed her attention to the young man who approached her.

He walked with stiff determination and stopped a few feet away from her. All arms and legs, he topped six feet already. He had his mother's dark hair and his father's pale blue eyes—eyes that shimmered with remorse. "I came to apologize, Mrs. Hooper. I'm really, really sorry about running into you yesterday." He glanced down at her foot and his cheeks flamed. "Is it broken?"

She drew in a deep breath. Here she was, feeling as bruised and battered as if she had been hit by a truck, and he apparently did not have more than a little scrape on his chin. But he wasn't a truck. He wasn't even an adult. He was just a kid. A good kid.

As much as she wanted to lash out at him and hurl every well-deserved criticism she could fathom, she did not have the heart. He looked scared. He looked penitent. He looked genuinely concerned about her well-being. "It's a bad sprain, but the doctor said I might be better off if I had broken it. Apparently, it's going to take a while to heal."

Jamie swallowed so hard, Andrea could see his Adam's apple move up and down. "I sprained my ankle once. Hurt like anything."

Andrea caught a glimpse of Doris, quietly slipping behind Jamie and out the front door. "Skateboarding?" she asked.

He cleared his throat. "Yeah. I mean, yes." He stared at the floor for a moment. When he looked up, his eyes were clear. He straightened his shoulders. "I won't be skateboarding for a while."

She cocked one brow. "You've been grounded," she murmured, and wondered if he would notice the pun.

His eyes twinkled. "Yes, ma'am. For the rest of the summer, at least. Mom and Dad said they'd decide then when I could get my skateboard back. It all depends…"

"Depends on what?"

"How I spend my summer. They left it up to me. I thought about it all night and talked it over with them at breakfast. They agreed with my idea. Dad wanted to come with me." He nodded toward the window. "I asked him to wait for me across the street."

Curious and impressed that he had apparently not been forced to come to apologize in person, Andrea nevertheless remained silent.

"Anyway, here's my idea," Jamie went on. "Instead of working at the school like I've been doing, painting and cleaning gum off the desks and stuff, I'd like to work for you. As a volunteer," he added quickly. "I feel real bad that you won't be able to get around because of what I did, so I figured you could use my help. I can be here to help you get inside when you get to work. I can go to the post office and mail stuff for you. Pick up lunch and bring it back for you. Take out the trash…whatever you can't do because you're on crutches, I can do. If you'll let me."

Stunned, Andrea sat up a little straighter. "You'd work here all summer?"

"Yes, ma'am."

"For free."

He never even blinked. "Yes, ma'am."

She narrowed her eyes. "What about your responsibility to your job at the school?"

"I called my friend, Matt. He's been looking for a job. Then I called my boss, Mr. Potter. He said it was all right if Matt took my place. I just have to call back this afternoon and let them both know if—"

"If I'll let you do your penance here?"

He nodded. "Yes ma'am."

Moved, Andrea glanced at the ridiculous crutches Madge had given her and steepled her hands. The conversation she had had with Madge about forgiveness and the greater blessings received when able to forgive someone else replayed in her mind. Instinctively, her heart reached out and claimed those blessings—for herself and for Jamie. "I'd need you here at quarter to nine. Sharp. You can help me get from the car to the office Monday through Saturday. You can leave at three. We'll try it for a week, see how it goes, and go from there."

Relief washed over his features. "When do I start?"

She smiled. "How do you feel about moving some furniture right now?"

* * *

That night, Andrea crawled into bed early and switched out her light. Well, *crawled* wasn't exactly how to describe the way that she had scooted and scrunched into a sleeping position, but it was the best she could manage. Her shoulder was still sore. Pain throbbed in her ankle. But her spirit was hopeful as she waited for the pain medication to start working so she could fall asleep, and she had the "girls" to keep her company until she did.

"I'm sleeping late tomorrow. It's Sunday. Jenny and Michael won't be picking me up until eleven for late services," she murmured to the cats, as Redd found her usual spot and settled down against Andrea's cheek. Redd's sisters, Sandy and Missy, curled up on either side of Andrea's bandaged ankle.

Andrea sighed and closed her eyes. Normally, she could not sleep on her back, but tonight, she could have slept lying upside down. "What a different day this has been from yesterday. Thank you," she whispered. She had scarcely begun her evening prayers when the doorbell rang, startling her.

She groaned, reached over and turned on the light.

Chapter Ten

Madge hit the doorbell a second time and reached into her handbag for the key. She was not anxious to repeat what had happened the last time she had let herself into Andrea's house, but she did not want Andrea to try to get up from the couch to answer the door, either.

She let herself in, punched in the code to deactivate the alarm and knew in a single glance Andrea was not on the couch reading or watching television. "It's only me," she yelled, setting her tote bag and purse down on the floor next to the door. Since the kitchen was dark, Madge immediately went to Andrea's bedroom and found her sister in bed. "I'm sorry. It's only half-past eight. I saw the light on in the living room and thought maybe you were still up reading or watching television."

Andrea covered a yawn with the back of her hand and

patted the mattress next to her. "Sit for a minute. Sorry, I had a busy day."

The moment Madge eased next to her sister, the cats scattered, as always. "I heard. I thought the doctor wanted you to rest for a week or so before you—"

"I'm resting now," Andrea explained.

"That's not the same thing, and you know it," Madge insisted.

"You're looking very glamorous tonight. I don't think I've seen that dress before. I would have remembered one with lavender sequins. Big date?"

Madge waved an objection. "Don't be ridiculous. Russell's still in Ohio. The county horticultural society's annual banquet was tonight. I left right after the awards ceremony so I could stop by and show you the plaque I received."

Andrea's eyes widened. "That was tonight? Oh, I'm sorry, Madge. I forgot all about it. Why didn't you remind me? I know Jenny couldn't go, but with Russell away, I would have gone with you."

"You have enough on your mind. Besides, you're supposed to stay at home to recuperate."

"I can sit and recuperate almost anywhere," Andrea protested, "especially at a dinner where my sister is being honored."

Madge lifted a brow. "Or at your office? I heard you went to work today," she admonished.

"Doris went with me. She's a treasure. Thank you. She took me to the office so we could work out our arrangement. We had to move the furniture around a bit to make room for her, but I feel much better having someone so capable handling all the legwork."

Madge's relief was short-lived. "Don't tell me you helped move furniture!"

The doorbell rang. Andrea grinned. "Saved by the bell?"

"No, you're not," Madge warned before she left to answer the door. "I'll be right back to get an answer."

"If I'm not here, I'll be out jogging."

Madge poked her head back into Andrea's room. "Not funny," she snapped, and hurried to the front door. She peered through the peephole, saw Jenny standing on the porch and let her in. "What brings you over?"

Jenny held out one bag, then another with her other hand. "Treats. I was going to your house next. The girls fell asleep on the way home, and Michael wanted to spend a little time on the computer, so I thought I'd make a few special deliveries. Besides, I needed to check on Andrea and I wanted to see your plaque. How did it go tonight?"

Madge could not have held back a grin if she tried and retrieved her tote bag. "It was so nice. Everyone applauded. I mentioned you and Andrea in my speech, and Russell, too. He called me on my cell phone right after I got the award. The banquet manager promised me a copy of the videotape so I could show Russell when he gets back next week. Then you can have it. I'll have copies made to send to the boys."

"I can't wait. Is Andrea still awake?"

Madge led her sister to the bedroom. "Did you know she went to work today?"

Jenny frowned. "I heard. She's got to be tired. Maybe we can look at the plaque together, have a quick treat, and let her get some rest." She yawned and covered her mouth with the back of her arm.

"You look beat."

"Long day, like always, but the bride was radiant and the food at the reception was yummy. I brought some wedding cake home."

They found Andrea sitting up in bed and grinning when they entered her room. "Did I hear you say wedding cake? Let's have a picnic right here."

Madge set down her tote bag. "I'll get some forks and plates."

"Got 'em," Jenny said. She climbed up on the far side of the bed, crossed her legs Indian-style and opened her bags of cake while Madge settled in on Andrea's other side. Within moments, they were nibbling away.

"This is great cake!" Madge took another bite, certain the cake was McAllister's famous pound cake. "I was so excited at the banquet, and so many people came up to talk to me that I never did get to eat my dessert tonight."

"It's been a great day, and this is a perfect way to celebrate all the blessings we've been given," Andrea remarked.

Jenny looked from Madge to Andrea and back again, wearing a puzzled expression. "I know why you're celebrating, Madge. Come on, unveil your plaque."

Madge leaned over, pulled the plaque from her tote bag, and held up the wooden frame with her fingertips so both of her sisters could see it.

Andrea traced the border of raised flowers on the ceramic inlay. "It's lovely."

Jenny read the inscription aloud: "Madge Stevens. Forty-First Home Gardener of the Year. Tilton County Horticultural Society." She sighed. "I'm so proud of you."

"Me, too," Andrea murmured.

Madge turned the plaque around, studied the face again and smiled as she stored the plaque back in her tote bag.

"What about you?" Jenny asked Andrea. "What could you possibly be celebrating today?"

"I'm actually celebrating two things," Andrea told her. "First, I've hired my first employee. Temporarily, of course. Doris Blake will be helping me at the office until I can back on my feet. Thanks to Madge."

Jenny looked as relieved as Madge felt. She had not really been sure how Andrea would take her meddling, as good intentioned as it was to ask Doris to work for Andrea before she'd consulted with her.

Jenny took another bite. "And the second?"

"I agreed to let Jamie Martin work in the office this summer, too," Andrea announced.

Madge nearly choked. So did Jenny.

Andrea quickly explained her decision. By the time she'd finished, Madge was so overwhelmed she had to blink back tears. Andrea's capacity to forgive was a model of faith that she would have to spend the rest of her life emulating. "You're an amazing woman," she whispered.

Jenny beamed. "I'm so proud of you."

Andrea actually blushed. "Enough. You both would have done the same thing. So…Madge and I both have a lot to celebrate tonight. What about you, Jenny? We shouldn't leave you out. Have you got something to celebrate today?"

When her baby sister grinned, she caught and held Madge's attention. "As a matter of fact…I do. Michael and I do have something to celebrate."

Madge clapped her hands. "He finished his book, and

now he can go back to teaching so you can stay home with your little ones!"

Jenny's smile faded. "No. But it won't be long now. He's hoping to have it done by the end of the summer. Then he'll be sending it out in the hope of finding a literary agent, but there's no guarantee this book will ever find an agent or get published. In the meantime," she added defensively, "I plan to keep working and supporting him while he pursues his dream."

Andrea jumped into the conversation and changed the focus from Michael and his book to her sister. "I know! You got promoted to nursing supervisor, and with your raise, you're putting in a pool for the girls," she suggested.

Jenny shook her head. "No promotion for me, thank you. I like it right where I am. And *no pool!* The umbrella sprinkler is quite enough for now," she added with a chuckle.

"So you can forget any ideas you have about swimming fully clothed," Madge teased. "Let's see…something to celebrate. You're getting a new car?"

Jenny grinned. "Wrong."

Andrea tried again. "You've decided to move and you need me to help you find another house?"

"Wrong again. You two must be getting old. Here. I'll give you a hint." Jenny rested both of her palms on top of her stomach and smiled. "Ready to guess again now?"

"A baby! You're having a baby!" Madge squealed, and Andrea's voice joined in unison.

"Finally!" Jenny beamed. "Katy and Hannah are going to have a baby brother or a baby sister in February."

After hugs and kisses all around, a bit restrained to accommodate Andrea's injury, Madge and Jenny left for home. Jenny waited until Madge drove away in her purple convertible before starting her own car. Instead of pulling out, however, she gripped the steering wheel and took several long, deep gulps of air to clear her mind and to try to understand why she was feeling so emotional after being with her sisters tonight. She was thrilled for Madge and her award. She was worried for Andrea and concerned about her accident, while cautiously optimistic about her chances for beating cancer. She was ecstatic about having another baby, but she was…jealous. She wanted to have the free time Madge had. She wanted to be home with her girls and with this new baby. She wanted to support Michael's dream of becoming a writer, but what about her own dreams? Her own needs?

The moment Andrea's image flashed through her mind, guilt grabbed hold of her heart and nipped at the self-pity that seemed to consume her right now. Andrea was in a virtual battle for her life, a reality that was more than sobering.

Humbled, Jenny brushed away her tears. She pulled away and drove toward home. All she needed was a good night's sleep. She'd feel better in the morning, wouldn't she?

Chapter Eleven

When the Sunday service ended, Andrea did not argue about staying with Michael and Jenny and the girls for the Summer Sunday Social. The church youth group was sponsoring the event as a service project that was planned for every Sunday in July and August.

While Katy and Hannah were in another room playing games with the other children under the supervision of youth group volunteers, Jenny and Michael offered to serve some of the light refreshments to Andrea while she sat at their table with her back to the wall. The long white tablecloth concealed her foot elevated on a box beneath the table, thanks to Michael's thoughtfulness. She was rather comfortable now, although her arms ached from using crutches. Using little stuffed squirrels as protective pads on the crutches was no help, and she made a mental note to try to replace the squirrels as soon as she could.

Across the room, Madge was holding court, receiving congratulations on her award. She looked stunning, as always. Her pale blond hair was perfect, not a hair out of place. She wore a long aqua dress, printed with sprigs of violets, that looked cool and was very becoming. As Madge chatted, however, Andrea noted just a touch of sadness in her eyes—a sadness Andrea suspected lay in the fact that Russell had not been able to come home to share in his wife's joy at receiving her award.

Not that Madge ever complained. She never protested about how much time Russell had to spend on the road. Ever. Not about missed birthdays or anniversaries. Not about spending so much time apart. Not now and not when their boys had been growing up.

Madge was too loyal, too committed to her marriage and too much in love with her husband to utter a word against him.

Andrea let out a sigh. Whether it was inspired by a little jealousy or a sister's protective instinct, she was not sure. All she knew was that if Russell Stevens loved his wife as much as Madge loved him, he would have come home by plane, train, car or on horseback, if necessary, and shared Madge's special moment last night and attended services with her today, too.

"Judge not," she murmured, hoping to retrieve some of the grace she had lost by letting her love for her sister lead her to selfish thoughts. She opened the church bulletin to distract herself and saw the advertisement for the new Shawl Ministry that Madge had mentioned the other day.

The advertisement filled a quarter-page box inside a border decorated with small crosses formed from pairs of knitting needles. It read:

Announcing the newly formed
Church of Holy Faith
Shawl Ministry
Wanted: Volunteers committed to prayer, fellowship
and the desire to serve Him by ministering
to others
Required: Willing hands and loving hearts
Knitting skills desirable, but not necessary
Come two afternoons a month to knit or teach
others to knit!
New Members Meeting: August 14, 7 p.m.
Welleswood Community Center
Donations of materials also appreciated

Memories began to surface, but before they came into focus, Andrea heard someone approaching. When she looked up, Peggy Fallon greeted her with a smile. "I heard about what happened. You look great, considering." She sat down next to Andrea. "Do you feel as good as you look?"

Andrea groaned. "You're a sweetheart. I certainly hope I look a lot better than I feel. Mostly, I just tire out a whole lot faster than I like these days."

"Who doesn't?" She tapped the advertisement Andrea had been reading. "I think the Shawl Ministry is a great idea. Tim's going to print some signs to put up around town to see how many people we can get involved."

"He's got a good heart," Andrea murmured.

Peggy laughed. "And you've got a very persuasive sister."

"Madge?" Andrea asked, although she knew only too well how persuasive Madge could be. Who else could have convinced Andrea to attend the meeting for the Shawl Ministry?

"None other. But the printing won't take too much time. Since Tim runs the church bulletin, he already has the ad in the computer. Touch a few buttons and keys, and he's got the size he needs for the signs. They should be ready by noon tomorrow. He's got a lot of work to do, and we were wondering if maybe you could let Jamie Martin take some time off tomorrow to pick up the signs and distribute them to the businesses in town? We need to get the signs into shop windows as quickly as we can. Otherwise, Jamie can stop in as soon as he finishes up work."

Andrea toyed with the corner of the bulletin. "I didn't realize you knew Jamie was going to be helping out at the agency. Word sure does spread fast."

Peggy patted Andrea's hand. "Good news, bad news and all the news in-between. That means, fortunately, for Jamie's sake, that yesterday's news gets forgotten rather quickly. He really impressed a lot of people by volunteering to help you while you recuperate. You've impressed them even more by letting him."

Andrea waved away the compliment. "He's a good kid. It was just an accident." She paused. "I'm not sure I would ask him to distribute the signs, though. Talking to the different business owners, some of whom might want to take him to task for—"

"He knows that. He said he would do it, but only if you gave your permission."

"Jamie already agreed? Are you sure?"

"He's right next door helping with the little ones. You could ask him yourself."

"No. It's fine. If Jamie wants to do it, then sure. He can see Tim at noon."

Peggy stood up. "Thanks. I'll tell Tim. Oh, I almost forgot. Tim said to tell you to send Doris Blake over early. Say nine-thirty? He'll try to get those business cards finished by the end of the day. And if you need anything, anything at all…"

"I will. Thank you."

As Peggy made her way back to her husband, a clamor of voices drew Andrea's attention. When she looked in the direction of the disturbance, which had evolved into a round of applause, she clapped her hand to her heart.

Russell Stevens, her brother-in-law, had entered the room and was approaching his wife with a bouquet of purple daisies in one hand and a dazzling smile on his face. At two inches over six feet, he was still as trim and good-looking as he had been in college when Madge first met him and brought him home to meet the family. True, he now sported a few gray hairs at his temples, and the years had etched character into his face, but he still commanded attention in any gathering.

Attentive and handsome, he was the husband every woman dreamed of claiming for their own. Generous and outgoing, he was the neighbor everyone wanted living next door. In short, he was the town's favorite adopted son, active in community affairs and local politics whenever he was home from his travels.

Andrea's eyes filled with tears of joy as Madge hurried

into her husband's embrace. He hugged her to him and swung her off her feet, much to the delight of the crowd. As charming as ever, Russell Stevens conquered every heart in the room, including Andrea's, and guilt tugged at her conscience. "Judge not," she repeated, and offered a quick prayer as penance for her earlier negative thoughts.

Madge beamed as she led Russell over to the table. Surprise and joy had erased all signs of sadness in her eyes. "You're here. I can't believe you're actually here," she gushed. "Look, Andrea. Russell's here!"

Andrea laughed. "As you can see, you've made my sister very happy. Thanks, Russell. The award means so much more, now that you're here to share it with her."

He put his arm around his wife's shoulders. "I wanted to get back in time for the banquet last night. Unfortunately, I had some car trouble on the way. I couldn't get my hands on a rental until late last night." He paused, and his expression grew troubled. "I'm sorry to hear about…about everything. Then to have such an avoidable accident with that boy. I'm terribly sorry," he murmured.

Grateful that he did not mention the word *cancer* with so many people around who might overhear, Andrea swallowed hard. "I appreciate your concern, but I'm doing pretty well. Madge is taking good care of me. Jenny, too."

He squeezed Madge to his side. "That's my girl." He looked down at her. "What kind of plans have you made for the afternoon?"

Madge blushed. "I—I promised Andrea I would come by and work on her garden."

"Don't be silly," Andrea countered. "The flower beds can

survive another day or two. Go. Spend some time with your husband," she urged.

Russell grinned. "I've made reservations at La Casita for four o'clock. Think you're up to celebrating with us, Andrea? I called Michael early this morning. He and Jenny are coming."

Madge elbowed him. "Michael knew you were coming home today?"

He feigned injury. "Not until this morning. What do you say, Andrea? Are you feeling up to coming? It would mean a lot if you could."

Andrea hesitated. Her shoulder was still very sore, and her ankle was throbbing. She was also a little tired. But the mere mention of La Casita, the new Mexican restaurant on the avenue, had her mouth watering and eased every ache and pain in her body. "I'd walk a mile on these ridiculous crutches to have one of their tortilla samplers. All I need is a nap first," she replied.

"We'll pick you up," Madge offered.

"And we'll take you home whenever you've decided you've had enough," Russell added, just as Jenny and Michael arrived with plates of cookies and glasses of punch. After a hug from Jenny and a handshake from Michael, Russell took Madge's hand. "If you folks don't mind, we're going to start making our way out of here. Michael, we'll see you and Jenny at the restaurant. Andrea, we'll pick you up at quarter to four." Without waiting for any of them to respond, Russell guided Madge back through a maze of well-wishers.

Michael excused himself to check on the girls, but Jenny sat down next to Andrea and sighed. "I'd love a nap. How about you?"

"Already have one planned."

Jenny smiled. "I'm sure Russell and Madge will 'take a nap,' too. Sometimes I wish…I wish you had someone, too, like me and Madge."

Andrea moistened her lips. "It's okay. I don't mind so much anymore. Once in a while, though, I wonder what it would be like if Peter had lived." She shook away the sadness that nearly enveloped her. "But it's okay. I have you and Madge. I have my business and my clients. And the kids. I call them a lot."

"I know, but it's not the same as having a husband."

Andrea lowered her eyes. Jenny was right. It was not the same. Even with all the blessings she had received, it just was not the same.

It was different, this being alone. She was not lonely. She was just…alone. Always alone. She nearly fell into the trap of self-pity before she brightened. "I have the 'girls' now."

Jenny nibbled on a coconut bar. "They're cats. They don't count."

"They snuggle. They purr. And they never complain," Andrea argued. She took a brownie and broke it in half.

"Like Ed Miller did?"

Andrea chuckled. She had dated Ed Miller for all of two weeks before realizing he was more interested in having a maid or housekeeper than a wife. "I haven't thought of him in years."

"Little wonder. What about Duane Allen?"

"Derek," Andrea corrected, popping the half brownie into her mouth and savoring the taste of chocolate.

Jenny shrugged. "Duane, Derek, whatever. He didn't last very long, either."

Andrea swallowed her brownie and took a sip of punch. "I didn't find it endearing to have my date suggest, on the third date, mind you, that I could remodel my home to accommodate *his* collection of Sinatra memorabilia and I could fit a new three-car garage on my property to house the antique cars he was going to restore with part of my salary. After we were married, of course."

Jenny gasped. "He didn't!"

"Did you ever ride by Linda Sullivan's house? I mean, before she married Derek and became Linda Allen? She didn't have a three-car garage when she started to date him."

Jenny held up her hand. "Okay. You're right. Point taken. There are a lot of frogs out there." She paused to cover a yawn with the back of her hand. "Tell me about Robert St. Helen. You dated him for what? Two years? Madge was absolutely convinced you were going to marry him."

Andrea stiffened. She had never told anyone why she had suddenly stopped dating Robert, even after he moved away from Welleswood. "Two years, three months and sixteen days. Then he hit me for the first and last time."

Jenny grabbed Andrea's arm. "He hit you? He *hit* you? Robert?"

"Charming men aren't always quite as charming as they appear. They're not all like Michael or Russell," Andrea whispered. At the time, the pain of disappointment had been far deeper than the pain of the bruise he had inflicted, but even now, the memory of the dreams he had destroyed in a single burst of anger was very real. "Being alone isn't being lonely. It's just being alone. Considering some of the possible alternatives, I think I'm better off that way," she whispered, wondering whether she was trying harder to convince Jenny or herself.

Chapter Twelve

The only businesses open on Sunday afternoon in Welleswood were the restaurants. A cloud of international aromas from a Mexican, French, Italian, Chinese, Thai and two traditional American restaurants hung together in the warm humid air and mingled with the gentler scent of potted summer flowers that added the vibrant color of summer to the avenue.

From her seat in La Casita, Madge could see pedestrians strolling along the new brick-and-concrete sidewalks, but there was little automobile traffic today. Groups of seniors had gathered to sit on benches beneath the shade of trees also gnarled and wrinkled with age. Surrounded by her sisters, and with her husband at her side, Madge was utterly and completely content for the first time in weeks.

She leaned closer to Russell as he tapped the side of his

water glass with the tip of his spoon to get everyone's attention. Then he started to lift his glass.

"Another toast?" she teased.

He smiled. "Just one more." He held up his glass. "To sand and sea and beach homes."

Her heart skipped a beat, but before she could say a word, he pressed a finger to her lips and continued. "As of last Friday, I've been named Regional Sales Manager for the Mid-Atlantic Region, which means that tomorrow, you and I are driving down to Sea Gate to pick out that summer beach house you've always wanted."

"Russell!" She threw her arms around his neck and barely heard the congratulations everyone offered to them both. "I'm so proud of you. Regional Sales Manager! Do you mean it? Can we really afford a place at the beach?"

He hugged her with one arm. "We can now, although I'm not sure how much time I'll be able to spend there. Not for a while yet. I'll still have to travel a lot, but Drew and Brett will probably find their way home more often if we have a beach house."

Madge settled back and gazed at her sisters. "You'll come and spend some time with me at the beach, too, won't you? Katy and Hannah would love it. We'll teach them how to swim and use a belly-board, how to build sand castles—"

"And how to dig for sand crabs?" Andrea teased.

Madge felt her cheeks warm. "Did you have to mention the sand crabs?"

Jenny looked from Andrea to Madge, back to Andrea again, and furrowed her brow. "Is this another story about something I'm too young to remember?"

Andrea laughed. "Yep."

Michael looked at Russell and shook his head. "Sounds like we're about to hear another sister story. Go ahead, Andrea."

"No, this is my story, too," Madge argued. She tilted up her chin. "Once upon a time, when there was just Mother and Daddy and the 'big three,'" she began with a wink in Jenny's direction, "before we started camping as a family, we used to go on vacation for a week or two—"

"Usually two," Andrea noted.

"In Sea Gate," Madge continued. "Mother and Daddy would rent a house right on the beach. Anyway, the year I was four—"

"And I was six," Andrea interjected.

Madge sighed.

Andrea held up her hand in mock surrender. "Okay. Tell it by yourself. I just don't want you to take all the blame. We were in it together, remember?"

Madge grinned. "Every detail, and since you were the oldest, you should take most of the blame. One year, Andrea and I decided we were going to take some sand crabs home, so the last day of vacation, while Daddy was loading the car and Mother was sweeping the sand out of the house one more time, Andrea and I sneaked down to the shoreline. Sandra was just a baby," she explained. "We dug up a dozen or so sand crabs, hid them in a big peanut butter jar we had taken out of the trash, added some sand and ocean water and sneaked it home."

She paused when the waitress returned with the dessert tray Russell had ordered, waited until she left and waved away dessert to continue her story. "Daddy's birthday was the following day, you see, and we wanted to give him a special present. He had a small aquarium he kept in his office at home."

Jenny shook her head. "I don't remember him ever having an aquarium."

Andrea giggled. "He didn't have one for very long."

Russell looked at Madge with anticipated dread. "Was it a salt-water aquarium?" When she shook her head, he groaned. "I know where this story is headed."

She laughed with him. "As soon as we got home, we sneaked into his office and dumped everything into the aquarium—sand, ocean water, sand crabs and even a little peanut butter went in, too."

Jenny cupped her hand at her brow and groaned. "I can't ever tell my girls this story, especially if we get an aquarium. What did Daddy do?"

Andrea held up her hand, and Madge sat back to let her older sister finish the story. "He didn't do anything. Not then. He didn't know what we'd done until his birthday the next day. Right after breakfast, we made him go into his office. We were so excited and so sure he'd be pleased with our present."

Michael grimaced. "Did anything survive?"

"Only the sand crabs," Andrea replied. "When I look back now, I wonder at Daddy's patience. He didn't yell. He didn't threaten. He just listened to our explanation, told us he understood our good intentions—"

"And then he punished us," Madge murmured, and fidgeted in her seat.

"A good solid spanking?" Russell asked.

"No, Daddy never spanked any of us," Jenny offered. "At least, not the little two."

Andrea smiled. "Not the big three, either."

Madge nodded. "I think I might have forgotten a spanking, but I'll never, ever forget how he carried that aquarium out to the backyard, set it on the ground, and helped us take out every one of those dead tropical fish. One by one, he'd tell us the species and lay the fish on the ground so we could see how beautiful it was."

"He made us kneel down and pray, right then and there to ask God's forgiveness for destroying His creatures, even though we didn't kill them on purpose," Andrea continued. "We buried them together in a little grave, and Daddy glued a couple of Popsicle sticks together to make a little cross."

"What happened to the sand crabs?" Michael asked.

"They only lived for a few more days. When they died, we repeated the little ritual and buried them alongside the fish," Madge explained.

Andrea yawned. "And that's the end of the sand-crab story. Unfortunately, there are many, many more stories in which I led my little sister astray."

Madge studied her older sister, noted the dark circles under her eyes and her pale features, and tapped the tabletop with her fingertips. "You're exhausted. Maybe we should save the other stories for next time. Right now, I think it would be a good idea for Russell and me to take you home." To her surprise, Andrea offered no argument.

Within half an hour, Andrea was home in bed and Madge was on her way home with Russell. "Were you really serious about going to the shore tomorrow? What about work?"

He chuckled. "I'm the Regional Sales Manager now. I can take a few days off."

"A few days?"

"I talked to Dan Myers at the social today. He slipped the keys to his house in Sea Gate right off his key ring and said we could stay a week if we wanted to. I'm not sure, but I might be able to stretch out a few more days off."

She sighed. "I have a meeting for the Shawl Ministry on Wednesday I really can't miss. Thursday I promised to take Andrea for chemo, which reminds me. I have to call her and find out what time she has her appointment. Friday I have a nail appointment, then I'm getting my hair touched up. We could stay Monday and Tuesday, though. No problem."

Disappointment flashed briefly in Russell's eyes before he offered Madge a grin that made her heart flutter. "Monday and Tuesday will be great. I really shouldn't take off more than that, I guess. I talked to Blair Whitaker at Shore Realty last week. We were fraternity brothers, remember? Anyway, he's got several places lined up for us to see tomorrow. The market is loaded right now, and he thinks we might even be able to settle before the end of summer."

She gasped. "You—you set up appointments with a realtor before I even said I wanted a beach house?"

He cocked a brow. "Madge, we've been married for twenty-six years. I can't remember when you didn't want a beach house. Of course, if you've changed your mind…."

"No!" She said the word so abruptly she laughed out loud. "I'd love a beach house, and if we could get one before Labor Day…"

Her thoughts drifted to fall. By then, Andrea might need a place to rest between treatments, and there was no place as peaceful and quiet as the seashore after the season had ended and all the vacationers had gone home.

"We could be at the shore in an hour. How about heading down tonight? We can take a walk on the beach, watch the sun set and be ready to look at houses first thing in the morning," he suggested.

She hesitated, but she was reluctant to disappoint him again and smiled. "Just give me half an hour to change and pack."

He pulled into their driveway, turned off the ignition and kissed her. "Make it fifteen minutes and you've got a deal."

Chapter Thirteen

The following afternoon, Madge stood with both hands on the railing of a second-floor balcony off the master bedroom in a beachfront home in Sea Gate while Russell went back downstairs with Blair to inspect the heating and air-conditioning systems. On the beach below, sunbathers stretched out side by side and head to toe, creating a patch-work of color. Lifeguards with their noses coated white with zinc oxide perched on stands to protect the swimmers and keep rafters and surfers in their restricted areas. Scents from tropical tanning oils, citrus lotions and sunblock blended with the salt air. Overhead, seagulls cried and swooped down for prey in the water or an unguarded snack on shore while majestic osprey glided on wind currents.

Madge closed her eyes and lifted her face to the sun to let a cooling sea breeze caress her features. With her lips, she murmured a prayer, asking God to clear any obstacles that might block their purchase of this house. With her heart, she embraced the memories of her loved ones, especially Sandra, who had loved the beach almost as much as Madge did.

She blinked back tears and cupped her hand to her brow to cut the glare of the relentless sun. In the far distance near the horizon, a freighter of some sort, probably out of Philadelphia, was heading north. Closer, dozens of sailboats and catamarans danced atop the blue-gray waters of the Atlantic. A motorboat pulling a parasail hugged the shoreline just beyond the swimming limits.

Madge had not ventured deeper into the ocean than mid-thigh for forty years, and she had no desire to change her habits now. She was not tempted to leave shore. Not even for half a heartbeat. Until she glanced up at the person strapped into the harness hanging below the red-and-white-striped parasail. She tried to imagine what the view might be like from that height. If the parasail broke free and soared above one of the few clouds in the sky, would she be close enough to heaven to get a glimpse or sink straight back to earth and wind up suspended in the ocean by a life jacket?

She fingered the gold chain around her neck as one of her dangling earrings brushed her neck. "I'd sink for sure. I'd rather stick with my beach chair, thank you," she whispered. When she heard footsteps, she turned and saw Russell approaching her with a smile, but Blair was not with him. "Everything looks good from my end. The two-car garage will give us off-street parking, and there are outside showers to help keep the sand out of the house. How about you? What do you think of the place?"

She grinned. "The view is amazing, and the house is beyond everything I've ever dreamed about. Where's Blair?" she asked, reluctant to appear overanxious about buying the house.

"He had to leave for another appointment. I told him we'd take another walk-through and lock up when we left. If we decide this really is the one we want, I can call him later. I've got his cell-phone number."

She left the balcony and met him inside the master bedroom. Together, they revisited the three other bedrooms, each with adjoining baths. "There's plenty of room for the grandchildren, if Drew and Brett ever settle down and give us some. In the meantime, I hope the boys can come for a visit. If not, Michael and Jenny and the girls will come. Andrea, too."

They went up a six-step staircase to the family room in the loft that featured yet another balcony facing the ocean. "I could set up an office here in this alcove. There's room for a desk and my laptop," Russell suggested.

Madge grinned. "*Our* laptop. I'll need to keep tabs on what's happening at home." She led him back down the staircase, along a hallway past a laundry room, and up another mini-staircase to a great room. An island separated the kitchen from the living room, replete with cathedral ceilings, a gas fireplace, and a wall of windows that provided a breathtaking view of the ocean, as well as a wraparound balcony. In her mind's eyes, Madge envisioned the glory of the sun peaking over the horizon at daybreak and a wide beam of moonlight stretching from the water to the sky at night.

She placed her hand over her heart. "Are you sure we can afford this?"

Russell put his arm around her shoulders. "That's why banks created home-equity loans," he teased. "The house in Welleswood has been paid off for a few years now. Between what we can borrow against the house and the bonuses I've been setting aside, we can not only afford the house, but we can also furnish it. Within reason," he cautioned.

"Within reason," she murmured, but her mind was already racing ahead, planning a color scheme and listing the stores and shops she would use to make her plans become reality.

He cleared his throat. "There's only one little glitch."

Her heart skipped a beat.

"If they accept our offer, we can't settle until the day before Labor Day, which isn't really a problem for me. With starting the new position, I've got a number of commitments that have to be met in August. In fact, I'll probably be away the entire month."

She smiled. "They say September at the shore is wonderful. It's still warm outside and so is the ocean, but the vacationers are gone."

He reached into his pocket and frowned. "I guess I left my cell phone back at Dave's. Let's grab a bite to eat first, then we'll head back to the house to get my phone. I can call Blair from there."

"I don't think so." She opened her purse, took out her cell phone and handed it to him. "Ask Blair to meet us at his office so we can put in our offer before we grab lunch."

The following morning, Madge and Russell left the real estate office with a signed contract, a settlement date of just before Labor Day and an appointment scheduled for that very afternoon at the bank back in Welleswood to arrange for the home-equity loan.

"Things are happening so fast, I'm almost dizzy. I don't know how you can keep all those dates and figures straight. You're amazing," she remarked as she got into the car.

He waited until she had secured her seat belt before closing the door and getting behind the wheel. "Some of us have a head for figures. Some of us don't," he teased as he guided the car into traffic. "That's why I handle all the bills, remember?"

She patted his arm. "And you do a marvelous job. You always have. I'm lucky I don't have the worries that Andrea has had to carry every since Peter died, or to have to make a choice between supporting my husband's dream or staying home with my children like Jenny has had to do."

"She and Michael seem very happy," he suggested as they reached the Garden State Parkway entrance and headed north.

"I suppose they are, but with the new baby coming in February, it will be even harder for her to work."

"Maybe Michael will sell this new book of his. He seems pretty excited about it."

She waved his words away. "Michael is always excited about his newest book. At this point, with six or seven manuscripts all gathering dust and enough rejection slips to wallpaper every room in our new beach house, I'm surprised he hasn't gotten the message."

Russell took his eyes from the roadway for a moment and glanced at her. "What message?"

She shrugged. "That he gave this writing career he wanted so badly his best, but failed. With a wife and three children to support, it's time he faced up to his responsibilities. He was a great English teacher when Jenny first met him. I'm sure he wouldn't have any trouble finding a teaching position again. Then Jenny could stay home and raise her babies, like she should."

Russell fidgeted in his seat and readjusted his seat belt. "I guess it doesn't matter that both Michael and Jenny seem satisfied with their arrangement?"

"I know my sister," she snapped, surprised by the churlish tone of her own voice.

"Ouch!"

She drew in a deep breath. "I'm sorry. I didn't mean to snap at you. It's just frustrating. Jenny waited so long to get married and have children. It's hard to stand by and watch her miss out on all those precious years with Katy and Hannah, and now with the new baby, too…."

He cleared his throat. "What about Michael?"

She cocked a brow.

Russell slowed down, pulled up to the tollbooth, tossed thirty-five cents into the bin and accelerated as the light turned green. "I only meant that maybe it's not such a bad thing, Michael staying home with the girls."

"I'm not saying it's bad. It's a whole lot better than having the girls in day care with strangers. It's just…different." She shrugged her shoulder. "I guess I'm just plain old-fashioned, and I'm a lot more worried about Andrea. She says she's going to be fine, but—"

"You don't believe her?"

"No, I believe her. At least, I believe she's telling me what her doctor has said. I just feel badly for her, that's all."

"Be careful. I'm not sure how well she takes to sympathy," he murmured.

"She doesn't, and you know it, which is why I know I have to be careful. I can't let her see how worried I am. It's not as if all she had to worry about was getting through her treatments."

"Trying to run a business and maneuver about on crutches won't be easy."

She sighed. "I'd love to strangle that Jamie Martin. Trouble is, he's been so decent about taking responsibility for the accident, I'm more tempted to just hug him. I just wish she didn't have to worry about keeping a roof over her head. If her business ever fails, which is not out of the realm of possibilities, she could lose everything. Then what?"

He shrugged. "She's a fighter. She'd find a way to survive somehow."

Madge's heart began to race. "Which only proves my point. She shouldn't have to find a way to survive. She shouldn't have to carry her financial burden alone. It's not fair. Not that she ever gives the idea of marrying again any serious thought. She's far too busy playing superwoman."

Russell rubbed his brow. "Let me see if I understand you. You're upset because Jenny has chosen to support her husband's dream and work while he writes and takes care of the children, and you're also upset because Andrea is sick again and because she seems to like being an independent, self-supporting woman."

Madge chewed on her lower lip and shook her head. "I'm not upset. I'm just concerned, and I feel a little guilty, I guess."

"Guilty? Why?"

"Because you've always taken such good care of me. I never had to choose between supporting your career and the children, like Jenny, and I've never had to worry about going to work, day after day, week after week, like Andrea. Now with the new beach house, it almost seems like I'm being greedy or—or selfish. I have so much…."

"If that's how you feel, it's not too late to back out of the contract. There's a three-day grace period."

"No. I want the beach house, but I want Jenny and Andrea to have more."

"Maybe they do," he whispered. "Maybe they do."

Chapter Fourteen

On Wednesday, Andrea had a "to do" list in front of her that would have been daunting on a good day, and today ranked somewhere between awful and disaster.

And it was only ten-thirty in the morning.

While Jamie continued on his mission to get additional businesses to display the signs advertising the Shawl Ministry, Andrea sorted through the color-coded files on her desk for the third time, leaned back in her chair and ran her fingers through her hair. She glanced at the paperwork on top of the conference table that was Doris's temporary desk and saw the purple folder she wanted. It had to be the folder she wanted. It was the only purple folder in sight.

She sighed. Unless that folder had grown legs or sprouted wings, a possibility she did not dismiss easily given the day's downward spiral, someone had moved the folder and left it well out of her reach. "Someone named Doris," she whispered.

She recognized the irascible tone in her voice and steepled her hands. She had anticipated the need to make adjustments now that she had to share her office space with another person. Although Andrea and Doris's personalities were compatible in their approach to clients, when it came to paperwork and organizational details, they could not have been more opposite. Accommodating their different styles was turning out to be much harder than Andrea had thought it would be.

Anyone who glanced at Andrea's desk would know she was more than highly organized. She was the Queen of Order, and she could not function any other way. Colored file folders lay separated by topic in bins on the right side of her desk. Minibaskets in her desk drawers held supplies so she could almost grab what she needed without looking. Even the maze of cords connected to the computer, printer, telephone and fax machine had been tamed into submission.

She glanced at Doris's desk and shuddered. The only way to describe the surface of the woman's desk right now was total chaos. File folders, mail and telephone messages littered the top of her desk as though she had simply thrown everything into the air and let it all lay where it landed. Several of Andrea's giveaway mugs were home to pens, pencils and other supplies that were all jumbled together.

There! The purple folder for the Wheatley settlement tomorrow was smack in the middle of that…that mess.

Andrea gritted her teeth. With her chemo treatment

scheduled for nine-thirty tomorrow morning, she would not have time to get back to the office and review all the paperwork before the one-o'clock settlement. She needed to go over that file now, but her crutches were in the corner across the room where Jamie had inadvertently put them.

Bracing both hands against the edge of her desk, she pulled herself up to a standing position, then realized she could not let go of the desk to push her chair back any farther and out of her way without risking losing her balance. She gripped the desk hard. "Think, Andrea!" she muttered.

Not about calling one of the office superstores to order a swivel chair on wheels or a plastic mat to put on top of the rug so she could glide from one desk to the other. She could do that easily enough later. She had the Office Genie catalogue in her desk drawer. Not about the fact that Jamie could have gotten the folder for her if he had not been on an errand. And not about the fact that the folder would have been on her desk, right where she had put it, if Doris had not moved it and then forgotten to return it.

She closed her eyes, tightened her grip and turned to carefully nudge the chair with her right knee. She opened her eyes and tried again. Nothing. Not even an inch of more space. Frustrated, she managed a little hop, but when she heard the front door open, she was caught off guard, lost her balance and plopped rather awkwardly back into her seat.

"Andrea! Are you all right? What are you doing?"

She glared at Madge, hoisted herself back into a normal sitting position and pointed to Doris's desk. "I'm fine. I was just trying to get that folder. I need it to make sure everything is ready for settlement tomorrow."

Madge walked over to Doris's desk, picked up the purple folder and grinned. "This purple one?"

Andrea clenched her teeth. "Yes."

Madge placed the folder on the desk in front of Andrea. "Where's Doris?"

"Showing a house."

"What about Jamie? I thought he was supposed to be here to help you."

"He's out distributing the signs advertising the Shawl Ministry."

Another grin. "Good thing I stopped by, isn't it? What else can I do?"

Madge's smile and willing nature sweetened Andrea's sour mood, but she had no intention of getting her sister involved in her real-estate business. "Lend me your left ankle?"

"If I could—"

"I know you would." Andrea glanced at Doris's desk again and sighed. "I don't like this. Not even a little."

"What don't you like? Having someone else working here, being so dependent or having me catch you doing something dumb, like trying to hop your way to the other desk?"

Andrea blushed, even though it was rather comforting to have someone know her so well. "All of the above."

Madge pulled up a chair and glanced around the room. "I know it's hard, but things will work out with Doris. I think you'll even get to like having someone to share all this work, too." She grinned again. "And I've seen you do plenty of dumb things before, so don't worry about today."

"What dumb things? Other than the disaster with the sand crabs?" she countered.

Madge curled the fingers of one of her hands into half a fist, inspected her nails and frowned. "Oh, let me count the times." She looked up at the ceiling for a moment. "What about the time you dumped the entire contents of the salt shaker into the gravy Mother was making for Thanksgiving?"

Andrea stiffened her back. "That wasn't my fault. Sandra loosened the lid on the salt shaker because she was mad Mother wouldn't let her help, too."

"Hmm. There was the time you sprayed hair spray on the furniture instead of polish."

A little stiffer. "Again, not my fault. Mother said to use the can of polish she kept in the cabinet under the kitchen sink. She didn't know you kept a can of hair spray hidden there so I couldn't borrow it. Neither did I, so I just opened the cabinet and grabbed the first can I saw."

"Without bothering to read the label, which turned out to be pretty dumb," Madge teased. "Do you remember Miss Dillon?"

"Vaguely. She lived up the street with her brother, I think. As I recall, they had a lot of pets."

"Miss Dillon had a turtle that she kept in a cage in the backyard. She had drilled a little hole in its shell, and she'd attach a leash and let it out to hunt for bugs in her garden. Remember?"

"I—I think I do remember playing with the turtle a few times."

"You stole the turtle."

Andrea's pulse raced with disbelief. "I did? Are you sure I stole her turtle?"

"I remember it perfectly," Madge countered. "It was the Fourth of July. We had all gone to the parade, like we did every year. On the way home, we were excited about the fireworks planned for late that night, which meant we had to take a nap, of course."

Andrea nodded. She had no specific recollection of that particular Fourth of July, but Mother's insistence that they all take naps if they wanted to stay up for fireworks was a tradition that had lasted well into elementary school for all the girls.

"Well, you didn't take a nap that Fourth of July. You sneaked up to Miss Dillon's and snatched Willie."

"The turtle's name was Willie?"

"Yes, it was."

Andrea rolled her eyes. "You even remember the turtle's name?"

Madge shrugged. "I do. Don't you? Never mind. Obviously you don't. Anyway, you brought the turtle home and hid it under your bed and then took your nap."

"I did?" Andrea shook her head. She had absolutely no memory of doing anything of the kind.

"You did."

"Why? Why would I steal Miss Dillon's turtle?"

Madge chuckled. "As I recall, after Mother found the turtle walking down the hallway after he'd done his business on her new carpet runner, you told her you'd brought Willie home because the fireworks that night were going to scare him."

Andrea furrowed her brow and mentally flipped through her childhood memories. She remembered loving the sprays of dazzling color when each fireworks display lit the night sky, but the loud bangs had terrified her. An old, old memory finally surfaced from the fog created by many,

many years, along with the emotions she had felt as a young girl. "Oh, I remember Willie now. Miss Dillon had let me paint his name on the bottom of his shell with nail polish! And I did. I did take Willie home to protect him. I did!"

"See? I told you I'd be able to think of something dumb you did."

Andrea drew her head back. "That wasn't dumb. I was trying to do something kind for an animal that I loved. That wasn't dumb," she repeated.

Madge's eyes twinkled. "Of course it wasn't. The dumb part was not putting the turtle into a box or something so he couldn't escape from underneath your bed. I tried to warn you at the time, but you ignored me, as usual."

Andrea opened her mouth to argue, heard the whisper of a memory to back up Madge's claims and pursed her lips. "How on earth do you remember all this…this stuff?"

"Great mind. Pure talent. Or sheer brilliance. Take your pick."

Andrea laughed with her sister. "Honestly, how you manage all that minutiae—wait a minute! You're back from the shore! I forgot you went to Sea Gate to look at beach houses. Did Blair show you something you liked? No, that was a dumb question. What's not to like about any beach house in Sea Gate?"

Madge opened her purse, pulled out a fact sheet and handed it to Andrea. "As of September third, it's ours!"

Andrea listened carefully as Madge described the four-bedroom, five-bath summer home—a home Andrea or most average folks could not afford if it was their only home. Joy for her sister, however, eclipsed a wisp of jealousy. "It's beautiful."

"At the price we paid, it should be," Madge quipped, "although you wouldn't believe some of the monstrosities we saw. They're tearing down so many of those little cottages Mother and Daddy used to rent, you almost wouldn't recognize it as the same town. Not that that's a bad thing."

She leaned closer to the desk. "The best part is we're facing the beach and the views…" Her gaze grew distant. "Mother and Daddy would have loved this house."

"They loved it anywhere we could all be together," Andrea whispered.

"There's plenty of room in this house for all of us and maybe a few grandchildren someday if I can get either one of the boys to settle down and get married," Madge ventured, and the twinkle in her eyes sparkled even brighter. "We called Drew and Brett last night. Drew isn't sure if he can get any time off in September, but he said he'd try. After living in Washington State for the past two years, he said he'd love to come to a drier climate. Brett's a definite, though."

She tucked the fact sheet back into her purse. "He said he'd fly in for a long weekend. He's going to see if he can get a flight right into Atlantic City."

"Is be bringing Amy?"

"They broke up." Madge shook her head. "I liked her a lot."

Andrea chuckled. "You liked Mindy a lot, too."

"I've liked all Brett's girlfriends. One of these days—"

"Madge? What a surprise!" Doris swept into the office with a shopping bag in one hand and her briefcase in the other. She plopped both on top of her desk. Simultaneously, the telephone rang, Jamie returned from his errands, picked up the remaining signs and left again. Meanwhile, the fax machine started whining.

Andrea reached for the telephone, but Doris got there first. "Hooper Realty. Yes? Oh, I see. No, I suppose not. Thank you." She hung up the telephone. "That was Dr. Newton's office? I—I'm sorry. I didn't get a chance to tell her... I think the receptionist thought I was you. Your appointment has been changed to one o'clock tomorrow, the last appointment of the day. She said something about the doctor having to schedule additional surgery in the morning."

Andrea felt the blood drain from her face. No one outside of her family knew about her cancer recurrence or the regimen of treatments scheduled for the coming year. To think a simple mistake might have changed that left Andrea weak with disappointment. Though secondary, the conflict between her appointment and the Wheatley settlement now added frustration to her emotional distress.

Her pulse pounded against the wall of her chest. How much did Doris actually know and how much would she surmise? Andrea closed her eyes and prayed for the patience and strength to survive a bad day—one that was quickly heading straight toward disaster.

Chapter Fifteen

"Oh, that happens all the time. Changing appointments, I mean," Madge said, diverting attention from Andrea to herself. "I hope you haven't overdone it. If that ankle of yours isn't healing as it should, the doctor is not going to be happy. You know doctors. They can be more than a little arrogant, and that's on a good day. I'm glad I was here when the call came so I know to pick you up at twelve-thirty instead of earlier."

She got up, leaned over the desk and shook her finger at Andrea. "Up, up, up! Get that foot up on that footrest, or I'm not going with you to listen to that doctor's lecture." She paused and pretended to untangle the gold necklace she wore while she gave Andrea a wink.

Bless you. Andrea mouthed the words and wished she could have given her sister a hug, especially when she saw Doris nodding her agreement to Madge's comments.

"Russell is making copies of the contract for the beach house. If I bring them tomorrow, will you look them over for me? I know Russell trusts Blair completely, but I'd feel better if you told me everything is in order."

"Of course."

"I'll come early, then, and I'll bring lunch, too."

Andrea shook her head. Changing the time for her appointment also meant changing her mealtimes, too. "I'll have a late breakfast around ten. Don't bother with lunch."

"Then I'll bring breakfast at ten," Madge insisted. She gave Andrea another wink and headed out the door.

Doris sat down behind her desk. "I'll cover the Wheatley settlement for you. I thought I had the folder right here," she mumbled as she moved her briefcase and shopping bag to the floor and rummaged through the mess on her desk. When she came up empty-handed, she frowned. "I was sure I had it here somewhere."

Andrea held up the purple folder. "No, I've got it."

Doris shrugged, apparently oblivious to the fact that Andrea had had to retrieve the folder. "I could call and see if we could move the settlement to the morning, if you'd rather attend, but I doubt that would work. If I recall correctly, the Wheatleys are settling on their old house at ten." She reached down, retrieved her shopping bag and set it back on top of the desk.

To Andrea's surprise, Doris handed her a small bag. "From me to you, for being so gracious with your time and helping me to get situated."

"A gift? You bought me a gift? That wasn't necessary."

Doris lifted a brow. "Yes, it was. Open it. I think you'll agree."

Curious, Andrea opened the bag, pulled out a pair of paisley cushions for the armrests on her crutches and smiled. "No more squirrels! Thank you so much," she murmured, feeling all the more guilty for staring at the other things Doris had bought.

Doris retrieved Andrea's crutches from the corner, removed the old gray squirrel cushions and worked the paisley ones into place. "There. Better?" she asked with a grin.

"Much better. You were right. Thank you." Andrea put the squirrels into the bag and stored it in one of the drawers of her desk. She turned the page on her daily planner to the next day and made a note to remind herself to give the bag to Madge. By then, the guilt she felt for being annoyed at Doris, who was being so thoughtful, had eased.

Doris returned the crutches to the corner. "I found the paisley cushions at the medical-supply store at the mall." She paused and looked around as if checking to see if anyone had overheard her. "Sorry. My sister tells me that mentioning the mall can get me into trouble here in Welleswood, let alone admitting to shopping there."

Andrea laughed. "I think you're safe. Besides, we don't have a medical-supply store on the avenue."

"No, but you have Over the Edge. What a great little shop! I finally found everything I wanted to make my desk more attractive. Ellen, I think she's the owner? She helped me coordinate everything." One by one, Doris set out her purchases on top of her desk. "What do you think?"

Andrea leaned back in her chair, too shocked by the items to do more than gape. She did not even try to reconcile Doris's promise to organize her workspace with her efforts today to make her desktop more attractive.

In all honesty, Andrea could only describe the floral arrangement as "over the edge," pun intended. The mother-of-pearl ceramic dish that held the silk flowers might have passed muster if it had not been shaped like a candle that had been stored in an attic over the summer and melted into a shapeless blob. By themselves, the silk flowers would have been lovely, especially with fewer of them, but the fan of peacock feathers at the back of the arrangement was more than a few degrees past garish.

The matching desk set, which included a business-card holder that featured a single peacock feather did not inspire a kind thought, either, so Andrea kept her attention on the floral piece. "The feathers add an…an interesting touch," she managed.

From the opposite side of her desk, Doris folded her arms over her chest and tilted her head. "It's better than interesting. It's perfect. You can't see a bit of the clutter. We wouldn't want the clients to think I wasn't organized," she added.

Before Andrea could think of an appropriate response, Jamie returned. He took one look at Doris's desk and grinned. "Looks cool, Mrs. Blake."

So much for hoping Jamie would be an ally.

"How did you do with the last of the signs?" Andrea asked, hoping to avoid discussing the horror on Doris's desk any further.

He held out his empty hands. "I had a very successful morning."

Doris beamed. "Didn't we all?"

"Didn't we," Andrea muttered. She checked her watch. Eleven-fifteen. Still plenty of time for the day to swing around.

* * *

At two-thirty, Andrea sent Jamie to the post office and home for the day. By four, the situation in the office was still status quo—no new problems, but nothing to celebrate, either. In fact, Andrea had managed to make a lot of progress on the settlement for Jane Huxbaugh, which was only days away. Unless she hit an unexpected pothole, the rest of the road to settlement looked smooth. Doris was prepared for tomorrow's settlement with the Wheatleys, too, and she had left early for a dental appointment.

The phone had not rung for over an hour. Andrea tapped her pencil eraser against the top of her desk. Something was nagging at her. What was it she still had to do? Her "to do" list gave her no help. Everything had been crossed off except making a call to Office Genie. But there was something else she had to do. She was sure of it. She just could not quite put her finger on it. But it was there, and she would not be able to go home today until she had figured out what she was supposed to do.

She leaned back in her chair, readjusted her foot on the footrest and looked up at the ceiling to minimize any distractions. She chose a hairline crack in the ceiling to stare at and mentally reviewed her day, starting with when she had arrived at the office. Whatever it was she had to do, did not involve Jamie or Madge.

That left Doris. Whatever was nagging Andrea did not involve either Doris's desk or the bizarre decorative elements she had added. There was the mix-up when the doctor's office called, but Andrea had already put that behind her. Doris seemed convinced the appointment was for Andrea's ankle, and Andrea had already talked with the office to inform them of the error so they could update their records to indicate Andrea no longer worked alone.

That left the Wheatley settlement. No help there. Doris was ready for that. If the settlement went smoothly, she would be back at the office by three at the latest, and the Wheatleys would be on their way to their new home. A thought rushed out, and she punched her pencil down so hard on the desk the eraser snapped off. "That's it! The Wheatleys! I forgot to tell Doris to take the present for them."

She tossed the pencil into the trash, along with the eraser, and double-checked her "to do" list on her daily planner. She always gave her buyers American flag kits for their new homes. She should have had it on her list for today. Why didn't she? Settlement was...tomorrow. On impulse, she flipped her daily planner to the next day and there it was, right next to one o'clock: *Wheatley settlement. Gift!*

Below, she had penciled a reminder to check the reorder for a new case of flag kits. She sighed. No wonder she hadn't written down the reminder for today. She had planned to go to the settlement herself tomorrow and she would have...if her appointment for her chemo treatment had not been changed today.

She sighed again. "Okay, so I'm not losing it. I was just a little...distracted."

No problem, though. She kept a supply of flag kits already wrapped and stored in a closet in one of the conference rooms. She would be here in the morning to tell Doris about the tradition she had started. Besides, she had already written a reminder in her planner in case she forgot.

With her mind at ease, she pulled out the Office Genie

catalogue and chose a new chair for herself, along with a
plastic mat for the floor. After she wrote down the product
and page numbers, she placed her call to the 800 number.
Ten minutes later, she had a confirmation number for her
order and a promise of delivery on Friday.

Feeling rather upbeat by three o'clock and with her day
decidedly on the upswing, she made her first executive decision as the owner of a two-woman office. She would close
early today. She made a second decision to leave her briefcase at her desk. By three-thirty, she had secured the office.
She had even managed to hold on to her purse as she maneuvered her way down to the conference room on her way
to her car.

She had her hand on the closet doorknob when a sense
of doom evaporated her optimism. The moment she
opened the door, looked inside and saw the empty shelf,
she remembered using the last flag kit just last week. "One
step forward. Two steps back," she grumbled. Losing
ground was not part of her nature. Losing ground on
crutches was a monumental pain that made closing early
today less of a gift to herself and more of a necessity if she
had any hope of pulling herself together.

She was not used to forgetting anything, especially
where her business was concerned. She did not like it—
not even a little.

She closed the closet door and leaned on her crutches. She
could wait until tomorrow morning to send Jamie down to
the hardware store to buy a flag kit. Or she could send Doris.
No. Scratch that idea. Doris would have to pass Over the
Edge along the way and might be tempted to get something
for the Wheatleys there instead. Andrea could go herself to-

morrow. Wrong again. Madge was coming with breakfast at ten.

As much as she wanted to go home, it looked like now or never, and the only question to resolve was whether to drive to the hardware store or walk. If she drove, she would have to get in and out of the car and back in again before finally driving home. She was still too awkward at that process, so she decided to walk the two blocks instead.

"Time for some real exercise, old girl." She returned to the front office and set her purse on the seat of her chair. After taking out money to pay for the flag kit, which she folded and stuffed into her pocket, she started for the front door. Though she had turned out all the lights, enough late-afternoon sunlight streamed in through the window in the top half of the door to guide her safely.

She was only a few feet away from the door when a man approached and tried the knob.

She froze in place and tightened her grip on her crutches. She stared at him, unable to speak, barely able to breathe.

He stared back and knocked harder.

Her pulse skipped right to triple time, and her heart pounded against the wall of her chest. Her mouth went dry. Fear melted every thought in her mind.

She was alone.

She was too far from her telephone or her cell phone to call for help.

"Dear Lord, protect me," she prayed. "Bill Sanderson is at my door."

Chapter Sixteen

Bill Sanderson locked his gaze on Andrea. "Mrs. Hooper! I need to talk to you."

She barely managed to swallow the lump of fear lodged in her throat. "Go," she croaked. She cleared her throat and pointed the tip of one of her crutches at him. "Leave now. The…the police are on their way."

He shook his head and apparently dismissed her threat for what it was—pure bluff. "I doubt that. Let me in. Please. I'm not trying to frighten you. I just need to talk."

"We have nothing to discuss," she insisted and leaned her weight on both her crutches again. Where, oh, where were the bicycle cops when you needed one? Probably busy chasing skateboarders, which had seemed to be the priority ever since that emergency meeting the mayor had called. "Thank you, Mr. Mayor," she grumbled. No doubt the police were too preoccupied harassing teenagers to notice a wanted fugitive standing on the avenue in the center of town!

His eyes flashed. "Don't you read the papers?"

She glared at him.

"Watch TV? You know, CNN? MSNBC? Fox News?" he went on.

She moistened her lips. "I work for a living. I don't have a lot of free time," she snapped.

He backed away from the door, pulled a paper from his pocket and held it up to the glass in the top half of the door. "Read this."

What a brazen man! She took a step back. She had no intention of getting close enough to the door to read whatever he had plastered against the glass, even if the door was securely bolted. Out of the corner of her eye, she saw traffic passing by on the avenue and a number of people walking down the street. No one, however, seemed to notice the stranger at her door.

Curiosity, however, kept her from turning around and calling the police, and intuition warned her to at least listen to what he had to say or read what appeared to be a newspaper article. He might be brazen, but he was not stupid enough to do anything that would call attention to himself, not in a town this small.

"You read it," she countered.

He smiled. "Fair enough."

She listened to every word he said, then made him read the whole article again. Disbelief gave way to relief, but caution kept a tight rein on her instinct to let him into her office.

Frustration flashed across his face. "Fine. Don't believe

me. I made it all up and had a fake article printed up just to fool you." He shook his head. "Chief Jackson said you were smart and pretty fair-minded. I guess he was wrong." He shoved the paper into his pocket, turned and walked away from her door.

Stunned, she hesitated for a moment, realized her colossal mistake and got to the door as fast as she could. By the time she got the door open and swung herself outside, he should have been a block away. She found him leaning against the storefront next door with his arms crossed over his chest and a smile on his face. She tilted up her chin. "Did you say Chief Jackson?"

"Chief Warren Jackson."

She tightened her jaw.

He grinned. "He said he appreciated the fact that I stopped by the police station as soon as I got to town, what with all the notoriety surrounding the case." His expression grew serious. "You've got to be the only person I've met in the past week who hasn't read the papers or watched TV. I'm sorry. I really didn't want to frighten you. I thought you knew what had happened."

Her cheeks flushed hot. "No. I'm sorry."

Her neighbor, Joe Bocatelli, who operated the tailor shop next door, came outside. He ignored Bill for a moment, stretched to his full height of five feet and four inches, and spoke directly to her. "Is there something I can do for you, Andrea?"

"No, thanks. I was going to close up early today, but it looks like I almost turned away a customer." She smiled and nodded to Sanderson. "Why don't we go inside where it's cooler?"

He pushed away from the storefront. "I can come back first thing in the morning, if that's more convenient."

"No. Now is fine," she insisted, anxious to get them both away the moment she saw Joe's eyes begin to glimmer with recognition.

Sanderson followed her back into her office and took a seat in front of her desk while she maneuvered into her own seat as gracefully as she could.

"You look like you've had a harder time than I did since we last met."

She sighed. "Skateboarder. He won. I lost. But you… you've survived a terrible experience."

He shrugged. "Being hijacked wasn't as bad as being hog-tied and left to die in an abandoned farmhouse. I just figured the good Lord was in control. All I had to do was trust Him to get me home safe and sound. I prayed a lot," he admitted.

"Did they catch whoever did this to you?"

His face darkened. "Not yet, but they will. Once the authorities realized I wasn't involved, they started to develop leads. I understand the investigation is going pretty well." He paused. "I guess I lost the house?"

She grimaced. "I'm sorry. Your check bounced."

He exhaled slowly and shook his head. "I was afraid that had happened. The authorities froze everything, but that's all cleared up now. I guess that means it's back to house hunting again."

"You're still serious about relocating here?"

"I need a place to live, and I need your help. My lease is up in a matter of weeks. I don't really have the time to start all over with another real-estate agent or to investigate other areas."

"This is a small town. You'll be a bit of a celebrity for a while," she cautioned.

He shrugged. "Only to folks who read the papers or—"

"Or watch television. I know." She ran her fingers through her hair. "Sorry. I've been pretty busy lately."

"Are you really showing houses?" he asked. "Using those crutches can't be easy, especially in your line of work."

"I've hired a woman to help out for a while." Quickly, she explained Doris's credentials and professional background, but she did not share her disappointment with him about having to let Doris take over many of her duties. She did not discuss with him how much resentment had filled her heart because she was forced to step back from the central role she had played in her business—a role that would likely diminish over the course of the next year, not improve. Given his obvious faith in God, after all he had been through in the past week, he might very well remind her to remember that God was in control, to trust Him and to pray a lot.

Humbled, she turned her attention to the business at hand. "Why don't we go over some of the listings I have available now? If you see something you like, I can schedule appointments for tomorrow morning and Doris can take you to see the homes."

Definitely before Madge shows up at ten, she added mentally.

He leaned forward. "Let's see what you've got."

The following morning, Andrea got to work at nine sharp. Despite the extra time she had spent on her morning prayers, she still carried a heavy burden. The way her injury was slowing her down was less frustrating than the way her treatment interfered with her day. In fact, ever since her cancer recurrence, she had felt she had a very short leash tugging at her—a leash that kept her from leading a normal life.

She had only just begun her treatments. She still had eleven and a half months ahead of her.

She might have felt better today if Jamie had not called in sick and he had been able to help her from her car to the office as he usually did. She would have felt better if she had been able to take Bill Sanderson out this morning to look at prospective homes, but she definitely would have felt better attending the Wheatley settlement instead of going for chemo.

Fortunately, Madge showed up at ten-thirty with Jenny, as well as breakfast, and Andrea's mood shifted a notch closer to happy and further away from the pity party she was having for herself.

"I'm late as usual," Madge quipped as she flashed her new wristwatch, "but it wasn't my fault."

Jenny held up a hand. "It's not my fault, either. I worked some overtime today, but I was home by nine and ready to go by nine-thirty."

"Pull up some chairs," Andrea suggested. "I'm starving. I can't wait to hear who gets blamed, as long as it isn't me."

Jenny's eyes twinkled, although she looked exhausted. "We were in the bakery when Madge's alarm went off."

"And they all loved it," Madge added as she set out paper plates, plastic cups, utensils, several white bakery boxes and an insulated carafe on top of the vinyl tablecloth that Andrea had spread out on her desk to protect it. "I think we've got every one of your favorites, plus here's a container of yogurt. You need protein, too."

Andrea's stomach growled. "Other than preferring miniatures, I don't really have a favorite."

Madge grinned. "That's why we got a few of everything they make in miniature." She pointed to the three opened boxes. "Here we have miniature cinnamon buns, with and without walnuts. They all come with raisins. Next, we have an assortment of Danishes—blueberry, cherry, lemon and cheese. They won't make peach until next month. Finally, we have minimuffins. There are bran, blueberry, orange crumb and cranberry-apple."

"There's enough here to feed most of the women in Welleswood!" Andrea ignored the yogurt and sampled a cranberry-apple muffin while Jenny poured lemonade into their cups. "You two are really spoiling me."

Madge made a mock bow. "Nothing is too good for our princess."

Andrea rolled her eyes. "You still didn't tell me who made you late."

Madge handed Andrea a napkin. "You did."

Andrea looked to Jenny for help.

Her baby sister nodded. "Madge refused to leave the bakery until we had samples of every miniature they made, so we had to wait."

"The muffins weren't ready," Madge explained.

Andrea blinked hard and swallowed the last bite of her muffin. "So because you decided to wait for the muffins, it's *my* fault you're late?"

"Of course," they replied in unison.

"That's ridiculous," Andrea argued.

"No it's not," Madge countered.

Andrea cocked a brow. "You can't be serious."

Madge shrugged. "What have you eaten so far?"

"A cranberry-apple muffin." She reached for a blueberry muffin, thought better of her choice and immediately grabbed a cheese Danish.

"Ha! See? I was right! You wanted the blueberry muffin, but you wouldn't take one because you didn't want me to know I was right. Muffins are your favorite," Madge crowed.

"I don't have a favorite."

"You have to have a favorite from McAllister's. It's almost a tradition," Jenny insisted. "Spinners were Sandra's favorite. The chocolate cake with the butter-cream icing is mine."

Madge nodded. "And mine are the éclairs, but only the ones stuffed with whipped cream, not the custard ones. Traditions, Andrea. They're important, so just admit it. Muffins are your favorite."

Andrea polished off the evidence in two bites. "Either I'm a little daffy today or you're making no sense at all. Do you have a fever or something?"

"No, she's fine. She's making perfect sense," Jenny offered. "As Madge sees it, you really like the muffins better than anything else, which meant she had to wait at the bakery for them. If she hadn't, you would have been disappointed. So it's your fault. If the Danish or the cinnamon buns were your favorite, we could have been on time. Got it?"

Andrea burst out laughing. Only Madge could get away with such convoluted thinking, and only Jenny would be able to explain it. Better yet, Andrea decided as she looked at each of them, only sisters would know just how to bring a little sunshine and a whole lot of God's love into her day.

Chapter Seventeen

❧

As always, the dog days of August blessed Welleswood with stifling heat and excessive humidity. No one was in the community more anxious than Andrea to see September arrive next week and let autumn snap the leash that held them all within summer's sweaty grasp. Even though she had tried to change her perspective, the other leash that had kept her from living a normal life did not show any signs of disappearing.

Last Friday, the day after her last weekly chemo treatment, she had gone to the hair salon. Her stylist, Judy, was on vacation, but Andrea could not wait. She had a new stylist cut her hair as short as she could and prayed the new growth would not feel like steel wool. That same afternoon, she had her final visit to the orthopedist and traded in her crutches for good. Her ankle and the muscles in her left leg, however, were stiff, and facing physical therapy three times a week for the next month certainly infringed on the freedom she had envisioned for herself now that she had a full month off between chemo treatments.

On the Wednesday before Labor Day, she arrived at work a little earlier than usual and limped a bit on her way to her desk. She took one look at the chaos on Doris's desk as well as her own and groaned. Not even that hideous flower arrangement was big enough to hide this disaster. And now her desk was a mess, too?

Working side by side with Doris for the past six weeks Andrea had watched the woman with a combination of awe and disdain. Truthfully, Doris also had a remarkable mind. She could remember the slightest detail surrounding a real estate transaction, and the clients absolutely loved her. Unfortunately, she was also a veritable hurricane when it came to paperwork. In a matter of minutes, she could wreak havoc on the organized papers Andrea gave her. Obviously, leaving Doris alone for the afternoon yesterday while Andrea had gone to physical therapy had been a major mistake.

"I can't work like this. I won't work like this. I shouldn't have to work like this," Andrea muttered to herself while she simply took the mess of papers from her desk and dumped them on top of Doris's desk. "There! That's my first executive decision of the day. My second is that Doris will sit here and put everything in order before she takes a step out of here today. Or touches the phone," she added when she caught a glimpse of the light blinking the number nine on the answering machine.

She sat down at her desk, pulled her daily planner from

the drawer where she kept it from meddling hands and took out a fresh memo pad.

First things first. She flipped the planner open to check the appointments for the day and gasped. "She wrote in my planner? In pen? In *red* pen?" Her pulse quickened and her cheeks flushed hot. "Nothing is sacred here anymore. Nothing is mine anymore," she griped.

So much for trying to hide her planner.

She noted the reminder that today was Jamie's last day. The meeting for the Shawl Ministry was tonight at seven, and she regretted, once again, letting Madge talk her into attending. She had one appointment with Bill Sanderson set for noon. Great. She had not had a client as fussy as this man for years, but at least he was her client and not Doris's. Actually, Doris had three appointments scheduled for that afternoon, but none for the morning. No settlements today for either of them.

She closed the daily planner, picked up a pencil and pressed the button on the answering machine to listen to the nine messages waiting to be retrieved. She wrote the number one on the memo pad, circled it and wrote as she listened to the first message: *Mrs. Malloy, confirming two-o'clock appointment with Doris.* Message two: *Alex Boxley. Needs certificate confirming home-owners' insurance for the Potter settlement.*

"Good. I can do that."

She continued through the next seven messages. Some were requests to see a listing. Two were requests to set up appointments to sign listing agreements. One was a hang-up. All of the messages had been left for Doris. None were for Andrea, except the Boxley call. Dismayed but not defeated, she listened to the last call and wrote automatically: *Call from Doris. She's having a body massage this morning. She'll be in at one o'clock for her first appointment.*

She stared at the message and tossed her pen into the air. "A body massage? You left this mess in my office and you're having a body massage?" She felt the tears well and held them back.

The pen fell to the desk, bounced and landed point first on the back of Andrea's hand. She yelped and rubbed the back of her hand. No real damage, but it sure did smart! "That about says it all, doesn't it? This day is going to be pure torture. Nothing can save the day now. It's already ruined."

As if on cue, the front door opened and Max Feldman came in with a vase of mixed flowers so big she could scarcely see the top half of his body. That was no easy task, given the three hundred pounds he carried on his frame. Her mood immediately shifted from agitated to overjoyed. "Flowers!"

He peeked over the flowers and chuckled. "That's why I've been in this business for thirty-four years. I make people smile every day. Arlene said to bring this over first thing. We've got so many deliveries to make outside of town, I probably won't be back to the avenue again until suppertime." His upbeat mood disappeared the moment he spied the artificial arrangement on Doris' desk, and he paused mid-stride between the front door and the two desks. "Tell me you haven't had to look at that for more than a day or two."

"Try six weeks!"

"Six weeks? Whoever made that…no, never mind. I know

where that came from. I'd better not say another word or Arlene will have conniptions. She's friends with you-know-who." He set the vase of flowers on top of Andrea's desk and removed the clear plastic wrapped over the top. He paused to take a deep breath and smiled again. "You can't do that with artificial flowers, can you? Enjoy. Don't forget to add fresh water every day," he instructed before he continued on his way.

She was fairly certain the flowers had come from either Madge or Jenny or both of her sisters. They were such dears. It was just like them to send her flowers to mark the end of her weekly chemo treatments. She found the little envelope lying upside down, opened it, and read the card that had been inside. Then she read it again out loud. "To the best real estate agent ever! Thank you for selling our home. The Finleys."

She gasped. "The Finleys? Tom and Susan Finley sent me flowers?"

She had not sold the Finley home. Dread pooled in the pit of her stomach. She found the little envelope again and turned it over. She was right. The Finleys had not sent her flowers. They had sent them to Doris. Hurricane Doris. The Doris who was, at this very moment, having a body massage while Andrea was at work.

Andrea shut her eyes and gripped the sides of her chair, but she had the awful feeling the day was sliding fast toward disaster.

Determined not to be pulled into despair, Andrea had restored order to the paperwork that had been on her desk as well as Doris's by midmorning. She had taken care of all the things she had to do for Jamie's last day and faxed a copy of the home-owners insurance certificate to Alex Boxley. She had even put the vase of flowers on Doris's desk and stored the ugly artificial arrangement in one of the conference rooms.

When Jamie arrived, Andrea's day began looking even better. She checked her watch and greeted him with a smile. "That makes it official. You've been on time every single day. I'd have to add 'punctual' and 'reliable' to that letter of recommendation I promised to write for you, if I hadn't done that already."

He blushed. "Thanks, Mrs. Hooper. I—I really appreciate how nice you've been all summer."

"You make it easy," she responded. "As a matter of fact, I have two copies of that letter right here." She pulled two of the envelopes that she had paper-clipped together from the middle tier of the bin on her desk and handed them to him. "One is a sealed copy. Sometimes colleges insist on that. The other one isn't sealed, so you can make a copy if you need one for your employer if you're job-hunting next summer, or your counselor at school can make copies when you get around to applying to colleges. If you need anything else, just let me know."

His blush deepened. "Thanks."

"Have your Mom and Dad decided when you're getting your skateboard back?"

He shrugged his shoulders. "Not yet."

"Tell them to read the letter, too. Maybe it'll help."

He dropped his gaze for a moment. When he looked at her again, he cleared his throat and squared his shoulders. "I was wondering if I could ask you to do a favor for me and for some of the other kids. I still feel pretty bad about what happened. You've been really nice about that. I really appreciate the letters of recommendation and all, and I'll understand if you don't want to help. I just…have to ask."

She leaned forward in her chair. "Ask me what?"

"There's a meeting a week from this Friday at seven o'clock. The town council is going to be talking about building that special section in Welleswood Park for skateboarders. I was wondering if you could come and if you'd speak up for us and say it's a good idea." He let out a sigh. "If you could. If not, well, we'll understand."

His words had poured out so fast, she knew he must have rehearsed them for days. She had received a notice about the town meeting, of course, and Jamie had mentioned it every day for the past week. She had suspected he was going to ask her to speak out in favor of the new skateboarding facility, and she was ready with her answer. "I wish I could attend," she replied. "Unfortunately, I've been invited to my sister's new beach house for that weekend and we're leaving early Friday afternoon."

He nodded stiffly. "Sure. I understand. My dad didn't think I should have asked you."

She grinned. "Well, once in a while, dads can be wrong. Not often," she cautioned. She took another envelope form the tiered bin. "I've already spoken to several of the commissioners, but I'd like you to take this letter to the meeting and read it to everyone for me. Can you do that?"

He took the envelope and stared at it as if it were made of gold. "Yes, ma'am. Thanks, Mrs. Hooper!"

"I'm not sure how much it will help, but all we can do is

try to get all of you a safe place to use those skateboards of yours."

"I think it's going to help a lot, having our own place to skate, I mean," he gushed. His shoulders relaxed as if he had shed a heavy burden. "What do you have for me to do for you today?"

"One errand, then you're free for the rest of the day."

"Just one?"

She nodded and handed him a fourth and final envelope. "I need you to take a deposit to the bank."

"That's it? You're sure?"

"That's it. The deposit ticket is inside."

"I'll bring the receipt right back, unless you want me to ask them to hold it for you like last time."

"Sounds good to me."

He caught her gaze and held it. "Thanks for everything, Mrs. Hooper. I mean it. You're a nice lady."

"And you're a great volunteer. Now get moving. You know how long the lines get at the bank right before a weekend."

She watched him walk out the door. She would have given anything to be at the bank when the teller opened the envelope, saw the check Andrea had made out to him for $1,000, and asked him to put his account number on the deposit ticket and endorse the check. She had already cleared her plan with his parents, who had only agreed to let Jamie accept the check if it was deposited directly into the savings account earmarked for his college education.

Instead, she turned her attention to the appointment she had with Bill Sanderson and prayed the man might be a whole lot less picky about the home he claimed he wanted to buy in Welleswood. On the bright side, the celebrity status surrounding his misadventure had faded, and the shift from a negative thought to a positive one made her less apprehensive about their appointment today.

She started reviewing the fact sheets for the two properties they were scheduled to see today. After making some telephone calls to resolve a few questions she had, she put all of the information into an orange folder, a color that designated potential properties a client had expressed an interest in seeing.

"Some potential," she grumbled. He was not going to like the first property, not that she did not try to convince him not to waste time visiting this one. The lot was too small, and there was not much either one of them could do about that. He was not going to like the second one, either. At least, he should not like it. It was a woman's house, top to bottom, and definitely not a house for a middle-aged bachelor.

She ran her fingers through her closely cropped hair and glanced at the two desks, which were now neatly organized, just the way she liked them. The very thought of Doris sailing into the office, fresh from her body massage, while Andrea was out on a wild-goose chase with Mr. Bill "Fussy" Sanderson, inspired a groan. Unless she covered each desk with shrink-wrap, there was no way to stop Hurricane Doris from hitting, short of changing the locks on the doors and sandbagging both entrances.

"Lucky, lucky me," she muttered. "I'm destined to spend the next month in Hurricane Alley unless…" She grabbed a sudden thought, found the catalogue for Office Genie and dialed customer service.

"Office Genie. This is Genie Cassandra. Is there an office problem I can solve for you today?"

Andrea sat back in her chair and relaxed. "Yes, I believe there is."

Chapter Eighteen

If Bill Sanderson was not her only client and if she had not made a real fool of herself when he had returned to Welleswood, Andrea would have left him at the first property and told him to give Doris a call to see anything else.

She was that desperate.

Unfortunately, he was her only client at the moment. The memory of how she had treated him like a fugitive instead of a victim was still very fresh in her mind, and Doris had her afternoon already booked.

At the second property Andrea led him up the stairs from the finished basement to the kitchen. She wished she could simply walk away and leave him behind, but sooner or later, the owner would come home, and Andrea would have had some real explaining to do.

"Watch your head. The ceiling is still low," she cautioned.

Abide with Me

He waited until they were in the doll-sized kitchen before he stretched back up to his full height, which was a few inches over six feet. "That was…interesting," he noted with a twinkle in his eyes.

She almost sighed, but held on to her patience. "As I said, the basement would probably not work for you."

He glanced around the kitchen and shook his head. "You're sure all the appliances are here?"

"They were custom-ordered. The refrigerator is here." She opened a cabinet door to show him.

"I had a refrigerator larger than that in my dorm room at college."

"For a lot of single, working women, especially women who don't have the time to cook, this refrigerator works well. It holds most of the essentials, but not much more," she countered. "There's a microwave and a toaster-oven in a cabinet, too, and the range is countertop. The owner has done a great job of maximizing space."

He grimaced. "That's for sure." He glanced at the countertop. "I don't think I've ever seen a two-burner stove before. I guess that was a custom-order, too. I'd never be able to cook much on that." He inched past her to the bistro table and single chair and chuckled. "I wouldn't even try sitting on that."

She chuckled. "That's probably a good idea. There's not much else that would fit, though. Did you want to see the rest of the house again?"

He shrugged his shoulders. "All three rooms?" He chuckled. "I guess not. You were right. This house is much too small for someone my size. The location is so ideal I was thinking that if the lot was a little bigger than a postage stamp, I could contemplate an addition. Are you sure that side lot doesn't go with the property?"

"Definitely. I called to check that this morning."

"And the owner isn't willing to sell the lot separately?"

She shook her head.

"How did they ever get a permit to build the house on a lot this small in the first place?"

"They didn't need one. The house predates all of the new laws."

He shrugged his shoulders. "It looks like you were right in the first place. This house isn't going to pass muster. I guess we'll just have to keep looking. Shall we make a date for Friday afternoon?"

She saw his eyes begin to twinkle and suddenly, his words took on a meaning that nearly knocked her off her feet. A date. He did not mean a date, as in "appointment." She looked into his eyes and knew she was right. Call it woman's intuition or just plain chemistry. He was making a "date" with her, as in a meeting between a man and a woman, as in "relationship."

Great. He was the one client she had, and now it turned out he was a potential suitor? How absurd was that? How could she have been so blind?

The past few weeks replayed in her mind, as if rewinding a movie, and she realized why he had been so insistent on seeing properties that she knew would not interest him. He was making appointments not because he was interested in buying a house, but because he was interested in…her!

The idea was so ridiculous she almost laughed out loud. The man was a full decade younger than she was. He was definitely not her type. She liked men… Wait a minute. She did not have a type. She did like men, but the idea of dating was in the back of her mind, behind weeding her gardens and way below surviving cancer. Most men probably would not find dating a woman with cancer at the top of their list, in any case.

"I'm sorry. I'm not making any appointments for next Friday," she replied. "I'm leaving for a weekend at the shore. Shall we?" She left her card on the bistro table and led him through the living room and out onto the front porch.

While she looked up, he leaned against the gingerbread railing. "Oh. What about Wednesday? I could get a few hours off in the morning. Or Thursday afternoon would work."

"I'll have to check my calendar, but we really shouldn't make a definite appointment until we know that there's a house that's come on the market that would be suitable."

He followed her down the porch steps. "Actually, I was thinking maybe I should take another look at the house on West Walnut."

She rolled her eyes, pasted a smile on her face and turned to face him when they reached the cobblestone walkway. "The West Walnut house? The one you said needed more work than Noah's Ark if and when it was ever found? That house?"

"Did I say that?"

"You did."

"Hmm. Maybe I did. What about the house on East Locust?"

"Sold," she told him.

"And the house on Mulberry? I forget if it was East or West."

"Sold, remember? That was the house you originally wanted, but you were…well…"

"Hog-tied and left to die, without water or food," he supplied. Then undaunted, he went on, "Speaking of food, why don't we continue our discussion of possible houses for me to see at lunch? There's a great little restaurant in town. The Diner, I think. It's close to your office so you wouldn't have to walk far to get back to work."

If Andrea had lunch with any man other than her brothers-in-law, that would be news. If she had lunch with Bill Sanderson at The Diner, a man so much younger than she, that would inspire more gossip than Andrea wanted to contemplate. It would also send the message that she was interested in seeing him on a personal level, which she was not.

"I don't think that's a good idea," she replied.

"What isn't a good idea? Having lunch or having lunch with me?"

She winced and tossed caution to the wind. "For a man who has led me on one goose chase after another on the pretext of looking for a home, you're certainly being direct, aren't you?"

He laughed and raised his hands in mock surrender. "Guilty as charged. So what is it? Having lunch or having lunch with me?"

"Having lunch with you," she blurted. Surprised by her own directness, she felt her cheeks warm. "I'm sorry. I didn't mean to be rude."

He laughed again. "Being direct isn't rude. You couldn't be rude if you tried. And you did try, as I recall. The day I came back to Welleswood?"

Her cheeks got hotter. "It didn't seem to work very well then," she admitted.

"I'm a persistent man."

"I'm a stubborn woman."

"So I noticed." He checked his watch. "I've got to run. Call me next week and let me know which day works best for you," he said. He left her standing there, mouth agape, while he got into his pickup truck.

"You still want me to take you to see houses?"

He grinned. "Unless you'd rather meet for lunch. Or dinner. That would work for me, too." He threw his truck into gear and pulled away before she could answer.

Persistent, brazen man.

Andrea entered the Community Center for the meeting for the Shawl Ministry half an hour late with a headache that would have been called a migraine if she had had the mental wherewithal to name it. To make matters worse, Madge had begged off attending the meeting tonight, pleading total exhaustion after spending the day with a decorator for her beach house. Andrea had a bag holding a dozen skeins of green yarn that must have dated back to the 1970s and a pair of gold aluminum knitting needles hanging from one arm and Jane Huxbaugh walking on the other.

Who said life wasn't grand?

She and Jane quickly found seats in the arc of chairs arranged in the center of the room, while Eleanor Hadley, the coordinator, spoke about their ministry. Andrea set her bag on the floor. She was disappointed in the low turnout. Only six women besides Andrea and Jane had shown up. She was rather pleased, however, to learn that the Shawl Ministry was exactly that: a ministry where women of faith could gather together to pray and to knit shawls that would be given to folks in need of comfort. Each session would begin and end with prayers the members had written themselves, and each shawl would carry with it a prayer they would write especially for the recipient. All Andrea had to do was learn how to knit, something Madge had assured her the other women would be more than willing to teach her.

After a brief round of questions, the women broke for some light refreshments. Eleanor Hadley came to sit beside Andrea, while Jane wandered off to find the ladies' room. "Thank you so much for coming tonight, Andrea," Eleanor said. "I thought Madge was coming, too."

Andrea dutifully made Madge's excuses. "She said to tell you that she'll call you tomorrow and explain."

Eleanor patted Andrea's knee. "I've been meaning to talk to you about something for quite some time. Now just seems the right time to me," she said softly. "You remember Mrs. Calloway, don't you?"

"I remember her as Auntie Lynn. She died a few years back, didn't she?"

"Yes," Eleanor remarked with a smile. "She was a direct descendent of Mary Welles Johnson, you know."

"The woman who founded Welleswood?" Andrea asked.

"Yes. Mrs. Calloway was her last direct descendent," Eleanor added. "She lived on East Walnut. You know where the playground is now?"

Andrea nodded.

"That's where her house stood. She had the most unbelievable gardens and a gazebo with a brass roof. She donated the property to the children of Welleswood in her will. Eventually, her inheritance finally ran dry. She got behind in her taxes, and with only her Social Security check to live on, she was forced to consider selling the family home and moving into the senior-citizen complex."

Eleanor paused to take a sip of punch. "Do you remember when your sister Sandra took out a home-equity loan on her house?"

Andrea shrugged her shoulders. "Vaguely."

"Well, I helped her with the paperwork. Sandra had to tutor on Saturdays for a long time to pay that loan off."

"She had to pay off her credit-card bills somehow," Andrea insisted. "What's that got to do with Auntie Lynn?"

Eleanor smiled. "Sandra had credit-card bills because she had taken cash advances. Lots of them. She had used the credit-card money to pay Auntie Lynn's back taxes, then used the money from the home-equity loan for the current taxes and Mrs. Calloway's living expenses until the day Mrs. Calloway died."

Andrea's heart skipped a beat. "I never knew that. Are you sure? Sandra would have told me or one of my sisters."

"Actually, she never told me the whole story, either. I was the executor for Mrs. Calloway's estate. I found the paperwork when I was going through her papers to get everything ready for the lawyer. Sandra was like that. She helped people without revealing it."

"Thank you for telling me," Andrea whispered, anxious to share this Sandra story with both Madge and Jenny. "Sandra was one-of-a-kind."

"So are you," Eleanor replied. "I know you've had a hard time getting around lately and you've barely recovered, yet you're still willing to volunteer your time to help others, just like your sister."

Tears welled, but Andrea brushed them away the moment she spied Jane standing by the door with a look on her face that told Andrea in no uncertain terms that she was ready to leave. Andrea bid Eleanor a good-night, added a hug for good measure and escorted Jane outside.

She led her elderly companion to her car and held the door until she got inside. "Do you need help with your seat belt?"

Jane sent her a withering look. "Not as much help as you're going to need learning how to knit. If you hurry, I can be home in time for my television show."

Andrea did not bother asking what show. Keeping conversation to a minimum seemed to work best when it came to getting along with Jane. She simply closed the door and walked around the car. As Andrea was sliding into the driver's seat, Jane said, "I was hoping Eleanor would keep the meeting short. I don't like to go out late at night."

After latching her own seat belt, Andrea started the car and headed toward Jane's house. "Most people don't," she replied. She'd known from the other women's expressions when Jane had walked in the door this evening that they were not particularly pleased that she had come, even if she was donating bags of yarn. "I suppose that's why the members voted to meet in the afternoons at the Community Center."

"Saturday afternoons," Jane added. "That's perfect for me, too. I wouldn't want to give up volunteering at the thrift shop."

"No. I guess more people are working now, too, and Saturday is better for them than a weekday."

Jane guffawed. "You're the only one young enough to work that showed up tonight. The rest of us are retired. We volunteer these days, which is just as well. You can't trust young people today to do much in the way of volunteering. It's the seniors who haven't forgotten the value of helping others."

Andrea listened to Jane's comments with only half an ear while she made a mental note to thank Madge for suggesting the ministry to her, although she had serious doubts about her ability to learn how to knit. The Shawl Ministry had an old-fashioned, small-community feel to it that appealed to Andrea. With her own world in upheaval, she hoped the ministry would help to keep her grounded and focused on something other than her own troubles.

When she pulled up along the curb in front of Jane's house, the elderly woman unlatched her seat belt before Andrea even slowed to a stop. "Go on up the driveway. It's shorter for me to walk."

"No problem." She backed up, turned into the driveway and stopped just short of the walkway that led to the porch.

"Next time you drive me home, you'd better come to a full stop at the stop sign," Jane grumbled, and let herself out of the car before Andrea had a chance to turn off the ignition.

Andrea watched the woman climb the steps and let herself into the house before backing out of the driveway. Then, eager to end her own day, she headed for home.

All in all, the day hadn't turned out to be too bad. She had ordered a new credenza for the office—with locks, and there was no way Doris would ever find the keys. Andrea had every intention to wear them on a chain around her neck if she had to, just to protect her paperwork.

Now wasn't that just wonderful. On top of dealing with a cancer recurrence and treatments, hair the texture of a scouring pad, physical-therapy appointments three times a week, a new agent in her office who was taking most of her clients, a man who was interested in dating her, leading her on goose chases and a promise to take Jane home every week, Andrea was now going to have a bunch of keys hanging from a chain around her neck.

Madge would be thrilled that Andrea was finally going to wear some sort of jewelry.

At least someone was going to find something about Andrea's life that made somebody happy.

Chapter Nineteen

By the third week in September, warm, sunny days were giving way to chilly evenings. Vacations were memories, captured in photographs to be arranged in scrapbooks, shared through e-mail with relatives or on videotapes that would provide entertainment over the winter months to come. Children were trading bathing suits and beach toys for new school clothes, backpacks and lunch boxes. The ritual of work, fall housecleaning and monitoring home-work was keeping the adults busy.

Most people had neither the time nor the inclination to spend a weekend at the shore, much to the relief of the folks who were residents of towns like Sea Gate.

Lucky folks. No, not lucky—blessed, Madge decided. She carried a tray of fresh fruit out to the beach where the last of her guests sat together in beach chairs. Russell had come home for the settlement in early September, but only managed to stay a few days before being summoned back to work. He hoped to be home next week, and Madge was anxious for him to see the house fully furnished. Drew and Brett had been able to spend four days at the new beach house, but both of her sons had left earlier that morning to catch flights home.

Fortunately, Madge was still surrounded by family. Her nieces, Katy and Hannah, were sitting in a pool of water the morning tide had left behind, making mud pies, under Michael's watch, while Jenny napped with her hands cupped protectively over the gentle mound of her tummy. Andrea was still arguing with a pair of knitting needles that flashed reflections of the sun each time she attempted another stitch with the green yarn that lay in a tangled mess on her lap.

As Madge approached, Katy and Hannah squealed and raced to meet her with Michael close on their heels.

Katy arrived first and tugged on Madge's arm. "Can I have some watermelon, Aunt Madge?"

"I want gwapes," Hannah cried as she wrapped her little arms around one of Madge's legs.

"Whoa, ladies! Give Aunt Madge a break," Michael warned.

Madge grinned down at the upturned faces of the two little girls. Dressed in matching bathing suits, with dainty barrettes in their dark hair, their eyes shining with innocence, they were utterly adorable. They also soothed the tiny ache that still remained in Madge's heart, even after all these years, for the daughter she had wanted, but never had. "Rinse off your hands first. Daddy will help you," she urged.

"Clean hands first. That's the rule." Michael scooped up his daughters, one in each arm. "You can both have a snack, then it's naptime." He caught Madge's eyes as the girls wriggled to get free and whined about taking a nap. "I don't suppose you have any more fruit inside?"

"Well, sure, but—"

"I think it would be easier if I take the girls inside for their snack and away from the beach. Are there any towels left in the outside shower?"

"I hope so. Here, babies. Take a little treat before you go," she insisted. She tugged a grape from one of the bunches and broke a piece of watermelon in half. The girls opened their mouths like baby birds, and Madge plopped their treat inside. "Aunt Madge has lots more in the refrigerator, and if you take a good nap, I'll show you how to dig for sand crabs when you get up."

The girls clapped their hands, spraying sand on their daddy, but Madge was quick enough to turn and protect the fruit from a sand shower.

"Dig for sand crabs? I don't think so," Michael replied sternly, but his eyes were twinkling. "I think we should find some pretty seashells to paint, especially since we're going to stay at Aunt Madge's for a few more days," he murmured as he carried his girls away. "Aunt Madge loves seashells, especially purple ones."

"And I love you," she called, and waved to the girls.

"I love you, too, but I'll love you more if you give me some fruit," Jenny teased.

Madge turned and smiled at her baby sister. "You're awake?"

Jenny tugged on the arms of her beach chair until the

back was in an upright position. "I'm awake, and I'm starving, as usual." She yawned and patted her tummy. "A growing baby makes for a hungry mama."

Madge offered Jenny some fruit first. "Here, princess. Take some for you and some for the baby."

Andrea set aside her knitting for a moment and raised the brim of her sun visor. "Princess? You called Jenny a princess? What about me?"

Jenny snagged a bunch of grapes and popped a plump green one into her mouth. "Sorry, big sister. Now that you've ditched your crutches and you're walking on your own two feet again, Madge gave the crown to me."

Madge laughed. "Besides, you're the oldest. You really shouldn't be a princess anyway, but if you insist on a title, would you settle for queen?"

"A queen without a country or a crown, that's what I am," Andrea grumbled. She picked up her knitting, ripped out the last few stitches and started again.

"The queen's a little cranky," Madge whispered as she sat down in between her sisters and put the tray on her lap.

"I'm not cranky," Andrea countered. "I'm frustrated." She tossed her knitting needles into the sand, along with her sorry attempt at creating an even row of stitches. "So much for that brilliant idea. It looks like the Shawl Ministry will have to manage without me, and Miss Jane Huxbaugh will just have to find someone else to drive her home." She reached over and grabbed a slice of honeydew melon. After she polished it off, she looked from one sister to the other. "Okay, so I'm cranky, but I'm frustrated, too," she admitted, stretching out her left leg and rotating her ankle.

"How long before your physical therapy ends?" Madge asked, avoiding the entire topic of her sister's mood.

"I had my last session last week."

Jenny frowned. "You stopped physical therapy or it ended?"

Andrea shrugged and munched on a pineapple stick.

Madge shook her head. She knew Andrea well enough to be able to read through her words to the truth. "You just stopped going, didn't you?"

"As a matter of fact, I did. Somehow, between the weekly chemo treatments and physical therapy three times a week, I'm supposed to be running a business." She snorted. "Something had to go. It's not like I can't continue the exercises on my own at home," she added defensively.

"Your weekly treatments ended three weeks ago," Jenny reminded her sister in a gentle voice. "You only have to go every month now."

Andrea hugged her knees to her chest. Her eyes glistened with tears, a sight so rare Madge's heart trembled. When Andrea began to speak, her voice was just above a whisper. "That's true. That leash I've been wearing isn't quite so short anymore, but it's still there, tugging me back to reality when I can forget, for one very short moment, that I have cancer. Unless I'm scheduled for a cysto. They're joyful. I can't tell you how much fun I have, lying there on the table and holding my breath during the examination, wondering if the doctor isn't saying anything during the exam because she doesn't see any new growths or because she sees them and wants to wait until she's finished before she tells me the chemo isn't working."

She swiped at a tear that had escaped. "Look at me. I'm

a mess. My energy level isn't half of what it used to be, and my hair feels like a steel-wool scouring pad." She leaned toward Madge. "Go ahead. Touch it. Be careful not to disturb any of the hairs that prefer to stick out straight so I look like a porcupine having a bad-hair day. I can hardly wait to see how I look by the end of the treatments."

Madge swallowed hard. She pressed a kiss to Andrea's head and tried to smooth a few errant gray hairs back into place. "Stubborn little wisdom hairs, aren't they? At least you still have them. Kathleen and Sandra lost every hair on their heads, remember?" she murmured. "I thought you were going to see Judy at the salon and ask her to recommend something."

Andrea sat back in her chair and closed her eyes. "I haven't had time," she whispered. Her voice cracked as she visibly struggled for control. "I've been a little busy trying to help clients who seem so happy dealing with Doris they're not the least bit interested in talking to me. Maybe it's the chain of keys I have to wear around my neck. The clients aren't sure if I'm a real estate agent or a warden. Of course, Doris doesn't have to miss as much floor time as I do, and she doesn't have to reschedule clients to keep outside appointments for herself, either. I would have let her go weeks ago when my ankle was finally healed, even though I'm not up to running the agency completely on my own, but she's endeared herself to the clients and the community to the point that I can't let her go, not without looking like an ogre."

"I have an appointment with Judy on Thursday. I'll get her to recommend some hair-care product, and I'll bring it with me on Friday. Your chemo is at ten, right?" Madge offered, trying to do something that might make Andrea feel better.

Andrea barely nodded, and when Madge opened her mouth to speak again, Jenny stopped her by laying her hand on Madge's arm. Jenny's gaze, however, reflected the same troubled emotions that tugged so hard on Madge's heartstrings. In all honesty, she had never seen Andrea so despondent. Of the three of them, Andrea was the rock, steady and solid against every challenge life had thrown at her, steady and solid when life dared to threaten either of her sisters.

Andrea could be their mother, their friend, their confidante and their confessor, but most of all, she was their big sister, and Madge could not bear to see her so sad and so shaken. She took Jenny's hand and gave it a squeeze before she spoke to Andrea again. "You're right, you know."

Andrea opened one eye. "Right about what?"

"You're frustrated."

"And a teeny, weenie bit cranky," Jenny teased.

Andrea opened her other eye. "Great. This is just great. I pour out my troubles for the first time in decades, I lay my soul bare so you can see what an ungrateful wretch I've become, and I let you see that my faith is about as steady as…as that piece of seaweed blowing across the sand, and the only thing my sisters, the only family or real friends I have near me, can say to me is that I'm frustrated and cranky?"

"Just a teeny bit," Jenny repeated.

Andrea huffed. "You're sick! Both of you! Sicker than I am, too."

"But there's a cure," Madge argued.

Andrea looked at her as if she had grown a third eye on the tip of her nose.

"There is," Madge insisted. "Isn't there, Jenny?"

"Um. Sure. If you say there is, then I believe you." She leaned around Madge and looked at Andrea. "You should believe her, too."

Andrea did not smile, but her face relaxed. "The last time I trusted Madge to cure something, we both ended up in trouble. I think I'll pass. I'm actually getting used to being frustrated and a little cranky. It's a refreshing change."

Jenny scooted forward in her chair and looked from one big sister to the other, clearly ready to hear the story.

Madge pursed her lips and tilted her chin.

Andrea actually produced a lopsided grin.

Madge held up her foot and watched the sunlight sparkle on her anklet. "Andrea was the one who climbed over the fence to steal our neighbor's peaches and wound up with poison ivy."

"Which spread to every pore of my skin. I even had blisters on my ears, thanks to your so-called cure, Madge."

"You begged me to help so Mother wouldn't find out what you'd done." Madge defended herself.

"You ate the peaches, too."

"But I didn't steal them!" Madge cried.

"You dared me to steal them!" Andrea retorted.

Jenny played referee and held up her hands. "Let's skip to the cure, shall we?"

Andrea smirked.

Madge huffed. "I told her to scratch at the blisters so they'd go away."

"So I did," Andrea added. "I scratched like crazy."

Jenny laughed out loud.

"It worked for bug bites. Sometimes," Madge said defensively.

Jenny held her hands up in mock surrender. "You're right, Andrea. I'm switching sides. I don't think Madge has a good record when it comes to cures."

"Traitor! You'll wish you hadn't," Madge warned. "You'll both wish you had listened to me." She set the tray aside, stood up and brushed the sand from her legs.

"Where are you going," Jenny asked.

"With both of you siding against me, I'm feeling a little frustrated and a little bit cranky, so I'm going to get a cure for myself. Not that you should care." She picked up the tray and started back to the house.

Andrea's voice rang out first. "Wait! Aren't you at least going to tell us what the cure is?"

Madge smiled to herself, but kept walking until Jenny called out, "There's no cure. You're just teasing us."

That did it.

Madge turned around and faced her sisters, now some twenty feet away. "My cure, ladies, is not a joke. Definitely not. A Monsoon Sundae at French's is no joke. It's a cure. It's also healthy. There's a lot of calcium in five scoops of ice cream. Then there's the hot-fudge sauce, toasted walnuts, crushed cherries, sliced bananas and homemade whipped cream that's so stiff you can stick a spoon into it and the spoon will stand up straight. And if a Monsoon Sundae doesn't cure whatever ails you, then you've got one foot inside the Pearly Gates and you don't want to be cured!"

Jenny scrambled out of her chair first. She took two

steps, then rocked still. "Wait a minute. French's isn't open after Labor Day, is it?"

"Only on weekends from Labor Day through the end of October."

Madge smiled when Jenny started racing forward again, but her smile stretched straight to her heart the moment Andrea got out of her chair and started running, as well as she could, to catch up to her sisters with a grin on her face and her eyes sparkling with joy instead of sadness.

"God's love and your sisters' love. That's the real cure," Madge whispered. "Come on, Andrea. We'll help you through this…if you'll let us."

Chapter Twenty

The following Thursday arrived with heavy winds and rain and a forecast of yet another day before the northeaster would pass.

Humming softly, Madge left the master bedroom just as the hall clock in the little alcove at the top of the stairs chimed the last of eight bells. For once she was early, and she had time for a nice breakfast before she was due to pick up Andrea at nine-thirty. She'd wakened feeling nostalgic this morning, and as she approached the top of the stairs, memories surfaced. In her mind's eye, instead of the clock in the alcove, she saw the huge toy garage that had once stood there, housing the boys' amazing collection of miniature cars. Instead of the cream carpet runner bordered by a gleaming hardwood floor, she saw the scars left from those little cars as the boys raced them, hour after hour, over the wooden hallway floor.

She started down the stairs and held on to the railing—the same railing Drew had ridden straight to the emergency room. He'd gotten six stitches in his head that time. Or had it been Brett? Before her two sons had left for college, Madge had probably logged enough hours in the emergency room at Tipton Medical Center to qualify for a volunteer pin. She chuckled to herself now, although she had not thought it was very humorous at the time. Wasn't it funny what a difference a few years and a new perspective could make?

She paused at the bottom of the stairs and held on to the banister as the present merged with the past. While the boys were growing up, she had been so busy playing mother and father while Russell's job kept him traveling the surrounding states that she had never had time to just enjoy the boys. At least, that's how she had felt at the time. With the passing of years, she realized she could have made the time. She could have let them have a pet, too.

Like the shoemaker's children who had no shoes, Russell's sons had never had any pets. Not a dog, a cat, a lizard, a snake, a hamster or a fish. Russell was the top salesman for a pet-food company, yet he had never permitted his own sons to have a pet—a paradox Madge had never solved.

If she were raising her sons now, she'd let them have a pet. And she'd have more time for her boys and the wisdom to know how to use it better. Unfortunately, the boys had not waited for her. They had grown up. "That's what grandchildren are for. To do it better the second time around," she told herself. She said a quick prayer that both of her boys would find a special someone, marry and start a family, preferably in that order. Given the declining moral standards so evident in popular culture, she was more than relieved that she had made the time to raise the boys with a strong faith in God, a faith they still claimed and followed as young men.

She gave the banister a pat and put her memories aside. When she got to the kitchen, she popped a frozen sesame bagel into the microwave for twenty seconds and poured a cup of coffee. Thank goodness for modern technology, especially the coffeemaker with a timer. When the microwave bell rang, she removed the bagel, split it open and layered each side with cheddar cheese and bacon pieces before setting both halves into the toaster oven. She set the temperature to 400 degrees and carried her mug of coffee with her to look out the window over the kitchen sink to see how her back gardens were faring in the storm.

Or she tried to look. The rain was so heavy and the wind was so strong, she would need windshield wipers to be able to see anything beyond the sheets of water trailing down the window. Poor little flowers. They were probably already beaten to the ground, creating purple puddles everywhere. Even though she had already ordered the fall mums, she had been hoping to enjoy another week or two of her summer blooms.

"Not this year," she muttered. She shivered and took a sip of coffee. Today was definitely a great day to curl up on the couch with a good book or to clean out the attic. To venture outside, she would need her ankle-length raincoat, the one with the hood. An umbrella would be useless today. The wind would blow it inside out before she even got to the car, which she had left in the driveway and forgotten to pull into the garage.

She flinched when thunder cracked overhead and the storm intensified. It really did not matter what she wore today. She would still get soaked to the skin, and she wanted very badly to stay home. Guilt tugged at her heart. Andrea had no choice. She had to go out today. She had a chemo treatment, and all Madge could do was worry about getting wet?

She shook her head, retrieved her breakfast from the toaster oven, and let it cool a bit on a plate. As she turned off the toaster oven, she suddenly remembered she had promised to bring Andrea the hair conditioner Judy had given to her. The conditioner was upstairs. "Next to my purse," she grumbled.

She tried a bite of bagel. The cheese stuck to the roof of her mouth and burned her tongue. She gritted her teeth. "Swell. This day's already getting worse, and I haven't left the house yet."

She tossed the bagel back onto the plate and went back upstairs. She grabbed the conditioner and her purse, then went into the spare room and got two fold-up umbrellas, just in case the wind died down. She sorted through her four raincoats, chose the longest one with a hood and folded it over her arm.

She was halfway down the hall before she turned around and went back into the spare room. She took a second raincoat out, just in case Andrea needed it. She folded that one over her arm, too. She straightened her shoulders. Having two raincoats on one arm and holding her purse, the conditioner and the two umbrellas in the opposite hand, she was fairly well-balanced, but she took her time going back down the stairs.

She had almost reached the bottom step when the doorbell rang.

Startled, she leaned against the banister for support and managed to get safely down the final step. "Who on earth…?" She struggled with the raincoats until she had them draped over the back of a chair in the living room.

The doorbell rang again.

"Coming!" She tossed her purse and the conditioner onto the seat of the chair and went to the front door. She checked the door chain to make sure it was secure, unlocked the door and opened it a crack—just enough to see the face of the man at her door. She sighed. "Russell? Why on earth are you standing outside ringing the bell? Did you forget your key?" She reclosed the door without waiting for him to answer, released the chain and swung the door open.

Russell did not rush into the house. He just stood under the porch roof. He was soaking wet. His hair was plastered against his scalp. Rivulets of water flowed over his features, and the wind blew rain past him into the house.

It wasn't the cold rain on her face that made Madge gasp. It wasn't her husband's obvious physical distress that made her gasp. It wasn't even his grim, almost fearful expression, either.

It was the little girl, fast asleep, that he was cradling in his arms that claimed every breath of air in her lungs. Tiny little thing, the child could not be more than two or three years old.

Madge pressed the palm of her hand to her heart and

gripped the edge of the doorjamb. So many questions rose in her thoughts she grew dizzy. Had he had an accident? Had he hit the little girl? How badly was she hurt? Where were her parents? Was Russell hurt, too?"

"Russell! Oh my mercy! Should I dial nine-one-one? Do we need an ambulance?"

"No. Don't call anyone. Just let us in," he pleaded. "I— I've driven all night through this storm to get here. Please let us in. We have…nowhere else to go."

Andrea paced back and forth across her living room, with the "girls" watching her. She checked her watch. It was nine thirty-five. Madge was late again. "I should have called her earlier," she grumbled. She took out her cell phone, pressed the phone book to get to Madge's cell phone number, and hit Send. She tapped her foot in rhythm with each ring. After ten rings, she got Madge's voice mail and hung up.

Andrea started pacing again. "She should have answered her cell phone. Unless she left it at home. She should have been here by now! She knows I can't be late." Her pulse quickened and tears welled. She swiped them away. She would have to ask Dr. Newton about the emotional pendulum she seemed to have been swinging on for the past few weeks. She checked her watch again. Nine-forty. "I am not happy," she murmured. "I wasn't happy when I went to bed last night, I wasn't happy when I got up, but now I am *really* not happy. I'm getting mad. I don't want to be mad. I want to go to the doctor's and be on time for my appointment. I want to get my treatment so I can get home to roll around in my bed for two hours. The later I get the treatment, the later I'll get to work."

She paused, closed her eyes for a moment and took a deep breath. "I don't have to be late. I can drive myself to the doctor's office and I can drive myself home. Whatever excuse Madge cares to make for being late will have to wait. I have to go."

Without bothering to check her watch again, Andrea called Madge's cell phone one more time, hung up without leaving a message, then called Madge's house phone. No answer there, either, but Andrea decided to leave a message this time. "Madge? This is Andrea. I'm leaving for the doctor's office. I'll call you when I get back." She grabbed her raincoat and headed toward the door.

The moment she opened the door and felt the full brunt of the storm, she realized how difficult driving must be. Had Madge had an accident? Was that why she was late? Or had she been delayed by someone else's accident? Worry mixed with guilt, and Andrea whispered a prayer before she dashed to her car. "Please, God, wherever Madge is, please watch over her, and for anyone who has had an accident this day, please watch over them, too."

By the time she managed to get into her car, her stockings were plastered against her legs and she had to stop to wipe the rain from her face before starting the car. She drove up to the avenue, but instead of turning right to go to Dr. Newton's, she turned left and went directly to Madge's house. The moment she spied Madge's car in the driveway, with Russell's car parked directly behind, relief washed over her. "I guess I can't blame you for being late. Russell must have surprised you and come home early!"

She smiled and continued on her way. She would have fun teasing Madge about being late this time! After she had her treatment. After she had spent her "rolling time." After she had gone in to the office. And definitely after Madge and Russell had had some time alone.

Chapter Twenty-One

$\approx$

Madge pulled the front door open wider. "Come in? Of course you can come in. This is your home, too, but I don't understand…"

Russell stepped into the foyer, looked into the living room, and back at Madge. His eyes were dark, with anguish so profound it could only have come from the very depths of his soul. Sorrow had deepened the creases in his forehead. His shoulders sagged. "I—I need…we need to talk, but first…" He shifted the bundle in his arms. "I need to get her tucked into bed."

Madge felt as if she were on a live reality television show, and her brain was on a seven-second delay. By the time she had processed Russell's words and understood the meaning behind them, he was halfway up the steps. She shut the front door against the wind and the rain, but she sensed there was a greater storm brewing inside her home.

She turned back to the stairs and saw the water and dirt he was tracking up the steps and cried out. "Wait!"

He stopped, but he did not turn around.

"What's going on?" Her chest heaved. Confusion and fear made her pulse race. "Russell? What are you doing? You can't just suddenly appear at the door with some unnamed child in your arms and go charging up the stair carrying whatever disaster you've…you've created for yourself and expect me to stand here patiently and wait for an explanation. Somebody else must know what…what happened. Somebody will be looking for her. If not her parents, then who? The police? What do I do if they come to the door looking for her or looking for you?"

He sighed. "Her name is Sarah. No one will be looking for her…or for me," he whispered.

Madge cocked her head. "Why not?"

He bowed his head.

Her pulse began to race. "Russell? What's going on? Why wouldn't anyone be looking for her? She's just a little girl. Isn't her mother worried about her? Why not? And why do you have her?"

He turned and locked his gaze with Madge's. "Her mother loved her very much, but she's dead. She died ten days ago in an automobile accident."

Madge clapped her hand to her heart. "So you brought Sarah here?"

He drew in a deep breath and nodded. "Yes."

"Because…?"

"Because she's only three years old and she was all

alone. Because she has no other family." He clutched the little one closer to his chest. "But most of all, because she's my daughter."

My daughter.

My daughter.

His words echoed in Madge's muddled brain, but somehow, she could not make any sense of them. They were only two little words: my daughter. She closed her eyes and struggled to understand what they meant. "My daughter," she whispered. Sarah is Russell's daughter? That was crazy. Sarah is Russell's daughter? Impossible. Russell didn't have a daughter. He could not have a daughter. He had two grown sons. He did not have a little daughter.

Reality crashed through her disbelief. The weeks he spent each month away from home. The occasional phone calls that pulled him back on the road, especially the last few years. The summons that ended his planned vacation at their new beach house just days ago. Ten days ago...

Her eyes snapped open. The staircase was empty.

Russell was gone.

Sarah was gone.

Madge blinked hard. When the room started to spin, she grabbed on to the banister for support. She gulped in long breaths of air and prayed her heart would stop pounding. She felt she had been sucked into a horrible nightmare. She wiped the beads of perspiration from her forehead and upper lips. Leaning on the banister post, she rested her forehead in the palm of her hand and closed her eyes.

Her heart trembled. She told herself she was only having a nightmare. This could not be real.

She was real. She could feel her pulse pounding against

her fingertips. The banister was rock solid and real. She opened her eyes. Her gaze followed the tracks of dirt and water up the carpet stairs. With a trembling hand, she reached out and touched the stain on the closest step.

It was no illusion. The water was cold and wet and real. So very, very real.

Dr. Newton came into the examining room, read Andrea's chart and smiled. "Everything looks good today. We can go ahead with the treatment. You know the routine. Do you have any questions before you get changed and we start?"

Andrea sighed and leaned against the back of the chair next to the examining table. "No. No questions. Not really."

"No trouble with mood swings?" the doctor asked as she set out the equipment.

"A little. My sisters tell me I'm getting cranky, or at least I'm crankier than normal."

"Are they right?"

Andrea sighed again. "Maybe. Sometimes I feel as if I'm the most ungrateful woman who ever lived, and I think that's what makes me cranky."

The doctor sat down in an adjacent chair. "How are you ungrateful? Or what makes you feel that you are?"

Andrea shrugged. "I think of Sandra. My sister died less than a year ago, from liver cancer. It spread to her brain."

"That must have been hard to watch," the doctor said softly.

"It was harder for Sandra to endure, I'm sure," Andrea whispered. She toyed with the hem on her blouse. "My sister, Kathleen, died from leukemia. She wasn't even thirty-five. She died eight years ago, but I remember...."

Dr. Newton laid her hand on top of Andrea's. "And you feel guilty? Why? Because we're going to cure your cancer? Because you're going to survive?"

Andrea swallowed hard. "Sometimes, I really can get myself into a snit when I think about how easy this treatment is compared to what they had to endure." She closed her eyes and blocked other painful memories of her parents' valiant struggles against the cancers that had ravaged their bodies, only to succumb in the end.

The doctor squeezed Andrea's hand. "So sometimes, when you're in this snit, as you call it, you're also feeling…what?"

Andrea clenched her jaw. Baring her soul did not come easily. "Sometimes, when I really do believe the chemo will work, when I dare to think I have a future that will last more than a few years, I get all filled up with hate." She lowered her voice to a whisper, ashamed of her feelings and her failure to be in control of them. "I hate this cancer. I hate the chemo. I hate the appointments. And I hate all the restrictions on my life now."

She paused and gently rubbed the base of her throat. When she spoke again, her words overflowed like a river swollen with heavy rains and came pouring out. "Most days, I feel like I have a collar around my neck, and there's a leash attached to it. A very short leash that keeps me from doing all the things I want to do. Simple, but necessary things, like…like taking my clients to see some homes or attending a settlement or having a meal when I want to eat it without having to check my calendar or the clock to see if I have a treatment or a cysto scheduled." She shivered. "I hate cystos, too. A lot."

Dr. Newton smiled. "Me, too."

Andrea turned and met her gaze. "You, too?"

"I'm a bladder cancer survivor, Andrea. It's been six years now, but I have my annual cysto, like it or not."

"Oh."

"I know the hate you're feeling. Hate's a strong, bitter emotion, a destructive one. It can tug on that leash and tighten that collar around your neck until you think you'll choke on life itself."

"Exactly," Andrea whispered.

"Unless you change your perspective, it will. Trust me, it will."

Andrea searched the depth of the other woman's eyes. Goodness and honesty stared back at her, and she trembled. "How did you do it? Change your perspective, I mean?"

"Faith. Trust in God, in the belief that His plan is always perfect." The doctor smiled and laced her fingers with Andrea's. "You can't get rid of the leash, Andrea, any more than you can reject the treatments or change your original diagnosis, but you can change your perspective."

"How?"

The doctor tugged on her hand. "Let me show you. First, close your eyes."

Andrea did, and the doctor went on, "Now, tell me what your leash looks like. What is it made of? Leather? Nylon cord? How wide is it? What color is it? Look hard."

Andrea squeezed her eyes closed tighter. "It's leather, I think, about three inches wide, and it's…it's purple," she blurted. She nearly choked. *Purple?* Where did that come from? She must have Madge on her mind.

"Look at the leash a little closer," the doctor instructed. "Can you break it?"

"No. It's...it's too strong."

"Why?"

Frustrated, Andrea opened her eyes. "Because it is. Look, it doesn't really matter. I can't break the leash, and I can't get rid of the leash. I don't have any choice about that, not if I want to live," she snapped, and pulled her hand away.

"Exactly wrong," the doctor murmured. "You have a choice. He always gives you a choice. Let's try again, shall we?"

Andrea blushed. "I'm sorry. I'm tired and I'm getting a little—"

"Cranky. No problem. We can talk about this next time, okay?"

Andrea moistened her lips. She had gone this far, she might as well finish whatever exercise Dr. Newton had in mind. She took the doctor's hand and closed her eyes.

The doctor squeezed her hand. "Take a look at that leash again. That three-inch purple leather leash. The one you think you must have."

Andrea nodded.

"Now imagine that it's gone. I've given you a new one. It's still pretty short. In fact, it's exactly the same length as the one you have now, but it's different. See? It's not leather anymore, and it's not purple. It's made of your favorite colors, the most beautiful colors God ever created for his flowers. In fact, if you look very closely, the leash is nothing but flowers. Your favorite flowers. And they're held together, leaf to leaf, petal to beautiful petal, with nothing but God's grace, because He made this leash of flowers just for you."

In her mind's eye, Andrea saw the purple leash disappear, inch by inch, until there was nothing but a row of magnificent flowers held together by grace that touched the very essence of her soul. The warmth of His love filled her spirit, leaving not a breath of room for hatred. Her body relaxed. Peace settled over her troubled thoughts. She felt safe. She felt loved.

"Can you smell the flowers, Andrea? What kind of flowers are they?"

She inhaled. "Roses. Red roses. And white lilacs."

"Fragile, aren't they?" the doctor asked.

Andrea smiled.

"They're meant to be fragile. Flowers are gifts, Andrea. You can plant them, you can water them, you can even feed them, but only God can inspire them to grow. He created them for all of us to enjoy, but these flowers He created and arranged together especially for you. Not for your sisters Sandra or Kathleen. For you. The leash of flowers is yours to keep and protect or to enjoy for as long as your treatments continue, and you can feel safe and warm, surrounded by His love and protection and by His grace. The leash of flowers may be short, but He created it for you. Only you can ask Him to reveal His plan for you so you can use this time for His work, not yours, and you can see all the other gifts He has given to you, as well."

She paused and squeezed Andrea's hand again. "On the other hand, you can choose to struggle against His will. You can let bitterness and frustration eat away at the grace He so freely gives to you until the flowers break apart and lie crushed beneath your feet. It's your choice," she murmured. "It's always been your choice to love Him, to trust Him and to believe in Him with all of your heart. Just remember that whatever you do, He loves you."

Tears streamed down Andrea's cheeks.

Why she had been given a more treatable form of cancer than her parents or either of her sisters was still a question that kept her spirit in turmoil. Of all the illnesses she could have gotten, cancer was probably the scariest. It was the fear that the treatments might fail or the cancer might have already spread that nibbled at her faith—even now.

Chapter Twenty-Two

When Jenny finally got home, she pulled into the driveway, cut the engine and released her seat belt. She looked out of the car window, saw the rain blowing sideways and pressed her forehead against the top of the steering wheel.

If working nine hours straight with only a fifteen-minute break on her first day back from vacation had not erased all the benefits of relaxing on the beach for a few days, driving home in this storm certainly did. She was exhausted and drenched to the bone from racing to her car at the end of her shift. She was in no mood to battle the elements again to get inside the house. She was hungry enough to eat her way through two breakfast specials at The Diner, but she wanted nothing more than to collapse into bed.

"A nice, warm, very dry bed," she murmured. She took a deep breath, secured the hood on her raincoat and got out of the car. As one gust of wind carried her forward, another blew her hood back, and she splashed her way to the front door. The moment she stepped inside the house, she realized something must be wrong. The silence was eerie. If she had not detected the tantalizing aromas coming from the kitchen, she would have thought Michael had taken the girls on an outing.

She shook her head. He would not have done that. Not on a day like today.

"Katy? Hannah? Mommy's home. Michael?"

While she waited for her family to come running, she eased out of her dripping raincoat. Without stepping off the plastic mat Michael had put down to protect the hardwood floors, she hung her raincoat on the hall tree. She untied her shoes and slipped them off, along with her socks. Miraculously, her scrubs were dry, except for the hems of her pants. Her hair had fared far worse. Water dripped down her face and into her eyes, as well as the back of her neck. She looked around for something to dry off her head and face when she saw Michael coming down the stairs carrying a large bath towel.

She smiled. "You're a lifesaver. I called out to let you know I was home, but you didn't answer."

"Sorry. I heard you pull into the driveway so I went upstairs to get you a towel. I had a feeling you'd carry half the storm in with you. Rough night?"

She shivered. "Not as rough as the ride home through the storm. Traffic on the Ben Franklin was so slow it was more like a parking lot than a bridge. Where are the girls?"

"Spending the day with their cousins."

She stopped toweling her hair. "You took them to your brother's? In this storm?"

He frowned. "Of course not. David called last night, right before supper, remember? He picked up the girls around seven for a sleepover? He's bringing them back after lunch, or as soon as the storm subsides a bit."

"Oh. I forgot."

He stepped behind her and took over toweling her hair. "Tired?"

She leaned back against his chest and closed her eyes. "Double tired."

When she shivered, he wrapped his arms around her. "I've got a hot bath drawn and waiting for you upstairs. Why don't you go on up? I'll have breakfast ready by the time you're done."

She tilted her head back and stared into his eyes. "You really are a man of many talents."

He grinned. "And I will be happy to remind you of my talents the next time you try to tell me otherwise." He eased her away. "Now scoot. The bathwater is going to get cold, and I have to check on breakfast before it burns."

"I won't be long. I'll be back down—"

"Up with you." He pointed to the stairs. "It's a breakfast-in-bed day. I suppose I forgot to tell you that, so don't come back down."

She giggled. "Breakfast in bed? We just got back from vacation, Michael. This is crazy."

"No, it's not crazy. It's a celebration."

Her heart skipped a beat. "A celebration?"

He laid his hand on top of her tummy. "Yes, a celebration. We could celebrate the fact that we're blessed to be having another child."

She nodded. "We could celebrate having a little time alone together."

The twinkle in his eyes grew brighter. "We could. Then again, we could celebrate the fact that precisely one hour and ten minutes ago, Annie Mitchell, president of The Mitchell Literary Agency called and agreed to represent me. I have an agent, Jenny."

"Michael!" She threw her arms around his neck.

He hugged her close. "She liked this book. No, she loved this book! She faxed me an agency contract, I signed it and faxed it back. She's sending my manuscript out by courier to four editors this afternoon. She thinks they'll all do a weekend read."

Jenny laid her head on his shoulder. "I'm so happy for you. I'm so proud of you. You did it! You really did it!"

He chuckled. "I haven't sold the book yet," he cautioned, "but this is really a big step in that direction."

"But you'll know soon. If one of the editors likes your book, you'll know Monday. You could sell the book by Monday, right?"

"Or not." He set her back and kissed her forehead. "I'm taking us all away for the weekend. Don't ask where. It's a surprise. I don't even want to think about what could or could not happen next week because that's not real. Not yet anyway. Getting an agent to represent my book? That's real. But having my family? That's a true blessing, and that's what we'll celebrate this weekend!"

"Yes, we will," she murmured. With a prayer in her heart that Michael might actually have his dream of becoming a published author come true, she held him tight, even as her own dream of becoming a stay-at-home mom took one step closer to becoming true as well. In the depths of her heart, however, fear nudged at her joy—fear that cancer might one day claim the life Jenny and Michael shared together.

Madge raced up the staircase, following the trail Russell had left on the cream carpet. She found him in the guest room across the hall from the master bedroom. He was tucking his little girl into the antique iron bed that had once belonged to Madge's Grandmother Poore.

Standing in the doorway, her heart trembled with anguish as she watched Russell tucking his child into bed. *His daughter.* Sarah was his daughter. She was another woman's child, and she was *here,* in Madge's home.

Madge did not want to look at this child any more than she wanted the girl to exist. But Sarah did exist. She was still fast asleep as Russell knelt by the side of the bed and struggled to untangle the blankets wrapped around her.

Madge's eyes misted with tears. Sarah was just a wisp of a thing. Blond ringlets, damp from the rain or from sleeping within a cocoon of covers, framed her heart-shaped face. She stirred and whimpered a bit when Russell settled her head on the pillow, but her lips never lost their grip on her thumb. As soon as he pulled the quilt up to her chin, Sarah curled onto her side, facing Madge, and started sucking on her thumb.

Such an innocent lamb.

Madge's heart ached when Russell pressed a kiss to his daughter's forehead, and she couldn't control her curiosity. Had Sarah been conceived in one rare moment when Russell had been too weak to resist the temptation of sin? Or had this child been born to Russell and another woman he had been seeing for…how long? Several years, at least, if Sarah was three years old.

Who was the woman who had been Sarah's mother?

Who was this man, the man who had been Madge's husband for all these years?

Reeling from questions that had no answers, she watched him as he pressed his forehead to the pillow next to his daughter. When his shoulders trembled and she heard him choke back his sobs, she sagged against the frame of the door.

He loved this little girl.

Madge had thought he had loved her, too, and his betrayal and the vision of the evidence of his betrayal sliced through her, opening a wound in her heart that she knew would never heal, not in this lifetime.

In that moment, watching her husband kneeling next to his love child, the world she had known crashed and shattered into pieces: The marriage she had treasured for twenty-six years? Gone. The vows they had taken, pledging devotion and forsaking all others? Broken. The husband she had loved? A traitor. The life they had shared together? An illusion.

When images of their sons flashed in her mind, Madge clenched her jaw to silence a moan. How could she tell Drew and Brett their father had been unfaithful? Or that he had brought his love child home?

Tears welled and streamed down her cheeks. Her heart hurt. How could Russell have done this to her and to their sons?

Another image flashed through her mind, a premonition

of days to come. Like the storm outside that carried rain and destruction with every gust of wind, news of Russell's infidelity would spread throughout the community. Welleswood's favorite adopted son would be branded with shame and scandal. And so would she.

Welleswood was a small town. It was Madge's hometown. Her family had lived here for four generations. Her roots were deep, but this nightmare would strangle every aspect of her life here until she had nothing left. And what about Jenny and Andrea? They could be tainted by this scandal, too, simply because they were her sisters!

Madge pressed her fist to her mouth. Too late. Wrapped in anguish, her sobs tore free and echoed in the room. Her soul cried out in pain. Her spirit yearned for justice.

Oh, God. Why have You forsaken me?

Russell stood up and walked toward her.

She backed into the hallway.

He came out of the room and closed the door behind him. "Please. Let me explain—"

"Explain? Explain what? That you've betrayed me? That you've broken your vows? I can see that." With tears streaming down her face, she pointed to the door. "The proof is in that room. The evidence against you is here in my home."

He blanched. "She's my daughter."

"Yes, she's your daughter, but she's another woman's daughter, not mine," Madge whispered. "What kind of woman takes another woman's husband and bears his child? Tell me, Russell. Was she a fling? Was she a…a prostitute? Or was she a woman who deliberately tried to trap you by getting pregnant?"

He shook his head. Fresh tears began to fall down his cheeks, which were darkened by several days' stubble and stained from tears he had already spent. "She wasn't like that," he murmured.

Madge stared at him, refusing to make it easy, refusing to back down.

Russell dropped his gaze to the floor and twisted the wedding ring he had worn since their wedding day. When he finally looked up at her, his eyes were steady yet filled with remorse. "Stacy was a good woman. She was Sarah's mother, and she was a good mother." He drew in a long, deep breath. "She was also my wife."

Chapter Twenty-Three

Madge could not keep the incredulous giggles from bubbling out. "Your wife? Did you say this woman was your *wife*? That's…ridiculous. I'm your wife, and I've been your wife for twenty-six years."

A horrific possibility grabbed her by the throat and made it nearly impossible for her to ask him if it was true. "Unless…unless you weren't free when you married me. Is that it, Russell? Is our marriage even valid? Were you single when we got married or are you trying to tell me—"

Disbelief flashed through his eyes. "Of course I was." Shivering, he brushed back several strands of damp hair from his forehead, pulled his wet shirt away from his torso and glanced back at the door behind him. "I need to get into some dry clothes, and I sure could use some coffee to warm up. Maybe we should talk about this downstairs in the kitchen? This isn't something we can settle in a few minutes," he whispered.

Her mouth dropped open. "I'm not even sure I want to be in the same house with you, let alone sit across from you at a table in the same room. Not until I get an explanation!" She gritted her words through clenched teeth and managed to keep her voice low to keep from waking Sarah. The last thing Madge wanted was a distraction or an interruption that would prevent Russell from giving her a full explanation.

Now.

"I'll forget the dry clothes, then. At least go downstairs with me."

When he tried to take her arm, she yanked away and caught another glimpse of her soiled hallway carpet. "Get changed while I make some coffee. You've already tracked up enough of the house."

"Five minutes. That's all I'll need," he promised.

She nodded and swallowed hard. Five minutes or fifty minutes from now would not make much difference. Her life had already been ruined. When he went into the bedroom and closed the door, she turned and followed the muddy footprints back downstairs. To her surprise, questions were not peppering her mind. She felt hollow. Her senses were numb. Her emotions lay frozen deep inside of her, beneath a brittle but protective shell that allowed her to function…until she started across the foyer, looked into the living room and saw the tube of conditioner lying next to her purse on the chair. She braced to a sudden halt, slipped on a puddle of water and slammed to the tiled floor. She landed hard on her knees and scraped the heels of both hands. Pain jolted through her body and cracked the shell that had kept her in shock. Tears sprang and gushed from her eyes.

Gasping, she leaned back on her haunches and wrapped her arms about her waist. "Andrea! I forgot all about Andrea." She groaned and tucked her chin to her chest. By now, Andrea had no doubt gone to her doctor's appointment alone, and she had probably been late, too.

Madge sighed. The thought that she had completely forgotten about her sister and let her sister down was yet another blow to her bruised and battered spirit. The mere possibility that Andrea might stop on her way home to make sure Madge was okay or to find out why Madge had not even bothered to call to let her know she would not be able to take her to the doctor's nearly crippled her. Panic, however, pumped new fear through her veins.

She could not see Andrea right now. She could not talk to her right now, either.

Scrambling back to her feet. What to do? What to do first? Secure the chain on the front door. Andrea had a key. Madge skirted the puddles of water and put the security chain back into place. Then she remembered that Andrea had to go straight home from getting the chemo for "rolling time," which meant she should not be stopping by.

Good. What next? The telephone? No problem there. Madge did not have to take Andrea's call. She had an answering service. She had voice mail on her cell phone, too. Her cell phone! She raced back to the living room to her purse, pulled out her cell phone, sighed and slipped it back inside. She had not remembered to turn it on before packing it into her purse earlier. Sometimes being a little forgetful was not a bad thing.

Cornered, she went to the telephone in the kitchen and lifted the receiver. When she heard a series of rapid beeps, her heart started pounding. She retrieved the message and heard Andrea's voice:

"Madge? This is Andrea. I'm leaving for the doctor's office. I'll call you when I get back."

Madge sighed and hung up the telephone. At least Andrea had not sounded too awfully upset with her.

Eventually, however, if she did not return Andrea's call, Andrea would worry and drive over. Once she saw Madge's car in the driveway, as well as Russell's, she would not stop banging on the door until one of them answered and reassured her nothing was terribly wrong. Terribly wrong? That might be the understatement of Madge's life, at least at this moment.

She closed the living-room drapes to keep the outside world from looking in, at least temporarily, and went to the kitchen where she made a quick call to Andrea's home and left an apology in a brief message explaining about Russell being ill and coming home unexpectedly. She made a fresh pot of coffee and set the table with lavender place mats and matching pedestal mugs. After she poured the French vanilla creamer that Russell loved into a pitcher, she set it alongside the sugar bowl.

When she finished, she stood with her back to the sink and leaned against the counter for support. The smell of fresh-brewing coffee and the sight of the table set for two presented a vision of domesticity and marital bliss and held an aura of intimacy that poured salt into the gaping wounds in her heart. Abruptly, she turned away and faced the window, but she could not escape the sting of Russell's betrayal.

Sobs tore through her throat. Tears blurred her vision. Like the torrential rain cascading down the window glass, her tears washed the salt from her wounds and helped to clear the debris of guilt littering her thoughts.

She had not done anything to destroy her marriage. She had not broken her vows. She had not been unfaithful. She was entitled to know why her husband had done this to her. To himself. To *them*.

Madge dried her tears with a tea towel and straightened the gold chain that had tangled about her neck. Overhead, she heard Russell pulling open dresser drawers, then the sound of water. He was taking a shower. With shoulders squared, she took a deep breath, marched to Russell's seat at the head of the table and sat down to wait for him.

She folded and unfolded her hands. She tapped her foot, but she refused to let the questions that demanded answers take root. She wanted a very clear mind when he finally appeared. She checked the clock. "You said five minutes, not fifteen," she grumbled. She listened hard, but she could not hear the shower. She could not even hear him moving around anymore.

A chill trickled up her spine, and she knew without looking up that she was being watched. She turned in her seat to face the doorway, ready to confront him for sneaking downstairs and observing her without letting her know he was there.

The reprimand died on Madge's lips.

Little Sarah was standing within the frame of the doorway, a picture of sweet innocence if one ever existed. Her eyes were the color of the summer bluebells that grew wild in the garden. Her blond ringlets were still damp and curled around her face. With her rosy cheeks, rosebud mouth and porcelain skin, she would have looked like a china doll if it weren't for the frown and the rumpled denim overalls she wore. She was staring right at Madge, and her eyes were wide with interest.

Madge's first instinct was to pick up the little waif and give her a big hug. She resisted. Sarah was not an orphan. She still had her father. "Your name is Sarah, isn't it?"

She bobbed her head. "Poppy seepin'."

"Poppy? You mean your daddy?"

Another nod.

"He's sleeping?" Madge asked, certain the little girl was mistaken. Russell could not be asleep. Not at a time like this. Even if he were asleep, she doubted Sarah could manage turning the knob and opening the door to the bedroom. She must have thought he was asleep because she had been sleeping.

"Poppy seepin' in bed."

"Oh, dear. No darlin'." Madge got up from her chair, walked over to the little girl and knelt down to eye level. "Your daddy isn't sleeping. He's just changing. He got all wet in the rain. How did you ever manage to get down here all by yourself without falling down the steps?"

Sarah tugged on Madge's hand. "Find Baby."

"Baby? Did you lose your baby?" Madge asked. She did not remember seeing a baby doll anywhere. She had watched Russell unwrap the covers around Sarah earlier when he had tucked her into bed. If he had found her baby doll, he would have put it in the bed with her, if only to make her feel more at home when she woke up in a strange bed in a strange room in a strange house.

"Find Baby," Sarah insisted.

She was more determined than upset, judging by the set of her shoulders and the twinkle of stubbornness in her eyes. Good. The last thing Madge needed was an inconsolable child on her hands. She brushed a ringlet from Sarah's forehead. "Did you have your baby in the car? Daddy probably left it there. We'll have Daddy go outside and get it for you as soon as he gets downstairs," she crooned.

The little girl's blue eyes glistened with tears. "Find Baby. Baby hungwy."

Madge smiled. "You must be hungry, too. How about we get you something to eat, and when Daddy comes downstairs—"

"Poppy seepin'. Find Baby," she wailed. She scrunched her little face, flushed scarlet, and began to shed tears the size of marbles.

Madge scooped the toddler up into her arms, but Sarah pushed and struggled to get down and cried harder. "Hush now. I'll…I'll get the baby for you. Don't cry."

Sarah stilled so quickly Madge thought she might have simply pressed a button from *On* to *Off*. When Sarah smiled at her without a single new tear waiting to fall, Madge knew she was face-to-face with one very strong-willed, spoiled little girl. Rather than get into a contest of wills, she cocked a brow. "You win this round, but don't get any ideas about winning the next one. Let's go find your baby and we'll wait until Daddy gets downstairs before we negotiate breakfast."

"Poppy seepin'."

"He better not be," Madge muttered. She carried Sarah to the foyer and sat her down on the bottom step. "You must sit right here while I go outside."

"Find Baby?"

"Yes, I'm going to find your baby." Madge opened the front door. By some chance, which had to be the first good one in what had become the most miserable day of her life, the rain has stopped. Overhead, clouds in the distance approached like a runaway herd of black sheep. The break in the storm would not last long. Madge said a quick prayer that Russell had not locked the car, warned Sarah to sit still again and charged out to the car. She saw the car seat in the back, opened the rear door and gasped.

There was no baby doll in the back seat. No stuffed animal, either. Only a little brown fur ball that lifted up its head, opened both golden eyes and yawned.

This was Sarah's baby?

This kitten was Sarah's baby?

Russell let his daughter have a pet? He had never allowed the boys to have pets of any kind. Was there no limit to this man's gall?

Madge reached in, picked up the kitten and cuddled it against her chest. Then she slammed the car door shut and marched back to the house. Her heart pumped in outrage.

The moment she reached the porch, little Sarah leaped up from the step. "Baby!" she cried, and held out her arms.

Madge handed over the kitten and picked them both up. "I think we should go and find Daddy now," she murmured. She carried the now-contented child up the steps and down the hall to the master bedroom. She kept a tight hold on her emotions and had no intention of making a fuss about the kitten.

Not now. Not with little Sarah here. But later, Madge

would blister that man's ears or her name was not Margaret Louise Long Stevens!

For now, she would have to settle for a glare so cold Russell would take one look at her face and instantly freeze. She rather liked the mental image of Russell's face coated with ice crystals, his body frozen solid, especially that lying, cheating heart of his. She set her features, opened the door and stepped into the bedroom. When she saw him lying on the bed, sound asleep just like Sarah had said, she rocked back on her heels and wrapped both arms around Sarah and Baby.

With her mouth agape, she stared at the bed where he had apparently sat down to put on his socks but fell asleep instead. He was sprawled on his side with a sock in one hand. The other was on the floor. Exhaustion etched in his face, even in sleep. Grief and shame, she hoped, gave an ashen-gray cast to his skin. He looked tired and beat, as if the world had become a place too difficult for him to be in anymore.

"Your world, Russell. The world you created. The world you destroyed for both of us," she whispered.

"Find Poppy!" Sarah squealed, and tried to wriggle free, which prompted the kitten to meow.

Madge was half tempted to let the child free to wake up Russell, but she had no desire to let Baby loose—not until she had a litter pan set up. Besides, waking Russell now would not accomplish much. He and Madge would not be able to talk freely until Sarah was napping.

"Hush now. Hold still. See? We found your daddy for you, but you were right. He's sleeping, and he needs to rest a little while longer."

Sarah's eyes opened wide and she smiled. "Mommy restin' too. Find Mommy. Find Mommy now!"

Madge gazed down at Sarah and swallowed hard. She could not explain to this little girl that her mommy was dead. Death was not a concept this three-year-old would be able to grasp. With time, she would eventually understand that death was a permanent state and her separation from her mother would last for all of Sarah's lifetime. Their reunion would come in the next world, not this one. The days and weeks, even years, ahead would be filled with confusion and uncertainty and grief so real she would cry from the pain that would rack her soul as she struggled to find a new place herself. A place where she felt secure and loved again. A place where she would once again find the joy and love that would ease the pain of her loss.

Just like Madge would have to do.

Inexplicably drawn to this child by a bond forged in mutual pain and loss, Madge hugged Sarah to her breast and left the room, closing the door behind her. She started down the hall. "It looks like we're both in the same sinking boat," she told the child. Without life vests, without a pair of oars, a compass or emergency flares, and the captain who had steered them into this mess was asleep! "What are we going to do?"

She hoisted Sarah to her hip, while the kitten held on to Madge's blouse with sharp claws that pinched her skin. She settled the kitten back into Sarah's arms.

With her bottom lip quivering, Sarah looked up at her. "Find Mommy?"

Madge sighed. "You know, if I could find your mommy, I would. I surely would."

Chapter Twenty-Four

By eight o'clock that night, the storm that had badgered Welleswood all day had swept father east and closer to sea. The heavy rains had become a drizzly mist. The winds had softened, but heavy clouds still guarded the moon and stars.

Madge, however, remained stuck in the eye of the storm that had swept into her home. After negotiating through a few tantrums, she and Sarah had managed through breakfast, lunch, dinner and bedtime. Sarah had a surprisingly good appetite. Their major battle had been over milk. Sarah had refused to drink a drop, but Madge's distaste for regular milk as a child made her sympathetic rather than upset. She would have given anything for a bottle of chocolate syrup; instead, she had taken a few of the imported French chocolates that Russell had given to her, melted them in the microwave with a little milk, and stirred the chocolate sauce into Sarah's glass of milk.

With that problem solved, Madge had moved on to the next. She had found a suitcase filled with the clothes Russell had brought along for his daughter in the trunk of his car, along with his luggage. She left his suitcases where they were, but Sarah's clothes now filled the dresser in the guest room, where the toddler had fallen asleep once Madge had taken the night-light from the hall and put it into her room.

Getting Baby situated required a little more ingenuity. Luckily, Russell kept stores of samples of various pet foods and supplies in the basement. For food and water bowls, Madge used two of the small silver bowls that Russell had received as awards at one time or another. Somehow, the idea that the kitten would be eating food and lapping water from bowls that had Salesman of the Year inscribed on the bottom seemed rather fitting since the man had obviously been catting around with at least one woman and who knows how many more.

The only thing she had not found was a plastic pan for the litter. After searching through the other half of the basement where Russell kept the tools he rarely used and the old "treasures" he intended to restore someday, she settled on an old wooden soda crate that had once held quart bottles of carbonated water. Once Madge had lined the crate with plastic, it made an adequate makeshift litter pan, which Baby used almost before Madge had added the last of the litter.

With Sarah tucked into bed and Baby snuggling in beside her, Madge sat alone in the living room in the dark. Russell was still upstairs sleeping, she supposed. She had not heard him stir or move about, but she had not had the nerve to open the door to their bedroom and check on him. She might never go back into that room, not while Russell was there. Maybe not after he had gone, either.

She toyed with her wedding ring and knocked her diamond engagement ring each time she twisted the narrow gold band round and round her finger. How could he sleep through the entire day? Was he *that* exhausted?

He knew she would not be able to take out her anger on a little girl. He knew how much she loved little children, especially her nieces, Katy and Hannah, now that their boys were grown. She loved children. Period.

Her backbone stiffened. Did he really think she would simply forgive him—or forgive him more easily for the sake of his daughter?

"She's your daughter, not mine," she whispered. She tried to imagine what Sarah's mother had looked like. Was she young and fair, like Sarah? Was she—?

A thud, followed by a groan upstairs ended her musings. She heard Russell limp his way down the hall and turn on the foyer light. Hidden by the shadows, Madge remained in her chair, silent and still. She felt no guilt for taking the night-light from the hallway. After all, she had moved it for his daughter. When she heard Russell descending the steps, she lowered her gaze, and said a prayer. *Please, God. Help me to be strong. Help me to bear the pain to come.*

"Madge? Are you in there?"

She swallowed hard. "Yes, I'm here."

He stepped into the room, saw her sitting in the chair and dropped into the chair directly across from her. "What happened to the night-light?" he asked as he crossed one leg over his knee and massaged his foot. "I think I might have broken a toe."

"Sarah needed it. I put it in her room."

He froze for a moment, then nodded and put both feet back on the floor. "I stopped to see her on my way downstairs. I'm sorry. I didn't mean to fall asleep—"

"Or sleep all day?" She asked the question, but she knew the haggard look he still wore was real.

He ran his fingers through his hair. "I'm sorry. It's been a while since I've gotten any sleep. Deep sleep, that is."

She wanted to take the lump out of her throat and throw it at him. "I'm sure it's been very difficult. Losing your *wife,* that is. And so suddenly. I'm sure you weren't prepared for that to happen. How inconvenient for you."

The blood drained from his face. "I suppose I should have expected that."

"Expected what, Russell? My anger? My disappointment? Or has it just now occurred to you that you're also going to lose this wife and you'll be alone, unless there's a third wife you've hidden away somewhere. How many wives do you have left now, anyway?"

He closed his eyes for a moment and moistened his lips. "You're the only wife I have."

"Now," she cautioned, although some deep part of her was relieved to know there weren't any more women calling themselves Mrs. Russell Stevens. Unless he was lying.

When he did not respond, she held silent. She had no intention of making this easier for him. She let the silence build between them, as cold and stiff as the wall his betrayal had already built.

He dropped his gaze to the floor. "I'm sorry. I know I've

hurt you…the boys…I'm not going to make any excuses for what I've done. I—I just don't know where to begin or if you'll even stop hating me for what I've done long enough to listen to what I have to say."

Her mind screamed for vengeance and created one bitter response after another to hurl at him. Already wounded, her heart trembled with the fear his words would deliver a fatal blow that would forever destroy the love she had for him. Her soul, filled with faith, begged her to let patience and understanding prevail. "Begin at the beginning," she whispered.

His eyes glistened with tears, which he swiped away with the back of one hand. "The beginning… The beginning was only a few years ago when I met Stacy. She is…was a lot like you, but I suppose you don't want to hear that."

"No, actually, I don't."

He drew in a deep breath. "I met Stacy through work. She had just moved to the Pittsburgh area and she started working as a secretary for the Sales Director at Noah's Ark. Their headquarters are in Collsworth, right outside the city."

Madge nodded. Noah's Ark was a major pet store chain on the East Coast and one of Russell's largest accounts. A mental image of the biblical ark formed in her mind. She shook her head to get rid of the image.

"Stacy…she had a flat tire in the parking lot one day. I changed it for her. From there…well…you can see how things ended up." He released the sigh of a totally defeated man, tilted his head and laid it against the back of his chair. His body slumped, as if his muscles were too tired to hold his body erect, and he closed his eyes, as if ready to surrender to death, to escape the nightmare he had created for himself.

The part of Madge that loved Russell yearned to take him into her arms and comfort him. The part of her that wanted justice urged her to pack a bag, walk out of this house and head straight to the best barracuda of a lawyer she could afford.

She decided to wait to learn more before she made any decision at all. "There's a lot that happened between meeting this woman and now. I deserve to know what happened, what made you take another wife without bothering to divorce the one you already had," she insisted. She was proud of herself for the even tone of voice she had used.

He sat upright and stared at her. "I never wanted a divorce. I never stopped loving you. Never. It's just…I was weak, I'll admit that. I sinned. Yes, I sinned. I broke my vows and I betrayed you, but I never wanted to hurt you. But things got…complicated. I didn't know what else to do. God help me, I didn't know what to do," he whispered.

Her throat constricted. "You mean what to do about Sarah?"

When he spoke again, his voice cracked. "I was already prepared to end the affair when Stacy told me she was pregnant. She didn't know I was married. I couldn't let her have the baby alone or raise the baby alone, either. She had no one. No family at all. She was all alone, living in a strange new town. Marrying her seemed the only option."

"So you lied to her, too. Did she ever find out—"

"No," he whispered. "She never knew I was already married to you. I couldn't tell her, especially after Sarah was born. I couldn't tell you, either. I didn't know when or how either one of you would find out, but I never dreamed it would be like this."

"Lies always come home to roost. My grandmother told me that more than once when I was a little girl. I guess it's true, isn't it?" Madge murmured. "What…what are your plans now? What did you think would happen when you came home to me with your daughter?"

Russell locked his gaze with hers. "I—I don't have any plans. Not beyond staying here for a few days. I—I won't fight a divorce…if that's what you want. Beyond that, I guess it's up to you, isn't it?"

She stiffened. Was it up to her? Did she have a choice? Could she find it in her heart to forgive him, or was the wall he had built between them so strong and so filled with anger and resentment that it was impenetrable?

She bowed her head, but her heart was too weakened to attempt to find the answers to her questions. She was blessed that her wounded heart was able to beat at all.

Suddenly, she was tired, so very, very tired. Without answering him, she stood up and walked to the staircase in the foyer. She paused at the bottom step, but she did not turn to look over at him. "There are leftovers in the refrigerator if you're hungry. I'm going to get a few of my things and go to bed. I'll be in Drew's room."

"No, please. Don't do that. I'll take his room."

She started up the stairs without answering him. When she got to the master bedroom, the room where both of her sons had been conceived, she paused and turned away. She went straight to Drew's room down the hall and closed the door behind her. She did not bother to turn on the light or take off her clothes. She just stepped out of her shoes, crawled into the single bed and pulled the covers up to her neck.

When the dam finally burst, when all of her emotions finally broke free, she buried her face in the pillow to stifle her sobs. She curled into a ball and cried as if her heart had broken, because it had. She cried as if she still loved this man, because she did. She cried as if all that she had treasured in the world was now slipping from her grasp, because it was. And she cried as if she had no other choice to make now about her marriage, because deep in her heart she knew she had no other choice but one.

When her tears were spent and her body was limp with exhaustion, she barely had the strength to pray. When she finished, the answer to her pleas for guidance spoke directly to her heart, but she did not find the answer any easier to bear than her husband's betrayal.

"This isn't my fault. I shouldn't have to do this. I'm fifty-five years old. I shouldn't have to start over again," she whispered with a breath of defiance, "and I won't do it."

But you must.

"I can't do this."

Yes, you can.

"Not alone. I can't do this alone."

You are never alone. He is always with you.

"But I'm not strong enough. I'm not strong, like Andrea."

He is stronger. Lean on Him.

She shook her head. "I'll fail. I'll still fall."

He knows.

"Soon everyone will know. The scandal will be unbearable." She paused. "My life will never be the same. No one will love me. Not like they do now."

He will. He'll always love you.

She wept until the moment she fell asleep, still too heart-broken to believe in much of anything beyond the pain that pierced the very essence of her spirit.

Chapter Twenty-Five

Trouble practically met Andrea at the door when she got to work on Friday morning, even though she thought she had put this particular trouble behind her.

She did not even have time to check her calendar for the day or retrieve the messages from the answering machine when six-feet-something of trouble sauntered into her office, pulled up a chair and sat down in front of her desk.

She met Bill Sanderson's gaze and matched his obvious determination by squaring her shoulders. "We didn't have an appointment today."

He shook his head. "No, I don't believe we did. You haven't called, and you haven't set another date to show me any more houses, either."

"An appointment. I didn't set another appointment. We've never had a date," she insisted.

"We really should do something about that."

She almost let out a sigh, but caught herself. "I'm not interested."

"Sure you are, but before you get all steamed up—"

"I don't get 'steamed up.' I'm simply getting frustrated. You don't seem to be getting my message."

He chuckled. "Oh, I've gotten the message. You like me. You're just too stubborn to admit it."

"And you're too persistent for your own good. Now, if you'll excuse me, I have a business to run and clients who respect the time I spend trying to find them a home, unlike other so-called clients who only pretend to be interested in moving to Welleswood," she snapped.

He ducked as if he were trying to avoid her words. "I'm glad I don't fit into that last category."

Her eyes widened. Rather than use words to defend herself and prove him wrong, she grabbed at the keys hanging from the lanyard around her neck and unlocked her new credenza.

"That's an interesting necklace you're wearing. Having trouble with thieves getting to your files?"

"No, only hurricanes," she muttered, pulled his file and put it on the desk between them. "Take a look. It's your file. Count the number of houses I've shown to you over the past two months."

He thumbed through the file so fast he could not possibly have counted them all. "Sixteen. I believe that's accurate."

"Sixteen exactly. And how many did you consider seriously enough to make an offer?"

He shrugged, but his eyes were twinkling. "Only the first one."

"Which you reneged on."

"Like I had a choice?"

"There were fifteen others," she countered, to change the subject rather than admit he was right. It had not been his fault that he had been victimized by hijackers.

"They weren't quite right."

She meant to wave his words away, but her gesture was more like a swing. "You weren't really serious about any of those houses. You only looked at them because you…I mean…" Feeling a little foolish to say she thought he only wanted an excuse to see her, she faltered—until she saw that twinkle in his eyes again. "You only looked at them because you wanted an excuse to see me."

He smiled. "I warned you I was persistent."

"And I distinctly told you that I'm—"

"Stubborn. I remember. Scared, too, I gather. One date would fix that."

She stared at him. "Were you born this brazen or is it an acquired fault?"

He laughed out loud. "Probably a little of both. At the moment, though, I guess I'm just interested in knowing one reason why you're not interested."

"In you?" she asked.

"Yes. Other than the age thing."

She cocked a brow.

He shrugged again. "It bothers some people."

"But not you."

"Obviously."

"Okay then, it bothers me. I'm fifty-seven years old. You're…"

"Forty-six."

"I was eleven years old when you were born!" Andrea exclaimed.

"A lot of people were. Now aside from the age difference, which neither one of us can change—"

"I'm not interested. I'm perfectly happy being single, so there's no need to date you or anyone else," she insisted. She was not going to explain anything beyond that because she did not need to. He just could not argue with that reason.

"I've been single for the past eight years. Being single is lousy, so I know better. Try again."

"I'm too busy to date. I have a business to run. Even if I wanted to date, I don't have the time." There. Argue with that, she thought, triumphantly.

His brow furrowed. "From what I hear, you do have the time. Mrs. Blake is a lot busier here at the office than you are, and she's been seeing the pastor's brother-in-law for the past few weeks."

"D-Doris? And the pastor's brother?"

"I also heard he's a few years her junior, too." He winked, and his smile had victory written all over it.

She could feel her heart pounding, and her temper slipped right out of her grasp. Even hours later, she could not figure out whether it was desperation or sheer orneriness that had prompted her to be so blatantly honest with him. "I'm not well, which means I'm not exactly dating material right now."

"Your ankle has been healed now—"

"I have bladder cancer. For the second time," she blurted. "I've been taking chemotherapy treatments since the end of July. I had one yesterday, and I have eight more months of chemo ahead of me. Which means I shouldn't even be thinking of dating you or anyone else right now because I don't have the time or the inclination to think about it because if I were interested, it wouldn't matter anyway. I can't date you because I'm not sure the chemo is going to work or not. I can't see my own future clearly, let alone anyone else's. Not right now. Understand? That's the truth, the awful truth, and nothing but the truth. So please don't worry about hurting my feelings. Just don't slam the door on your way out, and if you tell one person on this entire planet or any other what I just told you, I will find some way to haunt you for the rest of your natural life."

With her chest heaving, she watched his expression change from brazen and playful to serious and thoughtful. Her hands clenched into fists, ready to pound on her desk if she saw even the slightest hint of pity in his eyes. She steeled herself, certain he would get up and walk out the door, like any other man would do.

Instead, he took a deep breath. "What's better for you? I can make dinner reservations for eight at La Casita, or I can pack a picnic, pick you up at six, and we can head for the shore. I have it on very good authority that the storm is long gone. After we watch the sun set, we can take a walk on the beach."

When her mouth dropped open, she slammed it shut and almost bit her tongue. "You will what? Are you serious? I just told you that I—"

"You have cancer," he whispered. "I heard you."

"And you still want a date?"

"Yes."

"Why?"

"Why? I thought that was pretty obvious."

"Not good enough," she argued. "Give me one good reason why you'd want to date me. An honest reason," she cautioned, trying to toss his earlier challenge to her right back at him.

He smiled and held up the index finger on his right hand. "One, I find you incredibly fascinating. Two," he said as he held up his middle finger, "you have more gumption than any other woman I've ever met."

When she tried to protest that he had gone beyond the one reason she had asked for, he silenced her by adding a third finger. "Third, I happen to find stubborn women very appealing. Do you need a fourth reason or a fifth? I've got those ready, too."

She swallowed hard. If the persistent man wanted a date, she would give him one he would remember for a very long time. "Make it for the beach at six-thirty. I'm on standby. If Doris isn't finished her three-o'clock settlement, I'm showing a house for her at four-thirty."

He grinned, stood up and started toward the door. He had barely stepped outside and shut the door before he opened it again and peeked inside. "Make sure you bring a sweatshirt. The beach gets cold after sundown," he suggested, then shut the door again before she could answer him.

When the door opened again, only seconds later, she sighed. "What now? A reminder to bring a flashlight?"

Jenny strolled in, backward, then turned around and shut the door. "Wasn't that Bill Sanderson?"

"None other."

"Why do you need a flashlight? Don't tell me you're taking him to see a house at night that doesn't have electricity."

"Of course not." Andrea fiddled with the papers in a blue folder labeled Sanderson, the color she reserved for impossible-to-please clients. She could feel a hot blush rushing up from her neck to her cheeks. Women her age did not blush. They had hot flashes, but they did not blush.

Jenny sat down in the chair that Bill had just vacated. "Then what do you need a flashlight for?"

"Nothing. It's just a…a joke. The man's impossible. I told you that. What brings you here? I thought you were going to see Madge this morning."

Jenny put one of her hands on top of the folder to stop Andrea from fiddling. "What kind of joke?"

Andrea finally met her sister's gaze. "It's nothing. It's not really a joke. I was just telling him—"

"I don't believe it!" Jenny chuckled and leaned back in the chair. "He asked you out. You have a date with him!"

Andrea caught a lie before it slipped out. Jenny was her sister, and she would know it was a lie before Andrea finished telling half of it. "It's not really a date. We're just having dinner."

Jenny cocked a brow.

"All right. It's just a picnic at the beach," Andrea admitted. "Tonight?"

Andrea nodded. If life were fair, she and Bill would be able to slip out of town unnoticed and head for the shore, and no one in town would be any the wiser. "It's only one date. I couldn't talk him out of it," she added defensively.

"Are you crazy?" Jenny asked.

Andrea bristled. "Crazy for going on a date with him? I've been asking myself the same question for the fifteen seconds I had to myself between the time he left and you got here."

"No, silly. I think you were crazy for trying to talk him out of it."

"Well, I tried hard, but the man is annoyingly persistent, not to mention he has an ego that is boundless. I told him I wasn't interested in dating, that I like being single."

"And he said you were full of soup, as Mother used to say."

Andrea chuckled and ran her fingers through her hair. "Something like that. Good grief, what am I going to do with this mop of mine?"

Jenny pulled out a tube of conditioner and placed it next to the blue folder. "Madge asked me to give this to you."

"She and Russell are feeling better? I called, but she's still not answering the telephone."

"I guess not. I stopped on my way home from work, just to see if I could do something for her, but she wouldn't let me in. She only opened the door wide enough to pass the conditioner out to me. She's afraid to spread whatever Russell brought home with him." Jenny shrugged her shoulders. "Like I'm not exposed to a hundred things worse than the flu five nights a week," she grumbled before covering a yawn. "What else did you say?"

"When?" Andrea asked, startled.

"When you were trying to convince Bill you didn't want a date."

"Oh, only that I was too busy to date."

"A woman should never be too busy to date."

"That's what he said, more or less. He was so sure of himself, I lost my temper."

Jenny grinned. "You did? Why do I find that a little too unbelievable?"

"Well, I did. I—I even told him about the cancer. That

didn't stop him. What kind of a man would want to date a woman with cancer?"

Jenny stood up, walked around the desk, and put her arms around Andrea's shoulders. "Exactly the kind of man we'd want dating our sister," she answered.

Andrea leaned into her sister's embrace. "What kind of man is that?"

"Just the kind of man who could love you as much as we do."

There was only one man Andrea knew who had loved her like that, and Peter had died so long ago. "Maybe I should call Bill and cancel," she murmured.

"No you don't! You go on that date and have a good time. Now, forget the date for a minute and put on your thinking cap. We have a mystery to solve, or I won't be able to get a wink of sleep."

Grateful for the opportunity to change the subject, Andrea looked up at her sister. "What kind of mystery?"

"Russell's car, which is in the driveway behind Madge's."

"That's your mystery? Is there something wrong with the car?"

"No. The car is fine, but there's a child's car seat in the rear seat. What's Russell doing with a car seat?"

"I don't know."

"Neither do I. He certainly doesn't need one."

Andrea laughed. "Since Drew and Brett aren't even married yet, it's a little early to anticipate grandchildren."

"Especially for Russell. Madge might think that far ahead, but even for Madge—"

"Maybe she said something to Russell about needing a car seat for Katy or Hannah."

Jenny nodded. "She did mention wanting to take Katy to the beach house for a few days, and that she couldn't do that without a car seat. I guess that's it."

"Mystery solved."

"What about the other mystery?" Jenny asked with an impish grin.

"What other mystery?"

"What are you wearing for your big date tonight?"

"A T-shirt and a pair of jeans, and I'm taking a sweatshirt. We're going to the beach, remember?"

Jenny tugged Andrea out of her chair. "Come on. We have to hurry. Michael is taking us away for the weekend, and I promised I'd be home by eleven."

Andrea pulled back. "What are you doing?"

"Dragging you to Jolene's. Kick and scream if you want, but we're going to Jolene's to get you something new to wear tonight."

Andrea laughed and let herself be dragged to her feet. "Okay."

"Okay? You'll go?" Jenny asked.

"Sure. I haven't bought much in the way of clothes for a while."

Jenny laid her hand on Andrea's forehead. "No fever. Must be love."

"Wrong, little sister. This is all about right and wrong. One date with me, and Bill Sanderson will know I was right and he was wrong."

"About what?"

Andrea stiffened her back. "He really doesn't want to date me. He wants to prove a point."

"Which is…?"

"He thinks he's irresistible. I'm going to prove otherwise. After one date with me, he'll be very happy to leave me alone."

Which was precisely what Andrea wanted.

Wasn't it?

Chapter Twenty-Six

Madge banished both Sarah and Russell to the first floor and spent most of Friday morning on her hands and knees cleaning the stains from the carpet runner on the stairs and in the upstairs hallway. She had only just started when Jenny arrived unexpectedly, and she had sent her sister off without too much trouble.

Thinking about the story she had invented about she and Russell being ill, she scrubbed at a difficult stain with a vengeance. "All I had to do was lie to my sister. I hate lies. I hate the fact he's forcing me to lie," she spit, grumbling her words to match the rhythm of her arms as she worked the last stain from the carpet. Her arms ached and her back ached, but her heart ached more.

She leaned back on her haunches and wiped the perspiration from her brow with the back of her hand. She could hear Sarah and Russell's laughter as they played with Baby in the kitchen below. "How fair is that?" she asked herself. "Russell gets to play while I have to clean up the mess he made."

She stared down the length of the carpet runner and clenched the scrub brush so hard her knuckles ached. Her life was a far bigger mess than this carpet had been, and she would have to work even harder to clear the stain of the scandal that would ruin her reputation and Russell's. She did not have much time before the scandal broke. She could not hide Sarah forever. Sooner or later, someone would realize that Russell had brought home more than samples for a new line of pet food.

But Madge needed time. Time to let her seething anger cool, to decide what she really wanted to do, to make some sort of peace with herself before either she or Russell could contemplate the next chapter of their lives. Unfortunately, Welleswood was just too small a community to hide much of anything, let alone a three-year-old child. Madge did not have the time she needed. Not here.

The day after tomorrow was Sunday. The moment services ended, everyone would wonder why she was not there. As soon as Andrea and Jenny repeated Madge's lie about illness, Madge and Russell would be inundated with calls, and casseroles would appear at their doorstep. "Lies always come home to roost," she whispered, unwilling to let one snowball into another and smash into her life when she could prevent it.

When she dropped the scrub brush into the bucket, droplets of water splashed her arms and face and the solution to her immediate problem hit her. The beach house!

If she and Russell could slip out of town with Sarah, unnoticed, Madge could get a reprieve and have a few weeks, at the very least, to work through this mess.

At this time of year, most of the folks in most of the resort towns were either retirees who wanted to take advantage of off-season rates or full-time residents who were too busy to pay much attention to the fact that Madge and Russell had decided to spend a few weeks in their new beach house. The fact that the house just happened to be located at the tip of the town near the inlet, about as remote as one could get in a resort town, was an added bonus.

Madge wiped her hands, stood up and carried the bucket of cleaning solution to the bathroom and dumped it into the sink. She could not go downstairs for several hours until the carpet was dry. By then, she could have their suitcases packed and ready to go. She could put fresh linens on the beds and close up the upstairs, and while Sarah napped this afternoon, Madge would sit Russell down and explain her plan.

Or as much of the plan as she could.

She knew where they would spend the next few weeks, assuming Russell had arranged for some time off from work. If he hadn't, then he would have to do it now.

They both needed time to be together to take a good, hard look at their relationship to understand how and why they had ended up mired in this difficult situation and explore the possibility of professional counseling.

She knew she needed time alone, time to pray and search the depths of her spirit, time to find the strength to begin a new phase of her life. Without bitterness. Without resentment. Without anger.

She also knew Russell needed time to fully realize what he had done, time to seek forgiveness from God, as well as Madge, and time to prepare for the months and years ahead. Living at the beach house would give both of them the time they needed before they returned to Welleswood and faced the gossip and the condemnation the world would slap at them all, even Sarah.

Madge set the bucket and scrub brush on the floor to dry and walked straight to the master bedroom. She put her hand on the doorknob, took a deep breath and went inside where memories lay in wait, like thieves in the night, ready to steal her resolve to put the past behind her and focus only on the present.

Using her fingertips, Andrea fluffed her hair into place. The conditioner Madge had gotten from Judy had worked wonders! Andrea's hair might be short, but it was silky again and every unruly wisdom hair had been tamed to lie flat.

She smiled and stepped back from the mirror. True, the beige Capri set she had bought at Jolene's was stylish and flattered her slim figure, but it was the joy of finding the outfit on the seventy-five-percent-off rack that made her the happiest. No sense wasting money on the one and only date she would have with Bill Sanderson.

She grabbed her zip-up, hooded sweatshirt off a hanger in her closet and her sports bag, which she had already packed with a bottle of diet peach tea, and waited by the front door. The "girls" were perched along the back of her couch looking out the picture window. "He's got a dark blue pickup truck," she told them, although she knew the cats were really preoccupied by the activity at the bird feeders she had filled that morning. Half-a-dozen sparrows competed tenaciously at one feeder while several goldfinch fed at another. A pair of mourning doves pecked at the seed that had fallen to the ground.

Andrea checked her watch. She was fifteen minutes early.

When she heard a vehicle approach and pull into her driveway, she frowned. He was early, too. She gave each of the girls a quick peck, opened the front door and stepped outside. The minute she spied his truck in the driveway, she took a step back.

He was not driving a dark blue pickup truck.

He was driving a Jeep. An all-terrain Jeep with no roof and no sides, just two front seats and a windshield.

So much for slipping out of town unnoticed.

She pasted a smile on her face and hopped into the passenger seat before he could undo his seat belt to help her. "New car?" she asked.

"I borrowed it from a friend. It's turned as warm as a summer day, so I thought we might have more fun in the Jeep. Phil's a lifeguard in Sea Gate. Well, he's actually a lieutenant or something." Bill tapped a decal on the windshield. "We can even drive on the beach."

He took her sweatshirt and put it in one of the two trunks on either side of a cooler, which filled the space where a rear seat would have been. "I had a feeling you'd be ready early."

"The sooner we start, the sooner we can—"

"I have a few stops to make on the way. Buckle up," he said, and threw the Jeep into reverse. When he got to the stop sign at the avenue, he put on his left blinker.

The instant she realized he intended to turn left and drive straight down the avenue through the center of town, she gulped down her horror. "If you turn right, you can get to the freeway faster."

He turned left. "Once I make a few stops, that's exactly where we're headed. I promised you a picnic, remember?"

She shut her eyes and counted to three before she opened them again. "You said you were going to pack a picnic."

"I am. I'm going to pack up the Caesar salads from The Diner, the rotisserie chicken and shrimp from the deli, and a tortilla sampler from La Casita as soon as I pick up the orders." He nodded toward the rear of the jeep. "I only had time to get the muffins from the bakery and fill the cooler with drinks."

Flabbergasted, she did not worry about being rude. She just stared at him, unable to say a word. How had he managed to find out every one of her favorites, especially the muffins that only her sisters knew were her favorites? If Andrea or Jenny had told him about the muffins, she would make them regret it!

He cocked a brow. "Aren't you going to ask me about the drinks? No? Well, I'll tell you anyway. Most of them are iced tea. That's all I knew for sure about what you liked, so I got some of everything. Regular and diet, flavored and unflavored. I like them all, so I'll just drink what you don't want. Fair enough?" he asked as he pulled into an open parking spot right in front of Ellie's Deli. "Sorry. If I'd been able to get this spot on my way to your house, I could have had everything packed up and still been on time."

There were never any open parking places on the avenue, especially not on a Friday night. Why tonight? Why now? "I don't suppose you'd care to tell me how you just happened to order some of my favorite foods, would you?"

He shrugged. "That was easy. I asked."

"You asked?"

"Sure. There aren't that many restaurants in town. I just called them up and asked them."

Her heart did a somersault. Twice. "You called and asked them? You told them my name and—"

"And I said I was taking you on a picnic and what would they recommend for a guy who wanted to make a really good impression on his first date with you."

"With me." She groaned. He might as well simply have placed an announcement in the Sunday bulletin at church. At least that would have kept the congregation from gossiping during the pastor's sermon. She also had a meeting Saturday afternoon for the Shawl Ministry, and she knew Miss Huxbaugh would have more than one comment to make about Andrea's date.

"I won't be long. I think I can pretty much hit all the stores and be back in ten or fifteen minutes."

"I'll be counting every second," she assured him. For two cents, she would have waited until he got into the deli, gotten out of the Jeep and marched herself home, but she was too much of a woman of her word to do that. She had agreed to one date, and she would make it through this date, by any and all means necessary.

She even tried imagining the leash that held her back from doing most everything she wanted, but by the time he got back, she was seething with embarrassment, to the point that the imaginary red roses and white lilacs had long since burned to a crisp. She had stopped counting the number of people she knew who had either passed by and waved from their cars or strolled by and stopped to say hello to her.

Seeing the flash of disbelief in their eyes that she would be on a date with a younger man did not bother her as much as she had thought it would. Seeing the flash of disbelief in their eyes that she was on a date, period? That hurt a little. So how long had it been since she had dated anyone? Who cared? Whose business was it anyway?

By the time they were headed south on the freeway, Andrea's stubborn streak had stiffened her backbone, and she held her head just a tad higher than usual. She was going to show them all! She was entitled to date, just like every other single woman in Welleswood, many of whom would give half of Sunday's collection to have a date with Bill Sanderson.

But he had asked her, hadn't he?

She was so busy defending herself and so determined to prove to herself that she was interesting enough to be asked for a date, she completely forgot that she had only agreed to this date to prove otherwise.

For the first time in her life, Madge prayed for clouds, thick, heavy clouds, to block out the moon and the stars overhead.

By eight o'clock Friday night, she gave up and told Russell to pack the suitcases into his car while she pulled her car into the garage. While Russell carried a sleeping Sarah from her bed, buckled her into her car seat and got Baby situated, Madge made two more calls. This time her prayers were answered, and she didn't have to speak directly with

Andrea or Jenny. She left messages, telling them she and Russell were feeling well enough to drive to the beach house where they would be staying for a few weeks.

Russell had the motor running when Madge got to the front porch. She caught her breath and prayed no one would see them leave. They were several blocks away before her pulse slowed to normal again.

"Thank you," Russell murmured. "You've been kinder to me than I deserved. I know we…you have some difficult decisions to make about…about us…. I promise to try not to make them any more difficult than they already are."

Tears welled in her eyes. Emotion choked her throat.

"I love you, Madge. I've always loved you," he whispered. "I don't know if you can ever love me again, not after what I've done. You probably hate me right now, but I'm praying that you'll be able to forgive me someday."

Someday soon? She doubted it. Someday, as in some day, some moment in the future when her anger had cooled, her heart had healed, and her prayers for strength and courage had been answered?

She hoped so, or life would be miserable for them all. She had no hope at all, however, if the faith she had treasured for all of her life was not stronger and deeper than the gaping wounds in her heart.

"Someday," she whispered, and wondered if it might possibly be someday soon…or ever.

Chapter Twenty-Seven

For Madge, nothing quite captured the awesome dignity and overwhelming presence of God like a night sky, especially at the beach.

Late Friday night, she stood alone on the patio facing the ocean with her face to the heavens while she waited for Russell to join her. Without the glare of streetlights or any of the other luminary trappings of modern civilization interfering, the night sky had a majesty and an intensity that took her breath away.

Thousands of stars nestled deep in the folds of the universe reflected the power of their Creator. Some were specks of light, as small as the grains of sand on the beach beyond the patio. Other stars, larger and more brilliant, created a jeweled mosaic so constant since the beginning of time, they had guided the earliest seafarers safely from shore to shore. The moon spread a stairway of light from the sea to the heavens, providing a visual link between the Creator and his creation, for those who needed to know they were never alone.

For the first time since Russell arrived home with Sarah, she felt a little less angry and a little more capable of making a decision about her marriage and her feelings for Russell. She just needed a little help from above to understand the course she believed He had set for her.

"Madge?"

Before she turned around and faced her husband, she wrapped her soul with God's love. "Sarah's all settled in?"

"I put the kitten with her, too."

She nodded.

"I have some things I need to say to you," he murmured.

She took a seat on a chaise lounge, but he remained standing. Even in the dim light, she could see a difference in him. He stood more erect. His shoulders were straight. Even his voice had lost the desperate quality that had testified to his state of mind.

He put his arms behind his back, as if ready for military inspection. "I want you to know that I'm willing to accept whatever terms you want. I won't fight you. Not on alimony or the house. Whatever you want, whatever you think is fair, then that's what you'll get."

"In a divorce?" she whispered.

He nodded stiffly. "I know you'll want to consult an attorney. There are a lot of things to consider and financial arrangements that have to be made."

She swallowed hard. "You know I don't have a clue about

our finances," she admitted, although she expected to change that very soon.

"I know. That's why you need to consult with an attorney before you make any definite plans for…for later. I have a pension plan, 401K, stocks and a company savings plan. All of this should be divided. You're entitled to half of everything."

"At least."

He cleared his throat. "You should also arrange for a financial advisor, someone who can help you sort through all of this, even after—"

"After a divorce?"

"Yes, after a divorce." He turned and looked at the beach house for a moment. "I'm sorry. I know you haven't even had this house for a month, but we'll have to sell it. I'll absorb the loss. If I repay the home-equity loan on the house in Welleswood, it'll be free and clear. If you can continue to live there without having to worry about a mortgage payment, you probably wouldn't have to work. Between the alimony and the other income generated from the settlement, you should be fine."

"I should be fine," she repeated. "After a divorce, I'll just have to learn how to cope with being alone, I suppose. What about you? What will you do?"

He shrugged. "I haven't got that figured out yet. I cleared a few weeks off to decide…you know…under the circumstances…"

"No, I don't know. Why don't you explain it to me?"

He sat down across from her. "You're not making this easy."

"Did you?"

He shook his head. "I need to decide whether I should find a place for Sarah and me in Welleswood or not. It might be better to take her back to Collsworth and get a condo there or just pick a new town and make a clean start for both of us."

"Would it be better or would it be easier?" she asked.

"Nothing about getting a divorce and moving away would be easy," he countered, "but staying in Welleswood would be harder."

"What about Drew and Brett? Are you going to divorce them, too?"

"Of course not. Once we've decided what we're each going to do, we'll tell them, or I'll tell them. Whatever you think is best."

She pressed him harder. "What will you tell them, Russell? That their father was a bigamist? That their father had another child with a woman who was not their mother and because of his mistakes, he's going to abandon everything, forsake every vow and promise he made before God and witnesses, and start a new life without them? Will you tell them or should I?"

A long silence stretched between them. When Russell finally spoke, his voice was just above a whisper. "I can't tell them what I did. They'll never understand, because I still don't know how it happened. They'll hate me for what I did, and I wouldn't have a single argument to use to defend myself."

"But you could tell me?"

"I had to tell you. I had nowhere else to turn. I prayed. I begged for a way to spare you from learning about what I'd done, but—"

"But instead, you came home to me," Madge finished for him.

"It's not fair to you, I know, but I knew if I ever hoped to redeem this sorry soul of mine, I finally had to be honest with you." He shook his head. "I—I need time before I can face the boys."

The lump in her throat was almost impossible to swallow. "And what about Sarah?"

"Sarah." His voice broke and he looked up at the sky. "She's the only light shining through this entire nightmare. I look into her eyes, and I can believe in a God who is generous as well as forgiving. I'll spend the rest of my days regretting what I did to you and the boys and praying all of you can forgive me someday, but I intend to spend the rest of my life raising Sarah to become the kind of person I did not turn out to be. A person like her mother. A person like…you." He paused. "I wish I could say Sarah had never been born, but I can't."

"You'll raise her alone?"

"I have no other choice."

"We always have choices," she murmured. "Some are just harder than others." No one knew that better than she did. Her own choice about her future was hard to make and even harder to accept, but in faith, she now knew she had no choice but one. "You could make different choices about the future you apparently have planned for yourself and Sarah. You don't have to move away," she offered.

"What? Stay in Welleswood?" He snorted. "Even if I deserve to be mocked and ridiculed, I won't have Sarah destroyed by the scandal that's going to brand her as a love child! As much as you must detest the very sight of her, you wouldn't want that for her. I know you wouldn't."

"She's an innocent child."

"She's also living, breathing proof that I betrayed you."

"She's God's child. He created her in His image, and He created her for His purpose, not yours or mine," she whispered, surprised by her own words. Or were they His? She paused and prayed for guidance so she would know the right words to say. "Other men have affairs. It's sinful and it's wrong, but sin happens. You say you had realized your mistake and you were going to end the affair. Other men do that, too, because faith and goodness can ultimately be stronger than the temptation of sin. For some men, like you, the choice to end the affair comes too late."

She leaned forward and turned toward him. "You were the man God chose to be Sarah's father. You were the man He trusted to raise her in faith and in love because He knew her mother would be called Home before Sarah had grown up."

Russell leaned toward her. "What are you saying?"

"I'm saying we both have to remember our marriage vows. We made those vows to one another for a lifetime. 'For better or for worse' aren't empty words. They mean that we promised to stay together through good times and bad times, whether we liked it or not. We pledged that we would never break those vows."

"Oh, I see. You want to rub my nose in my mistake. You want me to remember it's my fault our marriage ended. You want me to—"

"I want you to stop and listen. Really listen to me. I'm not sure I can say this exactly right, and I'm certain I won't be able to say it again. Not tonight. I'm still struggling to get this clear in my own mind, which isn't easy because my heart hurts so bad I think I might not be able to breathe for the pain every time I think about what's happened and because I'm still very angry with you. Not with Sarah. With you."

He nodded. "I know you are. I'm sorry. Yes. I'll listen. I owe you that much."

"You owe me more," she argued. "You owe yourself more. You owe Sarah more, but you owe God the most. And so do I. That's what I'm finally realizing tonight. We've been married for twenty-six years, and God has blessed us with a wonderful life together. You make a living well beyond most other men. We have not one home, but two. We have two handsome, intelligent, loving sons who have grown up to be men of faith and good character. We have shared our love for one another and our means with others less fortunate. Given all that's happened, I know I have a difficult choice to make. I can stand by my vows and open my heart to this little one and learn how to forgive you someday, or I can do what you did—break my vows and prepare to move on, alone. There isn't a soul in Welleswood who would blame me, either."

She bowed her head and blinked back tears before she continued, but her heart was filled with the peace of knowing she had been led to make the right choice. "Stay in Welleswood, Russell. Stay and make a home for Sarah with me. Stay because you really do love me and you can promise never to break the vows we made to one another ever again. Stay because even though you've made a terrible mistake, you are still a man of faith and a man of character. And stay because you can trust God to show us both the way."

She caught her breath and held it until, slowly, he turned his face to her and nodded.

For now, it was enough.

Although she had already begun to make a mental list of things she expected to change in their lives, she set it aside.

For now, she was content. She had done what she knew He wanted her to do.

Tomorrow, she prayed, He would help them both to understand how to do it.

Chapter Twenty-Eight

※

Midway through her first date with Bill Sanderson, Andrea could not decide if their date was a smashing success or a dismal failure.

Instead of a picnic on the beach, they ate supper on a patch of grass behind a metal barrier along the shoulder of the freeway ten miles from Sea Gate, while waiting for road service to arrive and fix not one, but two, flat tires. Instead of watching the sun dip below the horizon, they had seen only the slow descent of the sun before it disappeared behind a billboard advertising, ironically, Captain Jeremy's famous sunset cruises.

When they finally reached Sea Gate at nine-thirty, Bill drove directly to one of the two asphalt access roads that led to a sandy road to the beach, but he had to stop before the front tires left the asphalt. A heavy chain stretching across the entrance blocked their access, and the sign hanging from the chain read:

Beach Closed To All Vehicles

Sea Gate Ord. No. 56713

He took one look at the sign, laughed and threw up his hands. "I give up. You know, I've had my fair share of dates over the past eight years, but I've never had one go so completely haywire, especially not a first date."

She laughed with him. "This could be one for the Guinness Book of Records, if they have a category for first dates that went wrong."

"Or a movie, *How to Make a Woman Lose Interest on a First Date.* Comedies always play well at the box office," he suggested.

The fact that he had faced every problem tonight with good humor had done quite the opposite, as far as she was concerned. She found the prospect of spending a few more hours with him more than a little intriguing, much to her surprise. He was either one of those rare men who took life far less seriously than himself, or he was an eternal optimist, an even rarer breed of man.

"There's a parking lot a block or so back. I can leave the Jeep there, and we can put this date to one final test by attempting to take a walk along the beach, or we can call it a rather forgettable night and head home. I'll leave it up to you. I haven't done so well making plans tonight."

She stifled a yawn. He had not mentioned a third choice, simply resting on the beach, and she was loathe to admit that chemo, or more correctly, the side effects of yesterday's chemo, tugged her leash again. "I'd love a walk," she managed before the yawn finally escaped.

"A short one," he cautioned. He slipped out of his seat belt, walked around the Jeep, and helped her get down. "Save your energy and wait here. I'll park the Jeep and be back in three minutes."

Before she could argue, he was backing the Jeep down the street. She watched him maneuver the Jeep into a tight spot, and she was not surprised to see him jog his way back. She zipped up her sweatshirt, but left the hood down for now. After he helped her duck beneath the chain, he handed her a flashlight. Laughing, she turned it on. "Tell me you were a Boy Scout."

"Cub Scout, Boy Scout and Eagle Scout, thank you. I'm going to be working with the pastor and see if we can't get a troop started in Welleswood."

She sidestepped a huge rut in the roadway. "I told my sister I should bring a flashlight tonight, but I forgot. Thanks for remembering one for me, too."

He stopped dead. "You told your sister about me?"

She did not need to turn and shine the flashlight on his face to know he was smiling. "Why not? Jenny's my sister," she said as she continued without him. "I only told her. I haven't told Madge yet, but that will only be two people. You told half the town!"

He caught up with her in a few easy strides. "Are you angry?"

"Not really, but you have to understand something about living in a small town."

He cringed. "Gossip?"

"That, too, but Welleswood probably isn't like the other places you've lived. The twenty-first century may have dawned in bigger cities, but Welleswood is an old-fashioned, small town that hasn't figured that out yet. Folks here can be very…protective, especially when it comes to one of their own. You're new to town. Or you will be, if you ever buy a house," she explained as they walked side by side down the sandy road that ran through grassy dunes.

"I'm trying," he argued.

This time, she stopped and waited until he turned around to walk back to her.

"I'll try harder, I promise," he said. "I'm not going to waste your time. As a matter of fact, there's a house that faces the park that I like, and it's probably going on the market soon."

She furrowed her brow. "Which house?"

"Phil Yost's. He's thinking about retiring to Florida. I told him as soon as he was ready to call you first and me second. I've already seen the house inside and out. I'll pay whatever you set as an asking price."

She wanted to ask him how he had managed to find out Mr. Yost was thinking of retiring and selling out when she had not heard a whisper about it, but decided to let it pass. "I know the house. It's a lovely Victorian, but it should list for more than you told me you were prepared to pay."

"But I should qualify, according to the mortgage company that did the prequalification, so that shouldn't be a problem," he countered as he led her to the top of the dunes.

The beach on the other side stretched a good fifty feet ahead before meeting the surf. When she switched off her flashlight, they were surrounded by darkness, save for the weak light of the moon and a few stars. She felt she had been pitched into a deep abyss, where she alone faced a battle against the unseen enemy that had invaded her body. In the rest of the world, in the glare of lights behind her, most men and women lived normal lives without any of the fears that had stolen into her life.

Fatigued and daunted by the challenges she faced in the months ahead, she yawned again, but this time she made no attempt to hide it from him.

"Why don't we just sit and enjoy the view?" he suggested.

Without argument, she sat down and crossed her legs. To her surprise, he sat down behind her. "Rest your back against mine. It's a whole lot more comfortable."

"Forever the Boy Scout," she teased. When she leaned back against him, she uncrossed her legs and pulled her knees up. "That's much better. Thanks."

Anxious to steer the topic of conversation away from herself, she realized how little she really did know about him, especially the ordeal he had been through. "Have they caught the people who hijacked your truck?"

"It wasn't my rig. It was a company rig, but no. Not that anyone's told me."

She shivered. "If that happened to me, I think I'd be scared…and worried they'd be trying to find me."

"That would be easy enough for them to do, I guess, but they got what they wanted. They're not all that interested in me anymore."

"But you're an eyewitness! You'd be able to identify them."

He chuckled. "Not really, but if you ever see four figures standing next to an old brown van in the middle of a two-lane highway, miles from nowhere, who are dressed in SpongeBob SquarePants costumes, let me know."

She giggled. "I'm sorry. I know it isn't funny, but just imagining four adults dressed up like that goofy character and standing in the middle of a highway…" She giggled again.

"Don't apologize. I laughed, too. They really caught me off guard. I thought maybe they had broken down on their way to a county fair or something, so I pulled over. I didn't see their shotguns until it was too late to do much more than hand over my wallet and keys. They had it planned well. Two of them got into the rig and took off. The other two had me blindfolded and tied up in the back of their van before I realized I might not see another moonlit night like this one."

She wrapped her arms around her knees. "I would have been scared witless."

"That about sums up how I felt." He let out a deep breath. "When they finally hauled me out of the van, I thought they were going to shoot me, but I couldn't remember a single prayer to say. When they tossed me into the air like a sack of garbage, I didn't draw a breath until I landed. I hurt so bad I figured I couldn't be dead. Then I heard a door slam and the van drove off. That's when I started to believe I actually might see a night sky again, and I let the good Lord figure out how somebody was going to find me."

She swallowed hard. "It took three or four days, didn't it?"

He sighed, and she could hear him tossing one stone after another into the darkness beyond them. "About fifty hours, give or take, before a couple of teenagers on horseback showed up. I sure did mess up their plans. Apparently, some of the kids who lived on the ranches in the area used to meet at the abandoned line shack for a little 'fun.'"

"I thought you said it was a farmhouse."

He tossed another stone. "Nope. Just one room with four walls, a door and a broken window. I knew there had to be a window. I could feel the fresh air. I would have given anything to have worked off that blindfold, but they'd hog-tied me real tight. So there I lay, in absolute darkness, without a single star or a sliver of moon to remind me that even in a universe as vast as this one, God had a plan for me and He hadn't forsaken me."

"How did you survive? How did you not lose faith that you'd be found alive?" she murmured.

"Prayers, mostly. I had plenty of time to remember those." He paused and his back grew rigid. "Don't misunderstand. I didn't just lie there, praying happily to while away the hours. It wasn't…well, it wasn't pretty, to be honest. I felt like I was tied to a pendulum. For a while, I'd be able to pray, confident He wouldn't let me die. Then I'd swing into anger or despair. I'd yell and holler and demand to know why this had happened to me. Then I'd swing the other way again." He grew silent for a moment. "I was in a local clinic for a few days before I could explain what had happened and they confirmed my identity. One of the doctors said I had probably been hallucinating a bit, but I think I just didn't trust God like I thought I should have. It's humbling, to say the least, but I knew if I survived, it was time to make some changes in my life."

Andrea bowed her head and tucked her chin to her chest. He had described his struggle with faith and his struggle to survive in a way that touched the core of her own humbling attempts to keep her faith strong as she battled her unseen enemy: cancer. He may have been blindfolded during his ordeal and denied the opportunity to look at a night sky like the one overhead, but she had been too blinded by her fears to truly see the night sky as he had described it.

She tilted her face to the sky and opened her heart to the one person she knew who might understand and not judge her too harshly. "Living with cancer can be a lot like swinging on a pendulum," she whispered, "but for me, it's more like I've been hooked to a leash, a very short leash. When I can pray, when my faith is strong enough to really believe in God and trust Him to carry me through the next year, the leash is made of nothing but fragile roses and lilacs and God's grace. I'm convinced the chemo will work and the cancer hasn't spread. Other times, the leash is made of leather. It's strong and it's unbreakable. No matter how I pray or struggle, my faith is just beyond my reach, and I get angry. I hate this disease. I hate what it's doing to my life. I hate that it took two of my sisters from me. I get afraid that God has forgotten me, that the chemo won't work or that the cancer has spread and by the time the doctors find it, it'll be too late."

He did not respond, not for several long heartbeats, and she thought she might have made a mistake.

"How much do you know about stars?" he asked.

"Stars? As in astronomy? As in—"

"As in, can you look at the sky and identify the constellations like the Big Dipper or the Little Dipper?"

She shrugged. "I couldn't name more than those two, and I couldn't find them in the sky if curing this cancer of mine depended on it."

He got to his feet. "Good. Let me show them to you." When she got to her feet, amazed that he could simply ignore the fact that she had poured her heart and soul out to him, he pointed to the moon. "Start there. You recognize the moon, right?"

"Yes, I know that's the moon," she replied. Apparently, he had not forgotten a thing since his scouting days, and he was more eager to show off his knowledge than commiserate with her troubles, a thought that soured her mood for the first time that night.

"Okay, now look a little to the left and scan the heavens. Can you find four stars grouped together that make a square or a rectangle?"

"I think I see four that sit like a corner on a square. Is that what you mean?"

"Exactly. That's called the Angel's Window. Actually, there are several of them, but you just found the biggest one. If you ever need an angel to give you a little help, even if you just don't want to feel alone, find four stars like this and pray. Your prayers will slip right through the Angel's Window to heaven and straight to the first angel waiting in line, according to legend," he added.

"Legend," she repeated. She did not know much about constellations, but she knew enough to suspect he had invented that legend all by himself.

"Now look way to the south. That's to your right."

"Got it. Looking south."

"There's a constellation there called Mount Blessing. Can you see it?"

She squinted hard. While there were dozens of stars, none seemed to join together to shape a mountain or even a small hill. "Are you sure it's there?"

"Look harder."

"Sorry. I can't see a mountain or a blessing, whatever that might look like."

"That's right," he murmured. "That's because you don't find blessings hidden in a mountain in the sky. His blessings are here on earth or they're tucked into your heart. The stars and the constellations are always there for you. Whenever you feel He's forgotten you, just look up into the sky. He's got thousands of reminders twinkling back at you."

She moistened her lips. "You made that up, just like you made up the legend about the Angel's Window."

He let out a sigh. "No, credit for both should go to my wife. She had multiple sclerosis. This is what she taught me during those awful years when she was confined to a wheelchair and then her deathbed," he whispered. "I promised myself I would share what she had taught me when I met someone who needed to learn this, too."

Humbled and overwhelmed, Andrea closed her eyes. She envisioned the leather leash, watched falling stars snip it into tiny pieces and let the wind carry them away. The leash reformed itself with imaginary roses and lilacs, but God's grace lifted each blossom and gently set each flower adrift at sea.

When she opened her eyes, she locked her gaze on the heavens. God's moon was not imaginary. It was real. She could see the beams of gentle light beckoning all to witness His glory. His stars were real. Some twinkled so close she could almost reach out and touch them. Others drifted far into the universe and closer to the Creator, their light dimmed by His brilliance. Her blessings were many on this earth, and for the first time, she could even see her cancer as one of them. She dismissed the idiocy of putting cancer into the same category as her other blessings. God did not shower sickness upon His children, but He did promise to be faithful, to provide the strength and yes, the wisdom for His children to prevail.

Cancer was not her enemy.

Lack of faith in Him. Lack of trust in Him. Those were her enemies. Those she could defeat, using God's love for her and the gifts He had sprinkled in the heavens, one star at a time.

"Thank you. I—I think I'm ready to go home now," she whispered. She flicked on her flashlight, and they walked silently back to the Jeep.

They were headed out of Sea Gate when he slowed and pulled over to the side of the road. "I almost forgot. On the way down, you mentioned your sister had just bought a house here. Do you still want me to drive by so I can see it?"

She hesitated only a moment. Madge and Russell's beach house was only minutes away, but it was late, nearly eleven o'clock, and Andrea had to get home and get to bed. She had a client coming in at nine o'clock tomorrow morning. "No. Maybe…next time."

Bill smiled and waited for her to realize what she had just said and change her reply.

She just smiled back.

Chapter Twenty-Nine

By midnight, Andrea's first date with Bill stretched beyond the boundaries of unforgettable and ended on the same note as the beginning.

The Jeep died a block after they got back underway again. The engine just stopped and they coasted silently back to the side of the road. After thirty minutes, he finally gave up trying to find the problem. By midnight, a sleepy road-service attendant arrived to tow the Jeep to a local garage.

When the tow truck disappeared around a corner, Bill shoved his hands into his pockets and looked up at the sky. Andrea waited, more tired than annoyed, and followed his gaze. "Looking through the Angel's Window? I think there's a Do Not Disturb sign. See it?"

He chuckled and shook his head. "I'm sorry. If I had

known that the Jeep was a disaster waiting to happen, I never would have borrowed it." He turned and looked down the road. "I think there's a motel back a ways. It's off season, so it shouldn't be a problem for us to get a couple of rooms for the night. Unless you know somewhere we could rent a car? I know you've got to be at work in the morning."

"Even if there was a car-rental agency, which there isn't, it wouldn't be open this late." She yawned. "The Pink Flamingo is probably the closest motel, but that's got to be a good two miles away." She hesitated, reluctant to suggest another alternative for fear he might misinterpret her meaning. "My sister's house is a lot closer, but there's only one problem. I don't have a key."

"No problem there. I can get you inside," he suggested.

"It's a large house. I mean, if you can get us inside, I could take one of the bedrooms on one floor. There'd be plenty of room for you in another. Under the circumstances—"

"Under the circumstances, I think it's a better idea if I get you to your sister's. I'll get a room at the motel and check in with the garage first thing in the morning. Welleswood's a small town, remember? Thanks to me, everyone knows we went out tonight. If I stayed at your sister's, sooner or later, someone would find out we spent the night under the same roof. That's a problem neither one of us needs."

"You're sure? I feel rather foolish, asking you to do that."

He chuckled. "Sorry. I get to keep all the 'foolish' to myself on this date."

They walked the six blocks to Madge's house and made plans for Bill to call Andrea on her cell phone by seven-thirty, after he spoke with the mechanic. With any luck, the problem could be easily fixed. If not, the garage might have a loaner vehicle that Bill could borrow long enough to take Andrea to the office by nine.

The house, of course, was dark. Jenny had said both Madge and Russell still weren't feeling well. Andrea felt comfortable they were both home in Welleswood and the beach house was empty, until they reached the back of the house and Andrea saw a light in the kitchen. She reached out and put her hand on Bill's arm. "I can't believe it, but they're here! Madge and Russell must have decided to recuperate at the beach house."

When she started toward the patio to cross to the kitchen door, he hesitated. "It's probably better to go around front and ring the bell. They'll be surprised enough to have visitors at this hour, let alone having someone knock at the back door."

"Don't be silly," she insisted. "The back door has a window, and there's no curtain on it to block the view. They'll see it's me right away." When he remained unconvinced, she compromised. "I'll look in first. If I don't see anyone, then we'll use the front door."

Without further protest, he followed her to the kitchen door. She looked inside and saw Russell. He was standing at the counter near the stove, stirring something in a small pot. He had his other hand on the lap of a small child, a little girl, holding her still as she sat on the countertop.

Andrea blinked hard while her mind tried to make sense out of what she was seeing. Her first reaction was that she had gotten confused in the dark and gone to the wrong house. She studied the man again. Even with his back to her, she knew it was Russell. He had been part of her family for over twenty-five years—a big part, especially since he had no family of his own.

She switched her attention to the little girl. She was a pretty little thing, even though her face was red and puffy from crying. She must have had a nightmare, but what was she doing here? Who was she? And where was Madge? Was she here at the beach house or home in Welleswood?

The mystery of the child's car seat suddenly seemed to have a very different solution than the one Andrea had suggested to Jenny earlier that afternoon, but the mystery had gotten even more complicated. The car seat, according to Jenny, had been in Russell's car, not Madge's. The little girl was in the kitchen now with Russell, not Madge.

From deep within, a primal urge to protect her sister rose, and Andrea knew she would have to unravel the mystery herself. She knocked on the window glass, oblivious to the man behind her.

Russell stiffened. He dropped the spoon and it sank into the pot. He wrapped his hands around the child's waist and lifted her to his chest before he turned around. When he saw Andrea, the element of surprise did not leave his eyes, but deepened into fear, and the blood literally drained from his face. Almost instinctively, at least to Andrea's eyes, he put his hand to the girl's back and held her even closer.

Russell set his shoulders and walked toward the door. His features were grim, his lips set. When he opened the door, he did not speak. He just stepped back and motioned for Andrea to come inside. The little girl, however, stared at Andrea with big blue eyes and a smile.

Andrea was not sure how she got inside. Her legs were

shaking and her heart was pounding, even as her mind reeled. "I—I'm sorry to barge in so late," she managed. "We were headed home when the Jeep broke down." She quickly introduced Bill to her brother-in-law. "I didn't have a key, but I was hoping to find a way inside for the night. Bill was going to the Pink Flamingo," she explained. Mystery or no mystery, Andrea did not want Russell to think she was going to use his home for anything improper. "I had no idea you and Madge would be here."

The color rushed back into Russell's cheeks. "I think she left you a message, about eight or so."

"We'd left by then," Andrea murmured.

Bill rushed past both of them and shut off the burner beneath the pot. The smell of scalded chocolate filled the air, and when Andrea looked at the stove, she saw that the hot chocolate Russell had been heating had boiled over. She did not know whether or not Bill had any notion of the mystery she had stumbled into, but he must have felt the tension in the air.

"Look, I'd better get moving. I'll call you in the morning?" he said.

She nodded, but kept her focus on Russell as Bill slipped out the back door. Her brother-in-law looked, well, he looked terrible. He had dark circles under his eyes, and his color was pasty. He certainly looked like he had been sick. When he seemed at a loss for words, Andrea turned her attention to the little girl. "Hi, sweetie. Did you have a bad dream?"

"Bad, bad, bad! Poppy come!" she announced, and snuggled closer to Russell.

"I was making Sarah some...hot chocolate," he explained. He took a deep breath. "Sarah is…Sarah is my daughter."

"No. That's not true. Sarah is *our* daughter."

At the sound of her sister's voice, Andrea spun around, but Madge walked past Andrea to stand next to Russell and Sarah.

"You have a…a daughter? I don't understand. Do you mean to tell me you've adopted a child?" she asked. She was not opposed to adoption, but she could not believe her sister would be considering adoption. Not at her age.

"We…that is…" Madge looked up at her husband. When he nodded, she let out a heavy sigh. "We need to talk."

"I'll take Sarah back upstairs," he murmured. He looked at the mess on the stove, filled a child's cup with apple juice and left the kitchen.

Before the silence between Andrea and her sister grew awkward, Andrea nodded toward the stove. "I can clean that up while you make a pot of coffee for yourself. I've got a bottle of iced tea in my bag."

For the next hour, Andrea sat with her sister. She listened to a tale that seemed to have come straight from the front page of one of those smarmy supermarket tabloids that screamed impossible headlines at shoppers, even those who tried to ignore them. The two sisters cried together as Andrea held Madge's hand. They even laughed together once or twice, a trait that some people might have misinterpreted as bizarre. Not every family could laugh in the midst of tragedy, but the Longs did.

By the time Madge had finished, the coffeepot was empty, Andrea's iced-tea bottle was ready for the recycle bin, and a ton of soggy tissues littered the table. They sat together, hand in hand, emotionally drained but strengthened by a bond of sisterhood that did not allow for anything but love.

"What are you going to do?" Andrea whispered.

"I'm fifty-five years old. I've been looking forward to playing with my grandchildren. I never planned on starting over and raising another child of my own, not at this stage of my life." Madge shook her head. "I'll do what I have to do. I love him. We've been married for twenty-six years. I can't throw that away. We'll both do what we have to do and raise Sarah together as our daughter."

"Are you sure you can? Are you sure you even want to?" Andrea asked. "After what Russell did, no one could expect you to stay married to him, let alone raise a child he had with another woman, even if she is gone."

Madge squeezed Andrea's hand. "Vows are forever."

"But he broke those vows," Andrea countered, remembering how often she'd been jealous of Madge. She was not jealous anymore.

"Yes, he did." Madge took several long breaths. "I haven't had a lot of time to think this through yet. I've been too angry. I haven't to talked to Russell about it, but I think one of the first things we've got to do is start marriage counseling. If it takes two people to make a marriage work, then two people must have some degree of responsibility when it doesn't. We need to find out how that happened to us so we know how to make sure it never happens again. I know we can, with God's help. Will you…will you tell Jenny for me? I don't think I'll be home for a while, and it's not something I want to tell her over the telephone."

Andrea nodded. Madge had always been so helpless when it came to handling trouble of any kind. How she had found the strength and the wisdom to deal with this crisis was a surprise to Andrea, unless Madge really had had the strength all along and only discovered it now, when her whole world was threatening to collapse. "I'll tell Jenny after she gets back," Andrea promised. "Michael took them all away for the weekend. I would think Pastor Staggart would be able to recommend a good counselor."

"Maybe," Madge responded. "I'll have to talk to Russell about it before I call anyone."

"Have you told the boys about Sarah?"

"Not yet. Russell and I still have a lot of things to settle between us."

"Settle?"

Madge bowed her head for a moment. "I don't have a clue about what we're going to do to try to put this marriage back together, and I'm not sure how we're going to explain about Sarah." When she looked up at Andrea, fresh tears welled and threatened to spill again. "She's such an innocent. I'm so worried what people will think about her." She found a fresh tissue and dabbed at her tears. "I can't bear to think that once everyone knows what really happened, she'll be…branded. For the rest of her life, people will see her and say, 'Oh, that's Sarah Stephens. She's really Russell's love child. He had an affair and then brought that child back to Madge to raise.' Sarah didn't do anything wrong. She doesn't deserve that kind of stigma. No child does, and I can't take her home until I make sure that won't happen to her. I won't let that happen," she vowed. "They can say what they want about Russell or me, but not Sarah."

Andrea squeezed her sister's hand again. "No one has to

know what really happened. You and Russell can just surprise everyone and tell them you both decided to adopt a child."

"You mean lie?"

"It's not a bad lie. It's a good one," Andrea argued.

Madge squared her shoulders. "A lie is a lie, and lies always come home to roost."

"Now you sound like Grandmother Poore."

Madge chuckled. "She was a stinker sometimes, but she also knew what she was talking about. I can't spend the rest of my life being afraid that someone, someday, will find out. Russell and I want to tell Sarah everything when she's older, of course, but I'd be afraid to let her out of my sight, just in case someone would find out and tell her before we did."

"Find out from whom? You and Russell aren't going to tell anyone. I'm never going to break your confidence, and Sarah's mother is dead. How could anyone find out?"

"She has a birth certificate, Andrea. My name isn't on it, but Russell's is. I won't be able to register her for school without it. That gives us two years. What do I do then?"

"But they'll know she's been adopted."

"You're not listening to me. Russell's name is on her birth certificate! They'll see his name alongside another woman's name. Got it?" She sighed.

"Oh. Got it. But you have two years before you have to worry about that. Right now, you need...you need to stop worrying. Come on. Get up, and come outside with me. I want to show you something."

"Now? Why?"

"Come on." Andrea tugged her sister to her feet. "There's

something I've got to show you. Have you ever heard of the Angel's Window? Of course you haven't, but just wait till I show it to you...."

Chapter Thirty

With no loaner car available, Bill and Andrea would have been forced to stay in Sea Gate until Monday, when the new computer module for the Jeep was expected to arrive. Instead, they had borrowed Russell's car, minus the car seat, and made it back to Welleswood in time for Andrea to make a quick change and get to the office by nine-thirty. They planned to return to Sea Gate Monday night, to return Russell's car and pick up the Jeep.

Andrea was half an hour late for her clients, probably the only couple in the mid-Atlantic region who did not have an answering machine so that Andrea could have left a message and told them she was running late. Fortunately—or unfortunately—Doris was scheduled to open the office on Saturday. Doris had many traits that annoyed Andrea, but she was always punctual, and she had an answering machine, too! She would be there to meet the Wilmots, and assuming she had retrieved Andrea's message, she would keep them occupied until Andrea arrived.

With a date set for Monday night for Andrea to drive Russell's car back to Sea Gate, with Bill following her to bring her back home again, they had parted company, but not before he had given his word not to discuss Sarah with anyone. He had been beyond patient and considerate and never once questioned her for an explanation.

Andrea parked her own car at the back door and rushed into the office. She slowed the moment she realized she had forgotten the keys to the credenza. When she reached the front office, her frown deepened. Her clients were not there. There was no sign of Doris, either, but one look at the mess on top of both desks, not to mention the broken lock on the credenza, told Andrea Doris had been there. Andrea could not decide whether to cry with frustration or run outside and scream for help.

Then she saw a note stapled to one of the outrageous peacock feathers in the arrangement on Doris's desk. She approached it with apprehension. She almost cried when she recognized Doris's handwriting and read:

The Wilmot's insisted on seeing the Locust Street property. Now! (You did mention they were cash buyers in your message.) Rather than upset them, I got the file, but please don't get mad. I called the locksmith. He'll be here by ten to fix the lock on the credenza.
Doris

Andrea read the note again and surveyed the damage to the credenza and the desks for a second time. Yesterday, she would have been horrified by the woman's gall and disregard for office property. Today, she simply marveled at the woman's tenacity and her refusal to let a client like the Wilmots slip away because Andrea had been late. She had had the listing for that house on Locust Street for months, but there were so many repairs that had to be made, there wasn't a bank or mortgage company willing to take the risk of holding a note for more than half the asking price, which was just over six figures.

"Maybe I needed a little bit of a hurricane in my life to shake things up right," she mumbled, but cheerfully set both desks back to right and made a call to Jamie Martin before the locksmith arrived. He did not show up until eleven, but when he left an hour later, he was no sooner out the door than Doris walked in without her clients.

Actually, Doris did not walk into the office. She just poked her head around the door. "Is it safe to come in or should I go to The Diner, have a cup of coffee and try again later?"

Andrea waved her inside. "It's more than safe."

When Doris walked in, she was carrying a white cardboard bakery box that she put on top of Andrea's desk.

"You didn't have to bring a peace offering." Andrea told her. "It's my fault I was late in the first place. I forgot the keys to the credenza anyway, so I probably would have done the same thing. The locksmith's already taken care of the repairs." With her stomach growling, reminding her that she had not had time for breakfast, Andrea fiddled with the knot in the string holding the box closed.

Doris glanced over Andrea's shoulder and grimaced. "What happened? He promised me he'd be able to put a new locking mechanism on today."

"I told him just to fill in the hole. We won't be needing a lock anymore." Andrea gave up with the knot, got a pair of scissors from her drawer and snipped the string. When she lifted the lid and looked inside, her mouth began to water. She was also surprised to see there was a message written in pale yellow icing on top of one of McAllister's giant, cream-filled crumb cakes. The message made it clear Doris had not brought a peace offering:

We did it! We have a sale on Locust Street!

She looked up at Doris, but she did not know what pleased her more—the sale of the house on Locust Street or the fact that Doris had used the word *we* instead of *I.* "They bought the house?"

With a proud smile on her face, Doris held up a signed agreement of sale that had two sets of signatures, the buyers' and the sellers'. "Signed and sealed, but not delivered yet. Settlement is set for October tenth. We really do make a great team, don't we?"

It took a few seconds for Doris's announcement to really register in Andrea's mind. "How on earth did you get all this done in a matter of hours?"

Doris tossed her briefcase on top of her desk. "I couldn't have done it without your help."

"My help?" Andrea chuckled. "Being late could have cost us a client and a sale. You were the one who saved the day, met the client, showed the house…and three hours later, you've not only got the buyer and seller to agree on a price, but a signed agreement, too? I've never had that happen so fast."

"You made it easy for me. All the obstacles that normally slow down the process, like a report from an independent house inspection to a termite inspection? You had them all done and ready to show the client. He was impressed, I must say. It didn't hurt that the sellers happened to be home, either, so I just drove over and got everything signed. We still need to get each of them their copies, though. I was so excited, I stopped at McAllister's and had them make this up. I don't care much for cake, but this cream-filled crumb cake is almost sinful."

"You're amazing," Andrea murmured, and she meant it.

Doris looked at her warily. "Are you feeling okay?"

Andrea nodded. "Actually, I'm feeling like maybe we should have a talk while we dig into this crumb cake." She rifled through her drawers looking for the leftover paper plates and plastic utensils, but came up empty.

Doris, however, ran across the street to The Diner and came back carrying a tray with real plates, stainless-steel utensils and two glasses of iced tea. "Caroline said to tell you to stop in sometime early this afternoon. She said something about the meeting for the Shawl Ministry. She needs to see you before you go."

Andrea grimaced. "I forgot about the meeting. I'll take the tray and glasses back then." She cut a generous serving of the crumb cake for each of them, scooped a forkful of the cream by itself, and let it melt in her mouth. "You're right. It's almost sinful." She enjoyed a bite of the crumb cake, then set her fork down. "I've been doing a lot of thinking," she began.

Doris set her fork down, too. "About the office?"

"Yes. When we first started working together, I think I made it very clear that the position was temporary. I feel a little awkward—"

"You're right. You did, and if I recall correctly, I also said I wasn't sure if I really wanted to work full-time. It's okay, really. You've been back on your own two feet again for a few weeks. I've been expecting you to tell me any day that you didn't need for me to continue any longer. I'd like to take next week to tie up some loose ends, if that's all right with you."

"No, it isn't. A week wouldn't be nearly enough time. I was thinking of a bit longer, somewhere in the neighborhood of at least a year or two. Even longer, if you're interested."

Doris cocked her head. "You want me to stay…permanently?"

"I do."

"But you—"

"I know. I've been really cranky, as my sisters have been quick to point out to me. I'd like to blame it on a lot of things, but mostly, it's just plain been my fault, and that's why I wanted to talk to you. First, to apologize." She held up her hand when Doris tried to interrupt. "Second, I know we have very different styles when it comes to paperwork. At first, I thought you were just totally and hopelessly disorganized, but now I know better. Your desk might be chaos, but it's an organized chaos. I don't know how you do it, but you know precisely where everything is in that…mess. Unfortunately, I'm your classic fussbudget. I can't operate on full steam unless I have complete order."

Doris smiled. "Type A, superachiever. I know."

Andrea chose not to respond. "Third, and this is really important, you really know your clients and you work very hard for them and for me. I'd really like you to stay because we balance one another well. We make a good team."

Doris beamed. "We do, don't we? To be honest, I told my sister, Betty, that I couldn't wait much longer. I was going to flat out ask you if there was any way I could stay. Begging was on my list, too."

Andrea's eyes widened. "You want to stay, even though I've been so cranky?"

"You had a lot to contend with after your accident."

"I wish I could use that as an excuse, but I can't," Andrea murmured. This was definitely not an occasion that called for her to play the cancer card. She knew she should tell Doris about the time off she would need each month, but she was not going to use her condition as an excuse for her behavior or as a plea to get Doris to agree to stay, either.

Doris took another forkful of the pastry. "I do have a few conditions, though. Mostly they're minor details, like setting up a little firmer schedule for floor time, that sort of thing."

"I think that's a good idea."

"We have to change the office arrangement, though. That's a must."

Andrea sipped her tea and tried not to smile. "Really?"

Doris' expression turned serious. "We make a good team, but we don't make good desk mates, if you get my drift. You've got two perfectly good rooms set aside as conference rooms that get dusted more often than they get used while the front office is crowded with our two desks. If we both have clients here at the same time, which has happened, or one of us has clients and the other doesn't, we can't help but overhear one another, and some of that information is or can be confidential. If I stay, which I'd very much like to do, we have to move things around a bit."

Before Andrea could respond, Jamie Martin walked in with three of his friends. If she had told Jamie the precise moment to arrive, she could not have timed it more perfectly.

He smiled at both of them. "Hey, Mrs. Hooper. Mrs. Blake. You've got some furniture for us to move?"

Andrea looked at Doris and grinned. "I told you we made a good team."

Four strong teenage boys made the work look easy, but they were sweating hard by the time they finished rearranging the entire office. They left with cash in their pockets and smiles on their faces, and they also left behind some news Andrea had not heard. By the fifteenth of October, the skateboarders would have their own place in Welleswood Park.

While Doris tried to decide where to put her flower arrangement in her new office, directly opposite Andrea's office in the other former conference room, Andrea took a tour and made notes of the surprisingly few changes that still had to be made. The wing chairs and coffee table that had once been scrunched together in the corner now occupied the space where the two desks had been and looked much more inviting. Andrea planned to use the former office as a reception area. She made a note to have another telephone jack installed and another electrical outlet. She already had someone in mind to hire as a receptionist, but there was no rush to do that today.

Her own office had been set up perfectly. No changes

needed there. Doris's office, on the other hand, would require some new office equipment. Andrea knocked on Doris's door and waited to be invited inside. When she found Doris on her hands and knees, she chuckled. "You don't have to resort to begging. Just ask. What do you need?"

Doris blew away a wisp of hair that had fallen in her face, looked up and winked. "I wouldn't dream of asking you to help me find two of those peacock feathers for me. I guess they got knocked out in the move."

Andrea looked at the arrangement and made a face. "How can you tell there are two missing?"

"There were twelve when I got that ugly flower arrangement. Now there are only ten."

"Did you say 'ugly'?"

"I'm sorry, but I can't pretend to like that arrangement for another second. It's ugly, awful, terrible, unattractive, tacky or ghastly. Take your pick."

"But I thought you liked it."

"When I stopped in the shop that day, the owner insisted that I take it as a 'Welcome to Welleswood' present. What was I going to do? Say no? I was so shocked, she talked me into buying the matching desk set and had it all wrapped up before I realized what I was doing. If she stops in, she'll expect to see the arrangement. I don't want to hurt her feelings."

Andrea spied the two peacock feathers in the corner, picked them up, and stuck them back into the arrangement. "Wait here," she said, went to the storage closet in her office, and returned with a large black plastic trash bag. "Put it in."

Doris scrambled to her feet. "The arrangement? I can't throw it out!"

"No. I agree," Andrea said as she bagged it up herself. She pulled the yellow drawstring closed and handed the bag to Doris. "Take it home. If the owner stops in, which I highly doubt, tell her you're getting so much more pleasure having the arrangement at home. You will enjoy it more, say, on a shelf in your sister's basement?"

Doris's smile was not slow in coming. "Yes, I do believe I will. You're one smart lady, Andrea Hooper."

"'Too soon old and too late smart,' to quote my grandmother," Andrea murmured. Thinking of her grandmother's quote reminded her of the one Madge had used last night. "Before I take the tray back, there's one more thing I wanted to tell you."

She closed the door behind her. If she and Doris were going to really make a good team, then she needed to be totally frank about her medical condition and the time off she would be taking for her checkups and monthly treatments. She did not want to broadcast the news, only share it with someone whose help she might need and who had earned her trust.

Chapter Thirty-One

$\approx$

With Doris handling the office, Andrea walked the tray back to The Diner, which was almost empty at midafternoon. She covered a yawn as she walked. After little sleep last night and a hectic morning, she had every intention to get in a good nap this afternoon. She had even thought about skipping the meeting for the Shawl Ministry. She still hadn't mastered knitting, but Jane Huxbaugh depended on her for a ride home so she had little choice and settled on getting to bed early tonight, very early.

When she got to The Diner, Caroline was at the cash register. She took the tray but refused to take Andrea's money for the beverages. "My treat. I insist. Consider it a celebration gift," she teased with a twinkle in her eye.

Andrea groaned. If Caroline said one word about celebrating Andrea's first date in years, she just might cry. She was that tired.

Caroline took one look at Andrea and laughed. "Don't get all defensive. We're celebrating the fact that you crossed the avenue safely this time. The last time you were here, you got run over by a skateboarder, remember?"

"Only too well. Yes, I suppose I should celebrate that," she admitted with relief.

"You thought I was going to mention your date, didn't you?"

"Honestly? Yes."

"Well, I won't say a word about it, but I did hear a lot. I guess you're not interested in knowing what I heard, though. Too bad."

Andrea let out a sigh. "Go ahead. After seeing half the town last night while I was waiting for Bill to pick up his orders, I had a strong suspicion we'd become the hot topic of conversation today."

"Actually, I think you're ahead. I'd say it's about sixty-forty right now. Maybe a little better than that."

Andrea lowered her voice. "Sixty-forty for what?"

"A second date, of course. Now I'm a God-fearing, churchgoing woman, like you are. I don't bet, and I don't gamble, even if some folks at the senior center do. But if I were a gambling woman and I wanted to add a few dollars to the pot they've got started, I'd put my money on you. That man doesn't stand a chance...not if you decide to set your cap for him."

"We had a date. One date. Let's let it go at that," Andrea countered. The very idea that some of the seniors had started a pool and were gambling on whether or not Andrea would have a second date with Bill did not sit well at all, especially knowing she already had that second date set for Monday night. She changed the subject. "Doris said you wanted to tell me something about the meeting for the Shawl Ministry this afternoon?"

"Right. You usually take Miss Huxbaugh home, don't you?"

"Usually. Why?"

Caroline looked around as if making sure no one could overhear and leaned forward over the counter. "She didn't want anyone to know, but she had her doctor call the thrift shop where she volunteers. Of course, by now, most everyone knows, but I don't want to be the one who gets blamed for spreading the news, but for all it's worth, I thought you should know so you wouldn't be caught by surprise at the meeting this afternoon." She paused and looked around again before continuing. "She's had a stroke. They transferred her to the coronary care unit last night. Word is she won't be there very long, either. She's had a bad heart for years, and the stroke only made matters worse. I thought maybe you'd want to visit her while there's still time. She's got no family and what friends she did have… She won't even let the pastor come. She made the doctor call him and tell him."

"I understand," Andrea whispered. She hardly considered Jane Huxbaugh to be a friend, and she doubted Miss Huxbaugh felt otherwise. Even so, Andrea did not want anyone to spend their last days on this earth alone, even someone as thoroughly miserable as Miss Huxbaugh had been for the past fifty years.

"Thanks for telling me. Do you know what hospital she's in?"

"Tilton Medical Center."

Andrea nodded.

"Just don't tell her I told you," Caroline requested. "If she surprises everyone and does recover, I don't want her charging in her and yelling at me. It upsets the customers."

"No, I'll make sure I don't. Thanks again," Andrea whispered. She returned to her office and replayed her conversation with Caroline in her mind. She did not blame Caroline or anyone else for being afraid of Jane Huxbaugh. The woman had had one nasty attitude for years. She had been abrupt with Andrea on more than one occasion, but never outright mean.

Andrea felt no obligation as either the woman's real estate agent or as her friend, which she was not, to visit her in the hospital. With all that was going on in Andrea's personal and business life, she certainly had a perfect excuse now to go home and get the sleep she needed.

Except for her obligation as a child of God to comfort one of the children He would soon call home. Andrea remembered the vigil that she and her sisters had kept for Sandra, as well as the vigils for Kathleen and Mother and Daddy. None of Andrea's loved ones had been alone in their last hours…and she could not let Jane Huxbaugh pass alone, either.

She went back to the office and explained to Doris that she'd be leaving for the hospital immediately.

Regardless of location or size or the wealth of the patients, there's a distinctive smell in every hospital. It's not the scent of disinfectant, disease or medical lotions. It's the subtle blend of hope and fear, despair and optimism, as some patients fight to live just a little longer while others pray for death to come.

Andrea hated hospitals. Maybe hated was too strong a word. She was trying not to hate anything these days, anyway. Hospitals made her feel…uncomfortable. Too many memories, too many times when she would have to rush to the hospital in the middle of the night or leave hours or days later, with yet one less family member here on earth.

When she arrived at the hospital, she went straight to the main visitors' desk and signed in. She checked her watch to write down the time. It was one-fifteen.

The elderly woman behind the desk put down her magazine and checked the sign-in log, saw Jane Huxbaugh listed as the patient being visited and Andrea's relationship listed as friend and shook her head. "Sorry. No visitors. Just got that written down in the book so I don't have to look it up."

"Doctor's orders or the patient's?" Andrea asked.

"The patient's orders. Don't blame me. I'm just a volunteer, and even if you wanted to visit, you couldn't. It's immediate family only in the coronary-care unit, and she doesn't have any family. I wrote that in the book, too."

Andrea dismissed the gentle reprimand, but she did not have to feign disappointment. "Oh, dear. That's a problem, isn't it?"

"Not for me," the volunteer receptionist quipped, and turned her attention back to her magazine.

Andrea did not know whether to ask to see someone else in charge or to try to see if she could get the woman to bend the rules. She did know she was not leaving, not without seeing Miss Huxbaugh. When Andrea noticed the old silver cross pinned on the woman's sweater, she decided to try persuasion. "I wonder if you might be able to help me," she murmured.

"Not unless there's another patient you want to visit," the woman replied without taking her eyes from the article she was reading.

"No, but it's very important for me to see Miss Huxbaugh. I could lie and say I was her daughter. I could even get very insistent and demand to see someone higher in authority," Andrea suggested. "I'd rather just tell you the truth and let you decide if you want to help me or not."

The woman raised her eyes and looked at Andrea. "Considerin' most folks would start yellin' or makin' a real fuss, that might be a refreshin' change. Go ahead. Make your case, not that it'll matter much. It just might be more interestin' than this magazine."

Andrea nodded. "Miss Huxbaugh is dying, and she's going to die alone unless you let me visit her. I've lost four members of my family, and not one of them died alone. But Miss Huxbaugh doesn't have any family. I just came because too many people die alone, that's all."

"But you're not related to her?"

"Only through faith."

The woman's gnarled fingers gently caressed the old silver cross for a moment, before she handed Andrea a turquoise pass. "There's a chapel you might want to visit. Go down the hall and take the second left, not the first one. If you take the first one, you'll be in the east wing. You don't want to go into the east wing because if you do, you'll pass right by the coronary-care unit and you can't go anywhere near there because Miss Huxbaugh isn't takin' any visitors. Now if you do make a wrong turn and somehow end up where you're not supposed to be and Miss Huxbaugh starts yellin', you hightail it outta there and explain you got lost goin' to the chapel. Understand?"

Andrea returned the woman's wink with one of her own. "Perfectly."

"Good. Now all I need for you to do is put your name and telephone number on this here slip of paper." She handed Andrea a pen and a piece of memo paper.

Without asking why, Andrea did as she was told and handed both back.

The old woman tucked the paper under the sleeve of her sweater. "I'm eighty-one years old come October. Got no family. I might need to call you up if I get real sick. That okay with you?"

Andrea's heart trembled. "You call me anytime. Day or night," she whispered, and started toward the hall. She took the first left, found the coronary-care unit without a single person to challenge her and slipped into the dim cubicle, where she found Miss Huxbaugh lying in bed, as expected. She was connected to a heart monitor and an IV, which probably carried some nutrition as well as medication.

Andrea approached the bed quietly. Miss Huxbaugh was resting peacefully with her eyes closed. If the stroke had weakened any of her muscles, they weren't the ones in her face. She just looked very old and frail, quite the opposite of her personality. Her breathing was slow and shallow; Andrea had to listen very hard to hear it. She carried a chair to the side of the bed and sat down.

After bowing her head, she said "The Lord's Prayer" silently. As she prayed, she placed her hand on top of Miss Huxbaugh's right hand, so very pale and cool to the touch. When a nurse suddenly appeared to check the IV bag, she wrote down something on the chart and smiled. "I didn't realize she'd changed her mind about visitors. I'm glad you're here. Even though she's sleeping right now, she's still lucid at times. The stroke hasn't affected her speech, so you may get to talk to her, though she's very weak. She doesn't have much longer."

Andrea swallowed the lump in her throat. "How much time—"

"Maybe till morning, but probably not that long. Under the circumstances, you can stay as long as you like. I can bring an extra pillow for you, or maybe a blanket? It gets a little chilly at night."

"No. Thank you. I'll be fine."

"Ring the buzzer if you need anything, or when the time comes," the nurse whispered before she left, closing the curtains around the bed and giving Andrea and Miss Huxbaugh a little privacy.

Andrea rested her forehead against the side of the bed and dozed off and on between prayers for what seemed an eternity. Once or twice, she thought she felt Miss Huxbaugh stir, but when she checked, the woman's eyes were still closed and she was still asleep. Andrea woke with a start when she heard a cart rumbling past the cubicle. She checked her watch. It was almost midnight.

The noise, however, had disturbed Miss Huxbaugh. She opened her eyes. When she saw Andrea, her eyes widened and filled with panic. With her right hand, she yanked on Andrea's sleeve. "Closer. Come…closer."

Andrea rose and leaned her face toward the woman's face.

"Get my keys…from my pocketbook."

"Your keys? You want me to get your keys from your pocketbook?"

"Hurry."

Andrea knew better, but she searched under the bed and the small metal chest of drawers anyway. Valuables and personal items were always stored away when patients were admitted to a hospital. "I'm sorry. They must have everything locked up for you for safekeeping. Your pocketbook isn't even here."

Miss Huxbaugh closed her eyes for a moment. When she opened them, she tugged on Andrea's hand until she had bent down closer to the woman's face. "Under a rock…in my garden…by the front door. There's a key…hidden there."

Andrea leaned even closer. The woman's voice was so low now she could barely hear her.

"Take it. Go inside. Under…under the bed, there are… boxes filled with…letters."

"I understand," Andrea whispered. "What do you want me to do with the letters?"

Tears streamed down Miss Huxbaugh's face. "Burn them. Don't…just throw away. Burn them. Please…burn them for me. Don't let…don't let anyone read them after…I'm gone."

"I will. I promise," Andrea crooned.

"Good girl. Good…girl…good…"

Miss Huxbaugh closed her eyes and drew in one last breath before she passed from this world to the next. Her hand slipped down to the bed. Andrea put the old woman's arm beneath the covers, but she remained where she was at the side of the bed and closed her own eyes.

There had been times in Andrea's life when she had felt close to God, but there had been other times when she had felt His very presence.

Times like now.

She had experienced the same feeling each time she had witnessed the passing of a loved one. First, Kathleen, then Daddy and Mother and, finally, Sandra. When they had passed, their sickrooms had filled with such holiness and inspired such awe, Andrea had felt as though she had been witnessing one of life's greatest wonders: the reunion of a soul with the Creator.

She filled with awe. She felt the holy presence of God. And she prayed for the soul of Miss Jane Huxbaugh. *May she finally find the joy in heaven she had never found in her journey here on earth.*

Chapter Thirty-Two

By the break of dawn, it would be too late for Andrea to keep her promise to Miss Huxbaugh. With flashlight in hand, she searched the bed of rocks in front of the house, found the key and slipped inside.

She was not a burglar, though she felt like one. If any of the neighbors caught a glimpse of light in this house at three o'clock in the morning, they would certainly assume the worst. The last thing Andrea wanted to do was to have to explain herself to the police, especially without Miss Huxbaugh alive to corroborate Andrea's story.

She kept the beam of the flashlight low. She got into a musty, first-floor bedroom that faced the street without any problem—until she walked straight into a rope of some sort that hit her in the chin. She yelped and her heart lurched against the wall of her chest. When she raised the flashlight beam from the floor and looked about the room, she gasped.

If she had not seen this with her own eyes, she would not have believed it. Clothesline hanging from hooks on the walls crisscrossed the room and still held a few pieces of laundry. Andrea lowered the beam and swept it over the carpet. Sure enough, lines of mold and mildew were like shadows beneath the clothesline overhead.

She backed out of the room. Why the older woman had chosen to hang her laundry indoors in a bedroom did not really matter. Andrea needed to find those letters and leave before anyone discovered her inside the house.

She had a little better success in the next room, which held a bedroom set straight out of the 1940s and smelled of old-fashioned toilet water. Andrea lowered herself to the floor, first on one side of the double bed and then the other. She was so exhausted she was tempted to put her head down and close her eyes. Unfortunately, her search only yielded seven pairs of slippers in varying degrees of disrepair, one screw-back earring, a free sample box of bran cereal, and a telephone directory from 1981.

She shoved everything back beneath the bed, brushed the dirt and dust from her hands, and moved on past the bathroom to the last bedroom at the end of the hall. Inside, she found a single bed against the wall, covered with an old chenille bedspread. When she reached beneath the bed and her fingers touched a box, she prayed she would find letters inside.

She slid the box out from beneath the bed. Before she stood up, she decided to shine the flashlight under the bed again, just to be sure she had not overlooked a second box.

That turned out to be a good idea. She did find a second box and a third and a fourth and a fifth! There were envelopes filled with letters in every one of them.

As far as the letters were concerned, Andrea did not see much. She only lifted each lid high enough to see there were letters inside before she closed the lid and moved on to the next box. Not that she was not curious. She was just more afraid of being caught rummaging through the house.

Stacked on top of one another, the boxes were perhaps two-and-a-half-feet high, and each box was the size of a man's shirt box. Andrea carried the boxes out the front door and set them down for a moment to bury the key again. She had parked her car around the block for fear someone would hear the engine or see the headlights. She looked up the street and saw nothing to indicate anyone in the neighborhood had been alerted by her presence.

She waited in the shadows until a transit train passed by before she headed back to her car with the letters that could perhaps unravel the fifty-year-old mystery surrounding the day Miss Huxbaugh had been left at the altar.

By the time she got home, Andrea only had enough energy to drop the boxes inside her front door, set the alarm and fall into bed with her "girls." She was asleep almost before her head hit the pillow.

Andrea woke with a start and a growling stomach. Groggy, she lifted her head, read the illuminated numbers on the digital clock and dropped her head back to the pillow. It was 10:41 p.m. She had slept through breakfast, Sunday services, lunch and dinner. She had also slept so late,

Jenny had not only come back from her weekend away but also left for her night shift.

With a groan, Andrea got up, headed straight for the shower and towel-dried her hair before she put on a night-gown and robe. She poured fresh food into the cats' bowls and chose a Southwestern omelet combination of some sort from a freezer full of entrées, and popped it into the micro-wave. She practically inhaled a couple of glasses of orange juice while she waited. Still flush with last night's success at retrieving Miss Huxbaugh's letters, she now faced a new challenge: how to fulfill the rest of her promise and burn the letters.

As far as she knew open, outdoor fires of any kind had been banned in Welleswood for years. Without a fireplace in her home or one of those newly popular garden chimineas, she had no way to burn the letters, at least not that many letters.

If she had found only a handful of letters, she would have been tempted to put them into one of her big pasta pots and set the letters on fire. Five boxes of letters made it easy for her to nix that idea. She could go to Madge's house. No one was home to see what she was going to do. Madge had a fireplace. A gas fireplace, she remembered. No help there. Jenny had a wood-burning fireplace in her house, but An-drea was reluctant to involve her or anyone else in Welles-wood. It was only the end of September. Someone would be bound to question why anyone would be using a fire-place when it was still so warm.

Madge's beach house would have been perfect, but it had a gas fireplace there, too. That left… A possible solution slowly dawned. She would need to make a telephone call to be sure, but it could work. She knew it could.

When the bell on the microwave rang, she put her meal onto a plate to rest for the required two or three minutes. She went down to the basement, got an old suitcase and scrunched all five boxes of letters inside before she stored the suitcase under her bed.

If her idea did work, then she only had to wait until tomorrow to fulfill the rest of her promises to Miss Huxbaugh and to Madge. By the time everyone found out on Monday that the elderly spinster had passed on, the secrets in her letters would be gone, too. By the time Jenny had to go to work again Monday night, she would know what had happened to Madge.

She sighed and sat down to eat. Everywhere she turned lately, she had found nothing but sadness. Tomorrow did not look to be an easy day at all.

Late the next afternoon, Andrea decided she had been wrong. Monday had turned out to be a rather productive day that took a rather dramatic turn at five o'clock.

Like most everyone else along the avenue, Andrea had gone outside when the fire whistle sounded and four fire trucks responded to a fire at the senior-citizen high-rise, only a few blocks from her office. Apparently, one of the elderly residents on the fifth floor had forgotten about a pot cooking on the stove. Miraculously, no one had been injured, but the one apartment had been heavily damaged by the fire and several other units had both smoke and water damage.

Rush-hour traffic had been blocked on the avenue for over an hour and side streets were clogged with detoured cars, trucks and buses. Conversation about the fire and senior citizens in general quickly sparked debates filled with gossip and innuendo that put the passing of Jane Huxbaugh into the category of old news.

Andrea decided the old woman would have liked it that way.

She drove to Jenny's house to talk to her about Madge. She had a little time before she needed to go home, switch to Russell's car, pick Bill up at work and drive to Sea Gate to pick up the Jeep and keep her promise to Miss Huxbaugh before coming all the way back to Welleswood. She parked in Jenny's driveway and followed some enticing aromas to the back patio. She had not planned on crashing supper, but she did not have a choice. She had to pick Bill up at seven o'clock.

When Andrea found Jenny at the barbecue grill instead of Michael, she was surprised. When she saw whole lobsters grilling alongside skewers of shrimp, she was impressed. "This must be some special occasion," she teased.

Jenny was beaming, but shrugged nonchalantly. "You might say that. I'm glad you stopped by. Michael bought tons too much." She turned one of the lobsters. "If you don't stay for supper, this little guy will go to waste."

"Normally, you wouldn't have to make me feel guilty to stay, not where lobster is involved. But I have plans for tonight. I can't stay. Where are Michael and the girls?"

"Picking up dessert."

"At the bakery?"

"Only for the girls. Michael made Aunt Elaine's coconut cake for us."

Andrea groaned. "Not the pound cake with fresh coconut and that special icing that makes you want to lick the bowl *and* the cake?"

Jenny laughed. "Like there's any other?"

Andrea took a long, delicious whiff. "So, are you going to tell me what the special occasion is, or are you going to keep me in suspense?"

Another nonchalant shrug. "Take a guess."

For a moment, Andrea caught her breath. "You sounded like Daddy just then."

"I did?"

"He used to do that with our birthday presents, remember? He'd wrap them up, put them on top of that old console TV at least a week before our birthdays, and make us guess what was inside."

Jenny chuckled. "I remember. Even if we guessed right, he'd just shrug, so we never really knew for sure if we were right or not until we opened the gift. It used to drive me crazy, but I think if he'd ever stopped the tradition, I would have been disappointed."

"You can't do that to me. If I guess the reason for your celebration, you have to admit to it."

Jenny shrugged again, then laughed. "Go ahead. You have three guesses. If you get it right, I finish grilling dinner. If you don't, then you have to take over. Fair?"

"Fair. Okay, let's see…let's start with the obvious, not that your tummy is all that big yet. You had an ultrasound today and found out you're having…twins!"

"Wrong."

"You're having a boy?"

Jenny frowned and flipped a skewer of shrimp. "Wrong again. Besides, you know Michael and I don't care about the baby's gender. We both love little girls. You have one guess left before I hand you the tongs."

"I have two guesses left. The ultrasound was one guess."

"One left," Jenny insisted. "Make it a good one."

"Oh, I don't know." Andrea did not have another good guess, so she blurted out the most incredible possibility she could think of. "Michael sold his book and got such a fabulous advance, you called work today and resigned so you can be a stay-at-home mom."

Jenny smiled and handed Andrea the tongs. "Nice try, but you're wrong again."

Andrea let out a sigh of defeat and took over at the barbecue, but she noticed Jenny's smile had turned the corner from teasing to smug. "What? Aren't I grilling to my lady's satisfaction?"

"No, you're doing just fine. But I like it when you're wrong. It doesn't happen very often. As it turns out, you were almost right about everything, except the last part. I'm not going to resign until tonight when I get to work."

Andrea stilled, then looked at her sister as her heart grabbed on to what Jenny had said and her mind let the words register. "Michael...sold his book?"

"To the highest bidder! There were three publishers fighting over it all day!"

"No!"

"Yes, yes, yes!"

Andrea threw the tongs up in the air. They embraced. They whooped and hollered and danced up and down. They cried and they laughed together until they both smelled the dinner burning. While Andrea retrieved the tongs, which had fallen to the lower deck, Jenny used an oven mitt to shove the dinner away from the hottest part of the grill. When Andrea returned, she flipped the lobster and shrimp and sighed. "I thought for sure dinner would be ruined."

"Nothing can ruin today," Jenny insisted, and held out a platter on which Andrea piled the food. "It's just too marvelous. Michael is so happy, and I'm so proud of him for being so talented and so persistent. He just never gave up, and now…"

She set the plate on top of the picnic table and patted her tummy. "Now I can stay home with all three of my babies."

Andrea's euphoria drained quickly. She did not want to spoil Jenny's day with the news about Madge, any more than she wanted to see Madge later and tell her she had not told Jenny, let alone tell Madge about Jenny's amazing news. Still, Madge and Jenny deserved to know the truth.

As the oldest, Andrea felt a particular obligation to both of her sisters. They were related, but they were friends and confidantes, too. They certainly were not cookie-cutter copies of one another. They were three different women with distinct personalities, different talents and faults, and different lives.

But the bond between them was strong. It was a bond that had been forged over their lifetimes where love and concern had always guided their relationship with one another. They had learned to balance the joys and troubles that life threw at them, often simultaneously. That's what friends did for one another, but more importantly, that's what sisters did—always.

Andrea's biggest problem now was putting that sense of sisterhood to the test. When she sat down at the picnic table, Jenny sat down beside her. "Do you remember what you said earlier about you and Michael loving little girls?"

"Sure."

"Madge loves little girls, too," Andrea began. "In fact, there's a little girl in her life now. Her name is Sarah. Madge is away for a few weeks, but she asked me to come and talk to you about Sarah."

Jenny listened as Andrea poured out the tale. When she finished explaining the decision Madge had made to try to save her marriage and make a home for Sarah, she and Jenny embraced. They cried mostly, but laughed a little, too. "I hope I didn't spoil your celebration too much," Andrea offered.

"I told you. Nothing could ruin this day for me. But Madge…I feel so bad for her, but I'm proud of her, too. She's a much stronger woman than I would be, I think." She dropped her gaze. "I'm not sure how this is going to work out for her. Even if she can forgive Russell, I—I think I'm going to have a hard time doing that. Part of me wants to wring his neck."

"I know. I've been wondering how to forgive him, too, but if Madge can manage to do it…"

"Then we'll have to forgive him, too," Jenny whispered. "Maybe you should wait to tell her about Michael's book and all. She's so unhappy right now. It doesn't seem fair that Michael and I both had our dreams come true while hers…"

Jenny's eyes widened with horror. "Oh, no, Andrea. What a goose I am! I'm sorry. Here I am all giggly and excited one minute and worried about Madge the next, and I forgot about you! You just look so good. I forgot for a moment that you're sick. You have your own worries. I'm really sorry."

Andrea put her arm around Jenny's shoulders. "Madge and I are your sisters. Even though her life is a mess right now and I'm fighting for my health, we can still be thrilled for you because we're more than just sisters. We're His children. That means we can do anything, as long as we let Him guide the way."

Jenny sniffled. "Tell Madge I love her and tell her to call me, too."

Andrea gave her sister a hug. "I'll tell her tonight when I take Russell's car back." When Jenny's eyes filled with confusion, Andrea explained what had happened to the Jeep on the way home from Sea Gate with Bill.

"So you're driving down, but Bill is going with you so he can bring you home in the Jeep?"

Andrea nodded. "He was pretty embarrassed."

Jenny grinned. "But he got what he wanted, didn't he?"

"Which was…"

"A second date!"

Andrea huffed. "It's not a second date. It's…it's just the end of the first date."

"Ha!"

"Ha, yourself!" Andrea stood up. "I'm going home to get Russell's car and pick Bill up at work so we can finish our *first* date." She put her hand on Jenny's shoulder when she tried to get up. "Sit. I can get back to the car by myself."

"Okay, but if Bill shows up with blueprints for a house, like Daddy did when he had his second date with Mother because he was so sure she would marry him, you're in trouble. Don't say I didn't warn you!"

"Trouble is having a baby sister who is an impossible matchmaker!"

"You love me anyway."

"I love you any way at all," Andrea replied, and left to fulfill a promise to an old woman who might have found a lot more joy in life if she had been blessed with a sister or two.

Chapter Thirty-Three

Heart-weary, Madge sat and watched the sun drooping low in the sky, just above the horizon. After a weekend alone with Russell and Sarah, she knew she had a difficult journey ahead. One day, they might be able to be a family together. With time and prayer, she and Russell would be able to fix their marriage, especially since he had agreed to start marriage counseling, but she was still worried about telling Drew and Brett they had a half sister.

Russell joined her on the patio and interrupted her thoughts. He sat down on the chair next to her, put his briefcase on the ground and let out a sigh. "She's finally asleep. She loves *Good Night, Moon* a little too much. I had to read it three times before she drifted off."

Madge felt a tug on her heartstrings and resentment flared briefly. The boys had both loved that classic story, too, but Russell had not been home very often to read it to them. Maybe Sarah was giving him a second chance at fatherhood, an idea that suggested to her that she also might be able to do things better on her second go-around at motherhood.

"I made those calls today that I mentioned over the weekend," he said. "Everything is set to go, but I want to run everything by you first to make sure you agree this is a good idea."

She was curious about his future at work and more than anxious to discuss something he had planned himself, since she had been the one to set so many conditions so far. Other than suggesting he had to make a few calls before he could make definite plans, he had told her little about what kind of changes he apparently had in mind. "I'm listening," she murmured.

"If we're going to make our marriage work better and make a home for Sarah together, the first thing I need to do is to be home more. Frankly, traveling so much in my job is getting tedious. It may pay well, but we've paid a high price, too. So…I want to quit my job."

Madge almost fell out of her chair. "Quit your job? How on earth can you do that and still support us?"

"We'd have to make some sacrifices. The beach house, for example. We'd have to sell it and absorb the loss, but I've got that all worked out." He took some papers from his briefcase and pulled his chair closer to hers so they could review the papers together. "I know you don't have much interest in finances, but that needs to change, too."

"I know." She glanced at the papers, which had a number of columns of figures and struggled to keep tears at bay. Was there no end to the pain he caused?

He pointed to the first column. "If I quit my job, this number represents the cash assets we can access. The second column represents the projected loss on the beach house and the repayment of the home-equity loan on the house in Welleswood. Are you with me so far?"

"So far, but what's the third column?"

"Start-up costs, projected expenses for the first two years of business, plus living expenses. If you compare that total with the total in the first column, you'll see we can do it, at least for two years. If the business fails or doesn't prove profitable by then, I'll have to get a job working for someone else again."

"Business? What business? You never mentioned going into business before."

"I guess I never thought long enough about it before," he responded. "Or maybe I just never felt the need like I do now. I need to be here at home with you to help raise Sarah, but I want to be home to do that, more than anything."

She agreed with him. He did need to stop traveling, but the prospect of starting a business at his age seemed a bit of a stretch financially. They could be ruined and have nothing left if the business failed. "What kind of business?" she asked.

"I only know one business. I know pet food and pet supplies, but I also know it very well. I've had to be one step ahead of the trends, and I'm convinced I'm on the right track." For the next half hour, he explained his plan to open a gourmet store catering to pampered felines. He had the statistics showing demand and some reports indicated that cats, not dogs, were the number-one choices for pets. He had the contacts he needed to provide the gourmet food, from snacks to meals. He could ask Andrea to check on storefronts available for rent or purchase on the avenue. He had even contacted Stan Anderson, the owner of The Cat's Meow, a grooming salon in Welleswood for cats only. The Cat's Meow would be a perfect "feeder" store. Stan's customers would be Russell's customers. Stan was doing so well, he had already been considering cutting out the accessories he carried to make more room for grooming, and Russell could add the accessories to his store.

But it was the commitment in Russell's voice and the excitement in his eyes that reminded Madge of the young man she had married so many years ago.

"I could make this work. I know I could," Russell vowed. "But I won't even consider it or bring it up again if you don't like the idea. I can stay where I am and travel. You won't have to give up the beach house, and things can stay pretty much as they are, at least financially."

She glanced down at the papers again. "The figures are right? You double-checked them?"

"Double- and triple-checked."

This change would be hard and potentially a financial disaster. Not changing, not taking the chance and having Russell continue to spend so much time away from home, however, would put much more than their financial future at risk. If saving their marriage was the priority, then change they must. The beach house was way down on her list of things she wanted now. "Did you have a name in mind for this business?" she asked, finding his enthusiasm contagious.

He shrugged.

She did not stifle her grin. "The Purrple Palace," she suggested, emphasizing the name by purring the first part of the word *purple*. "We could get a purple awning for the front window and have different kinds of cats stenciled on the awning in cream or lavender. Purple gingham curtains. Purple bags to hold the customers' purchases—"

He held up his hand. "Enough! Decorate the store any way you like. The name you picked is *purr*fect!"

They laughed together for the first time since he had brought Sarah home, but their laughter was not the only great thing that night. When Andrea arrived just before dark with Russell's car, and Bill walked down to the garage to get the Jeep, Andrea brought the good news about Michael selling his book and Jenny getting her dream of staying home with her babies. When the doorbell rang at eight-thirty, the time when Bill had agreed to return for Andrea, Madge walked her sister to the front door. "I wish there was something special happening for you today, too," she admitted. "Maybe Bill—"

"He's just a friend," Andrea insisted. "Don't start matchmaking. Jenny is bad enough."

"You shouldn't be alone," Madge said.

Andrea kissed her cheek. "I'm not alone. I have you and Jenny. I'll call you tomorrow and let you and Russell know which storefronts are available." She slipped out the door and closed it, avoiding an awkward meeting between Madge and Bill. Madge went to the window and watched her sister and the tall man walk to the Jeep and then pull away. Given the opportunity to choose between putting her marriage back together or being single again and part of the dating scene, Madge knew she had made a good decision. She did not envy Andrea, not even a little.

After Bill picked up Andrea at Madge's beach house, he drove them back to the beach area reserved for all-terrain vehicles and parked in the same parking lot he had used on Friday night. They walked together to the beach. Andrea carried the suitcase with Miss Huxbaugh's letters. Bill carried a stack of wood and everything else they would need to make a fire, including a special permit.

They chose a spot well away from the grassy dunes, although the night was calm, with nothing but a whisper of a breeze. While Bill got the fire started, Andrea sat quietly and thought about Miss Huxbaugh, the boxes of letters stored in the suitcase, the years wasted on bitterness and disappointment, and the mystery of the long-missing fiancé.

When the fire was ready, he helped her set the suitcase closer. "We'll have to feed the letters into the fire a few at a time, or they'll smother the flames."

She nodded and opened the suitcase. The lid blocked the light from the fire. She could see the outlines of the envelopes containing the letters, but it was too dim to be able to read any of the handwriting.

"Are you sure you don't want to read any first or at least note the return addresses?" Bill asked. "She's gone now. No one would be hurt."

Andrea shook her head. "I promised to burn them so no one could read them after she was gone. She'd never know I broke that promise, but I would."

He nodded.

"I feel we should say a prayer or something," she murmured.

He joined his hands with hers, and they bowed their heads. "Heavenly Father, we know You have called Miss Huxbaugh Home to be with You, and we pray she has found the love and happiness that so eluded her here on earth. We are burning these letters tonight to fulfill a promise because You have always been faithful to us and we believe in Your promise of life everlasting for those who claim You as Lord God. Amen."

Andrea blinked back tears. "That was beautiful. Thank you."

One handful at a time, they fed the letters into the fire. Bill had to add more wood twice. When the last letter had been reduced to ashes, they sat, back to back, and watched the fire until there was nothing left but embers. After he buried the remnants of the fire and the ashes that had not blown away, he helped her to her feet, picked up the suitcase and held out his hand. "Ready to go home?"

Hand in hand, they walked back to the Jeep. Bill headed out toward the freeway, but he pulled into an all-night diner before they left Sea Gate. "I don't know about you, but I'm starving. I know it's late, but I don't usually skip dinner and there's no way I can wait to eat until breakfast."

She did not have to respond. Her stomach growled loudly enough for him to hear it, too. "I thought you were going to get something to eat while I was at the house."

"And I thought you were going to eat at your sister's."

"I forgot."

"Me, too."

He smiled. "Eat in or take out?"

"Let's eat in."

"Great." He reached into the glove compartment and pulled out an envelope that had been folded in half lengthwise. "While we're eating, there's something I wanted to show you."

She laughed. "Sure. As long as it's not a set of blueprints."

"Blueprints?"

"You know. Blueprints. Like plans for a house. Or an office building," she added quickly.

He narrowed his gaze. "Did you peek or are you just as good at reading people's minds as you are at keeping promises?"

"This isn't our second date, right? It's only the end of the first date, which we started on Friday, but got interrupted when the Jeep died. Right?"

"Right. I think."

"Good answer. Okay, then. I'll take a look at the blueprints. Men who bring blueprints on the second date are pretty dangerous."

"Really?" he asked as he escorted her into the diner.

"Really," she replied, although she had a feeling that this man might be as dangerous and sure of himself as her father had been when he had courted her mother.

Chapter Thirty-Four

Brisk October air, waning daylight hours and brilliant displays of fall foliage proved the seasonal shift from summer to autumn was well underway. With vacations long over and school and work schedules becoming routine, weekends took on a festive flavor that was familiar to all who lived in Welleswood.

On Saturdays, soccer and midget football games sponsored by the Welleswood Youth Athletic Association (WYAA) filled the fields at Welles Park, not far from the new skateboard complex and a new sign indicating the fund-raising efforts for the girls' crew team were still less than halfway to the final goal. The cries of cheering fans and anxious parents carried to those at the open-air farmer's market, or shopping along the avenue, or at home doing yardwork or fall housecleaning. Sunday morning, church bells would call families from their homes to worship. With the heat of summer past, many people would walk to church again and gather on the lawn after services to chat while their children played together.

Not everyone greeted this particular weekend with joyful anticipation.

Too nervous and agitated to get very much sleep Friday night, Andrea had been up since dawn. Her "girls" had sensed her mood and stayed within sight but beyond her reach. At eight o'clock, she showered, dressed comfortably, grabbed her purse and a striped bag and left her house. She did not want to answer the telephone, and she had deliberately left her cell phone in the charger, too. She could not handle any calls from well-wishers, namely Madge and Jenny—not right now.

Out of habit, she went to check the clock in her car, but caught herself just in time. She had developed a real aversion to clocks lately and had even stopped wearing her wristwatch. She did not much care for calendars anymore, either. Unfortunately, her business demanded that she pay close attention to dates and times.

On this particular date at eleven-thirty, she would learn if the chemo she had started three months ago was working or not.

She pulled out of her driveway and headed toward Dr. Newton's office, but her mind was not focused on the road. She would be able to tolerate the cysto, which only lasted for a few minutes. The procedure itself, which would allow the doctor to actually see the interior of her bladder to check for any new growths, was uncomfortable rather than painful.

Still, there were a million different places she would rather go today and a zillion other things she would rather do. Or would she? Wouldn't knowing be better than just hoping the chemo was working?

"What if it isn't working?" she murmured. Negative thoughts had been threatening to overtake her for the past week, and she forced herself to think of something positive. She drove down the avenue past her office and managed a smile. She had hired Jeanne Drake two weeks ago. What a difference the retired chemistry teacher had made! Behind her ever-present smile and intelligent eyes lay a sharp mind and a strong will. She had become so efficient and so competent at running the office, Andrea had been able to spend only a few hours a day there and still keep tabs on everything, including Doris.

But not today. Andrea would not be able to work until Monday.

Up ahead, two blocks down on the opposite side of the avenue, she spied the purple-striped awning on the storefront Russell had rented for the *Purr*ple Palace. She slowed down and pulled over in front of the store. At this early hour, there were more open parking spaces than there were cars driving down the avenue.

Arched across the top half of the plate-glass window, workmen had already painted the name of the business, along with a pair of cats at either end of the lettering, all in shades of purple. Beyond that, Andrea could not see a thing. Inside the window in the door and the plate-glass window, huge sheets of white paper blocked the view, yet announced the Grand Opening for November sixth. The business was only one of the new beginnings Madge and

Russell were making to put their lives back together, but introducing Sarah at Sunday services tomorrow would be a far more important test of community reaction than the store would be.

Andrea's mind swept back to the present. Would today mark a new beginning for her, too? Or a slide back toward…the end? She pulled back into traffic, passed the street where Jenny and Michael lived, and smiled again. Of the three sisters, Jenny was certainly faring the best. Her world was filled with new beginnings. She had been home now for a few weeks and was loving every minute of it. She was feeling well. Her pregnancy was proceeding smoothly, while Michael worked hard on the revisions his editor at Sinai Press had requested.

With her spirit infused with positive energy, Andrea drove directly to the doctor's office. She parked the car and carried her purse and the striped bag with her as she walked around to the back. For the first time, she used the key Dr. Newton had given to her and let herself into the garden. She had not been here since that one time in July at her first post-op visit and the day she started chemotherapy.

She was surprised by the transformation that had taken place in three months. Against a backdrop of evergreens and conifers, hardy autumn flowers in shades of gold, mustard and burgundy had replaced the flowers painted in the soft palette of spring and the dazzling primary colors of summer. Even the air had changed. The heavy perfume of summer had faded to more subtle fragrances that no longer overpowered the scent of pine and cedar.

She followed a path bordered with white October daisies and sat down on a wrought-iron bench. She put her purse alongside her. Once she retrieved her knitting needles and the shawl she had started, she rested the striped bag on the ground at her feet.

Bathed in crisp sunshine, Andrea closed her eyes and recited the prayer she had written for herself as part of the Shawl Ministry. "With these hands, I reaffirm my love for You, dear Father. With this shawl, I will share my love with one of Your beloved children, so he or she may feel Your love and never feel alone. Amen."

She had to really concentrate on her knitting for the first few rows, and she had to accommodate Muffin, the curious calico cat that stopped by for a visit, until it got bored with playing with the yarn. Andrea was still too unsure of herself, but after she caught the rhythm, she relaxed and knitted away the time between now and her appointment.

She was not sure who would receive the shawl she was making. As each shawl was completed, the members would discuss the possible recipients and decide together who would receive the shawl. Andrea had missed a meeting or two, but as far as she knew, no one had finished a shawl yet. The dark green color of her shawl, which she had chosen in memory of Miss Huxbaugh, reminded her of the yarn the elderly woman had donated and which Andrea had used for practice.

She had received the listing to sell Miss Huxbaugh's house from the old woman's attorney, who insisted the house be sold as-is and fully furnished. Andrea had led a literal parade of people through the house in the first few days. Most had been curiosity-seekers. She had even had to stop some from rummaging through closets and drawers, proof that the mystery surrounding Miss Huxbaugh's past was still very much alive. Within a week, though, Andrea had sold the house to out-of-town cash buyers and settlement had just taken place earlier this week.

She stilled for a moment and laid her knitting on her lap. She thought of Bill and shook her head. The man had turned out to be one surprise after another, although he had kept his promise not to waste her time looking at houses anymore. He had not even asked to see Miss Huxbaugh's house when it went on the market.

Instead, he had decided to stay in the apartment he was renting and purchased the old schoolhouse on the avenue from the borough. Located at the south end of town, just a few blocks from the business district itself, the site was perfect for professional offices, and the old schoolyard would provide precious, off-street parking.

She chuckled and started knitting again. While looking over the blueprints with him in that all-night diner in Sea Gate, she had been surprised to learn he was an architect. Or he had been an architect. After the death of his wife, he had shut down his office, gotten a trucker's license and taken to the road, driving back and forth across the country. He believed his ordeal at the hands of hijackers, who still remained at large, was a blessing in disguise that only confirmed his decision to settle down in one place again. He was ready to resume the career that had once given him so much satisfaction, right here in Welleswood.

Thinking about Bill, who had not asked her out on a date again, led her to more confusing thoughts, and the reality of her visit to the doctor today hit hard. Driven by anxiety as the hour for her appointment drew closer, she put her knitting aside and got up from the bench. She strolled along the walkway until she reached the center of the garden, where all the other paths met to join a bricked courtyard. Circular benches surrounded a tarnished bronze sundial resting on a concrete bed at the feet of a marble angel. Andrea sat down on a bench and read the plaque at the base of the sundial:

I must find time to pray.
I must find time to love.
Because life is Thy most precious gift to me.
Though the journey is hard,
With Your angels to guide me,
Life can be all I discover through Thee.

Tears welled and choked her throat. For the past several weeks, Andrea did not have to pretend she was in perfect health. She honestly had almost forgotten about her cancer. After her last treatment in September, she had been tired, as usual, but with more rest, she had done almost everything she had wanted to do. She had even tried searching the Internet for information on bladder cancer and tried eating more nutritiously. She fared better, at least mentally, when she focused on everything but her cancer.

Prayer had helped.

Having Madge and Jenny's support had helped, too

But once the calendar read "October," she had found herself slipping back to fear again. She had not prayed as often. Today, with her appointment at hand, she wanted to run and hide or turn back the calendar to two years earlier before her first battle with cancer had begun.

Humbled by the words on the plaque, she bowed her head and folded her hands in prayer. "The journey is hard today," she whispered. She prayed with her heart, but she knew no one could travel this road with her today. She had to travel it alone.

On impulse, she looked up at the sky. A sliver of the moon was visible, but the sun was too bright for a single star to shine through. She closed her eyes and prayed for God to guide her.

"Andrea?"

She flinched. Her eyes snapped open, and she saw the receptionist, Nancy, standing behind the sundial.

"I'm sorry. I didn't mean to startle you, but Dr. Newton is ready for you now. I saw your things on the bench. I'll get them for you and keep them until you're finished."

Andrea nodded. Surrounded by His loving angels, she left her fears and anxiety on the bench and went inside. When she came out again half an hour later and returned to the garden, she stopped to offer a prayer. "Thank you, Father, for sending so many angels to help me. From now on, I'll try harder not to be such a weakling," she promised.

She left the garden before the doctor's good news truly sank in: The chemo was working perfectly. The joy in her heart erupted when she reached the parking lot, and she danced her way back to her car. She really did not care what anyone might think if they saw her, either!

Two weeks from now, when she faced chemo, she might be fearful again, but today was nothing but sheer joy. God was so good, even to weaklings like her.

Chapter Thirty-Five

Sunday services had been part of Madge's life for as long as she could remember, and this church held memories of the most important days in her life. She had grown in faith here. She had been married here. Drew and Brett had learned Bible verses here as little boys—Bible verses they still carried in their hearts when they came home last week to meet their new little sister. Mother and Daddy, Kathleen and Sandra had been here to receive one final blessing before being laid to rest. And it was here that Madge would find her way back to the loving marriage she so desperately wanted.

Today's service, however, was the first time she and Russell and Sarah would appear in public together as a family, although word of the adoption had spread quickly. Madge had had butterflies in her stomach when she woke up this morning. By the time she and Russell walked Sarah down the aisle and took their seats, there were only moments before the service was set to begin. She was half afraid to sing the opening hymn for fear a flock of Monarch butterflies would escape and really give the congregation something to talk about!

Reverend Staggart had been extremely helpful and very supportive when they had all met together several times over the course of the past week, and she kept her attention on him during the entire service. With her heart wrapped around the hope that the congregation would be just as accepting as the pastor had been, she tried to quell the guilt she carried for misleading everyone about how Sarah had come into their lives. It was harder to control the resentment that Russell had put her into this position in the first place.

She would have felt a whole lot easier if the adoption had already gone through and she had a new birth certificate for Sarah stored in their safe-deposit box.

She had seen more than a few shocked faces as the three of them passed down the aisle to their pew at the front of the church. Fortunately, Jenny and Michael and Andrea were already there, and Madge focused only on their smiles of support as they slid over to make more room.

Madge was not surprised to hear a few whispers behind them, either. Who could blame them anyone being surprised or curious? Madge and Russell were both old enough to be grandparents, not the adoptive parents of this little charmer.

She glanced at Sarah. She was sitting quietly. Next week, they might try letting her go to the nursery Sunday School, but not today. Poor little lamb. She still asked for help to find her mommy occasionally, and Madge prayed time would heal this little one's heart and leave room for Madge to fill the void left by her birth mother's passing.

As the voices of the congregation rose to sing the closing hymn, Russell reached over and squeezed Madge's hand. They still had a long, long way to go before they fully reconciled, but he was trying hard to make amends. His show of support now meant the world to her, but it would be her heavenly Father who would carry her through the next half hour after services ended and Sarah became the focus of everyone's attention.

The hymn ended. Instead of sending his flock back into the world to do the Lord's work in the coming week, the pastor urged everyone to be seated. "Today we have the pleasure of welcoming a new member into our community of faith. The Stephens have adopted a little girl. Madge and Russell? Would you bring Sarah forward at this time?"

Madge's heart flip-flopped. Sarah had already been baptized as an infant. What was the pastor doing? He had not mentioned anything about—"

"Madge?" Russell's voice cut through her panic. "We should take Sarah up now."

Madge nodded. Hand in hand, with Sarah in the middle, the three of them approached the altar. The pastor met them with a smile. "Relax," he whispered. "And smile!" he urged as he turned them to face the congregation. He stood behind Sarah to address everyone. "As you all know, we have a new women's ministry here and they've asked for a moment today when everyone was here. Mrs. Hadley?"

Eleanor Hadley and two other women stepped forward

and took places to Madge's right. Madge recognized Millie and Grace Hudson at once. They were carrying a pale pink shawl. She looked to Andrea for an explanation, but only saw a mirror of her own surprise and curiosity.

Eleanor began speaking in a clear but gentle voice. "As some of you know, I've been honored to be part of the women's Shawl Ministry. We've been meeting for some time now on Saturday afternoons to pray together and knit together, creating shawls we hope will bring joy and comfort to those who receive them. Together, we decided that our first shawl should be presented today to little Miss Sarah Stevens. Ladies?"

At her invitation, Millie and Grace approached Sarah, who let go of Madge's hand to cling to Russell's leg. She did not balk, however, when the two women wrapped the shawl around her shoulders and showed her how to tuck in the ends and hold the shawl in place with her arms. As they worked with Sarah, Eleanor recited a prayer. "With loving hands and giving hearts, we have made this shawl and present it to you, Sarah. We welcome you to our community of faith and promise to help you love and serve the God who has chosen Madge and Russell Stephens to be your loving parents. As you wrap yourself in the shawl, always remember that He is the source of all goodness and comfort and you are never, ever alone. He will stay with you always."

With one voice, the congregation said, "Amen."

Madge had not been present when Sarah had been baptized as an infant. The ceremony today and the words Eleanor had spoken went a long way toward easing her disappointment. Still, she wished Sarah had come into the family as a newborn. At three, she was too old for the traditional family ceremony Madge and her sisters used to welcome each of their children.

The spontaneous applause that erupted and the genuine smiles of welcome from the congregation, however, left Madge in tears that quickly turned to laughter when Sarah proceeded to pirouette and show off her shawl. The next few minutes were a blur, and before Madge knew it, she was standing next to the pastor in a receiving line in the church foyer. Russell stood on the other side of her with Sarah in his arms as friends and neighbors passed by to offer their congratulations.

True, there were more than a few raised eyebrows. Madge even overheard a few snide comments about her age, but by and large, most people seemed genuinely happy for her, which only added to her fear of what might happen if anyone discovered the truth. Madge was not Sarah's adoptive mother yet, and she wouldn't be for several years.

When Andrea appeared at the end of the line with Jenny and gave her a hug, Madge whispered in her ear, "You could have warned me what they were going to do today!"

Andrea hugged her back. "I didn't know a thing about it. I guess the other women were afraid I might have told you and ruined the surprise," she whispered back before Jenny playfully nudged Andrea aside. "I want a hug, too."

Madge hugged her baby sister, felt Jenny's extended tummy press against her and set her back. "Are you sure you're not due until February?"

"Positive." She kissed Sarah's cheek. "I like your shawl."

Sarah pulled away. "Mine!"

"Yes, sweetie, it sure is," Jenny assured her. "Uncle Michael went to get your cousins from Sunday School. Would you like to play with Katy and Hannah?"

Sarah buried herself deeper in Russell's arms.

"She's still a little shy," Madge explained.

Russell laughed. "Except when she's standing in front of the entire congregation!"

"Russell, why don't you take Sarah with you to find Michael and the girls while we make a quick stop back inside for a minute?"

Russell nodded, and Madge linked her arms with her sisters and ushered them back inside the foyer of the church before either one of them could argue. The church was empty now, but the memory of today's ceremony was still vivid enough to reignite Madge's fears. She paused just inside the foyer, forcing her sisters to stop as well, and bowed her head. "I can't do this. I can't mislead everyone. I can't lie like this," she whispered.

"Lie?" Jenny asked.

"About Russell. About Sarah," Madge whispered. "It's going to take a year or two for the adoption to go through and to get Sarah's birth certificate changed so both of our names are on it, not just Russell's. Until then, I have to continue to lie and pretend Russell isn't already her father—"

"That's not true," Andrea argued. "The circumstances of Sarah's birth and her adoption are private, and they should be. You and Russell have decided to raise Sarah together as her parents. That's all anyone needs to know."

"She's right," Jenny argued. "Listen to her."

"But if anyone finds out the truth, they'll know I misled them."

"They won't," Jenny insisted.

Madge took a deep breath. "But they could."

"Not if you could get the adoption approved and a new birth certificate issued quickly. Once that's done, the original can be sealed, even with the proviso that the records can be unsealed at Sarah's request when she's an adult, which she probably won't do because you and Russell are going to tell her the truth anyway. I assume Russell has her mother's death certificate?"

"I guess so." Madge's eyes lit with hope that quickly dimmed. "It's a good idea, Andrea, but I told you. Going through with the adoption and getting the birth certificate changed will take a good year, maybe longer."

"But what if you could get it done in a few weeks? What then?"

"Then I guess I'd feel much better than I do right now."

Andrea smiled. "Consider it done."

With her eyes wide, Madge leaned back, looked at Andrea, and sputtered. "C-consider it done? J-just like that?"

"Just like that. I have a friend, Trish Montgomery, who practices family law. She'll do it for me as a favor. I'll call her tomorrow for you."

"But you can't just call up your friend and expect her to drop everything to handle this for us. And what about the courts? They're clogged with enough cases to last through this millennium and the next, or so they say."

Andrea's smile turned into a grin. "Yes, I can. What did Sandra do every time she wanted something near…near the end when she was sick?"

"She played the cancer card."

"Right. Now it just so happens you have another sister who can do the same thing. I'll call Trish tomorrow and if

I have to, I'll play the cancer card. If it worked for Sandra, it'll work for me."

"You…you said you'd never do that! You told Sandra you thought it was terrible to play on people's sympathies like that!"

Andrea swallowed hard. "I know I did, but well, sometimes we have to do things because there's no other choice. I wouldn't play the cancer card otherwise. There's nothing I can do to make this all go away for you, so let me try to make it better. Please."

Madge did not bother to swipe away the next barrage of tears. "You'd do that? For Sarah and Russell and me? You said you didn't want anyone else to know your cancer was back."

"You're my sister," Andrea whispered. "Of course I will." Before they both got teary, she pinched Madge's upper arm.

"Ouch! What was that for?"

"Just a little victory pinch. I was right, wasn't I?"

Madge rubbed her arm. "Right about what?"

"Cancer. It isn't always so bad. Sometimes it's just plain good. Or it can be. It all depends on what you do with it. It's about time I made it work for good, don't you think?"

Madge sniffled. "I suppose."

"I suppose, too," Jenny teased before they shared a group hug.

Madge did not argue when Jenny and Andrea led her back outside where folks were still gathered, chatting together in groups on the church lawn. While searching for Russell and Sarah, Madge saw the leading members of the Shawl Ministry—Eleanor, Millie and Grace—talking with several women, no doubt recruiting new members. The sun felt warm on Madge's face, but her heart was already filled with enough peace now to make the weeks ahead easier. When she saw Bill Sanderson start walking toward them, she whispered in Andrea's ear. "There's someone coming who has his eye on you. I think he's a keeper, too."

Andrea scanned the crowd, saw Bill heading their way and nudged Madge with her elbow. "He's just a friend."

Jenny peered around Madge and made a face at Andrea. "A friend? How many dates have you had with him so far?"

"Two by your count, but it was really only one date," Andrea retorted.

Jenny's eyes sparkled when she looked at Madge. "The man can't be that much of a keeper if he's let the past few weeks go by without asking Andrea for another date. Do you think he's changed his mind about being interested in her, or is she just a little too cranky for his taste?"

Madge replied as if Andrea weren't even there. "I don't know. Maybe we should ask him."

"Good idea!"

Andrea groaned. "Have fun, ladies. I'll see you Tuesday for breakfast," she said, slipped free, and went to meet Bill before he got anywhere close to her sisters. Half the congregation might be watching, but together, Madge and Jenny were far more dangerous. "How are the renovations going?" she asked him as they met.

He held up a key ring with a set of keys on it. "I was coming over to ask if you'd like to see them if you're not busy. I wasn't sure if you'd be going out with your sisters to celebrate or not."

"No, I'd love to see them."

"We can walk or take my car. Maybe have some lunch

afterward? I know it's Sunday, but I have a little business proposition for you."

She nodded. She had a hunch about the business proposition, but let it go until later. "A walk and lunch sound perfect."

Before they left, she waved goodbye to her sisters. At least Sarah waved goodbye back. Her sisters gave her smirks.

Using the back streets, getting from the church to the old schoolhouse that he had purchased took about fifteen minutes. ET, the elevated train, passed by less frequently on Sundays, and Bill and Andrea walked beneath the tracks without a train rumbling by overhead. The parking lot, normally full by eight o'clock on weekdays, held only half a dozen cars.

"The contractor tells me the renovations will be finished by Thanksgiving. From the progress he's made so far, I'd say he's about on target. I've got my offices earmarked. Now all I need are some tenants." Bill nodded toward the tracks. "Having easy access to Philadelphia should help."

"For prospective tenants, but also for clients and employees," she suggested.

They turned, walked up one block and approached the old schoolhouse from the rear. He pointed to the schoolyard. "We'll resurface the blacktop after the construction work is done."

She noticed the rusted chain-link fence had been removed. "You'll have parking for what? Thirty or forty cars?"

"Thirty-five, plus allowances for handicapped parking," he replied as they crossed the pitted blacktop and followed a concrete path to the front of the brick building.

When they paused to take in a full view of the renovated school, she liked what she saw very much. The brickwork on the three-story building had been repointed. The oversize, rotting windows had been replaced with custom-made thermal windows. The old marble steps that led to a double set of doors had been repaired and polished. Even the concrete inset with the name of the school had been sandblasted to look brand-new, and the new name of the building had been engraved directly below the name of the school.

She read the inset:

Walt Whitman School
Where the Future Begins
Whitman Commons
Where Dreams Shape the Future

All she could say was "Wow."

"I'm glad you approve. Does being here bring back memories?"

She shook her head. "My sisters and I went to Welles School, on the other side of town. As the community grew, they built this one later. Now they're both obsolete. I wish they'd been able to save my school instead of tearing it down. Can we go inside now? I'd love to see what you've done."

"I haven't done anything. I'm just the dreamer. The contractor and subcontractors do all the work." He got them inside to the inner foyer where the smell of new wood and paint drying on drywall hung heavy in the air. Tools, sawdust and drywall dust littered the floor. "Follow me, and watch your step. They weren't expecting tourists," he teased.

From the inner foyer, he led her from the first floor to the second and third. He showed her where he would have his office on the third floor. The windows faced west, providing a skyline view of Philadelphia that would be even more magnificent at night. "What do you think so far?" he asked.

"I like what you've done here, but I like the fact that we've gotten to keep this building even more. I wouldn't worry. You shouldn't have any trouble getting tenants," she assured him.

He shook his head. "I'm a little busy at the moment trying to recruit clients for myself. You wouldn't happen to know a good broker, someone who might be interested in being the exclusive rental agent for Whitman Commons, would you?"

She laughed. Her hunch had been correct. "I had a feeling you'd be mentioning something like that."

"Well? Will you do it?"

"Sure. I'll have to do a little research first, maybe make a comparative study between rents here and in Philadelphia, as well as complexes nearby before I can suggest a fee schedule. I'll also need a list of all the suites, square footage, that sort of thing."

He grinned and patted his jacket pocket. "I've got that done. I thought we could look at the figures over lunch. We can stay in town or take a drive. I found a great little restaurant about an hour north of here we could try."

She furrowed her brow. "That depends. What are you driving?"

"Not the Jeep. Definitely not the Jeep. I've got my own car. My very reliable, well-running car."

"Then let's head north to this restaurant you've discovered," she suggested. Not because she did not want anyone in town to see them together again. Just because she liked the idea of spending the afternoon alone with this very nice…friend.

Chapter Thirty-Six

T rue and lasting friendships were like blessings, Andrea thought. Old or new, they never disappointed. They never judged. They just existed, waiting to be affirmed and reaffirmed, over and over again, and became more precious as time passed. To Andrea, some friends like Trish Montgomery, even become sisters-by-affection, as close as real sisters and just as special.

On Monday morning, Andrea said goodbye to Trish and hung up the telephone. Trish had switched into lawyer mode the minute Andrea had explained Madge's situation. She had promised to call Madge that afternoon after reviewing a few cases she had handled in the past that were, both fortunately and unfortunately, remarkably similar. Trish could not promise to have Sarah's adoption completed within a matter of weeks, but she did suggest it was not impossible.

Andrea bowed her head, turned the timing over to God and made a quick call to alert Madge that Trish would be calling her later that day.

On Tuesday, Jenny arrived first for another Sisters' Breakfast, this one marking Kathleen's birthday. But this time, Jenny did not have to drag herself to The Diner after working a full shift in the hospital emergency room and plop herself, half-asleep, into the corner booth. She did not have to feel guilty for not getting home in time to have breakfast with Katy and Hannah, either. She had fixed breakfast for Michael and the girls before she left home. Katy and Hannah had not eaten very much. They were too excited about their cousin, Sarah, coming over to play.

Instead of waiting for Madge, who now had a perfect excuse for being late, Jenny had left to be sure she would arrive first to get the full effect when her sisters saw her new look. Fully rested, though considerably rounder than when she had been here in July for Sandra's birthday, Jenny caught a glimpse of her reflection in the window and smiled.

No more ponytail. Staying home gave her more time with the girls. She had more time to spend on herself, too, like twenty minutes with a blow-dryer. The shoulder-length cut she had gotten yesterday at the hair salon was easy to manage and a lot more flattering. She had even painted her fingernails for the occasion, and her toes, too. She did not need makeup. Joy and contentment gave her all the glow she wanted or needed.

The Diner was usually busy today, but Caroline had still saved the booth for them. In between waiting tables and ringing up tabs at the cash register, she brought Jenny a cup of decaf and put an empty plate in the center of the table. "That's for the treats from the bakery that Madge will bring. What were Kathleen's favorites?"

Jenny laughed. "She had two, sort of. Knowing Madge, she'll get too much of both. We'll probably need another plate, but you can wait to bring it over. I'm not sure whether or not Madge will remember both."

Caroline looked at the waitress three tables up from them and shook her head. "Madge can remember something from twenty years ago, but these young girls I have to hire can't get the orders straight thirty seconds after they take them. I'll bring the plate."

When Andrea arrived a few minutes later, Jenny wished she had brought a camera to record the look on her sister's face. Eyes wide, Andrea slid into the booth across from Jenny. "You look wonderful! You cut your hair!"

Jenny held out her hands and wriggled her fingers. "I painted my fingernails, too."

"And your toes, I imagine."

Jenny laughed. "And Katy's and Hannah's. Michael drew the line, though. Speaking of looking good, you're not doing so bad yourself, for an old lady, that is. Tell me! Tell me! How was your date with Bill on Sunday?"

"It wasn't a date. We had a perfectly ordinary business meeting over lunch. He's asked me to handle renting the other offices in the building." She paused when Caroline delivered her usual glass of iced tea and left another empty plate on the table. "Naturally, I said yes."

"Naturally," Jenny quipped. "And just where did you have this business meeting?"

Andrea shrugged and added some artificial sweetener to her iced tea. "Just a restaurant. I'm sure you haven't heard of it. It's in a little town called Bayville, and the restaurant is right on Barnegat Bay. They have a place for boaters to pull in and dock during the summer, but it's getting too cold now. We saw some sailboats out on the bay, though. The water looks so dark now, when the sails caught the sunshine, they were a brilliant white that I've never seen before."

Jenny took a sip of coffee. "Yep. That sure sounds like a dull, ordinary business meeting to me."

"Don't start," Andrea warned.

Before Jenny could press for more details, Madge arrived in a whirlwind of apologies for being late, two bakery boxes and gushing compliments about Jenny's new look. "Sorry I'm late. Sarah slept a little later than usual today, and Russell had to leave earlier than usual to meet some deliveries for the store. Before I forget," she added as she slid in beside Andrea, "Michael said to tell you not to rush. He's going to take all three girls on a nature walk to collect leaves. Maybe after breakfast we can all go shopping and get the girls each a little scrapbook, the kind with the plastic pages?"

"Shop away, ladies. Some people have to work for a living," Andrea teased.

"We'll still have to press the leaves between waxed paper," Jenny cautioned as she slipped the string off one of the bakery boxes. She looked inside, saw half a dozen jelly doughnuts, and put three onto a plate. "Do you remember how to do that?"

Madge opened the second box, put two extralarge corn

muffins on the second plate, and winked. "I don't forget anything, little sister."

Caroline appeared with a cup of decaf for Madge and to take their orders. She saw the two plates filled with doughnuts and muffins and grinned at Madge. "I knew you wouldn't let me down. What's your pleasure today, ladies?"

Once she took their orders and left, Jenny followed tradition and did the honors. She cut the jelly doughnuts in half, just the way Kathleen had taught her. She sliced straight through the entire jelly center so each side was the full length of the doughnut. Next, she sliced the corn muffins, top to bottom, into six thin slivers. She used a spoon to scoop a bit of jelly from the doughnut and spread it on each slice of muffin.

They each took a piece and held it up as a toast.

With memories untouched by the passing of time, Jenny was able to speak from her heart through the tears that blurred her vision. "We remember you, Kathleen. Your sweet smile. Your sweet disposition, and the sweet sound of your laughter. Happy birthday, honeybun," she murmured. Her voice caught when she used the nickname she had given her sister. Kathleen had always laughed and said in return, "If I'm your honeybun, then you're my sugar cookie."

Jenny had not been able to eat sugar cookies for a long time after Kathleen's passing eight years ago.

"No tears today. That's the rule," Andrea teased. "Sisters' Breakfasts are supposed to be happy, remember?"

Jenny brushed away a tear. "I'm pregnant. I get weepy. I can't help it."

"I know," Andrea replied. "You were closer in age to

Kathleen than we were, so why don't you start today with a story. A funny one," she suggested before nibbling at her jelly muffin.

"And not the bunny story. You told that last year," Madge cautioned between bites.

Jenny took a couple of deep breaths, glimpsed her pink fingernails and smiled. "A funny story? Okay. How about the time Kathleen decided to play a joke and painted everyone's toenails while they were asleep? That was pretty funny."

Madge choked on her muffin. "That was not funny! She painted every one of our toenails a different color!"

Andrea nodded. "And those were the days when it took a lot of elbow grease to get that polish off."

Jenny frowned. "She painted Daddy's toes, too, and *he* thought it was funny."

"Daddy never got mad at anything," Andrea countered.

Madge shrugged. "We were sisters. We always got mad at something one of us did, but we got over it."

"Or we got a lecture from Mother," Jenny said.

Madge volunteered to go next, but she had to wait to tell her story until Caroline had delivered their breakfasts. "Once upon a time, you were just a baby, Jenny, so you don't remember this, but Andrea should. While the 'big three' were in school, Kathleen was home with Mother and you. Kathleen was helping Mother with the laundry. Mother had just gotten her first dryer, remember?"

Andrea smiled. "I remember. If she had turned down that dryer, I think I would have cried for a month of wash days."

Puzzled, Jenny stopped eating her omelet to listen as Andrea explained. "Mother and Daddy couldn't afford a dryer, so she used to hang her wash outside to dry. Summer or winter, it didn't matter. Unless it rained. Then she'd hang it downstairs in the basement to dry."

"Until we got old enough to help," Madge continued. "Usually, that meant coming in from school and taking down the wash. When you were born, that meant diapers. Lots and lots of cloth diapers. Disposable diapers hadn't been invented yet."

Andrea shivered. "Come winter, those diapers would freeze on the line and so would our fingers when we took the diapers down and brought them inside. They'd be as stiff as a board before they thawed enough to drape over the chairs in the kitchen to dry. That's why I wanted that dryer."

"Who gave it to her?" Jenny asked.

Madge giggled. "Her friend, Mrs. Riley, better known to her fellow fans at the racetrack as Bettin' Betty." She looked around and lowered her voice. "The poor soul was addicted to gambling, and she loved horse races the best. She'd slip over to the track during racing season, catch the first couple of races, and get home before the children got in from school. She won the Daily Double one day, used her winnings to buy a dryer and had it delivered to Mother as a surprise."

"Mother didn't know what to do," Andrea murmured. "The dryer was a gift, but it was bought with 'ill-gotten' gains. Daddy tried to talk her into accepting the dryer, but she had to talk to the pastor before she'd accept it, thank God."

"Actually, I think the pastor said, 'Thank God and say a prayer for Mrs. Riley every time you use the dryer.' So that's what Mother did," Madge explained.

Jenny resumed eating her omelet. "That's a good story about Mother that I've never heard before, but I don't see how that involves Kathleen, and it's not funny, either."

"I got sidetracked, but I'm not finished," Madge replied. "Okay, so now Mother had a dryer and Kathleen would help her. She decided that your plain white diapers were a little boring, so when Mother was busy setting the dial on the dryer, Kathleen tossed a handful of crayons inside on top of the wet diapers, and shut the door. When the load was finished drying, the diapers certainly weren't white anymore. Mother never did get all of the crayon out of them."

Jenny laughed out loud, but if either of her two girls had done that, it would not have been quite so funny.

"There's a theme here, one I hadn't realized about Kathleen before," Andrea suggested. "She loved color a lot, didn't she? I remember now how she loved her crayons and paints. That's all she ever asked for as presents."

"Maybe that's why she dreamed of becoming an interior designer," Madge murmured. "She never had much of a chance to make that dream come true. She was sick for so long…"

Jenny swallowed hard. Kathleen was first diagnosed with leukemia when she was a senior in high school. She had fought the disease, off and on, for the next seventeen years of her life. She had never finished college. She had never married or had children. She had been too busy trying to survive. Jenny took a deep breath and stifled her fears for Andrea's health and her own worries that cancer might one day invade her own world with Michael and the children. "Kathleen had a dream, but it never came true for her.

Maybe…maybe that's why it's important for us to hold on to our own dreams and to work as hard as we can to make them come true and to know how blessed we are when they do."

Madge nodded. "I thought I had my dream of a happy marriage, but now I know I took that dream for granted." She paused and lowered her voice to a whisper. "I still have that dream and with God's help, Russell and I will make our marriage happy and whole again. It's not easy right now. I know I'll never be able to forget what he did. I just keep praying I'll be able to forgive him completely. I'm just very, very grateful right now that Andrea's friend has agreed to help us get Sarah's adoption handled quickly."

Andrea smiled and reached down to take Madge's hand. "You both know my dream—good health. When I find myself growing weary of the battle, I try to remember Kathleen's strength and her sense of humor and her sweet smile when she told us she could no longer win the war."

The mood was more somber than usual as they finished eating. Jenny thought maybe it was because Kathleen had been gone for so long now and they realized how time was making their memories fade just a little. Maybe it was because so much had happened in the last three months since they had gotten together for Sandra's birthday.

Or maybe, just maybe, it was because the older they got, the more they all realized how precious dreams could really be and how little time they had to make those dreams come true.

Chapter Thirty-Seven

On a Sunday night in the beginning of November, Madge stared at the clock hanging on the wall above the front door of the *Purr*ple Palace. Was the clock broken already? It was only days old.

Russell came up behind her. "There's a battery inside that powers the minute hand to move once every sixty seconds. It doesn't operate on nervous energy," he teased.

She sighed. "I thought it was five minutes to seven over five minutes ago. I think I'm just as nervous about this grand-opening celebration as I was when I had my first party in high school."

He chuckled. "That was a long time ago."

She nudged him playfully with her elbow. "Well, I haven't forgotten how I felt right before everyone came to my fifteenth birthday party. I had this awful fear that no one would show up, but I was also afraid everyone who had been invited would come, and we didn't have room for them all. And what if someone crashed the party to make trouble because they hadn't been invited?" She shivered as the old memories returned. "This feels the same to me. My stomach hurts. My heart is pounding, and my head feels like there's a tight band of steel wrapped around it. I know tonight is just a party to celebrate opening the store and tomorrow is the first real day for business, but I'm still nervous."

He took her hand. "Me, too." Their gazes met. "We have a lot to lose if this venture fails, but if we don't have each other, then nothing else matters, anyway," he whispered.

She nodded and swallowed the lump in her throat. When the cat clock meowed seven times, Russell handed Madge the key to the inner lock on the front door. "Do the honors. If you hadn't supported me and helped me and given me a second chance, this store never would have happened."

She hesitated and wrapped her fingers around the key. Six months ago, she would have handed the key back to him and insisted he unlock the door for the first time. She would have been content to be in the background while Russell took center stage and accepted all the accolades, as well as responsibility for success or failure. Sadder and wiser now, she was committed to changing her past mistakes for the sake of a better future.

Russell had selected the site for the store, made all the major decisions about stock and planned the advertising. He would manage the store and the three employees ready to begin work tomorrow when the store opened. Madge, in addition to naming the store, had taken charge of the floor plan, decorating and arrangement of the stock. Once the store opened, her responsibilities as a wife and mother would be primary, but she would remain very much a part of the business as it evolved.

In truth, Russell had changed a lot these past few months. He had worked even harder at their marriage-counseling sessions than she had prayed he would. He had been honest and sometimes brutally hard on himself, and she had discovered ways in which she had failed, too.

Not that her failures had been as traitorous as his, which he was quick to point out during their counseling sessions.

When she examined the life they had led for the past few years with the same honesty, she realized she had put Russell and their marriage behind other things, like the roles she played within the community.

He should have been her first priority.

Their marriage should have been her first priority.

Tonight was a turning point in their relationship with each another, and she prayed for the courage and the wisdom to let him know she was now able to forgive him fully.

She urged Russell to go to the front door with her. She put the key into his hand and wrapped her hand around his and slid the key into the lock. The blessing of full forgiveness washed the anger from her spirit, once and for all. "For better or for worse, we'll work together as equal partners in our marriage and in every aspect of our lives. We've shared the job of getting the store ready to open for business, and we'll share the work of making it a success, each in our way, each with our own talents," she whispered.

When she tried to turn the key, he stopped her and

cleared his throat. "For better or for worse, we'll work together to make our marriage stronger. You have opened
your heart and offered forgiveness, and I pledge to you
with all my heart that I will honor and cherish you above
all others for the rest of my days as my wife and helpmate,"
he murmured, and turned the key. "Ready?"

She nodded, unable to speak, unable to see clearly until
she blinked away her tears. With a prayer of gratitude in
her heart, she stepped back from the door.

Russell had the door open and the vertical shades pulled
back before she had herself composed again. Fortunately,
at least for the moment, it was her family that poured into
the store. Michael and Jenny had brought Katy, Hannah and
Sarah with them, as planned, but Madge had to hide her
surprise when Andrea followed in with Bill Sanderson.

Andrea put her arm around Madge's shoulders while
Russell scooped Sarah into his arms. "We came on the dot
of seven to get the first tour."

"*If* anyone else comes. You do think they'll come, don't
you?" Madge asked.

"Of course they will," Jenny assured her. She put little
Hannah on her hip while Michael settled Katy on his shoulders. "Okay, the angels of destruction are secured. Better
hurry, though. This won't last long," he teased.

Madge smiled and nodded to Russell. "You're the official
tour guide."

He began where they stood, in the front of the store, and
methodically led the group in a mini-parade, through the
different sections. In the front, furniture, too old-fashioned
or scratched to be used in a home, but too young to be considered antiques, had been painted a soft cream color. Then

a local artist had painted scenes on them, featuring different breeds of cats, including their wild relatives from other lands. Stuffed felines in every shape, color and size filled bookcases, hutches and sideboards, along with fashion accessories for both the stuffed and live variety of cats, who claimed owners who wanted to spoil them.

Madge made everyone stop to let the girls pick out a stuffed animal for a keepsake, which would also keep them occupied. Katy chose a Siamese cat the size of her hand. Hannah took one identical to her sister's, but Sarah debated over two before she selected a pastel tiger with purple stripes. Madge beamed. "That's my girl!"

Before they continued, Russell made sure they looked above the purple gingham café curtains where a number of stained-glass ornaments and sun catchers hung, ready to catch tomorrow's sun, to dazzle window-shoppers before they followed the purple paw prints painted on the wooden floor to the center of the shop. Purple gingham fabric lined wooden crates that had been stacked to hold an assortment of trinkets for cats and their owners that ranged from all-weather scarves to zippered change purses. If they weren't shaped like cats, they had a cat stitched or painted or decoupaged on them.

The rear of the store, however, was Russell's greatest triumph. He waited until they were all together before he explained. "Up to here, Madge either organized everything you saw or decorated it. This is my one big contribution," he said as he waved his arm at the two chest-high glass cases in front of them. Much like the cases used in bakeries to display cakes and muffins or doughnuts and breads, the cases held all sorts of gourmet cat foods. The girls, however, squealed at the top of the cases, where plates of McAllister's butter cookies were set beside a tray of fresh vegetables and a bowl of dip. Smaller plates held squares of cheese, slices of pepperoni and crackers. Liquid refreshments were available at a side table.

Russell handed each of the girls a butter cookie to keep them quiet. "The case on the left isn't refrigerated. For anyone who has a special cat at home, we have all kinds of snacks shaped like mice, squirrels, rabbits and even a few breeds of dogs. They're made fresh every day, without preservatives or additives. On the bottom, I have sample cans of cat food. Most are imported, but I'm hoping to find a gourmet American brand soon."

Carrying Sarah, he stood behind the second case, where bowls of cat food were displayed like salads in a deli case. "Cats have a reputation for being finicky eaters, but I never knew what they really meant until Sarah's kitten proved it was true. I'm confident enough to make this guarantee to all of my customers— If there isn't something here your cat loves to eat, then I'll give you a full refund and a gift certificate for a free grooming at The Cat's Meow."

Bill peered into the case and shrugged. "Looks like ordinary cat food."

Russell grinned. "But it's not. I purchased the recipes from several sources, and I make everything from scratch using fresh, not frozen, ingredients. I only use the best cuts of meat and the freshest vegetables. I bake the dry food until it's crunchy on the outside, but tender on the inside. It's all nutritious, it's tasty and, best of all, it smells delicious to cats and to humans."

Andrea looked at the prices and winced. "It's a bit pricey, especially if you're feeding three at a time."

Madge chuckled. "You get a family discount, doesn't she, Russell?"

"Of course!"

Jenny shook her head and moved Hannah to her other hip. "You actually make the food yourself?"

"Not here. There isn't room for a kitchen, although I doubt I'd get a variance to put one in, even if I had the room," Russell responded.

"My gourmet kitchen at home is finally getting a good workout again, and I don't have to clean up his mess, either," Madge explained with a laugh.

Before her laughter died, their first official guests arrived. Jenny and Michael excused themselves and took the three girls home with them. Madge was more than a little anxious about letting Sarah go to her first sleepover, but Jenny promised to call, even if it was three o'clock in the morning, if Sarah woke up and wanted to go home.

"Bill and I will stay a while," Andrea told Madge, before Madge left with Russell to greet their guests.

The huge crush of people Madge had feared never happened. Over the next two hours, she and Russell greeted old friends, neighbors and other business owners who arrived in small groups, stayed for a while and left, making room for another wave of well-wishers or people curious about a business geared strictly for people who were owned by their cats.

At eight forty-five, the celebration night was winding down. Madge began to circulate among the guests who remained, while Russell took several men to the back storeroom. She stopped to chat with Caroline and her husband, the co-owners of The Diner, and another couple, who were also local merchants.

"You look tired, but probably not as tired as you're going to be tomorrow morning," Caroline suggested. "What time does Sarah get you up in the morning?"

Madge groaned. "Around seven," she answered before she remembered Sarah was staying with Jenny overnight.

Caroline looked around the store. "You've done wonders here. I hardly recognize the inside, although I haven't been inside for at least a year. That's when the old taxi company closed its doors." She sniffed the air. "I didn't think anyone would buy this place. I think the wood inhaled twenty years of cigarette and cigar smoke. How did you manage to get that out?"

Madge shrugged. "That was Russell's doing, not mine. I made the curtains, though."

"And handled the decorating, too," Caroline added with a smile of approval. "You two make a good team, just like we do," she said with a wink at her husband.

"I think we do," Madge murmured before the two couples offered one last wish for success and left.

Madge met Eleanor Hadley and her companions from the Shawl Ministry, Millie and Grace, on their way to the door. All three senior citizens smiled. "Lovely, lovely store, though we probably won't be buying any cat food, not on our limited budgets," Eleanor noted.

"The butter cookies are McAllister's, aren't they?" Millie asked before she popped a piece of a cookie into her mouth.

Madge chuckled, even when she saw the pockets bulging in all three women's sweaters. Grandmother Poore used to take little plastic doggie bags to events, too, and wondered if they shouldn't be called kitty bags, instead. "Are there any better butter cookies for a hundred miles? I wanted to thank you all, again. You made Sarah's introduction at church last month very special for all of us."

"We loved doing it for her, and for you, too," Eleanor replied. "You helped us to get started, remember? You even talked your sister into joining us. I don't suppose we could get you to join us, too?"

"I'd love to, but...I've got so much to do now."

Grace patted her arm. "That's okay, dearie. We understand. Little ones come first. Just pray for us, then, and be sure to let us know if you hear of someone who might need a shawl."

Madge agreed, bade them good-night, and moved on to the final group gathered at the rear of the store around the last of the refreshments. To her surprise, Andrea and Bill were still there, along with Carol Watson and another woman from the WYAA. By the time she reached them, Russell emerged from the storeroom with the women's husbands.

"This tour is over, and my day is done," he whispered as he joined her. "How about you? Tired?"

She nodded.

"I was just telling Andrea about the new girls' crew team," Carol said. "She made a donation a few months back. Can we count on your support, too, Russell?"

He ran his fingers through his hair and smiled. "Sure. I guess that's part of doing business, isn't it? Stop in during the week, and I'll have a check for you."

"You could have given the man a chance to open his door for business before you asked him," her husband chided.

"We only have a few months left to raise the money," Carol countered. "If we don't reach our goal by then, we'll never be able to buy the equipment and field a team in time for the spring meets."

Ginger Smith, co-chair of the fund-raising efforts with Carol, nodded. "Now that we finally have a name and a slogan selected from the contest we ran, maybe that will get donations flowing again."

"What's the name?" Andrea asked.

"The team will be called The Welleswood Sisters. The slogan is 'If we work together, we win together...in sports and in life.' I think that says it all about our purpose. We want the girls to feel good about themselves as athletes and competitors, but we hope they form friendships that will last a lifetime, as if they were sisters. What do you think?"

Ginger tapped her foot and stared up at the ceiling. "Personally, I think everyone will love the name and the slogan if the volunteer who promised to add the name and the slogan to our sign in the park ever gets around to keeping his promise."

Her husband blushed. "Tomorrow morning. I promise."

Ginger laughed with everyone else, but Madge noted a spark of interest in Andrea's eyes. Was she that interested in the girls' crew team, or was she reacting to the way Bill not only smiled his approval, but pledged a donation as well, even though his own business endeavor was still a few weeks from opening?

When Andrea covered a yawn, Bill called it a night. That prompted the others to leave, too. Russell locked the door and finally closed up at nine-thirty. Before he turned out the lights, he took Madge's hand and squeezed it. "Thank you. I couldn't have done this without you."

She squeezed back. "You're welcome. 'We done good,' as my grandmother used to say, but we'll do even better. We just need a little time and a lot of grace," she whispered, but she was not talking about the business.

He pressed a kiss to her forehead.

Just a gentle kiss that spoke to her, promising that time and God's grace could heal even a broken heart.

Chapter Thirty-Eight

❧

Winter blew into Welleswood with a vengeance. The earliest snowfall in eighty years hit the third weekend in November. The heaviest snowfall on record kept everyone at home on New Year's Eve, and it took three days before most people dug out to return to work or school.

By late January, Andrea had her second cysto. Good news again! The day she marked the midway point in her treatments, Whitman Commons finally opened with a ribbon-cutting ceremony at eleven o'clock in the morning, halfway through her "rolling time."

"Some days are just not long enough, and some winters are just too cold," she grumbled. She bundled herself up in an ankle-length, hooded down coat and laced up her fleece-lined boots. By the time she wrapped a wool scarf around the lower part of her face and neck and slipped into thermal mittens, the only part of her body that would be exposed to the elements were her eyes.

She stared at her reflection in the mirror and shrugged. She might look like an overstuffed, black snowman, but at least no one would comment on her gaunt look or the fatigue that showed up in new lines on her face. She had lost ten pounds, but it was not the chemo at work. She had just been uncommonly busy and often did not have the time to eat regular meals, even with Jeanne's and Doris's help at the office. When Andrea got home from work, she was too tired to fix anything beyond a frozen entrée. She just tired more easily now, and that was probably because of the chemo.

On impulse, she added a pair of sunglasses to cut the glare from the snow along the side of the roads. She did not have to rush. Bill knew why she had missed the ceremony. She had a feeling he had scheduled the luncheon that would follow for new tenants, other business owners and town officials for one o'clock to give her the time she needed to be able to attend.

Her presence at the luncheon was professional as well as personal. As exclusive rental agent, she had played an important role in luring prospective tenants to the complex, which was very similar to the work she had done on the Town Restoration Committee. As for the personal aspect, she and Bill remained business associates and friends.

Whether or not that friendship would grow into something else was a matter she set aside today, again. She had an appointment to keep before the luncheon—a settlement that had already been postponed twice. The minute she stepped outside, a howling, bitter wind almost took her

breath away. She got blown to her car. She turned the ignition and let the engine idle. When warm air finally came
out of the heater vents, she lowered her hood and scarf and
drove herself to the settlement, hoping she would be able
to get to the luncheon on time.

Just as Reverend Staggart stood up to say grace, Andrea
slipped into her seat next to Bill. "Sorry I'm late," she whispered as she stored her purse on the floor at her feet.

He looked at her with concern. "Are you feeling okay
after the...you know?" he whispered back.

She grinned. "Actually, I feel pretty terrific," she murmured before the pastor began the prayer and they bowed
their heads.

As luncheons go, there was not much to make this one
very different, especially the customary speeches. The town
officials spoke too long, and the president of the business
owners' association aired the usual call for a more cooper-
ative effort to keep the business district thriving. The food
rated a B plus, but it was Bill's short, poignant speech about
hoping to make a difference in Welleswood that drew the
most applause.

Then they wheeled in the dessert carts.

Instead of the usual dish of sorbet or slice of ice-cream
cake roll, the carts were filled with an amazing array of the
cakes that had made McAllister's nearly legendary. Each of
the three carts held a Black Forest Torte, a Baked Alaska,
an Italian cream cake and a strawberry shortcake with ber-
ries the size of a child's fist.

After the cakes had been pretty much devoured, Andrea
leaned toward Bill. "You made a lot of friends today with

your speech. They probably don't remember exactly what you said right now, but they'll never forget dessert."

His eyes twinkled. "Are you impressed?"

She polished off the strawberry she had saved for last. "Completely."

"Good. Then say you'll go out with me again."

She furrowed her brow. "We've gone out a dozen times."

"Except for our first date, we always talked business. This is different. Now that Whitman Commons is open and my office is up and running, I think we should have a real date. Maybe dinner and a show? Something fun. Something special tonight to celebrate. If you're up to it," he added.

Before she could answer him, her cell phone rang. Embarrassed that she had forgotten to turn it off, she apologized and grabbed for her purse. She got her phone out. She did not recognize the telephone number of the caller, but when she saw Tilton Medical Center displayed on the screen below the number, her heart skipped a beat. Had Jenny gone into labor early? She was not due for a few weeks yet.

She hit the button to take the call and eased out of her chair. "I have to take this call," she murmured before she stepped back from the table. She answered her phone. "Yes?"

"My name is Melanie Wilkins. I'm a nurse at Tilton Medical Center. I'm calling on behalf of Ethel Moore."

Andrea sighed. False alarm. "I'm sorry. You must have the wrong number."

"Is this 555-3058?"

"Yes it is, but I don't know anyone named Ethel Moore."

"She didn't think you'd remember her by name. She

asked me to mention another patient she helped you to see here. A Miss Huxbaugh. Does that help?"

Andrea immediately thought of the old woman at the visitors' desk and the promise Andrea had made to her. "Yes. Yes, that helps a lot."

"Mrs. Moore has been here for a few weeks, but yesterday she developed a few complications. The chaplain has been with her most of the day, but there's been a pileup on the freeway. I'm not sure he'll be able to come back to see her, and the nursing staff is shorthanded, as always. You might want to come as soon as you can."

"Yes, of course. Tell her my name is Andrea and I'm on my way, will you?"

"I will. Just stop at the visitors' desk for a pass. I'll call and tell them you're coming."

Andrea clicked off and hurried back to the table. "I'm sorry, Bill. I—I have to go. I'm not sure about tonight. I'll have to call you later."

"Is there something I can do to help? You look a little flustered."

When she saw her hands shaking as she slipped her cell phone back into her purse, she sighed. "Actually, I think I'm a lot flustered," she admitted. "I have to leave right away."

"Let's go. I'll drive." He ushered her to the coatroom and got their coats. She explained the emergency on the way to the hospital. "I don't know very much about her, except that she doesn't have anyone else, and she didn't want to die alone. I never dreamed the end might be so near or that she'd actually have someone call me."

"How old did you say she was?" he asked as he pulled into the hospital parking lot twenty minutes later.

"Eighty or eighty-one, I think."

He parked the car. "That's a good, long life, Andrea. Let's give her a proper send-off, shall we?"

Ten more minutes passed before they were headed to the elevator with passes in hand. She remembered rushing to the hospital to see Miss Huxbaugh and was glad she was not alone this time. They got off on the fourth floor. When she spied the sign prohibiting the use of cell phones, she stopped for a moment to turn hers off. Then they followed the signs to Room 418.

When Bill pulled the door open, a nurse stepped through the doorway. Her eyes were sad when she looked at Andrea. "Are you Andrea?"

"Yes," she replied. She recognized the nurse's voice from her telephone call.

"I'm sorry. Mrs. Moore passed away a little bit ago. I was just going to call you."

Disappointed, Andrea swallowed hard. "Was she alone at the end?"

"No. I decided to check on her instead of taking my break. I stayed when I realized the end was so near. She was a nice lady. I understand she had been one of our best volunteers. She's still here. Would you like a few moments to be with her?"

"Yes, I think we would. To say a prayer."

"Take as much time as you need. Just stop at the nurses' station on your way out and let me know you're leaving," the nurse said before she left.

Bill held the door open and followed Andrea inside the dimly lit room. Mrs. Moore looked very peaceful. Her face was turned toward the window, and she had a smile on her face as if she had seen the faces of angels as they had arrived to take her Home.

Andrea knelt by the side of the bed. Bill knelt beside her. Together, they prayed for the soul of this old woman who had no one else to pray for her. When they finished, Bill helped her to her feet. "I feel so badly that I didn't get here in time," she whispered.

"But she didn't die alone. I think she understands," he replied as he led her out of the room. When they stopped at the nurses' station, the nurse who had met them earlier walked around to the front of the counter. She reached into her pocket and handed something to Andrea. "She asked me to give this to you when you came, but only if you stayed to offer a prayer for her. I have a feeling she was a woman who lived life on her own terms. I know it isn't much, but she thought you might like to have it."

With tear-filled eyes, Andrea looked at the old silver cross with a safety pin still attached. "Thank you." When she tried to pin the cross to her coat, her fingers were trembling so hard she could not do it, but Bill completed the task for her.

"Were you related at all?" the nurse asked.

"We were…just acquaintances," she whispered as she fingered the cross, just as Mrs. Moore had done a few months ago, "but we were sisters in faith, too."

Chapter Thirty-Nine

Andrea was fighting as hard as she could, but she was quickly losing the battle to stay awake.

With her down coat as a comforter, she snuggled beneath the seat belt and nestled deeper into the passenger seat as Bill drove them home from the hospital. The windshield seemed to magnify the power of the late-afternoon sun that warmed her face. Soft jazz played on the radio. Between her treatment, her appointment with the lawyer, the luncheon, and the passing of Mrs. Monroe, she had had a pretty exhausting day.

Her eyelids drooped again, and she decided to let her eyes close for just a moment. Besides, she was wearing her sunglasses. Bill would not notice. Or so she thought. When he chuckled, she let out a sigh.

"I thought you might be asleep already," he murmured.

She smiled without opening her eyes. "I'm just resting my eyes for a minute. The sun feels so good."

"I had a feeling you might be part cat."

"What's that supposed to mean?"

"Nothing. You're just all curled up with your face to the sun. Cats do that all the time. They curl up, sleep for a bit, wake up, play or eat and then nap again. Hence the term, 'catnap.' Right?"

"They're pretty smart animals."

He laughed. "Go ahead. Take a catnap. That way you'll be all refreshed for our date tonight."

"Our date tonight?" She sighed again, but when she tried to open her eyes, they were just too heavy. "I think I'll take a little catnap first before we talk about whether or not we even have a date. Wake me up when we get to my house," she managed before slipping away….

Andrea stirred awake very slowly. She yawned. She rubbed the sleep from her eyes. She stretched—and banged her knee against a…dashboard?

Disoriented, she glanced about frantically in the dark. Through the windshield, she could see several open fires burning and skaters gathered around them to warm up frozen limbs before heading back to skate on the ice by the light of the fires and the moon. She recognized the place at once. She and her sisters had skated on the lake in Welles Park often enough as children, but she had not skated here for a long time. She had not realized they still allowed the campfires and had just assumed they had been banned for years. Firelight danced on a silver truck where hungry skaters stood in line to buy snacks. That was something new.

How did she get here? The last thing she remembered was driving home from the hospital with Bill, but that was hours ago! And where was Bill now?

The rap on the passenger window might have been gentle, but it was so unexpected, she flinched. With her heart racing, she turned, saw Bill standing alongside the car with a cardboard tray that held some food and beverages, and sighed with relief. She opened the door and picked up her sunglasses before they could fall and stuffed them into her pocket when she got out of the car.

"I didn't mean to startle you. Since you were sitting up, I thought you were awake."

She yawned. "I'm just getting there," she murmured. "The cold air helps." She stretched the muscles in her back, but before she buttoned up her coat, she shut the car door. "Can I assume I took a catnap that lasted the entire afternoon?"

He smiled. "Pretty much."

"You were supposed to wake me up when we got to my house."

He held the tray out and she took a cup of hot cocoa, but the hot dogs wrapped in waxed paper smelled delicious.

"I tried. That was after I remembered you'd left your car at the restaurant. I drove there first, but I couldn't wake you up. Then I drove you home." He chuckled. "I never saw anyone sleep that hard. When I couldn't wake you up, I thought maybe you needed the sleep, so I took us for a ride. I was headed back to your house when I saw the campfires. I just decided a few minutes ago to get us something to eat. I thought maybe the smell of food might wake you up," he teased.

"This is really embarrassing," she admitted.

"Actually, it worked out pretty well," he countered.

"Really?"

He shrugged. "Since you were asleep, I got to make the decision about our date tonight. You do remember we had a date?"

She took a sip of the cocoa and burned her tongue. Some things never change. "I distinctly remember you mentioning a date tonight, but I didn't accept. You were rather vague about the date itself."

"After the day you had, I didn't think you'd be in the mood for dinner and a show. I thought maybe you'd like to sit in front of an open fire, have a hot dog and maybe watch the stars, like we did on the beach. Sort of," he added. He nodded toward his left. "I think there's an empty log over there next to that fire."

She peeked onto the tray again. "I hope you brought mustard for the hot dogs."

He turned to show her his bulging pocket. "Packets of mustard, ketchup, relish and mayo. I wasn't sure what you liked, so I brought them all."

The log was not empty when they got to it, but the teenage couple sitting there left rather abruptly the minute Andrea and Bill arrived and returned to the ice. "I think we interrupted a special moment," she quipped, and sat down.

When he rested the cardboard tray on the log, she held it steady while he took a seat. "Probably," he replied. "Poor kids. They haven't got a chance."

They split the hot dogs, two apiece, and she smeared a couple of packets of mustard on both of hers. "'They haven't got a chance.' What's that supposed to mean?"

He pointed to a group of teenage boys. "Right there, he's got his five buddies waiting to find out if he stole a kiss." He pointed further to the right. "Over there, she's got her girlfriends waiting to find out if she got him to kiss her. The phone lines will hum all weekend. By Monday morning, when they're all back in school, two things will happen. The boy will have to decide in favor of hormones or hanging out with his buddies, and the girl will have to decide whether or not she wants to lead him on a merry chase or snatch him up fast before another girl does."

Andrea laughed. "Dating in high school was a complicated mess, sometimes, wasn't it?"

"It gets messier and a whole lot more complicated with age, trust me." He took a bite of his hot dog and held the rest out to make his point. "Take us, for example. At our age, you'd think dating would be easier, but we haven't been able to have a date yet that didn't wind up as a disaster or a business meeting, or better still, get cut short because of an emergency of one kind or another. I guess there's a message there."

"You forgot to mention that sometimes I fall asleep," she murmured and stared at the fire for a moment. She had not dated frequently over the years, but she had dated enough to know when she was about to be dumped, as teenagers called it. She should have been relieved. Oddly, she was not.

True, she and Bill had not had an official date that did not involve business one way or another since their first date. No matter what kind of disaster or unexpected interruption, however, he had shown himself to be a man of compassion, understanding, good humor and honor. More importantly, he did not leave his faith in his pew after Sunday services. He lived his faith every day.

Bill was the type of man who came along but once or twice in a woman's lifetime, if she was fortunate. Andrea had loved and married the first man she had known with those qualities. She would be foolish, indeed, to walk away from the man who could be the second, even if he was eleven years her junior. Character mattered a whole lot more than the number of candles on a birthday cake.

Unfortunately, if she read his meaning correctly, she might have discovered that even if she did want to seriously date him, it might be too late.

"Maybe you should have listened to me. I tried to warn you that dating me wasn't a good idea," she suggested, just to test the waters.

"And I definitely remember telling you otherwise."

"You're too persistent for your own good," she countered. Maybe it was not too late after all!

"And you're a little more stubborn than I thought. No problem," he insisted, and finished off his hot dog.

She shook her head. "No problem?"

"No. I might be persistent, but I'm also a patient man, in case you haven't noticed." He paused to get up and search around for another piece of wood and added it to the fire.

"Is that something you learned as a scout, too?" she asked, hopeful he really had not meant to stop dating or attempting to seriously date.

He sat down again. "What? Keeping a fire going?"

"No. I've seen you build a fire from scratch before. I meant being patient."

He put his hands behind his head and stared up at the stars. She followed his lead and looked overhead. There

weren't quite as many tonight as there had been on the beach, but just enough for her to be able to find an angel's window. When she did, she fingered the old silver cross that was pinned to her coat and said a prayer for both Mrs. Moore and Miss Huxbaugh.

"I learned patience from my mother," he murmured, "but I got my persistence from my dad. He was quite a fisherman. When I got old enough, he used to take me with him on Saturdays to the lake where he'd grown up and learned to fish as a boy. There's no ocean in Ohio," he explained. "I learned lots of things from him on that old fishing boat, things I couldn't learn from books."

She nodded, half-afraid he might still tell her they were finished as a couple, even before they really began. "Such as…?"

"Well, for one, you can drop bait into the water and reel in one fish after the other, if you're willing to settle for the little ones. To catch the best and the biggest, you have to take it slow. That big fish you want is smart and strong and stubborn. It'll fight you every inch. If you're not careful, it'll snap your line or wriggle that hook out of its mouth right when you're ready to pull it into the boat. You need patience to catch the best fish, and you need patience when you find a woman you think is the best, too."

She sputtered, spilled her cocoa and knocked the tray off the log. "You…you think dating is like fishing? You're comparing me to a…fish? A *fish*?"

He let her stew for a moment while he put the cardboard tray and cups into the fire. "Don't go getting all steamed up. You might wind up getting tangled in the line," he teased.

She pursed her lips. "You…you made that whole story up, didn't you? Fish, indeed!"

He burst out laughing. "Is it that obvious?"

She rolled her eyes. "You're impossible."

He grinned. "See that? We're making progress! I've gone from persistent to impossible. If you keep going backward alphabetically, you should get to the letter *d* pretty soon."

"*D* for difficult?" she teased, adding a bit of bait to her own line.

"Go back a little further. I was thinking of 'datable."

"You have a one-track mind."

"And you don't?" he argued. "Forget I said that. You've got a mind that can run over four tracks headed in different directions and switch back and forth pretty quickly. That's one of the things I liked about you right off." He cocked a brow. "Now about that date…"

She shrugged. Time to reel him in before he slipped off her hook. "How about an early dinner at my house tomorrow after church? Maybe it's time to let the 'girls' decide if we should date seriously."

"You're going to let your cats decide?"

She laughed. "Why not? You made up a story and compared me to a fish."

He stared at her. "You're teasing, right?"

"Maybe."

He checked his watch. "It's only eight. If we hurry, there's still time to catch a movie."

"Not unless tomorrow you want to eat a frozen entrée I've heated up for dinner. I need to get to the grocery store. There's one open twenty-four hours a day in Cherry Hill."

He stood up and helped her to her feet. "Show me how to get there. I'll take you to the store on the way back to the restaurant to pick up your car."

"My car! I forgot!"

"I do come in handy once in a while, don't I?"

When they got back to the car, he opened the door for her, and she spied her purse on the floor. She slid into her seat and checked her cell phone, dismayed she had forgotten to turn it back on after leaving the hospital. When she did turn it on, the phone beeped and flashed a little envelope in the lower right corner of the screen. She had messages.

"Head north on the avenue," she told him when he reached the end of the park. "I'll just be a minute. I need to check my messages."

He turned north.

She had three messages. She erased the first. Were the telemarketers invading cell phones, too? When she listened to the second message, which had been left more than three hours ago, she tugged on his arm. "Hurry. Turn around. We can't go to the grocery store. You have to take me back to the hospital. Jenny's having her baby!"

Chapter Forty

The maternity waiting room was the only waiting room in the hospital Andrea did not mind entering. Happy memories sailed through the door with her. She looked around the crowded room and headed for the far corner. She could not see the woman sitting behind a bouquet of half a dozen balloons, three pink ones that read, "It's a Girl!" and three blue ones that read, "It's a Boy!" But it had to be Madge. Who else would bring both?

With her heart racing, she stopped in front of the balloons and peeked through, just as the thought hit her that maybe someone was going to be delivering twins. The moment she saw Madge's face, however, she grinned. "Are you expecting twins or just trying to be prepared?" she teased.

"Andrea!" Her sister bolted to her feet and almost tripped

over her oversize purse and the ribbons tied to the balloons. "Where have you been? I called your office. I called your house and I called your cell phone. I left messages everywhere, and so did Jenny."

"I'm sorry. I was out with Bill, and I left my cell phone off for a few hours. He just dropped me off. Any news yet?"

Madge sat down again, and her smile was smug. "Jenny had the baby a little while ago. Michael came back and told me right away. He's with her now, but he promised I could see them once they'd taken Jenny to her room. I'm not sure I should tell you if she had a boy or a girl since you made me sit here all by myself while you were out on a date. Some sister you turned out to be."

"Jenny's due date is still three weeks away!"

"Not anymore."

Andrea plopped down into the chair next to her sister. "Well, I don't believe you. You're just trying to make me feel bad because you didn't like being here by yourself. If Jenny had had the baby already, you wouldn't be sitting here with pink and blue balloons right now. You would have gotten rid of one or the other color already."

Madge waved her arm. "Look around! This place is mobbed. I couldn't pop three of these balloons. I'd scare someone half to death!"

"You wouldn't pop the balloons. You'd give them to someone else who is waiting here, now if you don't tell me the truth right now, I'm going to burst."

Her sister shrugged her shoulders. "I did tell you the truth. Jenny had the baby, but you're right. I wouldn't pop the balloons. I just couldn't get rid of the balloons I didn't need."

"Then we'll just sit here and wait. As these families find out about the babies they're waiting for, you'll have a chance to give the balloons away."

"Not if they're all the same as Jenny's baby," Madge countered with a grin.

Andrea couldn't be certain if Madge was bluffing or not, but after being sisters for over fifty years, she still was not prepared to let Madge get the best of her, either. She sat back and hoped that some other family in the room would get some good news sooner rather than later.

She did not have to wait long.

A man burst into the room and raced straight to his family. "A daughter! I have a daughter!" As he provided details to his excited family, Andrea looked to her sister. If Jenny had had a girl, then Madge would not be able to give this family the pink balloons. If Jenny had had a boy, then Andrea would find out within moments.

Andrea's heart began to race when Madge pulled the balloons down, separated the pink ones from the blues one. "Let's see. Here. You take the blue balloons, and I'll take the pink ones."

Andrea held on to the ribbons attached to the balloons and waited to see if Madge would take the pink ones to the other family.

Madge's smile got bigger. "Oops. We'll have to wait to see if any of the others have a boy. We need the pink ones for Jenny."

"It's a girl? Jenny had a girl?"

"She had a girl!"

Balloons and all, they hugged and kissed and shed a few tears while Madge told Andrea all of the details. The quick, easy natural childbirth. Both mother and baby were doing fine.

Andrea toyed with the ribbons on the blue balloons. "Another girl," she murmured as they relaxed in their seats again. "She's just like Mother so far."

"I think Jenny's going to let Mother hold the record at five girls, though. Unless there's a surprise, I think Jenny's family is complete now. At least that's what she told me on the phone before she left for the hospital," Madge replied.

"Did they give her a name yet?" she asked.

"Michael said Jenny wanted to tell us." Madge checked her watch. "It's been half an hour since I talked to him. I hope we don't have to wait very long to see her and the baby."

A young man burst into the room and cried, "It's a boy!" His family rushed from their seats and surrounded him, showering him and each other with hugs and kisses and lots of tears. This time, Madge took the blue balloons and gave them to the family.

Andrea watched a similar scene repeated two more times over the course of the next forty-five minutes when two more proud new fathers announced the birth of a son and a daughter, respectively, and families left to see their new arrivals.

Madge and Andrea now had the waiting room to themselves. Andrea would have been nervous about waiting so long, but Michael had stopped back in to say all was well. There just had been some sort of mix-up about Jenny's room, and they would have to wait to see Jenny and the baby just a little longer.

Andrea found her thoughts wandering to her two sisters,

Kathleen and Sandra, and her parents, and she wished they could be here to share tonight's joy. She looked around the room, sighed and tried to sort through other thoughts linking life here on earth with life in heaven. "I wonder…do you think this is what it's like in heaven?"

When Madge looked at her, totally mystified, she tried again. "I mean, we know what it's like here when a new baby is being born and a soul begins its journey on earth. Families gather together, no matter what day it is or what time it is. They're so excited and anxious and they're ready to burst with joy the moment they hear the news that the baby arrived safely. We felt that way tonight, and we saw all the other families who were here. They did, too."

"Babies tend to make people happy. It's always like that when babies are born, I think," Madge replied. "What's that got to do with heaven?"

Andrea sighed. "I'm not sure. I just was wondering if the same thing happens when a soul is coming Home. Do families get together in heaven, all excited and anxious for the moment to arrive when they can be reunited once again and forever? We never know for sure when our days on earth are over. Maybe they only know the time is near, and they get together like all these families did tonight and wait for the moment that God has chosen, a time known only to Him. And when that soul finally arrives, it's the same sort of celebration."

Madge dabbed at her eyes. "I never thought of it that way."

"I never did, either, until just now." She handed Madge a tissue and kept one for herself. "Sorry. I spilled everything out of my purse. The tissue is a little mangled, but it's clean."

"It's times like this that I realize how much I miss them all," Madge whispered.

"Me, too, but maybe if they're all together in heaven, Mother and Daddy and Kathleen and Sandra, maybe they were there when God decided to send this little one to join our family. While we're all excited about the days and years ahead, they're already counting the days until they would be welcoming this little one Home."

Madge sniffled. "You never mentioned anything like this before."

"I guess I never really thought so much about life or death as I have…lately. After losing so many people I've loved, you'd think I would have thought about it before, but I didn't. Not until cancer hit me square in the chest…or bladder, I should say."

Madge took her hand. "You're doing well, though. You're halfway through your treatments and everything is fine, isn't it?"

The worry in Madge's voice tugged at Andrea's heartstrings. "Yes, I'm doing well. With God's grace, I'm going to beat this." She paused. "I—I took a lot of things for granted before, and I've finally realized that I can serve Him better if I stop charging through life and trying to control everything. I'm trying hard to surrender my will for His."

"I'm learning some lessons, too," Madge whispered. "I'm learning to trust in His goodness and His love for all of us. I—I heard from Trish this morning. Sarah's adoption should be final within a week or two."

Before Andrea could respond with more than a huge hug, Michael appeared and got another round of congratulatory hugs of his own from Andrea. While he went home to get Jenny some clothes, since he had dropped her suitcase and spilled everything out into the snow on their way into the hospital, Andrea and Madge went to see Jenny and the new baby. They promised to stay with her until he got back.

Carting balloons, purses and overcoats, they paraded to Jenny's room. Andrea stopped just outside the door and looked at the balloons. "I didn't bring anything for the baby," she whispered.

Madge held on to the balloons while she rifled through her oversized purse, which was more like a quilted shopping bag. She pulled out a stuffed pink kitten and handed it to Andrea. "I had a feeling you might need something. I checked the tag. It's fine for children under three."

"It's adorable." When Andrea tried to peek into Madge's bag, her sister zipped it shut.

"Yes, I brought a blue one, too, among other things," she quipped.

Laughing softly together, they went into the room. Jenny was resting in bed with the sleeping baby in her arms. After showering Jenny with more hugs and kisses, Andrea tossed their coats on a chair and put the stuffed kitten on Jenny's bedside table. Madge sat on the other side of the bed after she tied the balloons to the head of the bed.

Jenny placed the baby on her lap, all seven pounds four ounces of pure joy, and unwrapped the blanket swaddled around her. The infant stirred for a moment, but she did not wake up. "Poor baby girl. She's all tuckered out," she crooned. "She's beautiful, isn't she?"

Emotion choked Andrea for a moment. "She's so perfect,

but she's her own girl. She doesn't look like either Katy or Hannah. Oh, look at that! She's got a little dimple in her chin, just like Daddy did."

"She's got Mother's fair skin," Madge noted before she leaned closer to get a better look. "She doesn't have much hair, but I think there's some red in it, too."

Jenny beamed. "I knew you'd both see how much she resembles Mother and Daddy." She caressed the baby's head. "You're sleeping through your introductions. This is your aunt Andrea and your aunt Madge," she murmured before she looked up at both of her sisters. "And this is Joneve. Since she resembles her grandparents, I thought we should name her after them, too. Michael and I played around with their names a bit, but we decided there was only one way to put John and Evelyn together that sounded right. Do you like it?"

"I love her name, and I think they would love it, too," Madge gushed.

Andrea filled up with emotion again and had to dab away a fresh tear or two. "You always know just the right button to push," she teased.

"Wait until we start the ceremony," Jenny countered. "Are you two ready?"

Andrea nodded. So did Madge. They joined hands, with Andrea holding one of Joneve's hands and Madge holding the other, creating an unbroken circle that connected one generation to another. As the new mother, Jenny began the ceremony that was a tradition they had learned from their mother and she from their grandmother, although the words Jenny would speak came from her heart and not from rote. "My precious little Joneve, you are both a blessing and a responsibility that we all embrace with great joy and happiness. As your mother, I promise to love you and raise you with patience and wisdom and to teach you about the Creator who has entrusted you to our care. God has blessed you with two big sisters, and it is my prayer that you will grow up together and grow old together. You will be more than just sisters related by blood. You will be sisters united by faith and by friendship and by love. With God as your guide, life's joys will be all the more joyful and life's challenges all the easier to meet if you share them with one another."

When she pressed a kiss to the baby's head, Andrea continued the tradition, just as she had done for her other nieces and nephews on the day they had been born. "Remember, sweet Joneve, that your family is always here to support you—the family into which you were born and the family of Believers into which you will grow," she whispered.

"One day, little Joneve," Madge murmured, "you will be a woman, and we pray you will be blessed with children of your own. Love them well. Raise them to know and love God and to love one another always."

Jenny brought the traditional ceremony to a close after they bowed their heads. "Father, we thank You for this precious child. Share with us Your love so we may guide her wisely."

"Amen," they said in unison.

Andrea watched Jenny swaddle the baby again and smiled. "Joneve is now officially a member of our family." When she saw hurt flash through Madge's eyes, she thought she might know why and felt guilty for not thinking about this months ago when Sarah first came into their family. "I was wondering…maybe we should have something special like this for Sarah."

Madge's eyes lit up, then quickly dimmed. "The tradition is for newborns. Sarah is three years old."

"I think it's a wonderful idea," Jenny countered. "We should have thought of this before now. If you don't mind waiting a few weeks until I get back on my feet a bit, we could have it at my house and include Katy and Hannah, too. It's never too early to start teaching them about this tradition. They've learned others already."

"We've never had an adoption in our family before," Andrea noted, "but now that Sarah is here, we have the chance to change the tradition a bit, that's all."

Madge beamed. "Could we? Really?"

Andrea nodded. "Traditions are important, but they're not etched in stone. If traditions don't change or adapt, then they're bound to be forgotten and maybe they should be."

Madge sniffled again. "I don't know what to say, except I love you both so much," she managed before she dissolved into tears.

"You have to love us," Andrea teased.

"We're sisters, remember?" Jenny asked. "Sisters yesterday, today and tomorrow. Now stop blubbering, you big baby, and get my treat from McAllister's out of that bag of yours. I'm starving."

Madge dried her tears and hiccuped. "Who says I brought you something from McAllister's?"

"We do!" Jenny and Andrea cried together.

"What if I forgot?"

"Then you're officially expelled from the family," Jenny threatened.

Andrea pointed to the door. "Effective immediately, you're out!"

Madge grinned. "You can't expel me and you can't throw me out. We're sisters, remember? That's a lifetime commitment."

"And beyond," Andrea murmured.

Praise God.

Epilogue

The Diner was bustling with breakfast patrons when Andrea arrived for the second Sisters' Breakfast on Sandra's birthday the following summer. She was drenched from head to toe, thanks to a sudden cloudburst. She was almost half an hour late. When she saw Madge and Jenny waiting for her in the corner booth, she never lost a beat and the smile on her face just got bigger.

When she got to the table, she set her surprise on the table. "Sorry I'm late," she said. She tried to slide in next to Madge, stuck to the red vinyl seat and had to inch her way.

Madge peeled off the silver foil on Andrea's surprise, saw the squares of coffee cake heavy with fresh Jersey blueberries and crumb topping, and gasped. "You baked something? You?"

"Sandra loved Mother's Blueberry Boy Bait. Since it's her birthday today, I thought it was a good idea." She looked around the table. "It's a good thing I did. I don't see any Spinners here."

Jenny yawned. "McAllister's is closed for vacation. First time anyone can remember." She yawned again. "Sorry. Joneve's teething. I'm not getting a lot of sleep these days."

Andrea studied her baby sister's exhausted features and smiled when she noticed the ponytail was back. "You look beat."

Jenny gave her a fake smile. "Thank you. I'd say you looked like you forgot to take your clothes off when you took your shower, but I won't. I did that twice this week. Now I understand what it's like to be too tired to think." She shook herself, as if trying to stay awake. "Let's talk about something more positive, shall we? Like Madge's new car." She pointed out the window at the bright yellow SUV across the street.

Andrea took one look and laughed. "I think Kathleen would be very disappointed to see Madge didn't get another purple car."

Madge put a square of the crumb cake on a plate in front of each of them. "It's Sarah's favorite color. The brighter the yellow, the more she likes it. Besides, I had to get something new. A convertible isn't very safe for little ones."

"Neither is Vacation Bible School, which Katy and Hannah attended until two days ago." Jenny sighed and tears filled her bloodshot eyes. "The day before yesterday, when the counselors took all the children on a nature walk, my darling girls decided to add a pretty new leaf to their scrapbooks. Remember the ones we bought last year?" she asked Madge.

"I do. What's wrong with adding another leaf?"

"Nothing, except to get to the ones they wanted, they had to traipse through a patch of poison ivy. By last night, they were suffering so much, Michael had to take them to Dr. Burns. Apparently, they're both hyperallergic and completely miserable, of course. If I wasn't up the past two nights rocking Joneve, I was rocking one of her two big sisters or both at the same time."

Madge frowned. "Poor babies."

"Poor you," Andrea whispered. "You need something to pick you up."

Jenny sighed again. "I need sleep. Just a few hours of uninterrupted sleep. Michael's too exhausted to help. Between the galleys he has to proofread for his first book and the deadline for the sequel, he's barely able to get any sleep of his own. If he hadn't agreed to watch all three of the girls for a few hours this morning, I think I would have cried." She dabbed at her eyes with her napkin. "Quick. Somebody tell me something happy or I'll just keep whining."

Andrea looked at both of her sisters and found the smile she had tucked away for a moment. "We could celebrate my last chemo treatment or maybe you'd like the news that I'm now cancer-free? How's that for happy? Is that a good start?"

Jenny and Madge whooped and hollered and clapped, much to the curious stares of the other patrons. Their noise brought Caroline to the table. She took their orders and left, not quite certain to believe the story she had been told about celebrating Madge's new car.

"When did you find out?" Madge asked.

"I saw Dr. Newton yesterday."

Jenny frowned. "And you waited until today to tell us?"

"I wanted to tell you both in person at the same time."

"Okay, that's better than happy," Jenny said. "Now it's your turn, Madge."

Madge's eyes twinkled, but she took a bite of crumb cake before she responded. "Let's see. You already know about my car and that Sarah's got her own garden growing this summer. Catnip, naturally. Did I tell you Russell asked me to go away with him next weekend? He's got the shop covered for Saturday and it's closed on Sunday. All we need is a sitter for Sarah."

Jenny tried to smile, but failed. "I'd offer, but I don't know how the girls will be faring with their poison ivy."

"No. Let Sarah stay with me," Andrea countered. "She loves playing with the 'girls.' We'll make it a sleepover weekend. Girls only," she insisted. "Where are you two going?"

Madge beamed. "It's a spiritual retreat weekend at the shore that the marriage counselor recommended. It's for couples who want to renew their marriage vows."

Andrea hugged her sister. "I'm so happy for you."

Jenny reached across the table and patted Madge's arm. "Me, too."

"It's not that everything is perfect between us, but we've both learned a lot during the counseling. I think we're both ready to make a commitment to one another again, and I think we need time alone with other couples to pray together before we say our vows again."

Andrea swallowed the lump in her throat. She had not seen Madge this happy or as confident about her marriage in months. "Speaking of marriage vows…"

Jenny spied the engagement ring on Andrea's finger first and squealed. "He didn't!"

Andrea held out her hand and let her ring sparkle for her sisters. "He did. He asked me last night."

Madge clapped her hands. "You...you said yes!"

"Of course I did. He's a persistent man, which is good, especially where a stubborn woman like me is concerned. We called Rachel and David last night to tell them, and they're excited, too."

"What's the date?"

"We're going to see Reverend Staggart tonight. Bill and I both want a small ceremony. Just family and a few close friends, so don't get all carried away about planning an 'event.'"

Madge looked around at all of them and sighed. "Look at us, will you? We're so busy talking about ourselves, we've forgotten that it's Sandra's birthday."

"She'd be the first to congratulate both of you," Jenny whispered. "She'd be happy and proud and excited for you both." She closed her eyes for a moment. "And she'd be the first to tell me to stop whining and turning her birthday into a pity party. Big change from last year, isn't it?"

Andrea looked at Madge, who returned her unspoken question with a supportive wink, and spoke directly to Jenny. "In honor of Kathleen, we hereby declare war and as of this moment, you are our prisoner. After breakfast, you're going home to take a nap. I'm free all afternoon. I'll take care of the girls. And tell Michael that he's not working tonight. He needs a break, too."

Madge nodded approvingly. "I'm bringing supper over at six, so set your alarm for five o'clock. Get up, get a shower, blow-dry your hair and get dressed in something frilly. While your girls and I have supper and Russell takes Sarah out for a little father-daughter quality time, you and Michael are going out to dinner. Don't ask where you're going. I'll make the reservations and tell you when I get to your house."

"And I'll bring Bill with me later to spell Madge so you and Michael don't have to hurry home. There's a concert in the park tonight or you can take in a movie together, but you're not allowed home until you do something special together after dinner. Got it?"

"I can't. You're both so sweet, but I can't," Jenny murmured. "Madge should be having dinner with Russell and Sarah, and, Andrea, you have an appointment tonight to set your wedding date. I can't ask you both to drop everything because I'm having a hard time right now."

Andrea smiled. "Madge can have supper with her family tomorrow night, and Bill and I can set a wedding date anytime. You need us now. We're sisters. That's what we do for each other. We're up and we're down. We give and we take, and we even squabble a little from time to time, but in the end, we're sisters. That says it all, doesn't it?"

Afterword

The Shawl Ministry is not fictional. Two women, Janet Bristow and Victoria Cole-Galo, began the actual Shawl Ministry Program in 1998. To learn more about this loving program, please visit their Web site, www.shawlministry.com. You can read about how the program began, understand its purpose and goals, review sample prayers as guidelines to create your own, and view photographs of actual shawls.

Cancer, unfortunately, is not fictional, either. Cancer is all too real a challenge for victims of the disease, as well as their families and friends. Cancer treatments vary immensely. The best source of information, of course, is your physician or oncologist, along with the American Cancer Society, which provides valuable information and support through local chapters or on the Internet.

For those interested in recipes, below is my mother's recipe for Blueberry Boy Bait. There are others on the Internet that are very close. Recipes for other goodies in the book, like "Aunt Elaine's Coconut Cake," are posted on my Web site, www.deliaparr.com. Enjoy!

Mother's Blueberry Boy Bait

❧

2 cups sifted flour
1 1/2 cups sugar
2/3 cup Crisco (vegetable shortening)
1 cup milk
2 eggs, separated
1 tsp. baking powder
1 tsp. salt
Blueberries

Sift flour and sugar together. Cut in shortening until dough resembles small peas. Measure and save 3/4 cup for topping. Add baking powder, salt, 2 egg yolks and milk to leftover crumb mixture. Beat 3 minutes EXACTLY. Beat two egg whites until stiff peaks form and fold into batter.

Pour into well-greased and floured 13" x 9" pan. Sprinkle with blueberries and reserved crumbs. Bake at 350 degrees for 40-50 minutes. Remove and let cool. Dribble with confectioner's sugar before completely cool.

* * * * *

What happens next in Welleswood?
Watch for DAY BY DAY, the next book in
the Home Ties *miniseries*
On Sale April 2007

QUESTIONS FOR DISCUSSION

1. Sisterhood is a powerful theme in *Abide with Me*. How have your sisters or women in your family influenced your life? How have you been a "sister" to another person—someone not an actual relative? What does that mean to you?

2. Jenny and her husband face something of a role reversal when her full-time work supports his writing career. When have you taken on a new role to help out a family member? Why do we do such things?

3. The Sisters' Breakfast is a tradition the surviving Long sisters created as a time to remember their late family members. How do you honor family members who have passed on? What traditions have developed in those situations?

4. Russell's betrayal of Madge offered a chance for them to rebuild their marriage and renew their commitment to one another. How can painful experiences be transformed into second chances? How can we position ourselves to make good use of them?

5. Andrea was loath to relinquish control over certain aspects of her cancer treatment or to confide in her sisters. Was this the right approach? Why or why not? What Scripture would you share with her to encourage her to give her problem over to God?

6. The Shawl Ministry is a unique program created to help others—what ministries has your church developed to help those in need?

7. The sisters marvel at Andrea's ability to forgive when she hires Jamie Martin, but in what way does her sister Madge's ability to forgive come to the fore in this story? How would you have dealt with Russell's infidelity?

8. Working in a small office can cause friction between workers with different work habits. Though Andrea was the one to hire Doris, she quickly finds it difficult to work with her. How have you coped with difficult coworkers?

9. Bill Sanderson's romantic interest in Andrea is something she initially refuses to accept, given that she is struggling with cancer at the time. Share an instance when God's timing sent unexpected opportunities your way. What did you do?

10. What role does the beach house play for each sister? How does it differ character to character? Does it?

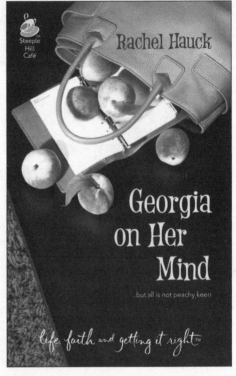

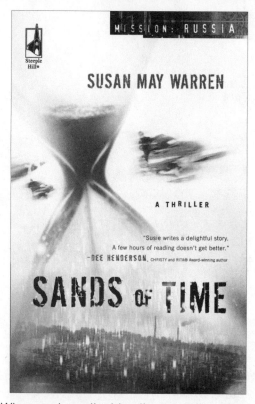